To Deb,
Thank you so much for ... have done this without you! Hearty Appetite Arnold

FROM TEAPOT TO TEMPEST

The Old Men's Cooking Club

ARNOLD BREMAN

'A Rollicking, Food-Filled Mystery'

FEATURING SECRET RECIPES FROM THE OLD MEN'S COOKING CLUB COLLECTION

Dedicated to the children I love Justin, Trillion, Zach and Dave

AUTHOR'S NOTE

There are many grandpas portrayed in The Old Men's Cooking Club but none of them are real people. This is a work of pure fiction.

A bouquet of bravas goes to Stephanie Meyers and Deborah Gants for their invaluable help in bringing the Old Men's Cooking Club into existence.

A special bravo to Zach Breman for his great devotion to this project.

A huge round of applause to artist, musician Kenneth Baldwin for his insight and wonderful ability to bring the old cooking chef's alive on the cover.

Cast of Characters

The Lay Senior Chefs

Dick Reynolds (75): Former CIA operative. The boys were more interested in his stories than his disastrous cooking.

Ernest Stubbs (86): Non-cooking, do-nothing, bigoted curmudgeon with a pock-marked heart of gold.

Art O'Neil (85): Lackadaisical modest good old boy from Arkansas who loves nothing more than working in his vegetable garden that yields prize-winning tomatoes.

Fred Davis (75): Men's Cooking Club leader and founder and excellent cook who spent his working life literally in garbage as a refuse executive.

Abe Kacynscy (80): Know-it-all about everything, especially food who isn't terribly discreet in letting everyone know.

Steve Quentin (76): Jolly self-proclaimed artist who is precariously obese but creates some of the most colorful meals.

Ed Fisher (72): Former boring scientist. His turn to cook lunch is like attending a science lab.

Joseph Jones (75): Retired, macho bartender and passionate Harley-Davidson biker who brings a touch of redneck and mouth-watering ribs to the mix.

Charles Hamilton (79): Aged homosexual and fanciful cook, who recently married his lover, Robert, after living together for more than 50 years.

Bill Foster (74): Wealthy, but painfully frugal, retired junk dealer called "the buy-one, get-one free" king.

Franz Schmidt (85): Newest member of the group, a German immigrant and former Third Reich soldier.

Supporting Characters

Harry Smith (Heinrich Schmidt): Investment broker, son of Franz Schmidt and head of the.......

Otto Schafer (85): Best friend of Franz Schmidt in Germany

Bessie Hudson: Twice-divorced wife and caretaker of Ernest Stubbs

Anneliese Schmidt: Wife of Franz Schmidt and mother of Harry Smith

Ingrid Smith: Wife of Harry Smith

Sally Adams: FBI Agent

Tom Prentice: FBI Agent

Leonetta Moore: Denny's theatrical waitress

Siegfried Schloss: Colleague of Otto Schafer in Germany

Herman Sharif: President of the United States

Sid Townsend: Vice President of the United States
Rabbi Joel Tannenbaum: Head of the Orlando Jewish community
Rabbi Seymour Auerbach: Another Jewish leader
Henry Thompson: Florida landscaping and nursery proprietor
Emil Watson: Celebrity event planner
Pete, Floyd, Ralph, Tom, Jim, Derek, David: Assorted supporting characters

FROM TEAPOT
TO TEMPEST

Part One
Another Fine Kettle of Fish

Prologue

Gloating, he said, "they were convinced that I was a Jew. Me! Can you believe it? I had a dense crop of black hair, charcoal-gray eyes and a Mediterranean, olive complexion." Franz's voice lowered and took on a somber tone. Franz Schmidt relished recounting his stories about World War II. A small group of his close friends had assembled for his 85th birthday in his home in Regensburg, Germany "It was 1939 and I remember the day, I was playing outside, kicking a ball or something on the street. We lived on the outskirts of Munich. So, anyway, the police pull up, confront me and drag me to their headquarters."

"Of course, I was scared and then I was so humiliated! I was 12 years old and could not convince them that I had Christian Germanic roots." He paused to make sure he had everyone's attention. "I needed to drop my pants to verify that I was uncut. Pure Aryan. The Reich officers crackled with laughter and told me not to worry: My miniature, shriveled penis would grow someday. "But for now," they said "… you are ready to join the Hitler Youth.""

Above the laughter, Anneliese, the love of Franz's life for 58 years, admonished him, "Oh, Franz, enough stories, it's time for us to feast. This is a celebration, not a memorial service."

She stood at the parted dining room doors and ushered the guests in.

A long serving table in front of a picture window displayed a colorful garden of luscious food delicacies. The rays of the afternoon sun illuminated the idyllic Bavarian countryside. Low grassy hills, lush trees, and vibrant flowers provided nature's own decorations for this milestone celebration. The hosts' contributions were the mouthwatering aromas encircling the room, emanating from the vast banquet of traditional Bavarian food.

At the doorway, Franz stood next to his oldest friend, Otto Schafer, as they allowed the other guests to enter before them. They had become best friends after they met in 1944 as prisoners of war at Fort Dix, New Jersey. Both were low-ranking soldiers in the German Armed Forces who had been captured by the allies and sent into exile. The two men were among hordes of German and Italian prisoners warehoused in the United States since it was deemed easier to control them here, rather than risking their escape into the European forests, back to the war to do more damage.

In this context, the two polar-opposite personalities: Otto, highfalutin' and angry-over-his-captivity, and Franz, more docile and reconciled to his fate. The buddies bonded and remained dear cronies for nearly 60 years.

At last all the guests had entered. Otto's ancient blue eyes brightened up as he glanced at the buffet.

"Ach, there is so much food to choose from."

"That was the plan, Otto. Go ahead. Gorge. Be decadent. It's a special day."

"I hardly know where to start. It's a feast for the eyes and a curse on the waistline."

"Start with a plate and fork," Franz laughed.

"Anneliese is such a superior cook."

"Anneliese, Anneliese? I created most of the dishes," Franz bragged.

"You cook too, Franz?"

"Why not, my wife and I spend many hours together in the kitchen."

The conversion ended as each man filled a plate with Leberkase, sauerkraut, potato casserole made with a pink meatloaf, and Frikadellen, a flattened pork dumpling served with a heap of thick kartoffersalat – potato salad.

Franz bemoaned the fact that there wasn't room for the other delacasies. He turned to Otto and winked. "… but then again there are always second helpings." A separate table overflowed with Bavarian beer, red Trollinger and white Riesling wines.

Anneliese paraded into the room carrying a lopsided lit candle atop a Bayerische cream cake. The group saluted Franz for his achievement of longevity by boisterously singing a traditional German birthday song.

"I'll cut the cake in a minute," Anneliese announced to the guests. "But, first, I have a surprise for Franz. This morning I received an e-mail from Heinrich. He's in the U.S., you know Florida."

Heinrich Schmidt, their youngest son, had morphed into Harry Smith with his move to Orlando ten years ago. He was now working as an investment banker and lived with his Bavarian-born wife, Ingrid, and their three children.

"Let me read what it says: 'Dear Papa. We are so sorry that we can't celebrate with you today. But if you watch the post over the next few days you will find airline tickets for you and Mama to visit us in Florida. Kiss Mama for us. We love you, Harry.'"

The guests cheered with approval. They ate, laughed, drank, consumed more, and lingered long.

The sun was slipping behind the Alpine foothills when the celebratory crowd began to leave, with a chorus of "Auf Wiedersehens" trailing off. The quiet was welcomed by Anneliese and Hilda, Otto's wife, who were in the kitchen cleaning up. The two longtime best friends sat in the rococó-style lounge in ornate gold-framed armchairs in front of the dormant fireplace. They shared groans of satiety as well as a bottle of plum-flavored schnapps. The spirits enabled them to talk more freely, but each knew there were still off-limits topics for their tight friendship.

Otto remained unfeeling about the war. In his heart he didn't believe that the machinations of the Third Reich were so appalling and never felt the need to be apologetic about it. He was not enamored with Jews and abhorred homosexuals. He had followed his orders with great passion.

Franz, however, carried a quiet guilt of the horrors every day of his life. He cared about people of every type. His opinions were unbiased, never discriminating. He became more and more humbled in his advancing years.

Breaking the silence, Otto complimented his friend, "You are not such a bad cook, Franz, a little heavy on the fat content maybe."

"Are you kidding? Fat adds richness and flavor to all foods. And what do you mean, 'not such a bad cook'?"

"You are right. You are a good cook. But the fat sets up barricades in your arteries," Otto retorted. "On the other hand, those marinated pigs' knuckles were especially fine and tender, I must concede."

"So, then," he asked, "you and Annaliese will you be off to the States? Soon?"

"Yes, shortly. We haven't seen Heinrich and his family in a number of years and now there is a new baby we never met."

"He has done well for himself in Florida."

"Indeed. To tell you the truth, I always worried about Heinrich," Franz confessed. "He was the most difficult of the children: very intense, argumentative and stiffly Germanic. He doesn't have his mother's warmth. At times he shows an unfortunate lack of compassion and sensitivity. He displays little concern for his siblings and doesn't seem interested in their well-being. He has a dark spot, Otto, and I don't know what it is. This bothers me."

"Ah, Franz, that's the schnapps talking."

"Maybe a little bit, but I have an unsettling feeling in my heart about him. Nevertheless. we shall have a good time there. They want to take us to Disney World. Hah! I'm too old for Mickey Mouse."

"But not too old to fuck Minnie, eh, Franz?" He bent over and gave his old friend a playful elbow to the ribs.

"You are a lecherous old man, Otto."

"Well, I still have my fantasies, Franz. I can't act on them much anymore, but they are still vivid and in technicolor."

"We know of someone in the States. It's been more than 60 years since I've seen him, and I don't have a clue where he is. He was a young American soldier; a military policeman at Fort Dix. Do you remember him, Otto? He was compassionate. He brought us cigarettes and other items to make life easier during our captivity. We were so young and in a strange enemy land. I was confused, lonely and afraid of what might happen. This guy looked out for us. He took charge. He cared. I think his name was Arthur or Art and he had a bushy head of Irish red hair. I wouldn't begin to know where or how to look for him."

"You paid more attention to all that than I did. Let me think about it. Maybe I can remember. How to find him? A needle in a haystack, Franz. I suspect the spirits are truly beginning to work on you. Let's go and have a little snack. How about a nice big slice of some of that Bayerische cream cake?"

"More cake, Otto? ... and you say I am a bit heavy with the fats?"

Like mischievous children, the cronies tiptoed into the darkened dining room to avoid lectures from their fraus about overeating. Back in their easy chairs in the lounge, they devoured the desserts quietly.

Otto seemed lost in his thoughts. He had a great deal on his mind. He reflected on the meeting of the Fourth Reich to be held the following week in Munich and of the anti-American plot they were about to unleash. This prompted him, as if from out-of-the-blue, to remember a thumb drive that was critical to get to the States.

"Franz, I have a special memento for your son. I will bring it for you to take when you travel to Florida. I know that he will want it.

"It will be a pleasure, Otto," Franz acknowledged without a hint of suspicion as his mind was on the kindly American soldier with the bushy mane of red hair.

Chapter 1
Fresh Ingredients

The dilapidated Orlando Senior Center was swarming with activity. The raucous sounds of banter, pots and pans clanging and the laughter from elderly men in the kitchen drifted throughout the building as it did most Thursdays when The Old Men's Cooking Club met to prepare and eat their weekly communal lunch.

CIA retiree Dick Reynolds shouted, "Hi fellas," and waved to all, after wandering into the antiquated kitchen – late as usual. The busy chefs looked up from their gastronomic chores, grunted and resumed their work.

Know-it-all Abe Kacynscy diced bright-red, beefy tomatoes with the theatricality of a Japanese hibachi chef, yelling "Banzai" for all to hear. To his left, bushy-haired Irishman Art O'Neil was sniffing and blinking from his flowing rivulets of tears as he chopped the onions. Club-leader Fred Davis shifted back and forth, tossing salad mix up in the air, then catching it in the bowl like a child at play.

There were only five of the ten elderly chefs in the kitchen today and each had double-duty to create today's lunch. Abe grabbed a basting brush and painted an open-face half of French bread with garlic, oil and gobs of butter. Art's eyes, still filled with tears from the onions, now sported fogged eyeglasses as he got ready to boil water for spaghetti, while a flustered smart-aleck Abe rushed over to the stove to ponder how to work the new high-tech stove the Center bought with Federal stimulus money. He muttered to himself, "I wonder if the government knew that those funds would be used to stimulate our stomachs rather than the economy."

Authoritarian-leader Fred flaunted his role as the club's designated chef of the week. He was now fondling chicken breasts with a look of exaggerated lust. Dick meandered over to the stove to watch his co-chef sprinkle a variety of spices on the plump fowls with passion.

"What's that smell? How are you seasoning the chicken today, Fred?"

"Shhh, if I told you, I would have to kill you," The chef du jour said as he lovingly prepared the chicken to be baked.

Dick took his place among the harried workers and stood over the sink feverishly trying to rub out an ugly, yellow turmeric stain on one of last week's serving plates. "Who the hell washed the dishes last?" he griped.

"You did!" The unanimous and resounding response filled the room with laughter and camaraderie.

Ernest Stubbs, the self-appointed kitchen "Grand Poohbah," held court while sitting in the middle of the cookery watching the frantic work of his four fellow chums and anticipating the fruits of their labors. Ernie didn't cook, and the group allowed him to get away with it. He was certainly no stranger to food consumption and proved it by having a voracious appetite and demonstrating his love of eating.

Ernie was fiercely proud of his longevity, thriving beyond his 86th birthday. As one of the oldest members of the club, he was quick to tell new acquaintances that he was around when the Dead Sea was only the Sick Sea. Few knew that he was once a tall, virile man since he was now stooped over, exposing his bald scalp and large brown benevolent eyes. He had an ill-fitting, below-the-knee prosthetic leg necessitated by a near-fatal car accident. An insurance company made him, once a poor man, financially fit for the rest of his life. He endured the amputation of his leg, a bout with lymphatic cancer, kidney failure, chronic heart problems and diabetes. Nevertheless, he boasted being the healthiest "sicko" in the club.

"Hey, Dickie boy," he called out across the room, looking for someone to pay attention to him.

Ernie laughed at Dick's quick retort: "I see you are doing your usual Thursday morning activity, Ernie: nothing."

"Now, now. You know I don't cook. I come by each week to give you guys an exquisitely hard time. Hell, I even take you all out for breakfast occasionally."

"Yeah, big spender. We go to Denny's. And, Ernie, each of us pays for our own food!"

Fred interrupted by offering Dick another kitchen job that his buddy could not ruin. "Hey, Dick, I need your help plating the desserts."

"Yeah, sure, go ahead. Let Dick do that," Ernie chortled with a mischievous smile. "That is if you don't mind upside-down cake."

Dick shook his head and mumbled, "You're hilarious, Ernie."

"It seems to me that after 43 years in the CIA, you should at least be able to boil an egg."

Abe joined in the fun. "Don't let him near the knives. The last time he chopped tomatoes, we couldn't tell the difference between his blood and the tomato drippings."

"Yeah," Fred said, as he lovingly caressed the plump fowl breasts with spices. "It took us several hours to clean up after the fire department left

6

when he fried bacon."

"What am I doing here?" Dick said shaking his head.

"Why did you join the club?" Abe asked.

"Great question. It's because my wife hoped that a cooking class would be a useful, as well as a challenging, activity to stimulate my mind and stomach."

"So, how long have you been here now, Dick?"

"Three months, since the day Ruth kicked me out of the house."

"Well, what do you think?"

"I thought I was coming here to learn how to cook," Dick smiled. "But you're a just a bunch of old farts who want to get away from your wives for a couple of hours a week."

"Wait, who are you calling old?" Ernie chirped in, rising slowly from his chair for the first time.

Ernie eyed Dick fumbling with the dessert pan and ambled over to harass him.

"For someone who spent so many years as a spymaster, you can't even find your way around a kitchen."

"Thanks, Ernie."

"Seriously, Dickie boy, when did you retire?"

"It's been seven years since they gave me my gold pin and shoved me out the door at Langley."

"Yeah, right. So, what did you do then?"

"Nothing. The forced retirement caused a fate worse than illness: boredom. My moderately glamorous career was grueling. Time had never been a commodity that I enjoyed before. Ruth went nuts with me around the house. She was frantically searching for activities to occupy my time and give her some peace. Her prayers were answered one morning, or so she thought, when she eyed a heaven-sent advertisement in a senior citizen newspaper promoting this men's cooking group."

Fred shuffled over to the stove, lifted a fork, stabbed a strand of spaghetti out of the boiling water and handed it to Art. "You think this is cooked enough?"

The Irishman tasted the floppy piece of pasta. "Nope, I think it needs more time."

"Here, Abe, you have a taste. Tell me what you think. Are we ready to eat?"

Abe dramatically took his time sloshing the spaghetti strand in his mouth. "Tastes ready to me," he smiled knowingly and flipped Art the "bird" with his wrinkled middle finger.

"Here, let me tell you if it's ready," the non-cooking Ernie was already standing in front of his permanent throne, grabbed a fork, fished for a strand of pasta from the bubbling pot and flicked it into the air towards the cabinet. The wormlike pasta stuck with a slapping sound.

"Yup, it's done," Ernie beamed with a victorious smile. The boys all stood there mesmerized, mouths agape as the pale, beige pasta strand stayed glued to the 1950's avocado-green cabinet door.

The silence was short-lived. One after another the cooking crew was energized. "Hey, let me try that."

"Me too"

"Give me one of those strands."

The pasta-tossing melee began and soon strips of sticky starch were all over the room. A piece of spaghetti dangled from the fly of Abe's outdated, plaid Bermuda shorts. "Is that spaghetti or your skinny wiener hanging out?" Ernie shouted causing loud laughter. Dick scratched his head as he watched the elder children at play.

Chairman Fred signaled for the end of the chaos. As co-founder of the club he was a natural- born leader. The impressive 75-year-old polymath was clearly one of the most educated of the lot. This led the group to assume that he had wasted his meritorious knowledge on garbage since his long-term career was in the waste management industry in New Jersey. Everyone speculated that he had worked for the Mafia. Along with his love of cooking, Fred, like Ernie, was a hearty eater.

When the club was inaugurated, ten years before, it was he who brought to the group a recipe to be implemented at the weekly gathering. As he expected, the boys followed through with the execution of the meal. At first, they eagerly anticipated his culinary creations since he was one of the top chefs of the group. Eventually, others in the group were also bursting with creative ideas. They ganged up on Fred to change that procedure. Now each member was assigned a week to create his own menu, and, with the help of the group's senior chef, assembled and prepared the lunch for all.

"Come and get it, guys!" boomed Fred. They rushed to line up along the kitchen counter. Each filled his paper plate to the brim, grabbed the plastic utensils and adjourned to their makeshift dining salon, the computer room across the hall. The starch course was sparse as most of the spaghetti was hanging on the walls or plastered to the floor of the kitchen.

Dick passed out cups of water to help wash down the sometimes-indigestible chow.

Art was the senior member of the clan. He sported an enviable mane of bushy white hair, quite a feat for an 86-year-old. As an old reserved

Southern boy from Arkansas, he loved nothing more than tending his vegetable garden.

Abe was a short stocky octogenarian who believed he knew everything about everything and wasn't shy about sharing this belief. He bragged about handling foundations for many years. Everyone surmised he worked in the construction or philanthropy field. Only later did they find out he specialized in designing and building women's girdles and bras.

Ernie finally joined the boys at the table. The outspoken grouch was always last in line, citing his good manners by letting them go ahead of him. But everyone knew he scooped up double portions of what was left after the rest had helped themselves. "Oh goody! Chicken; a healthy lunch for a change," Ernie said, eager to attack his heap of vittles.

"Healthy, my ass," Abe said with a skeptical look. "You call this healthy? The French bread alone is hemorrhaging butter and cholesterol. The tossed salad is coated with sugar-filled dressing. Our man-handled spaghetti with canned vodka sauce is swimming on top of the baked chicken breast."

"Screw you, Abe. Look how healthy I am," Ernie boasted.

The cooks almost choked on their food when they heard his big fat lie.

The voracious quintet assailed their delicious, if unhealthy, meal. Ernie took this to be a cue to begin his traditional, weekly government-bashing comments.

"Did anyone see where President Sharif used Helicopter One to take his damn dog to be groomed? And, on my money?"

"Where on earth did you hear that baloney?" Dick tried to make light of Ernie's mindless political ramblings.

Ernie smelled blood and continued passionately, "I hate Sharif. Can you imagine the President of the United States is a Muslim? He doesn't like Americans. He doesn't like us. Our White House has been reconfigured with Muslim decorations. Can you imagine that? Sharif is destroying us. We are all going to be ruined under his rule."

"Calm down, Ernie," Dick snapped. "How many times do I have to tell you that Sharif's a Christian. Born in the good old U.S.A. His parents were Egyptian Christians."

"That son-of-a-bitch Sharif just won re-election. I bet someone shoots him while he's in office. At least I hope someone does."

"Why don't you shoot him yourself?" Abe challenged.

"If I was thirty years younger, there might be no stopping me."

The room fell silent.

"Whoa, that's extremely dangerous talk, Ernie. You need to watch what you say before you get into real trouble!" Dick looked directly into Ernie's eyes, fearful that his friend was serious.

"You do know that even making a statement like that is a Federal offense?"

"The Prez hates Jews too," Ernie blurted out, totally ignoring Dick's remark.

"Do you hate Jews, Ernie?" Abe asked.

"Well, I like some Jews."

"I'm a Jew, Ernie. Do you like me?"

"No! I mean, yes. I thought you were Christian. I don't believe you're a Jew, Abe."

"You want me to open my fly?" Abe jumped up from his chair.

"Spare us the spectacle, Abe," someone shouted.

"Not a spectacle, a thrill."

"We never knew, Abe," Art added.

"Was there ever any reason to bring it up?" Abe sounded defensive.

"In the seven, heartburn-filled years that I have been in the club, I never knew Abe was a Jew."

Ernie looked puzzled.

"Fellas," Dick intervened, "let's change the subject, I think …"

Ernie, however, carried on his campaign, "Vice President Sid Townsend should be behind the big desk in the Oval Office instead of that bastard. I like Townsend. Although I understand he is a bit of a pansy."

Moans of disbelief could be heard.

"I'm not even going to ask you where you got that tidbit," Dick said.

"From an article I read in the National Gazette while I was waiting in the check-out line at the supermarket."

"Sheer nonsense! He's got a sexy wife with big tits. and four beefy-looking sons," Abe corrected him.

"So what if Townsend is gay?" Dick said, "Big effing deal."

"Because I don't like homos either."

Aggravated groans prevailed.

"Come on, Ernie. One of our own boys, Charles, is a homosexual."

"I don't mind if Charley's a fairy. I can tolerate him as long as he keeps his hands and rump to himself."

Dick piped in trying to change the subject once again, "Mm, mm. Art, these tomatoes in the salad are wonderful, so juicy and sweet."

"Those are my prize beefsteaks. I grow them with love."

Fred walked in from the kitchen holding a hot baking sheet and offered each of his fellow cooks a large brownie.

"Hey, are those marijuana-filled brownies, Fred? Magic brownies?"

"No such luck," Ernie said.

Abe and Art stood, relieved that the interruption had quieted Ernie, removed the plates and headed back to the kitchen to begin the cleanup ritual. Abe had a weird passion for scouring the stove to make it sparkle. Art, on the other hand, loved to get his hands in the soapy dishwater. Ernie sat alone, as usual, leaving the work to everyone else.

"How's Ruth, Dick?" Ernie asked, switching from terrible Mr. Hyde to Dr. Jekyll.

"She's struggling, Ernie. Doctors want her on a new cancer drug therapy. They say it will save her life, but Medicare may not cover it. It costs a fortune and will probably bankrupt me," Dick looked subdued.

"It's that frigging Egyptian Muslim Pharaoh, He's the one killing your wife. Listen, Dick, if you need some money, I have a nest egg from my accident settlement. I'd be happy to help you out, really."

Incredulous, Dick stared at his generous, if prejudiced, buddy. His offer was a total surprise. Ernie was such loose cannon, the most bigoted man he knew. He wondered how Bessie had tolerated him for so many years. He knew they had been married and divorced twice and she was now his caretaker and best friend.

"I am sure grateful for your offer, Ernie, but we'll manage somehow." Dick went to help the boys put the pots, pans and bridge chairs away.

"Who's cooking next week?" Fred asked.

"Me. I am," Art said.

"Great, more of your prized vegetables."

Ernie joined Dick as they left the building. They looked like the cartoon characters Mutt and Jeff. Dick, tall and lanky wearing his New York Yankees baseball cap, sauntering alongside Ernie who was stooped-over and hobbling. A most unlikely duo, they were the Old Men's Cooking Club's misfits; one couldn't cook and the other wouldn't.

"You know, Ernie, you never cease to amaze me. You are a dirty, old curmudgeon with a pockmarked heart of gold," Dick said, his arm around his buddy's shoulder.

"Stop that, Dick. Don't talk dirty to me."

The two senior cooks shook hands. Ernie got into his boxy white Scion to head for his lakeside condo in Altamonte Springs and favorite rocking chair. Dick eased himself up into his shiny-black SUV and headed home to the comfort of his rickety dock and trusty fishing poles. He marveled at how fate and food had brought them together, but also had a gnawing feeling that after listening to Ernie's rantings, their lives were about to tailspin from a simmering teapot to a boiling tempest.

Chapter 2
Passing the Torch

Like a beached whale, Otto Schafer's belly drooped over the blue and white checkered restaurant tablecloth. Hilda could do nothing to get him to lose weight.

"I've had this bulge for 80 years and it hasn't killed me yet," he constantly protested.

A passionate lover of food, drink and other excesses, food competed with sex throughout his marriage. Food had won. With a polished scalp, now free of blond hair, his once-bright blue eyes had turned smoky with age. Puffy jowls rounded out his face but there was a steely look in his eyes. Otto was a protean character resembling the side-by side-masks of comedy and tragedy. He could be charismatic and charming, yet cruel, calculating and controlling. He loved to laugh, yet there was a distinct coldness in his demeanor. He tended to be stiff and stuffy which Hilda was constantly defusing. Although he used a cane, he was buoyant and remarkably vigorous despite painful sciatic nerve damage from the war.

Starting as a lowly teller at a Munich bank after the war, Otto rose quickly within the ranks of senior management. He made money for his affluent and questionable Bavarian compatriots while they provided him with wealth and security. Always a deal maker, he was ruthless in achieving rewarding ends.

Sitting alone in his favorite restaurant, the Haus Heuport, Otto enjoyed looking out of the window at the beautiful church in Regensburg's old town center. The pealing of the church bells rang throughout the medieval town. The lunch plate before him was filled with his favorite delicacies. He was salivating at the thought of eating the fillet steak von rind, gushing with onions, dollops of butter, and German fries. The half empty bottle of a 2008 Riesling was the icing on the cake for this perfect meal.

Thinking about the lovely birthday party Anneliese had thrown for his buddy Franz, he mused, "If only Hilda could cook like that." She rarely allowed him in the kitchen since it was small, and his stomach got in the way. If he wasn't consuming excess space, he was always sampling more than the portions being prepared.

Hilda would tell him, "Otto, you are less dangerous in the dining room than the kitchen."

Although his dear friend, Franz Schmidt, was an old man, Otto never accepted that within a few months he too would cross that same milestone. Despite his years and bulk, he daily walked a mile each way to the bank, still participating in its transactions. Hilda would not permit Otto to retire, since if he just stayed at home, he would make her crazy.

Consuming everything he could about the World War II, he collected memorabilia from that era. Fiercely patriotic to the Fatherland from the time he served in the "Hitlerjugen" to when he returned to Germany in 1945 after internment in a prisoner of war camp in New Jersey. Otto continued to believe in the draconian practices of the Third Reich and even today was an active leader within the secret Fourth Reich. As a card-carrying member of the National Democratic Party of Germany, he attended covert meetings under the guise of his other hobbies. It was amazing that his best pal and former war buddy, Franz, didn't have a clue about his current activities. Hilda and his children were oblivious to that damaged part of his psyche as well. But never mind all of that, today was a glorious day and he was involved in his favorite pastime, gluttony.

Otto marveled at the tourists feeding the pigeons and taking photographs in the square. Witnessing a young man clad in a leather outfit drive up and park his motorcycle, he gazed up as the Aryan youth entered the eatery and was directed to his table.

"Herr Schafer?"

"Ya."

"A package for you."

"Danke," Otto said, reaching into his jacket pocket for some coins to tip him.

Opening the small parcel, he found another well-sealed package with a note. He tore it open:

Dear Otto,

To be given to Franz Schmidt to transport to his son Heinrich in Florida. Hope all is going well with the plans. I am looking forward to our upcoming lunch in Munich.

Heil Hitler!
Siegfried Schloss

As he prepared to attack the juicy steak, his cellphone rang out with the first four infamous notes of Beethoven's Fifth Symphony.

"Hallo"

"Uncle Otto, how are you?"

"Good, good, Heinrich. How are things in Orlando?" He asked as he begrudgingly put his knife and fork down.

"Fine. Did I call you at an inconvenient time?"

"No, I was just sitting at my favorite bistro, getting ready to devour a magnificent steak fillet."

"Then I won't keep you long. How are you feeling, Uncle?"

"Surprisingly well, my boy, for a very ancient fossil."

"And Aunt Hilda?"

"She is young, like a spring chicken."

"That's wonderful. How was my father's birthday? Did he get my e-mail? Was he pleased about the gift?"

"The party was lovely, and the food was mouth-watering. I didn't know he could cook so well."

"My father always loved to cook."

"And yes, your papa was ecstatic, he talked about the trip to Florida all evening."

"I'm very glad."

"How are things going there?" Otto asked, changing the subject quickly.

"We're making progress. Our plan will soon be complete," Heinrich reported.

"I anxiously await the details."

"Uncle, did you wire the money?"

"Ya, I deposited two hundred thousand dollars in your account on Friday at the Deutsche Bank, Cayman Islands."

"Excellent. I shall keep you posted," Heinrich said, very pleased. "What about the thumb drive? Is it in your possession?"

"I just received it moments ago. It's sealed in an envelope and I plan to stop by tonight to wish your folks a bon voyage and drop it off."

"Are you sure that my father doesn't suspect anything?"

"He thinks it's a special memento for you. I believe that everything is fine."

"Good," Heinrich said with slight trepidation in his voice.

"Give my love to your beautiful wife, Ingrid, kiss the children and keep up the excellent work. Bye, bye," Otto was euphoric. A legacy was being passed on to a new generation.

Chapter 3
Who Killed Bambi?

Although he seldom spoke, Art O'Neil was welcomed to the Old Men's Cooking Club as one of the boys. While not as nimble as many and certainly more reserved than Ernie, the bushy-haired 86-year-old hobbled into the kitchen lugging several shopping bags filled with the assorted ingredients needed for today's meal. Art's selection: venison stew.

As soon as Art rested his larder on the counter, Abe appeared as if from nowhere and began poking into the bagged food. "Hey, Art. What's in the bags?"

"Deer!"

"Thanks, honey. But what's in the bag?"

"Deer!" Art chuckled, defeated by Abe's quick response.

Dick quipped from across the room. "Aw! Who killed Bambi?"

"Probably Ernie" the elder ex-bartender biker, Joe, explained. "Who else?"

"Nah, my son Bob did. Bagged it while hunting up in the northern Panhandle," Art explained.

Macho-biker Joe, acting totally insensitive, asked, "So, who's on the menu for next week? Thumper? He shoots any rabbit while he's at it?" 75-year-old Joe Jones, a former bartender and Harley-Davison fanatic brought a touch of redneck and mouth-watering ribs to the fold.

The jovial laughter subsided, and men of the club came to order and focused on the task of preparing lunch. There was the full complement of cooks today and a flutter of activity ensued with percolating noises from the coffee pot and water boiling for corn on the cob providing the background music.

Fussy Charles Hamilton, an old homosexual and fanciful chef, delicately removed the bread wrapper, and sliced the fresh loaf in half. He reached over to get his basting brush sitting in warm butter and artistically painted the French bread with yellow pools of butter. The knock-off version of the Parisian favorite was baked in Orlando and served as a pacifying appetizer to keep the men in line while the meal was cooked.

Ernie held court on his perch, waxing poetic apropos of nothing.

Trawling the group with his comments, he waited for someone to strike the bait and issue a challenge.

Four of the members circled around Art, trying to decipher the recipe for this strange, never-before-served-in-this-kitchen entrée.

Abe was busy, scrubbing clean the beefsteak tomatoes that Art had harvested from his garden. Dick stood over the newspaper-covered table shucking the husks off the corn. The results: there was more silk on him than the yellow stalks ever had.

"Say, Bill. How much do we pay this week?" asked Ed Fisher, the boring scientist.

"Five bucks each," answered Bill Foster, the 74-year-old wealthy, retired junk dealer and the group's frugal banker. "And that's a good deal." The boys believed that he had the first nickel he'd ever earned, and nicknamed him the "Buy One, Get One Free King."

"I'm going to quit this group," protested Ernie. "It used to be two bucks a week. It's getting too damn expensive."

"Come on, Ernie. Where can you get a meal for two dollars?" Ed challenged the malcontent.

"At Burger King."

"I said 'meal,' Ernie, not a heart attack."

Preparations continued. The supply of buttered French bread dwindled. Attention now focused on the Chef of the Week.

Art was seen by all as a unexpressive, passive man except for his seldom heard, but infectious laugh. Although friendly, he could be non-committal, making it hard to decipher his feelings. Like most of the group, he had lost most of his hearing, making it challenging to communicate with him. His was a gentle soul, but his body revealed battles with the less-than-gentle adversary: time. Art's arms were covered with brown liver spots, purple bruises and assorted other colorful markings: his "merit badges": the tattoos of the AARP set. His thick, shaggy mane of hair was the envy of everyone in the room.

As a widower who'd lived alone for several years, Art missed his children who were dispersed around the country. Members of his sole social outlet, the cooking club, never learned what he had done for his career. But it was obvious that he was very proud to have served his country during World War II. Art was wounded as a soldier in 1944 on a German battlefield. He was returned to the States, and leaving the field hospital, proudly wore his Purple Heart to recuperate. Later, he was assigned to Fort Dix to guard German and Italian prisoners of war shipped there to work during the war. He was a good-natured soul who made a point of treating his charges with the respect he would have wanted.

In the crowded kitchen the cooking crew soldiered on with food prep and tomfoolery.

Abe, Art, Joe and Dick gathered around Fred by the stove trying to decipher the recipe for the main course.

"Where the heck did you get this 'mishugana' recipe?" Abe asked.

"I found it in the library in an old Scottish cookbook."

"Old is one thing, but readable would be good, don't you think?" Abe continued, "The print is so tiny, it's hard to focus on. Might just as well be a secret recipe?"

Art's laugh lifted everyone, "Let's hope that 'secret' means 'delicious' in Scotland.

"Okay, boys, let's get this show on the road," barked Fred.

"Let's see. What do we need?"

"We have the venison. It's trimmed and diced," Art said. "It marinated in herbs all night."

Dick was concerned about what anatomical part of the deer he would be eating. "Says here you need the shoulder of the deer. Are you sure that you have the right body part?"

"We've got what my son sent me. Who knows: could be the shoulder, could be the testicles? What you see is what we got."

"I'm not eating any stewed buck balls," boomed Ernie from across the room.

"So, Fred what else do we need?"

"¼ cup butter."

"Check"

"An 8 oz. piece of streaky fatty bacon cut into ¾ of an inch hard-ons."

"I got more than a ¾ inch hard on. I thought you said the shoulder." Joe volunteered.

"Let me see. Hand me the recipe." Dick said. "It says lardons, fellas."

"What the heck is a lardon?"

"What you need in order to have great sex." Ernie quipped.

Dick opened his cell phone and tapped the Google icon. "According to Google, 'a lardon is bacon, diced, blanched and fried.'"

"Never mind that crap. Just throw in the bacon," Abe said impatiently holding up the sizzling frying pan.

"Onions, carrots, celery and flour."

"Check, check, check. And check."

"Garlic"

"Lots of garlic," instructed Dick.

"You know what they say about garlic? 'A nickel will get you on the subway, but garlic will get you a seat.' Careful, Dick, put in too much and your wife won't kiss you or anything else you want," Ernie arched his eyebrows up and down a la Groucho Marx. He was amused by his own words of wisdom.

"Yeah, garlic is Italian birth control," Joe joined in and laughed.

Ernie stood and bellowed, "Birth control? Well, it sure as hell doesn't work. Look how many of them Eye-trall-yuns we have…"

"Stuff it, Ernie." Abe called. "Hey Ed, did you smuggle in the wine?"

"Got it right here in the Dr. Pepper bottle," he answered, lifting a cola-labeled, two-litre plastic bottle out of a shopping bag.

The Senior Center had strict prohibitions against any alcohol on the premises, but wine had been smuggled in by this group in various disguises for years.

"Says half a bottle," read Art.

"Oh, pour the whole damn thing in. You only live once," Dick commanded.

The countdown continued with everyone chiming in.

"Wine."

"Check."

"Salt and dark stock"

"Right here."

"Heaps of salt"

"That's not good for my high blood pressure," Ernie reported.

"That's why I said 'heaps.'"

Fred continued: "Red currant jelly?"

"I don't know what red currant jelly is, so I got some Welch's grape jam," Art explained.

"And finally: black pepper."

"Ernie only eats white pepper. You know him."

"Yeah, yeah, I got it. Well, he won't be eating any today unless he brought his own."

"Okay, then we're good to go."

Art and the gang sliced, mixed, stirred, diced, sautéed, simmered and seasoned the entrée to completion. Finally, lunch was served. They devoured the intriguingly unique venison stew, fresh salad and sweet corn.

"Save room for the batch of apple strudel I made for dessert, guys," Abe pointed to the oven and said, "Take a whiff. Boy, that's what heaven smells like."

"Speaking of German apple strudel," Dick interjected with a serious tone, "any of you read the piece in the newspaper this morning about hate groups in this area? Mostly in Bithlo, Mims and Christmas."

"The Klu Klux Klan and the Aryan Connection and a dozen other hate groups are always active out in the boonies."

"Maybe the Klan will shoot the president," exclaimed Ernie.

"So, are you saying that you'll shoot President Sharif, Ernie?" Joe blurted out, somewhat annoyed by the constant bilious political ravings of his cooking pal.

"I was thinking about it," Ernie smirked.

A chorus of boos and razzing erupted.

"From my experience," Dick interjected, "I'm more worried about the Aryan Connection. An active group of neo-Nazis in our backyard. Lord help us!" Dick gradually raised his voice.

"According to the news this hate group is following the principles of the World War II Nazis and is advocating the destruction of Jews, blacks and anyone who's not white. It's scary stuff. I mean, here? Now?"

"It was mighty horrific in Europe during the war but the thought of having this sort of budding holocaust right in our backyard is awful," Abe bellowed.

"Holocaust, my red, white and blue ass," Ernie proclaimed loudly. "I can't believe that the Holocaust actually happened." Ernie was being his ornery self again … only more so.

Dick gave him a look of horror. "You don't mean that, Ernie. You can't."

Abe attempted to remain calm. The cooking club was intended to be fun, but he started to feel his blood pressure rising.

"You, numb nuts, of course it took place, Ernie. My father lost eight brothers and sisters. Eight humans in one family alone!" Abe yelled, went over to Ernie and stared him in the eye. "We lived in Poland where they had a leather factory. In 1939, just before the war, my father brought us to the United States. I was seven. The rest of the family back home was arrested by the Gestapo. The Germans took over our factory." Abe's face mirrored the crimson of Art's tomatoes. "When they realized they couldn't operate this very technical business, they transported key members of my family from Auschwitz to run the company. And when they no longer needed them, they were shipped back to the camp – directly into the gas showers and ovens," Abe continued ranting at Ernie. "My father never saw any of his family again."

"Yeah, I saw the camps when I was in Europe during the war. They were nightmarish," Art confirmed in a wailing tone.

"I just don't believe anything I read in the press." Ernie recoiled and played a bit coy.

Without prompting, the usually closed-mouthed Art began telling a story about a prisoner he had met when he was a guard at Fort Dix.

"Ernie, I saw it with my own eyes. I'll never forget him; his name was Frantz. This guy was shot down and captured by the Americans. After being imprisoned in Bavaria, the military shipped him to the States. We were about the same age and I was assigned to watch over his unit." Art reminisced as a chill fell in the air.

"He was more civil than most, a sensitive lad, very different from the other Reich soldiers. He aspired to become a lawyer but there was no law left to practice under the Third Reich. We shared many hours together. Eventually he was shipped back to Germany after the war. I never knew what became of him."

"That's some story, Art. Have you ever tried to search for him?" Dick asked.

"For many years I have wanted to reconnect, but I didn't know where to start."

Dick looked at Art with a sympathetic grin and said, "That sounds like finding a needle in a haystack."

The group had never heard Art talk so much. Even Ernie listened intently to the poignant story.

"You know what? It's funny. I can't remember what I did yesterday, but I can remember vividly my relationship with Franz," Art, the Irish Catholic of the group, had become emotional. "The Holocaust was horrific. My association with Franz was the only good thing that I remember about the war."

"Why can't the CIA or FBI go into the woods and clear out those vermin," Abe pleaded to Dick.

"Because we don't have proof that they are breaking any law. And without proof, we have – how do you say it Abe – 'bubkes'?"

There was a long silence in the room. No one moved. Dick didn't know how much these boys were sympathetic to the plight of the Jews, but they had listened to these stories with rapt attention. A surprising tear slowly wound its way down Ernie's face. The group sat in silence, heads down. No one even tasted their strudel.

Chapter 4
The Cooked Goose

Dick Reynolds accelerated his car as he left the Senior Center with lots of troubling thoughts swirling around. Ruth's illness was always a major concern. Ernie's behavior bothered him. His cooking buddy was always off the wall, but his latest idiosyncrasies seemed to be getting out of hand.

Dick wanted, needed, and was trying to relax. He knew that fishing was the perfect prescription to release his tension and to relieve his mind. Once home, he changed into his fishing shoes and hat, collected his gear, a beer and strolled out to the dock behind his home.

His brown and green camouflage hat was a personalized token of his hobby. The colorful flies, leads and lures pinned to its crown jiggled in the light wind as Dick fished. Never without a hat, he usually wore his trusty NY Yankees cap, as he had earlier that day. Now he wore his lucky, military-style giggle hat, which he "knew" was essential for success in this sport. The cooking men constantly ribbed him that his hats covered the badly woven, colored hairpiece that Ruth made him wear.

An eerie quiet prevailed on the lake interrupted occasionally by the soft chirping of crickets and the distant croaking of bullfrogs. A vermillion sun was beginning to set in the distance. The heat of the day was, at last, subsiding.

Dick had retired from the CIA where he had seen and done it all. He had roamed the deserts of Africa dressed as a sheik and penetrated the souks of Afghanistan when it was extremely dangerous for any outsider. He paid his dues as a covert operative in the Soviet Union during the height of the Cold War. And then had a stint in New Mexico tracking UFOs on radar decades before "Star Trek." In later years he worked on subversive overseas operations from a desk at Langley. Dick's conjuring analytical mind was, by necessity, always percolating. Fishing was the antidote to keep him from that higher emotional plane.

The former agent had retired physically, but not mentally. He remained bright, enquiring, patient, and extremely methodical in his thinking. As always, his mind traveled a mile a minute over a highly familiar terrain. His daily therapy included completing The New York Times crossword puzzle

… in ink. Fishing from his backyard pier was a great passion, but he still itched for mind-challenging work.

Ironically, only his eyes itched and did so constantly from the pollen that permeated the humid Florida air. Even at a buoyant 75, he was not the healthiest of his chums. Years of high stress work had left its mark with damaged arteries and minor strokes.

Dick's first attempt to command the pots and pans at the Old Men's Cooking Club was a disaster. Always appreciating someone else's cooking abilities, he had never spent a moment in the kitchen until Ruth encouraged him to join the senior men's group.

Despite assurances that "It is almost impossible to ruin spaghetti and meat sauce," Dick did a grand job of achieving that goal. At his inaugural cooking session, he also dropped the tossed salad on the floor, burned the French bread, and his Jell-O mold failed to congeal. There was still little evidence of improvement in his cooking following his second and third attempts. His cooking-mate Ernie never attempted to cook, and although Dick tried, he never succeeded. He constantly entertained the cooking troops with stories of spy mastery and intrigue. They were good enough to serve as his credentials into the club. In fact, they were so good that they encouraged him to miss his turn on the cooking cycle. Although he always promised to do better the next time, everyone assured him that it was unnecessary.

The grey water in the lake was as still as glass. The red and white fishing bobbin lay motionless on the calm surface. Sitting low in his camping chair, rod in one hand and can of beer in the other, his long sinewy legs were stretched out across the dock. Finally, relaxation prevailed. The respite was ruined after too few minutes when he was startled by the obnoxious squawking of a pesky neighboring goose.

"I'm going get you, you son of a bitch," Dick yelled, positioning his cocked trigger fingers in the air; ready to shoot. "I'll get your goose, and when I do, you are going right into the pot at the Old Men's Cooking Club."

Ruth, Dick's cheerleader, came lumbering down the grassy hill from the house. She climbed the rickety steps to the pier and sat in the extra chair Dick always had set out for visitors.

"Who were you talking to, Dick?"

"Oh, no one, Ruth. I was just informing our neighborhood pest about his options for the future."

"I brought you a piece of apple pie," she offered.

"Thanks, hon, but I'm not hungry."

"Fish biting?"

"No"

"How was the cooking today?"

"It was okay."

"Dick, you seem so preoccupied. What's eating you?"

"Sorry, dear, I have a lot on my mind."

"Can I help?"

"You always help."

"Tell me."

"I'm worried about you, Ruth."

"We've been through so much together. We will both survive this setback as well."

"You have an amazing attitude, my lovely. No wonder I adore you so much."

Ruth was a survivor. She and Dick had been married for over 50 years. While his life was behind enemy lines, she sat alone for all those years waiting for the telephone to ring bearing bad news. He had put her through an endless number of sleepless nights. Even when his work attached him to a desk in Virginia, there was a reasonable and constant danger that some foreign agent could be after him. She never felt comfortable or safe.

Dick adored his three daughters but readily admitted that Ruth had single-handedly raised them. He, of course, provided for them financially, but he was seldom around to enjoy the spoils of their riches. Through thick and thin, she had adored him and knew that he was crazy about her.

"What else is troubling you, Dick?"

"I'm puzzled about Ernie. The older he gets, the more cantankerous he becomes. The boys say he was always a bit loony, but it seems like recently it's getting out of control. He said that the Holocaust never took place. Can you believe that? And, he was there, Ruth, right after the war. He hates the president and talks constantly about shooting him."

"I don't believe that one bit," Ruth cried out. "Oh, he must just be mouthing off, Dick. He's also not physically capable of carrying out something as dreadful as that."

"Ernie is an amazing sort. I don't know what he can do. But he is certainly capable of running off half-cocked with his loose lips which could land him in a messy stew."

"Can you talk to him?"

"I've told him to be careful who he says things like that to, but I don't think he listens."

Dick told Ruth about Ernie's generous offer of financial help. She sat there taking it in every word and shaking her head back and forth.

"Keep an eye on him, Dick. That's the best that you, or anyone, can do. I feel so sorry for Bessie."

"She deserves the Nobel Peace Prize for putting up with him all these years."

"Truly!"

"The funny thing is that beneath all that bluster, I truly believe there is a genuinely good person."

"It may be out of his hands, Dick. By the way, when do you cook next?"

"In three weeks, I guess."

"Have you thought about what you are going to make?"

"Besides a big mess? No, say, why don't you cook for me? I can bring it in, heat it up and the boys will never know the difference."

"That's cheating and besides they will definitely know the difference; anyone would."

"Well, we could burn the edges around the meat and overcook the vegetables slightly, so they will truly believe that it came from me."

"You can do that without me. You're always the plotter, Dick Reynolds, aren't you?"

They watched the sun sinking below the tree line, enjoying the cooling breeze and then walked slowly back up the path to the house, holding hands.

"I hope that Ernie is all right, Dick. Watch him. Protect him."

"I better or he will be the cooked goose."

Chapter 5
The Ponzi Chicken Scheme

"I gave my mother-in-law a burial plot for Christmas last year. 'What's the matter, no gift this year?' she complained. 'Well, you didn't use last year's,'" Club Leader Fred said and laughed.

"That was pretty lame," Abe said, grimacing.

The weekly meeting of the men's gastronomy group left the starters gate and was off and running.

Fred asked, "What's cookin' today, Bill?"

"Ponzu chicken and rice."

"Was it made by Bernie Madoff?"

"No, Art, that's Ponzi's a financial scam."

"I'm not eating any God-damned scammed chicken," echoed Ernie from across the room, seated on his usual do-nothing perch.

Money-man Bill set the record straight. "Don't worry, Ernie, Ponzu is a citrus-flavored sauce from Japan."

Once again, the Thursday morning lay chefs chopped, diced, and sautéed. The kitchen was alive with the sounds of cooking, coffee percolating, pots banging and dishes clattering. The boys were drooling for their pre-lunch snack of English muffins with mounds of butter, olive oil and cheese that were toasting in the oven.

"We have a special dessert today, guys. It's called spotted dick," Bill announced with a straight face.

"I'm not eating anyone's dick, let alone a spotted one," Ernie carried on in his loud voice.

"Ernie, calm down. It's just a flesh colored steamed pudding with dried fruit and a touch of custard on top. It originated in England."

"Speaking of spotted dick," Abe said, "Has anyone been reading about the new law going to the voters in San Francisco to ban circumcision? They say it violates one's choice about body mutilation."

Ernie began again in his usual bigoted manner. "I'll bet you that movement was instigated by our black Muslim president."

"Ernest!" a round of objections was heard.

"There he goes again with his passionate love for Muslims," Abe said, shaking his head.

"I wonder if Ernie would be so vocal if the president was just black?" came Bill.

"Ernie doesn't discriminate," Fred said.

Biker Joe was quick to respond, "With the economy in the shit house and American involvement in wars on so many fronts, I just can't imagine that cutting a boy's pecker is a priority on the president's desk."

Ignoring that remark, Ernie bantered on. "Next they'll want to build a mosque on the south lawn of the White House with direct access to the Oval Office."

"We keep telling you the president is Christian, Ernie. His parents were Coptic Christians from Egypt, and he was born right here in the good, old U.S.A," Dick repeated.

"Coptic, Coptic, what's that? I suspect that he used Coppertone to make himself look blacker."

"Ernie, you are exasperating."

"Yeah, he's Christian like I'm Jewish."

"Maybe you are Jewish, Ernie. Ever think of that. Are you circumcised?" Abe butted in.

"I'm not a Jew and I'm proud of my foreskin. I bet President Sharif is circumcised."

"Muslims perform the rite as well, Ernie," Charles said. "But unlike Jews, Muslims wait till the boys are twelve or so."

"Ouch, that's gotta hurt," Ernie said, grabbing his crotch.

"Everyone has it done nowadays," Dick added.

Club leader Fred jumped into the conversation, "They say that sex is better with a circumcision and it's a lot healthier for the boy."

"When the heck did, they start cutting off peckers anyway?" Ernie said, trying to be serious.

"Some say that there are drawings of this ritual on the walls of prehistoric caves. They can also trace the process back to ancient Egypt," know-it-all Abe told the group.

"I read that it began as a religious sacrifice marking the boy's entrance into manhood and symbolic to ensure virility and fertility," Fred added.

Charles chimed in, "I heard that in some parts of Africa the foreskin is dipped into brandy and eaten by the patient."

"You're into dick. You would know, buttercup," said Ernie.

"Stop that, Ern! You need to behave," Dick was getting hot under the collar.

"I am going on 86 and still have all of my parts. Well, most of them anyway."

"But it's never too late for your well-being. Hey, we could perform the circumcision surgery on you right now, here on the kitchen counter, Ernie," Abe said running over, brandishing an ominous meat cleaver. "Hold him down, boys."

"Don't come near me with that. Next, we will be eating foreskin stew," Ernie yelled across the room.

Shaking his head in disbelief, Dick just stood there staring at his warped buddy. Bill yelled while banging a pot loudly, "Fellas! Fellas! Lunch is served."

The plates were filled with the exotic Asian chicken over seasoned rice and peas with a salad of packaged shredded lettuce. Some of lunch's allure was lost with the discussion of the spotted dick.

Bill Foster, the chef of the day, was parsimonious. His food ingredients were generally generic, and portions were less than typical for the group's eating habits. Today's chicken packages boasted a buy one, get two free promotion, so lunch only cost $2.50 per head. This was especially popular with Ernie. The boys speculated that although he was the wealthiest member, They all thought that Bill probably still had every dollar he had ever earned. At a sprightly 74, one of the younger members, he had retired from his auto restoration parts business, or a glorified junk dealership. Operating junkyards in several states, he became rich selling obsolete auto parts. The seventeen-year-old jalopy he drove was kept running with parts from one of his yards. Bill had a passion for Dick's 1957 Edsel, believing he could get a mint for its parts. Dick had a bigger passion to keep this priceless lemon running forever and far from Bill's claws.

The boys hauled their less-than-loaded plates into their makeshift dining area and filled two tables. Dick and Ernie were odd men out and so sat together at the third one. Ernie shoveled down his green peas like there was no tomorrow, while Dick picked at his chicken.

"Mm, mm," announced Ernie ebulliently with green slime running down his chin. "This is the best meal we've had at the club since Ed served that canned chicken and dumplings."

"You have such wonderful taste in food, Ernie."

This was a rare and good opportunity for Dick to talk to Ernie alone. His buddy had been on a high horse all morning about blacks, Muslims, Jews, and his favorite topic: shooting the president.

So Dick began, "Ernie, you know that I am very fond of you."

"Oh, gee whiz!" Ernie said, not really knowing how to respond to this endearment from a male friend.

"I'd hate to see you get into trouble. I really respect your great patriotism and how loyal you feel towards this country. I spent my life protecting it. But you must be careful mouthing off about controversial topics like shooting President Sharif. You never know who might be listening." Dick was worried that Ernie would spout off at the wrong place and jeopardize his well-being.

"So, how is Ruth?" Ernie said, completely ignoring Dick's gentle warning.

"Ernie, this is not about Ruth. This is about your safety."

"Oh, you know that I don't always mean what I say," Ernie said with a large grin. "I'm just a big ol' teddy bear."

Dick wasn't so sure.

The spotted dick turned out to be a big hit, but Ernie didn't touch his. The boys headed to the kitchen to start the washing up ritual while Ernie sat on his perch and watched Bill portion out leftovers for the boys to take home. Soapsuds splashed everywhere as Art washed the dishes. Abe made love to the stove with a Brillo pad and Dick danced a mop around the floor.

"I won't be here next week. The grandkids are coming to town and I'm going to Disney World," Art explained.

Suddenly Bill asked loudly, "Anybody got some money to invest?"

"Don't look at me," Steve said. "All I own is time. Why are you asking?"

"Because I have this great young broker who's offering a deal that has a 15% guaranteed return. It's a small company from Georgia, AMACORP. This guy has given me some really good financial ideas before."

"I'm looking to put some money in silver," said Ernie, who had his nest egg from his lawsuit and liked to throw bits and pieces of money around.

"Silver is good, but this is a one-of-a-kind deal," Bill explained. "I've done research on the company and I'm going to invest a couple of grand."

"I could go a few, if you really think that it's a safe bet," Ed said.

"Me too," Fred and Art answered together.

"Must be a legitimate deal if cheap Bill's opening up his wallet," Fred whispered to Abe.

"With the banks paying less than one percent, this seems like a good thing." Bill said.

Abe was cautious, "I'd like to know more about it."

"Geez, guys, that's great. I'll give my broker, Harry Smith, a call and set the wheels in motion. I'm sure he'll meet with us and explain the details. Hey, Ernie, are you in?"

"Well, I don't know."

"Oh, come on, Ernie, I heard that you got a million bucks from your lawsuit," Steve said.

"I got some money for the accident and the loss of my leg, but the damn lawyers got half, the witnesses took their share, our Muslim Uncle Sam was next in line with his hand out, so that didn't leave me with much of a pot to piss in."

"But you should be able to take a small risk," Bill said.

"I've got a little cash, but I don't know, Bill, the deal smells to me like that scamming Ponzi chicken dish we had for lunch."

Chapter 6
The Pot Thickens

Senior investment-banker Harry Smith stared out the window of his plush penthouse office overlooking the city. Thinking how Orlando had blossomed since his wife, Ingrid, and he had settled here from Germany ten years ago. It was now a major city. Today, without a cloud in the sky, Harry could see the rafters of the nosebleed-high rollercoaster, 15 miles away, at the Universal Theme Park. His corner office had two walls of floor-to-ceiling windows. A cluster of oversized television screens bustled with banner-filled numbers depicting the economies of the world.

He was daydreaming about how fast the years had flown since he'd arrived in this country and remembering his first official American act: changing his name from Heinrich Schmidt to Harry Smith. His thoughts led him further back into his former life.

During his unremarkable upbringing, Heinrich had been doted on by his parents, Franz and Anneliese, but he had grown up angry and surly, so different from his warm, loving parents. An independent child, he went his own way and did his own thing. He was not particularly close to his older siblings who seemed to ignore him. He yearned for a close relationship with his father, but that never seemed to happen.

Although Franz was an affectionate, giving soul, he tended to be closed-mouthed, oblivious and distant. Heinrich desperately needed some male bonding and was constantly craving attention. He filled this gap by developing a close friendship with his father's wartime friend, Otto Schafer. Every day after primary school, Heinrich rode his bicycle to Otto's home and sat with him for hours in front of the fireplace, listening eagerly to his war stories.

Franz would not allow any discussion of war at home; it was a dark and shunned topic. With much hidden guilt, he buried the horrors into the far reaches of his mind. Otto, on the other hand, aggrandized his time as a Reich servant and proselytized proudly. He acted as a Dutch Uncle and taught Heinrich the history of the Third Reich with emphasis on the purity of the Aryan race. He coached him on the evils caused by non-Aryans and instilled a sense of hatred in his impressionable mind. Constantly vilifying the Zionist Jewish state, there was an excitement to his jingoistic views that was contagious. Heinrich became infected by Otto's passion. The abhorrence went farther than the Jews: Muslims, blacks, Hispanics, and homosexuals were viewed as a hindrance to a perfect life.

Since his father would not discuss the war, Heinrich did not reveal any signs of the shadowy cloud brewing in him. Unfortunately, Franz and Anneliese were oblivious to Heinrich's reprogramming. Otto cast a hypnotic spell over Heinrich. When his protégé graduated with a business degree from university, Otto gave him his first job at his bank. Under Uncle Otto's tutelage, Heinrich was lost forever. The otherwise clueless Franz was eternally indebted to his friend for taking the boy under his wing and supporting and developing his career.

From his high school years Heinrich was uncomfortable with girls and shied away from dating. Otto once again interfered, pushing him to date the "right" kind of German girl for the correct public perception. He introduced him to Ingrid, the daughter of another cherished friend and Reich compatriot. Heinrich and Ingrid had a long, platonic relationship and were finally married in the medieval church in Regensburg's main square. The Schmidt's refused to accept the reality that most of the guests at the wedding were subversive modern-day Nazis.

The young couple were naive about sex and their honeymoon was less than exhilarating since his passions were for politics and hatred. Those thoughts were erotic enough to give Heinrich his most powerful erections. Ingrid endured life as an obedient, old-fashioned German wife who wanted a path out of her rural town in Bavaria and Heinrich seemed to be the ticket. She was left out of the political entanglements and was kept ignorant of his shady leanings.

Otto initiated him into the draconian web of the New Reich and instructed him to disguise these activities with hobbies and other interests. Heinrich felt a contradicting pressure mounting which could not be contained. None of his friends waved flags of nationalistic prejudice. His family was devoted to love and goodness, while he was brainwashed into believing this hatred and evil. He was living within a conflicted world and at times felt like damaged goods. Although fiercely loyal to Otto, Heinrich felt smothered by him.

There was a strong need to flee from this rigid control and so he applied for a banking position in Florida. With his excellent credentials, he was hired immediately, and so Ingrid also was escaping Bavaria and Heinrich could run away.

"Harry" was six feet, two inches, ruggedly handsome with blondish hair that was turning grey at the temples and bright blue eyes. He conveyed a warm, charming demeanor, was an excellent salesman, bright and serious, yet ruthless in achieving his goals. He rapidly ascended the company ladder at the investment house and in his spare time took on leadership in an activity that created an outlet for his programmed mind: The Aryan Connection, a notorious American neo-Nazi organization.

Harry was jarred back to reality by the buzzing of his phone. Looking down at his lunch plate from Pineapple's, one of Orlando's tony restaurants, he mused to himself, "Uncle Otto's only positive influence was eating well." The glazed salmon drenched in pomegranate-port-molasses sauce was surrounded by boniato mash, a Caribbean sweet potato blended with heavy cream, butter, nutmeg, and a medley of spring vegetables.

In some ways Harry was a polygamist, married to both Ingrid and the appendage phone set that rested on his head.

"Harry Smith here," he said into the mouthpiece.

"Daddy, Daddy," a frantic cry. "There's a snake on our patio. It's big, red, yellow, and black and Mommy is hiding in the closet. I don't know what to do?"

"Just calm down, Anna. The snake is not going to come into the house. Call Mommy to the phone."

"But she's hiding."

"Just go get her! Please!"

Pause.

"Harry, you have to come home right away," pleaded Ingrid. "I'm so afraid. I don't know why we must live so far out in the country. Snakes on the patio, alligators on the golf course and even the cockroaches that come into the house are large enough to move our grand piano across the room. I'm so scared. What should I do, Harry?"

"Calm down, Ingrid. Call the police and tell them about the snake," he tried to calm her, "and call me back."

"Harry Smith" he said again.

"Heinrich, wie geht es der, mein Junge." The phone reception from Germany seemed choppy.

"Very well. Speak English, please. It's a bit difficult to hear you, Uncle Otto; I have been busy, Things have been turbulent all day."

"I hope that you are making lots of money."

"That seems secondary today."

"I visited your parents last night to wish them a bon voyage. They are excited about flying over. I gave your father the small package for you. The thumb drive contains all the necessary information. Be very careful with it."

"Does my father suspect anything?"

"I don't think so. I told him it was a little memento and advised him to keep it in his pocket to get past security without difficulty."

"Very good. I look forward to receiving it."

"Please let me know as soon as it's in your possession."

"I will. How is Hilda, Uncle?"

"Besides the aches and pains of being an old lady, she is surviving nicely."

"And you?"

"Busy as ever trying to start a revolution," Otto chuckled. "Hugs and kisses to Ingrid and the children. I'll speak with you very soon, auf wiedersehen."

"Auf wiederschen."

Harry savored a bite of the dehydrated fish as the phone buzzed again. It was a client who asked to purchase shares of stock, and he was grateful for some business today.

"Harry Smith," he said, trying to chew and talk at the same time.

"Heinrich, my son, I'm so glad I caught you."

"Ah, Mama! It's so lovely to hear your voice."

"Your papa can't decide what to pack. He wants to know what the weather is like in Florida? He has every shred of clothing he owns on the bed."

"Hold on, Mama. I have another call."

He rushed another customer who wanted to dump shares. Harry feverishly typed the order into his computer to get back to his mother.

"Sorry, Mama. Tell Papa to bring as little as possible: shorts, tee shirts. No one wears jackets and ties in Florida."

"Papa doesn't own shorts or tee shirts, only undershirts and underpants. He can't walk around in those. He must bring his suit. It's his uniform."

"Well, use your best judgment to steer him correctly, Mama."

"Uncle Otto dropped off a token for you. He says it's a memento that you would want to have. Papa will carry it on his person so as not to lose it."

"Very good."

She reminded him for the tenth time that they were arriving the day after tomorrow at 8:00 a.m. He told her that he would be at the airport with bells on and wished them a good flight.

While taking another quick bite of his soggy lunch, there was another rapid-fire ring.

"Harry Smith."

"Harry," said a frantic voice.

"Yes, Ingrid? How is the wildlife on the home front?"

"I called the police and pushed the children into the bedroom closet. Ten minutes later, two large police officers with their guns out came rushing into the house and ran onto the back porch. The next thing I knew a policeman was asking me to come out of hiding. They are now standing in our living room holding a three-foot-long spitting reptile. Thank God it wasn't poisonous but a harmless corn snake. They said it's good for the vegetation. It eats all kinds of insects and suggested that it should be put back in the garden. I told them to take the wriggling object and put it in the patrol car and drop it off 250 miles away in Miami. I can't live here in the woods much longer, Harry, please."

"Ingrid, right now you need to pull yourself together and continue preparing for my parents' visit."

"Easy for you to say, you are not here all day."

"Just keep me posted."

Ingrid did put up with a lot. She had wanted to live in one of the more affluent communities near downtown Orlando. They certainly had the resources, but Harry insisted on a rural area near Deland, 25 miles northeast of Orlando. When he wasn't working, he wanted peace and quiet and to be able to go into the woods and practice with his guns. She had spent most of her life in a rural town in Bavaria and this isolated area felt just as backward.

She needed to communicate with people and considered herself and the children prisoners. Dreading the upcoming visit of the in-laws, what would she do with them in the middle of nowhere? It would be good for the children to be with their grandparents, but she would be on her toes all the time and must invent things to do. This was not the utopia she hoped for.

"Harry Smith," he said again into the phone.

"Harry, this is Bill Foster."

"Hello, Bill, what's cooking?"

"Funny you should ask. Some of the guys in my men's cooking group are interested in talking to you about your investment offer with ANACORP. Any chance of a meeting?"

"Sure. That's terrific, a wise move. It's a wonderful opportunity. I'll call you back to set up a meeting," Harry was elated, more capital for the covert cause.

Then, he said, "Hello, Ingrid, what's the matter now?"

"Nothing now. I just want to remind you that on Sunday we are taking the family to Disney World. Don't make other plans."

"Yes, dear, I look forward to taking my 85-year-old father on Space Mountain."

"Don't be a smart-ass, Harry. Make sure it's on your calendar.

Harry got up and tried to stretch only to plunk back in his black leather executive chair with the buzzing of another call. It was an Ernest Stubbs, recommended by Bill Foster from the Old Men's Cooking Club. He listened attentively but thought Ernest a little strange, and zealously patriotic. The man babbled incessantly about investing in stocks exclusively from down-to-earth red, white and blue American companies. "No foreign stuff for me."

Claiming to have funds, Harry invited Ernie for lunch. Maybe this guy is rich, Harry thought. Perhaps he was interested in other things American. Worse comes to worst he would have a good lunch. No sooner than the phone clicked off than it buzzed again.

"Harry Smith, hello."

"It's Peter."

"You're not supposed to call on this line, Pete."

"You didn't answer your cell. I'll be brief. Is everything in order?"

"Yes, our little exercise is all set for Thursday morning, Ralph is raring to go."

"Good, and the thumb drive?"

"It is due to arrive from Regensburg the day after tomorrow in time for our meeting on Sunday."

"Shit" he mumbled under his breath. "I'm supposed to take my folks who are visiting from Germany, and my family to the Magic Kingdom on Sunday."

"Harry, this is a crucial meeting. We are formulating our project plans, and we must have our captain there to lead us."

Harry was dumbstruck. There was no question he had to be there on Sunday. How he maneuvered getting there would be challenging. He was already in the doghouse with Ingrid, and she would not forgive him for abandoning the family outing. He knew she felt isolated, lonely, ignored and constantly on edge as she says, "only a slave in the relationship." How could he put her in charge of the large family entourage for an all-day expedition to the theme park? How could he invent a credible excuse? He was damned either way. It was almost impossible that she and his folks would understand his absence. He threw his remaining lunch in the trash as his acid reflux started its heated dance.

"I guess Mickey Maus will have to wait," he said to Pete.

"Good, good. Heil Hitler, Heinrich."

Chapter 7
Top Banana

Smarty-pants Abe limped into the kitchen carrying a large bag of groceries and set it down on the counter. It was Thursday morning, and the cooking boys had already gathered in the culinary workshop, drinking their morning coffee busy dissecting the world situation. As top banana for the day and donning a floppy white chef's hat, he got right down to business. Abe Kacynsey was a roly poly man, with an infectious laugh and an infuriating know-it-all personality. He was short in stature, wide in girth, long in verbiage and had a remarkable head of dark hair for an 80-year-old.

As the chef du jour unloaded the ingredients, Fred, the group's leader, grabbed the coffee pot and began pouring a second round of the morning elixir for the cooks.

"Sure, you don't want some coffee, Ernie?"

"Nah, Fred, thanks anyway. I don't drink much coffee these days."

"Yeah, his favorite drink is Alka-Seltzer," Abe smirked.

"Fred, where's Dick?" asked Ernie.

"He never called to say that he wasn't coming today."

"I hope he's all right?" Ernie seemed genuinely concerned. "Ruth's not well and Dick seemed a little wobbly lately."

"I'm sure he's okay."

"If Art and Dick aren't here today, lunch will cost six bucks a head. Get the money up, fellows." Bill put out his hand to collect the funds and everyone forked over their lunch money.

Ernie muttered loudly under his breath, "Highway robbery."

"What's for lunch today anyway?" asked Steve the self-proclaimed artist. "I suppose it's something healthy."

"I'm going to Denny's," bellowed Ernie. "My doctor told me not to eat healthy."

"You won't live long with that attitude, Ernie," biker Joe said.

"Hell, I ain't dead yet. At my age I can put anything in my belly as long as I can get it down."

Gay Charles joined the conversation. "Do we have any other choice besides healthy?"

"As a child, my family's menu consisted of two choices: Take it or leave it," Abe said.

"I think when it comes to healthy food, I would leave it," continued Ernie.

Retired scientist Ed asked, "Speaking of healthy, does anyone here know the four food groups?"

"I do," Fred quickly responded. "Fast, frozen, junk and instant."

"You're wrong, Fred." The rotund Steve waddled over and said, "Everyone knows the four food groups are chocolate, milk chocolate, white chocolate and dark chocolate."

Joe smiled and said, "I don't want to burst your bubble, fellas, but the critical four food groups are definitely pizza, beer, chips and pussy."

"Guys, guys, today the four essential food groups are appetizer, salad, entrée and dessert and if we don't get crackin', we're all going to suffer from a serious, nutritional deficiency. And for you smart asses, lunch is not especially healthy today." Abe said in his "tirdy tird street and tird avenue" accent. He liked to call himself a street rat from Brooklyn and boasted that his childhood recreation included stickball on the streets where a broken window counted as a home run.

Abe was a closet Jew. He never spoke about religion or cooked traditional Jewish foods. No one in the group really talked about his spiritual affiliations. His surname was Kacynscy and since he came across as a strong right-wing, ultra-conservative Republican, all the boys automatically tagged him as a Polish Christian. Ernie envied him his career in foundations: girdles and bras, assuming that Abe did a great deal of personal fitting of the apparel. He was the least educated of the pack but had the highest level of street smarts.

Abe knew everything and didn't hesitate to tell you a bona fide know-it-all. Often, he was correct. Considering himself a master cook, he always came up with interesting concoctions. Much of his passion for food was displayed on his protruding belly that peeked from his Hawaiian shirt and yellow, tattered Bermuda shorts. One had to accept Abe with a grain of salt, but one could also learn a lot listening to him.

"Anyone interested in helping with the cooking?" Abe said.

All the men, except Ernie, got up to volunteer.

"Someone needs to lay out the corn muffins."

"Corn muffins? They're not exactly nutritious," Fred said, reading the label on the box.

"They're a lot healthier than the weekly French bread soaked in butter, garlic and oil."

"That's true."

"For our first course, we are having borscht with sour cream," the chef du jour announced.

"What the hell is a borscht?"

"It's a beet soup from Eastern Europe, Ernie"

"Oh, it's bad enough we have to eat Jewish food but now it's Polish Jewish."

"ERNIE!" Fred shouted, gently slapping his buddy on the head.

"Ernie, you want to do something to help?"

"NO."

"Useless," Abe whispered under his breath. "Art, would you please peel the potatoes for the borscht? I made the soup yesterday, but I like to serve it with fresh boiled potatoes and sour cream."

Would-be artist Steve asked. "What do you put in the borscht, Abe?"

"Beets, onions, carrots and cabbage."

"Cabbage makes me fart," piped up Ernie.

"I guess you're eating alone today," Joe said.

"I also put in some extra virgin olive oil."

Ernie joked about putting in the extra-virgin olive oil, telling the group that he hadn't been a virgin in 65 years.

"I can imagine what your deflowering was like, Ernie," Steve said.

Joe couldn't help but take this opportunity to put his two cents in, "With Ernie, it was a de-weeding."

"Hey, guys, that isn't fair."

"What was your first time like, Ernie? Can you remember that far back?" Joe said, adding some fun to the fire.

"I don't kiss and tell, fellas. You're never going to know."

"If we don't get back to our cooking, lunch will be spoiled for the first time," Abe yelled, annoyed now. "And now the piece de resistance: I add a sprinkling of kosher salt, viola!"

Everyone stopped, looked at Ernie, and waited for his comment.

"I'm not saying a word ... I don't mean to sound stupid or anything but since we only have one Jew boy here, why does the salt have to be kosher?"

"Kosher salt is used to make meat kosher. It has a much larger grain than table salt, so it helps soak and move blood from the meat. It is used primarily in cooking by the great chefs like me! It adds flavor for some reason," Abe said. "No, I don't know why, Ernie."

"Well, you learn something every day. You see I'm not prejudiced, especially against you, Abe."

The boys couldn't quite understand Ernie's aversions, especially toward

Jews. They all knew he had gone to Germany right after the war and must have witnessed the ravages first-hand. There is no way he avoided seeing the horror of the near annihilation of the Jewish race. It was a puzzle to all.

Abe took the aluminum foil off the large pan of meat-stuffed cabbage with rice, smothered in a tomato sauce and asked Art to sauté some string beans. Steve mixed lettuce, tomatoes, cucumbers and carrots for the salad. Joe slipped the cabbage rolls into the oven to bake and asked, "How will we know when they're ready?"

"Well, being the superb chef, I am, the answer is easy: when the smoke detector goes off," Abe said with a big smirk, and they all chuckled.

A half an hour later, lunch was ready, and Abe doled out the portions. The boys adjourned to their makeshift dining hall, juggling plates of borscht, salad and cabbage. Some of the spilled red soup left a trail to the kitchen.

"Hey, Bill," Ed yelled across the room. "Any news on that financial investment with your broker friend?"

"I talked to Harry Smith yesterday and he is anxious to meet with us. I'll set it up."

"Good deal."

"I have an additional surprise, fellas. I made a special dessert," Abe announced, and all the faces lit up like pumpkins on Halloween.

"Wow, we don't always have dessert," Steve said.

"I brought in some macaroon cookies, and they are healthy! I had made them before our last Passover dinner. They were so good I thought I would bake some for you guys. Some Jewish soul food. They are completely fat-free."

"Fat-free and Jewish cooking just don't seem to go together," Ernie said.

Suddenly there was a cacophony of sirens everywhere.

"What's that?" Abe shouted, looking around. No, there was no smoke in the kitchen. Police cars, fire trucks and ambulances raced past the Senior Center. The noise was shattering. Lucky they weren't baking a yeast cake, or it would have fallen. They all paused. It was distracting but the chefs resumed their eating as the sounds faded away.

"I hope those sirens weren't for Dick. He lives nearby. I'm worried. I hope he's okay," Ernie said, working himself up into a dither.

"Calm down, buddy," Fred said soothingly. "Let's give Dick a call and see what's up."

Fred dialed and it rang six times before it was answered. Fred listened and responded with a serious expression on his face.

"Oh, I see, okay."

"What's the matter, tell me. Don't hold back. I'm old enough to take it.

Is Dick okay?" Ernie babbled, grabbing his arm.

"Ernie, Ernie, Dick's fine, he fell asleep while he was fishing, and I just woke him up."

"Phew."

"Ernie, you look terrible. You have to calm down."

"He doesn't look as bad as Margie," Steve said pointing to the director of the senior center who was standing at the door looking disheveled and trying to catch her breath.

The men's chorus came alive.

"What's wrong?"

"Why are you out of breath?"

"Do you need help?"

"What should we do?"

"I heard those sirens, so I ran down the block to see what the commotion was. You wouldn't believe it, but there are two large black swastikas painted on the walls of the synagogue and the police suspect that the perpetrator is still in the area."

Abe became angry, "What an awful thing to do."

"It isn't safe to go anywhere anymore," Charles said.

To stir things up, Joe said, "I bet Ernie did it. He disappeared into the bathroom right about that time and stayed there a long time,"

"I wouldn't be surprised," came Bill.

"Hey guys, that's not fair. I'd never do that. As a matter of fact, if I had my gun with me now, I'd go out and blow that sucker from here to kingdom come. Let me at him. You know I like Jews."

A flummoxed Abe stood there staring at his flip-flopping co-cook, shaking his head.

Chapter 8
The Man Who Came to Dinner

Ernie was dressed to the nines when he arrived at Harry Smith's uppity rooftop club. His outfit, a forty-year-old blue plaid sports coat, beige polyester slacks, and a clashing yellow butterfly bowtie on his starched white shirt which barely buttoned, clearly made him out of his element. Harry greeted him warmly, ignoring his mismatched attire and escorted Ernie to a table with a view of the city.

"What will you have to drink, Ernie?"

"A beer would be fine, thanks."

The red-vested waiter enumerated at least ten varieties of international ales available on tap, but Ernie, being Ernie, asked for a Budweiser.

"So, Ernie, how've you been? Keeping busy?" Harry said, trying to make small talk.

"Pretty good. Between puttering around the house, spending time with my ex-wife Bessie, trying to get my money's worth from Medicare by keeping doctors all over town busy and going to my men's cooking group, I have plenty to do."

"Do you cook, Ernie, What's your specialty?"

"Oh, I don't cook; I just go to the weekly group to give the fellas a hard time."

"I'm sure they love that."

When the waiter brought menus, Ernie looked at the resplendent bill of fare and marveled at the fact he didn't understand most of it. He wondered to himself, why can't people just speak American? Why not just say, lamb with spaghetti instead of lamb cappellitti? Who the hell cares? It's all the same shit.

"What will you have, sir?" asked the waiter.

"Treat yourself to something special, Ernest. What appeals to you? The lamb here is superb as is the Key West snapper," Harry said.

"Let's me see, let me see. I'll have some … water sprout tomato soup to start."

"That is the Waterkist Farms tomato bisque, sir. And what can I bring you for your main course?"

"Well, yeah, one of those rare double cheeseburgers with American fries."

"Curled or waffled?"

"Curled or waffled what?

"The fries, sir?"

Ernie, relieved the ordeal of ordering was almost done, said. "Any way they make them in the kitchen is fine with me."

Harry ordered California Delta asparagus to start, a Vande Rose Farm pork schnitzel and a glass of Hogue Late Harvest Riesling.

Harry's cell phone jingled, and he checked the screen. "Excuse me, Ernie, but I need to take this call."

"No problem."

"Harry Smith."

"Mr. Smith, would you please hold for the Vice President of the United States." Then there was a pause.

"Harry, how are you? Keeping out of trouble?"

"Sure trying, Sid. What's going on there?"

"Politics as usual, I just wanted to let you know that I'll be in Orlando next week. I'm dedicating a pavilion at a hospital, not sure which one. It was named after a big political donor."

"Lucky you, will I get to see you while you're here?"

"I'll try. The mayor has me scheduled all around town. If not, I'll see you next month at our big house party in Washington. You and your lovely wife are planning on coming?"

"We wouldn't miss it for the world, Sid."

"Good, I've really missed you, Harry. See you then."

"Sorry, Ernie, that was the Vice President."

"The vice president of what?"

"Of the United States."

"Wow, you know the vice president?" Ernie was beside himself.

"Yeah, we're old friends."

"No shit. Sid Townsend, the real Vice President of the United States?"

"Yes, Ernie. The very real vice president."

"How do you know him?"

"We met a number of years ago at a political meeting and really hit it off," Harry said.

"Wow! Wow! Wow! I can't believe it. He should be president instead of that raghead that we have in office."

Harry listened carefully and began to size him up. The two unlikely luncheon companions continued to chat amicably about the weather, family and some potential investments for Ernie.

"I really want to invest in red-blooded U.S.A. companies," Ernie explained.

"You don't want to invest in the American company your cooking buddies are going to put money into? It will bring an excellent yield of profit."

"Nah, that seems a little too risky for me. I need to invest in something solid, like baby food. Gerber will never go out of business as long as babies keep popping out," Ernie was amused at his own analogy.

They talked more about investing and Ernie again made it clear he wanted to put his money in a company that flies the American Flag on its front lawn. Babbling on, he was vehemently opposed to committing any funds to a left-wing Communist-owned business. The conversation went awry when Ernie headed in the direction of politics.

"Did you see where the Tea Party got creamed in the last election? That Midwestern broad should have won against Sharif! Democrats must have tampered with the election results.

They do that here in Florida, you know. I just can't stand that guy Sharif. Someone has got to do him in."

Harry was listening very carefully and continuing to analyze every word.

Slurping down his third beer, Ernie said, "Whatever happened to good old red, white and blue values? Sharif panders to his brother ragheads and gives in to everything they want. I just don't know how we're going to survive the next four years under his rule. No one can get a job anymore. Our money is worth nothing. Do you know how much tomatoes cost? This president is fucking everything up. We've got to do something to get rid of him," a loose-lipped Ernie blasted on loudly.

"Shh, Ernie, watch it, not so loud. It isn't advisable for people to hear you talk like that," Harry said, looking around. Now very interested in his companion's diatribe, he decided to take a big gamble.

"Ernest, what are you doing Sunday? How would you like to come to a barbecue with a bunch of staunchly American guys?"

"What kind of barbecue?"

"Just a group of regular guys like you and me who are all for promoting the red, white and blue and the American Dream. We get together regularly to talk, drink beer, and eat some of the best barbecue in the state. It's sort of a community service organization. They have plans to do a lot for our country."

"Sounds like it's right up my alley," Ernie was interested. "Where is it going to be?"

"It's in Christmas, just a few miles north of town."

Ernie said enthusiastically, "How bad can the meeting be if it's in Christmas? I am free on Sunday. Count me in."

"Well, let me just make a phone call."

"Hello, Pete's Fish and Tackle," came the response to Harry's call.

"Pete, Harry here. I think I have a recruit for our group. I have invited him to our meeting on Sunday."

"Good, Harry, if you think he will fit in, but remember discretion is critical."

"We can convince him of that over beer and food. See you Sunday." Harry turned to Ernie,

"You're in, my friend. I'll e-mail you directions."

"Thanks, Harry. That's very kind of you."

Harry signed the check, said goodbye and drove back to his office. He thought about his new recruit. Ernest Stubbs may be their perfect scapegoat.

Chapter 9
The Mouse and the Maus

On Sunday morning, precisely at the same moment as the preachers of Orlando were sermonizing to their flocks, Art O'Neil and Franz Schmidt were worshipping separately at the temple of fun, the Magic Kingdom, at Disney World.

Franz felt his dentures slip as he plummeted down the short water flume in the adventurous "Pirates of the Caribbean" ride. His grandchildren were screaming in glee while poor Anneliese was holding on for dear life.

Ingrid was still pouting that Harry had abandoned them for the day.

Franz and his lovely bride had arrived on schedule from Germany and were embraced warmly with hugs and kisses from Harry, Ingrid and the children. An enormous number of suitcases were piled into the car before they headed off to the country. Franz seemed to have brought everything he owned. Harry was anxious to receive Otto's "special" package.

Anneliese adored the house and thought Ingrid had done a splendid job decorating the expansive five-bedroom ranch home. Franz did not like the isolation. The house guarded by skyscraping trees offered no neighbors and the adjacent woods seemed impenetrable. It might be fine for a vacation, but the remoteness was haunting to him. He continuously needed diversions to help elude the horrible war memories he still carried.

That night Harry outdid himself with a barbecue feast of pork ribs and salads around the lovely swimming pool. Harry made an excuse to go to his den to make a phone call.

"Peter, Harry here. I have the thumb drive from Otto. Father handed it to me immediately."

"Excellent. How did you manage to get out of the Disney excursion?"

"Don't ask. The bigger challenge is still ahead. See you tomorrow."

"We're having some really great food at the meeting tomorrow. It's an American-style barbecue, Harry."

"I know."

Harry pondered his strategy with Ingrid. Despite his lack of passion for her, he had to revive himself to make love to her, a less-than-frequent feat these days. Then after she was sexually satiated, he would tell her about his plans for Sunday. This seemed like his only avenue of choice, distasteful as it was to him.

"Why does it have to be this Sunday, Harry?" she complained bitterly despite feeling very relaxed and defenseless.

"I have to work, Ingrid. There's a major portfolio review Monday," he was sympathetic but firm.

"Somehow I find it hard to believe," she suspected a dalliance with another woman but didn't want to bring it up, especially now. He had been absent and pre-occupied too much lately.

"I'll make it up to you, dear. I promise." This was a commitment that he made and broke regularly.

"It's not the same," she said, tears sliding down her cheeks as she turned away to avoid exposing her vulnerability.

Reluctantly Ingrid took command of the Disney adventure the following day. No one anticipated the low stamina of the elderly in-laws. Anneliese wanted to do everything, but Franz tired quickly. They were in Tomorrow Land when the kids begged to go on the Buzz Lightyear's Space Rangers ride. All Franz wanted to do was sit in the shade and have a snack, so they parked him at a table. He told the family to take their time and have fun, assuring them he would be fine. At a kiosk he ordered a Coney Island hot hog and an iced tea.

Franz watched the enormous crowds parading by. He hadn't seen crowds like this since the war when masses lined the streets of Munich to pay allegiance to the Fuhrer. At that time peoples' arms were extended straight out in their salute. Here at Disney arms were flapping in every direction out of sheer enjoyment. A larger-than-life Minnie Mouse character came by and patted him on the head. He marveled at this foreign universe while biting into his overstuffed frankfurter.

The O'Neil family twirled like dervishes in a teacup on the Mad Tea Party ride in Fantasy Land. Art, frustrated, holding onto his panama hat, was dizzy and feeling much too old for this. "This is a lame ride," yelled one of the grandkids. It had been a busy week, constantly on the go with the kids in town. He was accustomed to a quieter life. His weekly excitement was usually picking radishes in his garden and cooking with the men on Thursdays. He missed them this week but was glad to be with the children.

"Papa, I want to go on Space Mountain now," one grandson pulled at Art. "It's in Tomorrow Land."

"I'll walk you there, but I need to sit and rest. Maybe I'll get a little something to nibble on."

The entourage crossed the bridge heading for the infamous rollercoaster.

Art found an outdoor table in the shade near a fast-food shack, bought a Philly steak hot dog and eased himself into a chair. He knew that there would be a never-ending line for the ride, and he would have lots of time to relax. Despite the crowds, he began to feel less overwhelmed.

"Why must they put all this stuff on these frankfurters," came a man's voice with a thick foreign accent. "All I wanted was a plain frankfurter and I got chili, mustard, onions and God knows what else. Who can eat all this? I can't even taste the sausage," Franz said, smiling.

"My hot dog is topped with onions, peppers, mushrooms and cheese sauce. It's so good. I don't want to taste the dog," Art replied.

Franz boasted, "This frankfurter comes from my part of the woods."

"Where are you from?" Art turned towards Franz.

"Germany. I am here on a holiday visiting my children and grandchildren."

"I didn't know that hot dogs originally came from Germany?"

"Ya, they go back to the 1850's when the butcher's guild in Frankfort developed a combined spiced and smoked sausage and enclosed it in a casing."

Art was amused.

"A German butcher shaped it after his loving dachshund and called it a dachshund sausage. The name 'hot dog" came much later from a hawker selling the sausage at a baseball game in New York who shouted, 'They're real hot, get your red-hot dachshund sausage while they're hot.'"

"Wow, hot dog, I didn't know that. Are you expert on food?"

"I'm just an ignorant man who's infatuated with food, loves to read with too much leisure time on his hands."

"Do you cook too?"

"I am a very good cook. My wife and I spend hours in the kitchen together. How about you?"

Art replied, "I cook very little since my wife died, but I belong to a weekly men's cooking group. We all take turns cooking and I manage my share."

"It sounds very convivial."

Art wasn't sure what that meant but smiled to be polite.

Franz took another bite of his fraudulent wiener. "There is nothing like a German sausage. A mouthwatering bockwurst is made from finely minced, spiked pork and then smoked. Or a Fleischwurst, which is a mildly smoked sausage served with steaks or added to spätzle. We are discussing real food here. Yum, yum, yum." Even though he had been in Florida for just four days, Franz suddenly felt slight pangs of homesickness.

"My wife used to make the most wonderful Irish bangers and mash. Now that was real sausage. Her corned beef and cabbage were to die for, except it used to stink up the house."

"I can imagine," Franz laughed.

"Have you ever been here in the States before?"

Franz was cautious about getting into a conversation about when he was a prisoner of war in New Jersey. But he was taken with Art's easy style and was feeling comfortable. There was also a pressing need to confess what he had only held in his heart for so many years. Since it felt better to talk to someone who didn't know him and would never see again, he took a bold step.

"Ya, I was here more than 65 years ago during the war."

"Were you a soldier?"

"Ya," Franz admitted. "What about you? Did you serve?"

"I was in the war when I was very young, I was sent overseas, saw combat in France and Germany but wasn't there very long because I was wounded. Shot in the back, rescued, and saved in a Red Cross hospital tent, then was returned to the States for more recuperation. It was hard. There were some very fierce battles. For such a naïve kid, it was a horrible experience," Art said.

"Did that disqualify you from the service?"

"No, after my convalescence, they sent me to guard Italian and German prisoners here in the States."

"What was that like?"

"I found them to be a good bunch of boys, mostly glad to be here, instead of on the battlefields."

Franz felt a bolt of lightning, sat up and looked at Art intently as he told his story. "Indeed, the war was horrific," Franz said.

"Did you fight?"

Responding to Art's sensitivity and warmth, he became even more comfortable to open the door a bit about his secret.

"I was a low-ranking soldier of the Third Reich. Flying for the Luftwaffe, I was captured by the Allies in 1944, and transported by ship to New Jersey."

"Why to the States?"

"We never knew why the Americans brought us here. I suspect it was easier to contain us here than to have us possibly escape back to the German forests where we could do more harm."

"So, you were a Nazi?"

"NO! I was not a registered Nazi!! I didn't believe in all that. I was

48

forced into the military. At thirteen years of age, coerced into the Hitlerjugen and indoctrinated. Of course, first I was strongly nationalistic and excited that Germany finally had powerful leadership to correct its terrible economy and the ills of the First World War. Hitler billed himself as a savior of the Reich. We were taught that pure German was the master race and everyone else didn't count. We sang, marched, saluted and strictly followed orders."

Art listened intently.

"Before that, I had Jewish friends and a homosexual chum at school, but then I was forced to ignore them. They had been my pals; I thought they were good people. When they disappeared, I became disillusioned and wanted out but got caught up in the heinous freak show," Franz couldn't stop talking.

"That's quite a story."

"There's more. For some reason I was trained as a fighter pilot and was shot down returning from a bombing mission. I parachuted out of my plunging ME 109 Messerschmitt, placing me in the heart of Allied territory. I was young and scared. The experience still gives me nightmares."

"What happened then?" Art asked.

"Your army kept me in Europe for a while and then sent me here to Fort Dix. When the war was over, I was repatriated back to Germany." Franz was choked up, having relived his past and finally sharing it with this stranger.

"Fort Dix, New Jersey?" Art was suddenly on the edge of his chair. "Did you say Fort Dix?"

"Yes, I did."

Art said, "Sometimes I don't remember what I did yesterday, but that was a period I remember vividly. I was an MP guarding prisoners at Fort Dix. My memory recalls two special German boys who were close friends. One of them was very friendly and emotional and the other was so angry and belligerent, and yet they were the best of buddies. I'll never forget them. I used to bring them cigarettes and extra rations. I think … Franz was the name of the kinder soul. I can't remember the other. To this day I wonder what happened to them."

"What! I am Franz, Franz Schmidt! And my dearest friend today in Germany is that same cantankerous kid who is now an old man, Otto Schaffer."

"Oh my God, I am Art O'Neil. Is it possible that I was your guard?" He said, now tears filled his eyes.

"It seems impossible, but possible."

Art went over to embrace Franz. Then they continued talking non-stop, oblivious to the crowds of people around them. Feeling totally energized and animated, Art bought a second round of sausages for them. Gobbling down the food, chatting about the war and the American prison camp, they also talked about Otto and their families. Franz told Art about his son, Harry, an investment banker in Orlando. Art passionately confided about his late wife, Irene, whom he had idolized for 50 years. He missed her dearly. They each bragged about their grandkids and proudly took out pictures.

"I saw in your local newspaper the other day that large swastikas were painted on the walls of one of your synagogues," Franz said, sipping his tea.

"Yes, that vandalism happened right down the street from our senior center. The police are still investigating."

"You would think that those days were over years ago, wouldn't you?"

"Especially in America, but there are still hate groups, even here in our area."

Their spirited conversation lasted for more than two hours, the time it took the family to ride Space Mountain twice. Before they parted, they vowed to spend more time together during Franz's visit and exchanged information.

"Franz, since you love to cook, why don't you come and be my guest chef at our men's cooking group?"

"What would I have to do?"

"Together we'll plan a menu and do the food shopping. The fellas help us prepare the meal and then we eat together."

"I wouldn't want to be an intruder in your group."

"You'd be a welcomed guest."

"Can we make a German meal?"

"What else?"

Franz was getting excited, "That could be fun."

"Yes, it'll be loads of fun."

"It would be an honor and a pleasure, Art."

They got up and Franz put his arm around Art's shoulder.

"Can you imagine the odds of this happening. There are more than seven billion people in the world and the two of us have been reunited under the watchful eye of a mouse!" They both laughed heartily and walked to meet their families.

Chapter 10
Pork Rinds And Provocations

Ernie was lost. Commandeering the boxy Scion aimlessly down a deserted road in the middle of nowhere, he passed gray scrub and dark forests. Giant green moss hung out threatening to swoop down and engulf him. Nearby in a meadow, grazing cows were startled by his erratic driving. "What am I doing out here?" He wondered. The sexy voice on his GPS advised him, "Make a left turn on Gator Creek Road." He had done that, miles back. He was heading to the Sunday barbecue and the club was supposed to be somewhere on this road. Realizing that the only civilization out here might be Native Americans, he also thought this could be a terrific spot to set up a still and make himself some moonshine.

"This sure doesn't look like the North Pole," he muttered to himself after he passed the red and green town sign announcing Christmas, Florida. "Boy, Santa could do better than living out here in this God-forsaken area. How can it be Christmas; there are mostly palm trees and sand?"

As he approached a clearing in the woods, he saw a cluster of vehicles. There were several dirt-encrusted pick-up trucks with gun racks, a bunch of expensive Harley-Davidson bikes and a few SUV's parked in the brush. He pulled into the grassy parking area and noticed he drove the only nerdy car in the group. He was followed into the lot by his broker Harry Smith, driving a black Mercedes 350 sedan.

Ernie got out of his car, looking around at the wilderness. Harry walked over to his potential recruit and extended his hand, "Glad you could make it, Ernest."

"Where the hell am I?" the bewildered Ernie asked, returning the gesture.

A large contingent of loudly squawking crows flying overhead masked a noise the two men didn't hear. Some strange clicking sounds came from behind a tree in the woods.

From the moment he entered the meeting area, Ernie felt it was a deja vu of his men's cooking club. Jim was tending a whole pig rotating on a spit; Floyd was stirring a pork and bean concoction; Tom handed out pork rinds as an appetizer and Lloyd basted chicken legs on the grill. Ralph shucked corn savagely and Al chopped up a juicy watermelon, Paul-Bunyan style. Several others clustered, sporting cold beers from a Styrofoam cooler. Alligator tail, fried dill pickles, okra with tomatoes and creamy coleslaw were spread out on the picnic table.

There was a round of "yee yaws" when Derek walked in carrying two homemade apple pies. Later the slices would be smothered with vanilla ice cream. This was cholesterol and sugar heaven for Ernie.

The meeting place was an oasis in the middle of a dark ominous forest. The grounds housed a cabin with a large patio where the barbecue festivities were being held. It seemed to Ernie that the dress code included mandated tattoos. Pete, wearing jeans and a Harley-Davidson tee shirt, excused himself from his group and sauntered over to greet Harry and meet Ernie.

"Pete, this is Ernest Stubbs."

"Welcome Ernie, glad you could join us. Why don't I bring you over and introduce you to the rest of the gang?"

Ernie obliged but secretly hoped that they would eat soon since he was famished. Then Harry pulled Pete aside and passed along the well-traveled package containing the thumb drive. Pete was relieved.

"I'll hand it over to Henry Johnson directly."

"Excellent," said Harry. "That will get things rolling."

"Say, Harry, this guy Ernie looks a little wobbly. Are you sure we can trust him?"

"Once we initiate him into our secret society, he'll be fine. He may also be the perfect dupe for our plans."

"Possibly," Pete said.

Harry explained to Pete, "We've had a significant boost in our treasury and have enough funds to make the down payment for the second part of the operation."

"Good, Harry, take care of it as soon as you can."

Harry and Pete rejoined the others and found Ernie in the middle of the group, telling stories, and making everyone laugh.

"What did the elephant say to the naked man?"

"I give up."

Ernie smirked, grabbing his crotch. "Isn't that thing cute, but can it pick up peanuts?"

"Oh, brother," they said and laughed.

The alcohol in the beers was working and the lively conversation progressed to tits and ass.

"So, I met my new doctor yesterday," Ernie rolled on.

"So, what?"

"Well, she was tall, blond, had triple E boobs hanging out of her coat and her shorts were up to her ass. She was drop-dead gorgeous."

"Shit, why can't I find a doctor like that?" Said one of the guys with his tongue hanging out.

"So, she said to me, 'Tell me what's wrong and I'll check it out.'"

"And what did you say?"

"I said that I was embarrassed. 'Don't worry I'm a professional. I've seen it all.' So, I told her that my wife thinks that my dick tastes funny." There was a roar of laughter and one of the men slapped Ernie on the back, nearly knocking him over. Ernie was having a ball being the center of attention. After exhausting the topic of sex, they moved onto politics.

"That broad didn't have a snowball's chance in hell to win the presidency against Sharif," Ernie said.

"She was pretty hot stuff."

"Yeah, some mighty fine white meat."

"She could ride on my bitch seat anytime."

"I don't know how we are going to survive another four years with that raghead in the Oval Office," Ernie was dead serious as he spoke.

"Someone said that he was related to bin Laden."

"We need a real American president, one who understands how important it is to promote the majority white society. Never mind the niggers, kikes and fags."

"I'll buy that," Ernie said, raising his beer bottle in salute.

The venting continued, "Them Jews continue to cause all the problems. We wouldn't be in such a financial mess if it weren't for kike interference in our economy."

"Sharif is such a Jewish ass-licker. I'll bet they pay him under the table."

"He's a Muslim bastard."

Ernie rose up and said, "Why doesn't anyone just shoot the son of a bitch."

"Hoo Ra, Hoo Ra!"

"Hoo Ra, Hoo Ra!"

"Yeah, we need Sid Townsend in the president's chair."

"Who knows, maybe that's going to happen," Pete said.

"Here, here!"

"Here, here!"

After that cheer the food was served. Plates were piled high with the gourmet redneck delicacies. The pig was succulent, and the chicken cooked to perfection. Ernie loved the alligator bits, and everyone gobbled down the pork rinds. After the fire was put out and the apple pie and ice cream consumed in huge portions, Pete convened the meeting. The men gathered their lawn chairs into a semi-circle around their leader. Harry Smith took the stand.

"I'm glad that we are gathered together, men. It's great to see that you gave a gracious welcome to our new patriot, Ernie Stubbs. Welcome, Ernie." A round of applause and hoo ras followed.

"Thank you, fellas," Ernie stood and waved.

"We really must continue our plans to achieve white superiority in this nation. The Germans had it right during the World War ll. We can't exist with a black Arab president and a Jewish secretary of state. We can't allow the Jews to control our financial destiny. It's a disgrace to allow bum fuckers to be married. It goes against the principles of God. The wet backs are climbing the walls into our South every day. Soon they will be taking over the country. This nation is fucked up and since no one else will, we need to take things into our own hands. We are the future of this nation." There was an electric tension in the air. "Our plans are moving along very nicely. Ralph, you did a great job with the swastikas on the synagogue last week." Everyone applauded. Hoo Ra!

Suddenly Ernie became confused. He didn't feel that he had that much hatred inside himself, but these guys did seem like a great bunch.

Harry continued. "Thanks to our friends in the Fatherland and some local investors, our treasury has had substantial increases in the last few weeks. We've got the funds in place to go forward and proceed with our plans. Onward and upward!"

"Onward and upward!" They all shouted.

As the group began to disperse, there were warm handshakes, fist bumps and well wishes. Ernie was in the middle of bidding goodbye to his new friends when Pete and Harry cornered him.

"So, did you have a good time?"

"Yeah, it was great."

"All the boys seemed to like you a lot and we'd like to make you a member of the group. You interested?"

"What do I have to do?"

"Since not everyone out there understands how important our mission is, just swear to us that you will keep completely quiet and not mention a word about this meeting, or our group, to anyone."

"I can do that," Ernie said, "That's easy enough."

"Remember we all, including you, will be in huge trouble if word of any of this gets out."

"You can count on me, chief," Ernie said, saluting Harry and Pete.

"By the way, Ernie, the red-blooded American stocks that I invested for you have done well over the past few days."

"Now, that's great news to end a perfect day."

Ernie climbed into his car and prepared for the long trek home. "I hope I can find my way out of here before Christmas," Ernie said joking to Harry, but he was half serious.

"Why don't you just follow me to the interstate? I'll be leaving in a minute."

Pete seemed to be more convinced about Ernie and agreed that he would be an excellent lamb to lead to the slaughter. They wished each other well, and Harry pulled out of the lot followed by the newest member of the Aryan Connection.

Ernie was still a little puzzled as he drove along on the deserted roads, but he felt good that everyone had liked and accepted him.

"Finally, there's a group of people who understand me," he said to himself.

Harry dialed a number in Germany as he drove home.

"Hallo, what time is it? Who's calling at this hour?" Hilda was terrified that one of her children was in trouble.

"I'm so sorry, Aunt Hilda. I forgot the time difference."

"Is everything all right, Heinrich?"

"Yes fine. Is Uncle Otto sleeping?"

"Well, just a moment, He is up now."

"Heinrich, what's going on?"

"The thumb drive was received and is on the way to Johnson."

"Zayer gut mein Junge. Zayer gut. Thank you, I don't mind you waking me to tell me that. I'll report it on this end. Good-night, lad. Very well done."

FBI agent Sally Adams was really annoyed. She and Tom Prentice sped downtown to their office after hiding in the woods outside the barbecue site and were trying to decipher the information. The FBI rarely screwed up, but they had royally this time. The camera worked from their vantage point, but the audio bug planted on the patio had failed. They were only able to process who had attended the session, not what had taken place. As they looked at the photos, they could identify many of the participants, except the elderly man with the plastic leg.

Chapter 11
Boys Will Be Boys

Ernie felt under the weather all week. The doctor assured him his restless sleep and constant headaches were the result of anxiety. Everything in his life had seemed to be going well and he couldn't imagine what precipitated this sudden tension. He had been accepted by a new group of friends who shared his American ideals; he and Bessie were getting along fine, and he wasn't scheduled to cook for the boys for a while.

Feeling lethargic, Ernie had weighed skipping the cooking group, but Dick was chef du jour and even though some of the boys would jump at any minor ache or pain as an excuse to miss the ex-spy master's cooking, he wanted to support his buddy. He roused himself from bed, hooked on his trusty leg, and donned a pair of blue plaid short pants with a brown-and-yellow striped tee shirt and bright red suspenders. This vision of fashion added a black belt as security against losing his pants.

The cooking boys were standing around the kitchen commiserating about the upcoming lunch when Dick sauntered in with Ruth, carrying four shopping bags filled with groceries.

"Hi guys," Dick said bubbling over with enthusiasm about the meal he would cook.

"Hey Dick," Abe called back. "I hear we are eating out today?"

"Eating out? My ass. I went to a lot of trouble preparing lunch for today."

The boys looked at each other with some disappointment. Ruth put her bags down, wished her husband well and was heading out when she ran into Ernie who was lumbering in.

"Hi ya, Ruth. How ya feeling?" Ernie asked, pushing aside his doldrums.

"Good, Ernie. One day at a time. You don't look so good yourself."

"I've been under the weather lately, but I didn't want to miss Dick's cooking."

"You're a brave- hearted soul, Ernie. Take care of yourself."

"I will, you too."

Back in the kitchen Dick unpacked the groceries while singing loudly and dreadfully off key; "When the moon hits your eye like a big pizza pie, that's amore."

Fred whispered, "Battle stations" and they all took their assigned spots. Steve posted himself at the fire extinguisher; Abe guarded the drawer with the knives; Joe protected the stove, and Fred rushed over to make the coffee. A new glass carafe was required after Dick brewed coffee the last time without filling it with water. Ed was commissioned to keep a close eye on the new microwave oven. Unfortunately, Dick burnt out the last one when he used it as a timer for his roast in the oven.

Dick knew that the boys were being protective, so he wasn't bothered by it. He had planned to make today's lunch flawless.

"What's on the menu, Dick?" Steve asked.

"Biscuits while we're cooking, boys, tomato soup, coleslaw, meatloaf, green peas, baked beans, mashed potatoes and fruited Jello for dessert."

"Are you sure that's enough?" Abe jested and was kicked in the leg by Fred.

"Mm, mm, mm, that's my kind of food," mumbled Ernie.

The lay chefs got down to serious business. Steve assaulted the biscuits. Charles divided the cans of soup, peas and baked beans into pots and arranged them on the stove to heat. Fred mastered the directions on the packages and executed the instant mashed potatoes. Art scooped out the coleslaw onto a large serving dish. Dick had created the meatloaf at home and put the pan into the oven.

"So far so good," Bill said to Fred.

Ernie sat sadly in his spot, not participating as usual in the cooking, or the banter.

The boys tried to let up on Dick and enjoyed their biscuits and coffee.

Thirty minutes later, Dick yelled out, "Viola" and gingerly lifted the meatloaf from the oven while the cooks spread out the side dishes on the counter. Art bent down to investigate the cabinet for cutlery. He came up empty-handed.

"Who was supposed to buy the plastic forks, knives and spoons this week?" Art said.

Fred pointed, "Joe was."

"Nah, don't lay it on me. Bill said he could get them cheaper and would pick them up."

Bill protested. "I never go shopping for the group."

"Well, we don't have any eating utensils," Art scowled.

Ernie piped in like a child. "I'm hungry; what are we going to do?"

"I'll guess we'll have to go out for lunch, Dick," Abe teased.

"Not after I prepared all this food."

Bill tried to rescue the day. "We can always send one of us to the supermarket."

"My food will get cold," Dick complained. "Let me have a look," and he bent down into cabinet where the cutlery was kept, looked around and came up with a large box of green Hefty garbage bags.

"It takes a former spy to come up with a logical solution to our cutlery dilemma."

"We can't eat with those," Abe said.

With a mischievous gleam in his eye, Dick announced. "We're not going to eat with them. We're going to wear them."

"Are you out of your fucking mind?" Abe said.

"Gentlemen, what would you do in the middle of the Sahara Desert with no fancy forks or spoons. You eat with your hands. Put on the garbage bags, everyone. We are going to eat with our hands."

The men's cooking chorus sang out loudly.

"The man has lost his marbles."

"He's been watching too many spy movies."

"He wrote the spy movies."

"This is the most ridiculous thing I ever heard of."

"Think of it as a lobster bib at the Ritz, Charlie," Fred said, holding up his enormous green makeshift bib.

"I think it sounds like fucking fun," said biker Joe as he poked a hole in his refuse apron to cover his expensive Harley-Davidson tee shirt.

"Hey Fred, how do you work this bag. You were in garbage," Ernie seemed to perk up with this new potential invention.

They appeared like a bunch of green munchkins as they carried their plastic bowls of tomato soup into the computer room. While the vessels were awkward, they managed to slurp down the blood-colored liquid without much of a problem but lots of laughter. Ernie was the first to decorate his face and apron in bright shades of red.

"Hey, that was fun," Abe said.

Ernie was bubbling over, "Let's get into the meat and potatoes."

"We are definitely going to be in the meat and potatoes," Joe was first in line to load up his plate. With the kitchen's few utensils, Joe filled his plate with mushy overcooked olive-green peas, slimy-looking burnt sienna baked beans, grainy beige mashed potatoes, watery yellow and orange coleslaw and dark leathery meatloaf. For dessert he spooned globs of fruited green Jello into a plastic bowl. They followed suit and adjourned to their dining hall.

What ensued was too painful for words. They chased peas around their plates with their fingers; stained their hands on the dark baked beans;

dripped coleslaw from their mouths and shoveled in the mashed potatoes in soggy clumps. They were good sports and laughed their way through their primitive gastronomical escapade. All was in the best of fun until Ernie picked up his slice of leathery meatloaf and thumped it on the table imitating Nikita Khrushchev banging his shoe during the Cuban missile crisis at the United Nations. Dick took offense at Ernie's humorous charade at the expense of his cooking and grabbed a handful of mashed potatoes and pitched it at Ernie, landing on his head. Ernie, flustered but revengeful, tossed a battery of peas at his buddy, hitting him squarely in the face. Conservative Republican Abe, jolted by a political remark that liberal Democrat Ed had made, threw a slew of slaw at his political adversary and Ed returned the volley by tossing a collection of dripping beans at Abe. These minor infractions started a major food fight.

Biker Joe getting into the action, emanating his hero Arnold Schwarzenegger, rose up, grabbed the family-size plastic ketchup, and squirted a fierce barrage of bloody sauce, wounding all his enemies around the room.

Dick, no stranger to automatic weapons started yelling, "Rat, Tat, Tat, Rat, Tat, Tat" and retaliated by shooting mustard at the macho man, wounding everyone in the yellow liquid's path. Food was flying everywhere, landing on the boys, the walls, floors and computers. Nothing was spared. This was male bonding at its best, a bunch of elderly children tossing food, laughing and whooping it up.

A rash of police sirens interrupted their play momentarily, but nothing could have been so important to take these comical warriors away from their battlefield.

"Maybe there were more swastikas painted on the synagogue," Joe said.

The would-be artist, Steve, looking like a plethora of color, said, "Ernie couldn't have done it this time, cause he was here and just hit me in the face with a plateful of disgusting baked beans."

Ernie retaliated by lifting his bowl of jiggling Jello and dumping it over Joe's head. Now the green jellied liquid was flying everywhere. The war was endless, and no one ate any more lunch. The noise grew unbearably loud when suddenly the boys heard a piercing shriek.

"OH MY GOD!" yelled the director of the center, standing in the doorway of the war-torn computer room next to several well-dressed guests. The boys looked up, ceased firing and bolted erect in less than a split second. Fred's red face matched the tomato soup on his plastic garment; Artist Steve resembled a walking Jackson Pollack painting. Biker Joe had a crop of green jellied hair and ponytail. Ed wore mountains of mashed potatoes on his full-length bib. Charles looked like the gay liberation rainbow flag covered with all the multi-colored food courses. Dick was wearing clumps of meatloaf all through his scalp and Art's enviable mane of hair was streaked with beige and orange coleslaw. Ernie, coated in slimy peas, dripping ketchup, mustard and tomato soup looked up, sheepishly grinned and saluted the vice president of the United States and the mayor of Orlando.

"OH MR. VICE PRESIDENT, MR MAYOR, I'M SO, SO SORRY!" the horrified director cried out, envisioning her job going down the drain.

"Boys will be boys," Vice President Sid Townsend said, and everyone burst out laughing wildly.

Chapter 12
The Riot Act

URGENT EMAIL
TO: ALL MEMBERS OF THE OLD MEN'S COOKING CLUB
FROM: Fred
SUBJECT: The Riot Act

Hi fellas, we have been ordered by the Senior Center High Command to report for cleanup duty at 8:00 a.m. tomorrow morning in the computer room. The room has been closed off and nothing has been touched. We must return it to how we found it: spic and span. Please bring a mop, pail, rags and cleaning detergents. It took me a lot of groveling with the director to allow our group to continue. We are in the doghouse big time and are on strict probation. We should all be terribly ashamed of ourselves, but it was a shitload of fun. See you tomorrow.

FROM: Ernie
TO: Fred
SUBJECT: Cooking

I don't clean! Furthermore, I have a doctor's appointment tomorrow morning at that time.

TO: Ernie
FROM: Fred
SUBJECT: Cleaning

CANCEL IT. You better get your ass down here with the others or we'll come and get you. Savvy?

TO: Fred
FROM: Art
SUBJECT: Guest Cook

I forgot to mention I have invited an old buddy who is here on vacation from Germany to cook with me next Thursday. We're planning a German lunch.

TO: Art
FROM: Fred
SUBJECT: Guest Cook

I don't care if you resurrected Joseph Goebbels to cook us. Just make sure that you and your co-cooks behave!

TO: Fred
FROM: Art
SUBJECT: Guest Cook

Ja Wohl, boss.

TO: Fred, Abe, Bill, Charles, Dick, Ed, Ernie, Joe, Steve
FROM: Art
SUBJECT: Guest Cook

Hi guys, I have invited a special guest from Germany to come and cook with me on Thursday. His name is Franz Schmidt. He's going to make some mighty fine German chow. Let's give him a special Old Men's Cooking Club welcome.

Chapter 13
The Sour Kraut

Rickety old Abe was teetering on an unsteady ancient step stool while scientist Ed was balancing on a shaky bridge chair on the other side of the room.

"A little higher," yelled Steve.

"A bit more to the left," Bill said.

"What are you talking about – it's perfect," shouted Abe from atop his post.

Dick piped in, "It's lopsided."

"Put your glasses on, will you?" Ed said.

"Only put a small piece of tape on the ceiling. The director will kill us if we mark up the plaster; we're still in the doghouse," Steve, who had created the masterpiece, barked instructions.

"WILLKOMMEN FRANZ" read the colorful banner.

"Looks terrific, fellas. Leave it just like that. It's perfect," Steve gave his final blessing.

The group munched on Twinkies with coffee for their mid-morning snack. The resplendent banner was to show support for Art's guest and co-cook from Germany.

When Art and Franz made their grand entrance lugging two boxes of goodies, everyone gathered to extend Franz a warm Old Men's Cooking Club welcome.

"Dankeschon, herren, Besten dank.

"What did he say?" Ernie asked.

From Dick, "It's German for thank you, many thanks."

"It's so nice to be with you, and I am honored to be able to cook for you today," Franz said in perfect English.

Franz wore his uniform, a brown pinstriped suit with a broad lapel, starched white shirt and a wide 1950's art deco-designed old man's tie. It was so different from the boys, who wore worn shorts and ratty tee shirts.

Ernie had continued to be subdued, and a bit less cantankerous, but this didn't stop him from getting into the conversation.

"We are having any of that sauerkraut stuff for lunch?"

"Yes," said Art, "with our sauerbraten."

"Any of you know the definition of sauerkraut?" asked Ernie.

The boys waited with bated breath, praying that Ernie would not cause a diplomatic incident and insult their guest right off the bat.

"A cranky old German," Ernie laughed. "Like me, except that I'm not German."

"That was from hunger, Ern," Abe said.

"No, it was from Hungry."

"Someone needs to do something about him," Dick whispered to Fred. "He's getting worse every day."

The members helped Franz out of his coat and tie, unloaded the bags and began their cooking assignments.

Art and Franz had met for coffee at Starbucks the previous Monday morning to strategize their plan for the lunch. Franz wanted to prepare sauerbraten, but the meat would have to be marinated for several days before cooking. The odd couple hobbled into the Publix supermarket, and, although both had the energy and agility to walk, they charged over to the handicap mobility scooters to make their assault. The octogenarians behaved like two kids on go karts, racing each other up and down the aisles. The meal would start with a potato soup and continue with sauerbraten, potato dumplings, sauerkraut and conclude with bundkuchen, or bundt cake, for dessert.

They faced their first big decision at the meat counter. The butcher suggested three different cuts, and Art asked Franz, "Chuck, round or rump roast?

"Chuck will not work, the round is possible, but I would prefer a rump," Franz said.

Art mused to himself, "So would dirty-minded Ernie."

They selected carrots, onions, potatoes, lemons, beef broth, flour, vegetable oil, butter, dark brown sugar, and gingersnap cookies. When they found the spices, they chose mustard seed, juniper berries, allspice, cassia, dill seed, bay leaves, cloves, ginger, star anise, tellicherry peppercorns, coriander, mace, cardamom and red chili peppers: fifteen different spices that alone would break the bank. The duo got in the way of each other, trying to read the labels. More than 200 jars of seasonings beckoned them. Franz had trouble with the label language and Art had difficulty seeing the numerous classifications. They were utterly frustrated when Art finally thought of a solution.

"Roll over here, Franz," Art said.

"Vas?" Picking up speed on his grocery go-cart.

"Look what I found, Knorr Sauerbraten Seasoning Mix!"

"Gut! We will cheat. Look at all the money and measuring it will save us too. Don't tell anyone."

They added bacon, chicken bouillon, potatoes, sour cream, eggs and parsley for the potato soup and cabbage for the sauerkraut to their carts. The shopping excursion was rounded out with ingredients for the spaetzli, dumplings, and bundkuchen.

"Do you have Dickmilch?" Franz asked a barely out of school store attendant.

"Are you for real, Pop?"

"Did I say something wrong? Dickmilch is rich fatty-soured milk we have in Germany. I use it for making bundt cake," he said to Art. "It has the best taste."

"It has a very different meaning here, Frantz," Art said pointing down to his crotch. "Let's just settle for whole milk."

On the way to the cashier, they nearly collided with Harry Smith.

"What are you doing here, son?" Franz asked.

"Hi, Papa. What a surprise. I was just going to meet with my friend Pete for a coffee break,"

Harry said, "What are you two up to?"

"We're doing the shopping for my cooking at the men's group Thursday," Franz boasted proudly.

"What are you cooking?"

"Sauerbraten."

"Oh, I love your sauerbraten. You need to invite me for lunch," Harry said.

"The cooking club is only for old men, Harry."

"These days I seem to be getting older by the minute. There's Pete now; I must go. Bring me home some sauerbraten, Pop."

"Knowing our boys, there won't be any left," Art said.

"Have fun, guys," Harry ended, heading to meet his partner.

Pete Stevens sauntered into Publix wearing tattered jeans and a smelly tee shirt boasting Pete's Fish and Tackle, his uniform for selling bait and cleaning fish. Harry, standing next to him in his Armani suit, completed the portrait of an authentic odd couple. They went over to the café to order coffee.

Franz and Art watched the duo. Franz, observing them closely, felt as if it looked like they were plotting something intense. He became suspicious of this strange combination and of their mid-day rendezvous.

"I drove over to Daytona this morning and gave the thumb drive to

Henry Johnson," Pete began.

"Any comments?" Harry asked.

"The plans look pretty complicated, but he feels the task is achievable. He must double the ingredients for two units and needs more cash. Wire him $10,000 today."

"Will do. I called Ernie this morning and reiterated our warm feelings for him. I invited him to join us for the shooting brunch next week. He says he owns a couple of guns but doesn't know how to use them. I told him we'd remedy that. He's in."

"Great."

Harry and Pete left in opposite directions.

Art's grocery bill came to more than $85.00 and he volunteered to subsidize the luncheon to prevent a revolution from the boys. Then they drove to Art's home to start marinating the meat and creating the bundt cake.

That Thursday in the Senior Center kitchen, Franz held up the magnificent roast of marinated meat, said, "This will make a spectacular sauerbraten."

"What type of meat is it?" Abe asked.

Art teased, "It's a mystery."

"Yeah, I can just see the headline now, 'Squirrel population dwindles as Senior Center's men's cooking group serves mystery meat for lunch,'" Abe said.

Franz admitted "It's actually a rump roast."

Strangely Ernie sat quietly. This would have been a perfect opportunity for one of his outbursts, but he was still unusually reserved. The group began piecing together the lunch puzzle. One group worked on the soup, several prepared the bread and a few focused on the meat course. Meanwhile the spätzle and dumplings simmered in separate pots of boiling water.

As Art peppered the meat, he let out a raucous sneeze.

"Gesundheit," said Franz quickly.

"See I told you that Franz speaks English very well," Ernie bubbled up.

Franz told his fellow cookers. "I love sauerbraten, It's my favorite dish. You know its origins go back more than a thousand years. Originally they used horse meat to make it."

Ernie yelled out, "So I guess Roy Rogers and Dale Evans had one hell of a sauerbraten before they stuffed and mounted their horse Trigger on their front lawn."

By noon each of the boys had slurped down a heaping portion of rich,

66

thick potato soup with bacon with sourdough bread, perfect for dunking. Then back to the kitchen to fill their plates with the moist, flavorful and exceedingly tender sauerbraten. The sauerkraut was stringy, yet luscious; the spätzle melted in their mouths and the dumplings were light as feathers. The plates were as bloated as their stomachs. Little energy was left for them to do the washing up.

"I read somewhere that Americans consume 387 million pounds of sauerkraut a year," Fred said.

"That's a hell of a lot of farting," Ernie said, trying to hide a gas bubble that was erupting from him.

Art asked Franz to tell the group a bit about life in Germany. Franz began to speak about his homeland, its culture, the climate, the idyllic scenery and family life. He bragged about the rich, wonderful food of his region and his passion for cooking and, most important, that he loved to eat. The boys listened intently. He quoted Euripides, "When a man's stomach is full, it makes no difference if he's rich or poor."

All agreed.

Ernie asked, "What did the German kid say when he pushed his brother off the cliff?"

"What, Ernie?" asked the group, waiting for a zinger.

"Look ma, no Hans."

"Boo"

"Boo"

Then Franz told the story of his miraculous reunion with Art at Disney World. "Can you imagine of all the places in the entire world, we meet in a Fantasy Land."

"Over a hot dog," Art added.

"Over a really terrible hot dog."

"We hadn't seen each other in 60 years. And before I left Germany last week, I mentioned to my wife that I knew someone here in America but with hundreds of millions of people in the United States who would ever believe we would meet.

"That's pretty amazing," Dick said.

Franz continued, "I was a pilot shot down by the Americans. They sent me here to the States. Young and terribly scared, I didn't know what they would do to us or why they bothered to ship us here. In the beginning there was a serious communication problem, I didn't understand much that was going on around me. I remember that Art was the first friendly face I met. He offered me a cigarette and then brought me chocolate. Slowly we started to communicate with each other. During my time here, he looked out for me and my buddy, Otto Schafter. After the war Otto and I both returned to Germany, and I lost touch with Art."

"You were a pretty good guy, but that friend of yours was a real handful," Art commented.

"Otto Schafer is 85 years old now, lives in my town and is still a bad handful," Franz laughed.

"I can't believe we were just eating hot dogs and started talking," Art kept repeating.

"Miracles do happen," Franz said.

Dick asked more about the war, but Franz ducked many of the details. He did reiterate how horrified he was at what took place. He explained that there were many unsympathetic Germans, including him, who could not opt out of the conflict. While it was true that many of the elite were horrible, guilty war criminals who claimed to just be following orders, the average German had no choice but to go along with it all. "There were many who believed the direction of the Third Reich, but lots of us were skeptical and were trapped."

He said nightmares still plague him about the horrors he experienced. "I was almost grateful to be captured and shipped to the States. It would never happen again," Franz said as he nibbled on his bundt cake.

Ernie was not so sure but sat quietly. Although usually he was his obnoxious self, but after this discussion, he became very sullen because of his painful secret. The others sensed something was wrong.

"Hey, Ernie, you've been really down lately. Are you feeling okay?" Dick asked.

"I'm all right, guys, just a bit under the weather. Thanks for asking."

The cooking club chorus was once again on stage.

"You need to buck up, Ernie."

"And take care of yourself."

"We really need you here, Ernie."

"Yeah, we love you, Ernie." Charles ran over to give him a big hug.

Ernie cringed with Charles's hug, but did brighten for a minute. He loved the attention, the warmth, and the acceptance of the group, but not the hug.

"Damn straight you need me," bellowed Ernie. "You need my plastic leg to stir the soup."

Chapter 14
Pre-Sunrise Shake Up

Ernie tossed and turned in his old, lumpy bed. He was drenched with perspiration which could have been avoided had he ignored his frugality and switched on the air conditioner. The round-faced alarm clock read 3:30 a.m. and the moonless sky was pitch-black. Laying wide awake and very perturbed, he thought, what have I gotten myself into?

The Aryan Connection barbecue had mixed up his emotions. On the one hand, he was finally feeling appreciated and worthy by a group, but it was causing a chilling effect inside him. It didn't help that Harry Smith had called the day before inviting him to another meeting, this time a "shooting brunch."

A shooting brunch? He kept wondering.

Ernie looked forward to the meal and the camaraderie of the men, but the shooting part scared him. He had inherited some pistols, but had never used them, nor did he expect to. In fact, he didn't even remember telling anyone he had them. Much of the virulent hatred expressed at the barbecue was too extreme even for him. Basically, he had some prejudices, but he didn't consider himself to be a hateful person.

Ernest Stubbs had endured a conflicted and isolated childhood. Growing up in a remote rural town in western Pennsylvania, he was never exposed to blacks, Hispanics, Jews or homosexuals. Those "elements" lived faraway on the other side of the railroad tracks. There was never any interaction with these minorities and his righteous parents constantly extolled the purity of being white and Catholic.

Until the morning he was caught in the sacristy imbibing on the sacramental wine and gulping down a handful of communion wafers, he had served as an altar boy in his family's church. He was an only child; lonely, naïve and gullible. His playful sense of humor went unappreciated since he had no one in his somber household to enjoy his cleverness.

Prejudiced teachings were constantly hammered into him, and they made an indelible impression. Ernie managed to plow through life despite those deeply bigoted ideas. He had little formal education but gained lots of street smarts.

Ernie was proud to serve his country in the Army during World War II. He was sent overseas after the armistice to help repair bridges in a fallen and defeated Germany. He witnessed the destruction and the results of the near annihilation of the Jewish race but had pushed this reality into to the far reaches of his mind, never speaking of it.

He flaunted his sexuality following the occupation, but ultimately returned home to Bessie, his high-school virgin sweetheart. They danced down the aisle twice to the same church altar, with the same results, each ceremony eventually resulting in a disastrous divorce. They had two children who fled to different ends of the country, forcing them to enjoy their grandchildren through photos and an occasional Skype call.

Bessie was Ernie's love, caretaker, best friend and lover. They simply were not able to live in peace together. She was a kind, sympathetic, and understanding person who knew how to tolerate Ernie and more than anyone, recognized and appreciated his core of goodness beneath all his bluster.

Throughout his career as a salesman of mechanical parts where his verbal skills were an asset, Ernie managed to get away with his racial beliefs without flaunting them publicly until later in life. It was no wonder that Ernie was a right-wing conservative who passionately disliked the current black "Muslim" president. He felt that the country was being taken away from the hopes, desires and basic beliefs of those who lived on the white side of the tracks.

He suffered his fair share of pain with many health issues and the loss of his right leg because of a nasty car accident. He was a most complex character who became more caustic and less tolerant as he aged. Despite perpetual crankiness, he was able to maintain his sense of humor which was boyish, mischievous and playful. He had an admirable streak as well. He couldn't do enough for those he liked. Beneath his curmudgeon veil, people found him warm, caring, charming, and very attentive.

Ernie was funny although often toxic and this complexity was evident in the reactions of those in the men's cooking ensemble. The guys understood him, looked the other way, mostly in his favor. His presence rounded out the overall diversity of the group and the good Ernie certainly brought a great deal of fun to the table.

Being mostly all mouth and no action, Ernie never subscribed to the hatred that resulted in physical violence. The Aryans at the barbecue were less talk and a great deal more action. Feeling completely in over his head with no way out, he had been sworn to secrecy and felt trapped. He was now involved up to his eyeballs. Opening his mouth to anyone would implicate him as an accomplice to their heinous schemes. His big mouth was usually his downfall, so he must keep quiet about the conspiracy.

He attached his prosthetic, got up and paced back and forth in his steamy bedroom. Picking up the phone several times, he opted out before completing any call. Then he finally found the courage and dialed.

"Bess?"

"Ernie, are you, all right?"

"Were you sleeping?"

"What else does one do at 3:30 in the morning?"

"I'm very upset. I need to see you right away."

"Ernie, should I call 911?" his ex-wife asked.

"No, I'm not ill, other than my sick mind." It was hardly the time for a humorous remark, so Bessie let it pass.

"We must meet now."

"Oh, please go back to sleep, Ernie. I'll come over in the morning."

"NO, NOW. Meet me at the all-night Steak 'n' Shake, please."

"Come on, Ernie." Bessie said, used to Ernie's theatrics.

"I'm upset enough to jump out of my window."

"Ernie, you live on the first floor."

"So, I'll go upstairs," Ernie was relentless, and she caved.

"I guess I can be there in half an hour."

Bessie became seriously worried. After surviving their marriages and many crises with this man, she knew him inside and out, but didn't remember hearing him this tormented. She couldn't imagine why he was so troubled. Ernie had money to take care of himself for the rest of his life and his health was stable now. She could only imagine what kind of trouble he had gotten himself into. As a betting woman, she would have put money on something to do with his loose lips. He tended to speak his mind without thinking and there were many times she had had to remove his foot from his mouth. Dressing quickly in the first mismatched clothing she could find, she hurried to meet her tormented ex-partner.

The only customer in the eatery, Ernie was hunched over the table in a corner leatherette booth. When he saw her, with some semblance of relief he said, "Bess, I'm so glad you're here."

"Ernie, what the hell is it? You're scaring me like never before."

A sleepy waitress appeared, asked, "What will you folks have?"

"I'll just have a cup of black decaf coffee," Bessie said in an agitated voice.

"I'm not very hungry so I'll have a double California cheeseburger, with fried onions, pickles, lettuce, tomatoes and mayonnaise. Don't leave out the

American fries and finish with an Oreo cookie milkshake."

"Ernie, it's 4:30 in the morning. What in the world are you doing?"

"Ordering my breakfast, Bess. I'm petrified. You know that I eat to relieve stress."

"What's going on? Tell Mama."

Ernie started to weep as he retold the story in full graphic detail, right down to the tattooed arms and the food at the barbecue.

"Oh my God, Ernie! Are you sure you're not exaggerating?"

"Could I make up a story like that?"

"Probably not."

"I have my quirks, but I'm not that demented. What should I do? I'm so lost. Help me."

"You should go to the police, or the FBI, or somebody."

"They'll find out and kill me. I'm sure of it. These guys are American Nazis and play rough. They swore me to secrecy."

Remembering Harry's cold warning, Ernie felt chills down his spine. "All of us, including you, are in a heap of trouble if this should get out?"

Interrupting their conversation, the sleepy server delivered a mountain of food for Ernie and a single cup of coffee for Bessie.

"Let me think," Bessie said, trying to hold the cup in her trembling hands.

"Help me, please."

"What about calling Dick? He would know what to do."

"I can't Bess; I just can't," Ernie continued, sobbing, his puffy face a cherry red from the trauma.

She pulled a handkerchief from her handbag, handed it to Ernie and said, "Okay, here's what you are going to do. You play along, act as natural as you can, be part of the pack, and we will find a way to get this information to the authorities."

"Are you sure?"

"It's the only way. And, Ernie, PROMISE ME, PROMISE ME, you will keep your big mouth shut. It's that mouth that has gotten you into this trouble."

"Yes, I know it has."

Ernie's entire body ached, and he felt awful. He was supposed to be enjoying his last few years on the planet, not wishing for their conclusion. Bessie was correct. He would do exactly what she said. But his depression stole his appetite, and so the food was left untouched, with the cheeseburger sagging, the lettuce wilted and the tomatoes shriveling up. The American fries looked un-patriotic and more and more unappetizing. Even the soggy

Oreo cookies had risen to the top of the parfait glass.

"I am in such a major pickle. I don't know how I will survive this," Ernie moaned.

"Buck up, Ernie, and do as I say, and you'll be fine. You are a true survivor," Bessie assured him lovingly.

"Not hungry, hon? Somethin' wrong with the food?" the bored waitress asked, as she put down the check.

"Lost my appetite," Ernie said, still terrified but perked up after unburdening his tale to his confidant. "Wrap it up, I'll have it all to go."

Chapter 15
It is in The Works

The two German fossils met monthly for lunch in a private dining room at an exclusive men's club. A chauffeur had driven Otto Schafer the 64 miles from Regensburg to Munich, the capital of Bavaria, Germany. The club, like the gentlemen, was antiquated, stiffly formal, laden with high ceilings, dark woodwork, faded art, chandeliers and cracked leather furniture.

Lunch was a long-drawn-out affair. It usually began with several rounds of aperitifs. Today they feasted on salad of quail breasts with artichokes and goose liver, filet of beef oxtail terrine with Périgord truffles and saddle of lamb. For dessert there was a selection of cheeses and strawberries with bourbon, vanilla meringues and lemon ice. The Riesling wine flowed throughout the meal. After this gluttony, they belched, farted, begged forgiveness from each other for their indiscretions, and laughed.

They talked about the football matches and the economic situation in Germany. Their conversations, however, always seemed to steer them back to the war. Each had a story of his involvement. Each had survived unscathed from the battles, strongly passionate to preserve many of the policies and practices of the former Third Reich. There was now a system of active webs throughout the country for comrades who felt the same way.

Present-day German industrialists funded their efforts. There were even modern-day sects of secret agents through these companies serving as covers for military research and intelligence. This cloak-and-dagger intrigue was all in preparation for National Socialism's return to power. For these two patriarchs of the movement, this was equivalent to the coming of Christ. One of their goals was to spread their clandestine operations to the United State that had already begun.

The main topic for their time together was always saved for last. They whispered discretely about the National Socialist Party and the growth of the Fourth Reich in their homeland. Otto Schafer reported about the covert activities taking place around the country. He headed the Bavarian Regional Council which was assigned to spearhead the Florida Project.

His luncheon companion, Siegfried Schloss, a nonagenarian, seethed with the uttermost venom. As a former officer in the Gestapo, he had escaped being captured by the skin of his teeth.

"Otto, did the money get wired to our Florida compatriots?" Siegfried asked.

"Yes, it was sent last week to their account in the Cayman Islands."

"Are you confident the group in Florida can carry out the complex plan?" Siegfried pressed.

"Yes. Heinrich Schmidt, their leader, is an extremely bright, capable man. I have known him since he was a boy and truly believe that they will succeed. He reports to me weekly and they are moving along. I am planning to make a trip there to help them accomplish our goals."

Schloss began to lecture, "We need to keep a close eye on the political situation in Washington. It is a travesty that Sid Townsend was only elected Vice President. He should be leading that nation instead of Sharif. Townsend stands for the white majority and understands the plight of the Caucasian red-blooded American. He believes that white Americans are an organically grown social order that is based on language, cultural history and heritage, which is the essence of humanity. All other races are in direct contradiction to this. His viewpoint matches those of the new Reich here in Germany. He is a strong right-wing, ultra-conservative politician who shares so many of our ideals."

"I agree fully. The Americans can't afford to have a black Muslim in the presidential chair, especially one who favors the Jews and their Zionist state. It doesn't fit with our plans," Otto concurred.

"The only reason that Sharif was reelected was because Townsend was on the ticket."

"That will all be taken care of soon," Otto said.

Sid Townsend was placed on the reelection ticket with Herman Sharif at the last moment as a compromise candidate because he was a public independent and was able to bring a vast number of swing votes from leaning conservatives. He was the consummate politician: outgoing, glad-handing with the ultimate charisma. Yet he was a secretive individual unique for a politician. Despite his high-profile persona, he managed to hide his deep racist and other prejudicial leanings. Deep-pocket backers of the Fourth Reich in Germany helped swing the American election for him and Sharif.

"When was the last time that we were in touch with Townsend?"

"Harry Smith spoke to him a week ago."

"Is he ready for the job?"

"Yes."

"Now we have to move on our plan."

"It is in the works."

Chapter 16
The Slam Dunk

Leonetta Moore had a queasy feeling in her stomach. Something told her she shouldn't have gotten out of bed and come to work this morning. The five-foot, three-inch buxom black waitress with a grey-shaded 1950's beehive hairdo was a star at Denny's Restaurant customer service employment program. Everyone enjoyed her dominant presence and comical demeanor. This Denny's was a food and theatrical experience and Leonetta was its floor show.

"Oh Lordy, it's that time of the month. The Old Men's Cooking Club will be invading again. Why don't they just stay in their own kitchen where they belong?" She said, setting the long table in the rear of the restaurant for the eleven diners.

Ernie was first in the door and promptly took his rightful seat at the head of the table.

"How you doing, sweetheart?" asked Leonetta.

"Not bad for an old fart."

"You ain't no old fart, just a big bag of wind."

"Thanks, Lee, I love you too," Ernie chuckled.

"Got a full group today?"

"Yep, and I'm the host."

"That means you're paying the check, right?" She asked, hopeful.

"Hell, no! It's separate checks all around."

"I knew this was the day to call in sick."

One by one the boys hobbled in. Everyone was glad to see that Art had brought Franz. Eventually the table became a cacophony of voices all talking at once. This once-serene breakfast haven had become a bustling beehive of activity. The boys checked the menus even though they already knew it by heart.

"I'll have a glass of diet water," Ernie yelled across the room.

"I'm having a Slam Dunk," Abe said, out loud to the others.

"That's a Grand Slam," Fred corrected.

"Me too."

"Me three."

"Why don't we all have Grand Slams. That will make it easier on everyone," came a welcome but foolhardy idea from artist Steve.

"Sold American," yelled Ernie above the fray.

Leonetta came over, took a deep breath, poised and ready to write. "What can I get you fellas today?"

"We're all having Grand Slams," club-leader Fred answered for all.

"Okay, who wants to go first?"

"I'll have bacon strips, buttermilk biscuits, pancakes with blueberry syrup, scrambled eggs well done, and coffee with cream and sugar," ordered Art.

Bill said, "I'll have oatmeal, hash browns, fried eggs over easy, sausage links, and an iced tea with lemon. Could I please have my oatmeal first?"

"Sure thing," she scribbled furiously.

"My turn?" said Abe. "Okay, three pancakes, chicken sausage, two poached eggs slightly hard, and an English muffin with butter and jam on the side. Bring me a black coffee too, dear."

"I don't know what I want. Let me see," said Fred.

"Take your time, sweetie. We're open 24 hours," Leonetta kidded.

"Okay, here goes coffee with cream and Sweet 'N Low, whole wheat pancakes, hash browns, soft scrambled eggs, and dry rye toast with jam. Yep, I think that'll do."

"Who's NEXT?"

"Me," said Dick. "I want seasonal fruit with no strawberries, but double the melon, runny sunny side up eggs, well-done grilled ham, whole wheat toast, and an orange juice."

"I'm having trouble deciding as well," Steve said. "Do I want scrambled eggs or poached eggs, whole wheat or sourdough toast? Decisions, decisions."

"That's all right, hon. I'll wait but may never live to see sixty-one next year."

"Oh, all right, I'll decide. Three fried eggs, a bagel with a heavy schmeer of cream cheese, grits, buttermilk pancakes with boysenberry sauce, and a cup of hot tea with lemon and milk."

"I swear, Pedro's gonna have a heart attack in the kitchen. He's gonna quit in the middle of this order." Leonetta was now flustered and writing feverishly.

Further down the table the boys ordered equally mixed up concoctions including turkey sausage, sunny side up and scrambled eggs, new potatoes and hash browns, oatmeal, pancakes both whole wheat and blueberry English Muffins, yogurt and every imaginable beverage combination.

78

"Scrambled eggs soft, lightly buttered whole wheat toast, delicately cooked bacon strips, pancakes, and a cup of tea with lemon and Sweet'N Low," Charles ordered.

"I'm gonna make extra sure that your bacon strips are real delicate. The cook is going to have a field day with that request," laughed Leonetta.

"Well, I've got a fragile stomach," Charlie said.

"That's okay, sweetie. If you want them delicate, you'll get them delicate. We aim to please at Denny's." Turning to Franz, she asked, "What about you, honey?"

"Franz is having some difficulty reading the English menu," Art explained.

"Take your time. The dinner rush doesn't start for another 30 minutes," she said, tapping the order pad impatiently.

"Ya, I will order yogurt, fresh fruit, no berries, oatmeal with fat milk, rye toast with butter, jam, and a cup of hot tea.

"Hey, Lee, I want to change my order," Ernie blurted out.

"YOU CAN'T!"

"Did you get all those orders straight, Leonetta?" Fred asked.

Ernie joked, "Maybe you should repeat the list."

"He's at it again," Abe said. "Screw you, Ernie."

"Where and when?" Ernie responded, cracking a big smile.

* * *

While the kitchen turned into chaos with the mishmash of orders, a man and a woman strolled in a different door. It was the front door of the Orlando Senior Center down the road. The center's director greeted them at the door.

"Hi, I'm Sally Adams and this is Tom Prentice. We are hoping to have a word with a gentleman named Ernest Stubbs."

"Well, he's usually here with the men's cooking group, but this week they all went out for breakfast, and frankly, I didn't ask them where they were going. One never knows with that group."

"Here's my card," said the professionally dressed middle-aged woman, "Tell him to give us a call when you see him. It's important. Thank you."

***

Meanwhile the boys were in full form around the long table.

"Hey, Leonetta, how old are you?" Ernie asked boldly

"Why Ernie, you know it ain't right to ask a woman her age. Few of us women will admit our age. But I'll sure tell you one thing; few men act theirs," she said pointing to the group.

"Good for you, Lee."

"You told him."

"Hey guys, what's the cheapest meat?" said Ernie.

"I give up" came the echo from around the table.

"Deer balls! They're under a buck." The only one laughing was Ernie who thought his joke was hilarious.

Retired CIA spook Dick and self-proclaimed artist Steve could be heard having a loud discussion at the other end of the table.

"There is no Betty Crocker," Steve said.

"Of course, there is. I grew up with her on television."

Steve argued, "Betty Crocker was a 1920's marketing promotion that has lasted the past 80 years."

"I don't believe you."

"I know I'm right. There have been at least a dozen different actresses who have portrayed the fictional baker over the years.

"Go on, I suppose you'll tell me that there's no Chef Boyardee?" said Dick, now a bit upset with Steve.

"Yes, there was a Chef Boyardee. He migrated from Italy to Cleveland in the early 1920's."

"I don't like that canned ravioli shit," Ernie chimed in, needing to add his two cents.

It required Leonetta, a bus boy and the manager to carry out the eleven breakfast orders. There was a considerable amount of passing around plates and drinks, but, by and large, they got the orders correct. The boys cheered the concerted effort and dug into their baseball-named dishes.

"Acht, this milk on the oatmeal is horrible. What they need here is Dickmilch, a rich creamy dairy product we have in Germany," Franz said.

"Sweet Charlie drinks dick milk here in Orlando," Ernie blurted out.

"ERNIE!" Dick gave him a look to kill. Charles became flustered but took Ernie's remark in stride.

Other patrons started to turn to listen to the sordid comical conversations.

"In Sweden they serve Jussi Pussi," said Fred. "It's a Swedish potato chip."

"And in Brazil they have a 'Prick' brand potato chip," continued Dick adding to the discussion of obscene titled foods.

80

Leonetta, a busy bee moving around the table refilling drinks, listened intently and getting a kick out of this month's men's club session.

"In Poland fart means good luck," Franz announced. He was getting considerably more comfortable letting his hair down and turned out to be quite the rascal too.

Fred desperately tried to change the subject. "I've been reading a lot of mystery books lately, and I'm not sure I understand the difference between the FBI and the CIA."

"One is intelligent, and the other isn't." Steve jumped in before Dick could clarify the difference.

"We handled international affairs at the CIA, the FBI is for domestic issues."

"Biker Joe handles domestic affairs." Then turning serious, Abe said, "The police still don't have any clues who painted the swastikas on the synagogue, do they?"

"That's shameful," Franz added, almost mournfully. "It's impossible to believe that this kind of activity would happen here in America."

"It's like a cancer. It just doesn't go away," bushy-haired Art said.

Ernie, listening intently, became very quiet.

"There is hatred all over the world, and there is acrimony here in Orlando as well. I guess that's what makes the world go around," scientist Ed said.

Dick proclaimed, "As a matter of fact, I am pretty sure there is a very strong neo-Nazi group somewhere in the backwoods outside of town."

"Could never happen here," said Bill.

"Don't be so sure." That was the first meaningful comment to come out of Ernie's mouth.

"What are you saying, Ernie?" Dick jumped on his comment.

"Oh, it's nothing. Just that there are bad people everywhere," Ernie said, not wanting to reveal anything.

"Well, that's true, Ernie," Dick said.

Steve, trying to change the subject, asked, "Anybody know why men die before their wives?"

"I give up," said Art.

"They want to!" With that, they all had a good laugh.

"So, who's cooking next week?" Fred asked.

"It's my turn," Charles raised his hand.

"We're going to have six faggots in gravy! What? It's an English dish, guys," Ernie told the group.

"You know, Ernie, it's a good thing that I take you with a grain of salt,"

Charles piped in. "But sometimes you just go too far."

"You can take me without the salt. I know I do, and I don't really mean it. You know that I love you, Charlie."

Bill asked, "Do you love him enough to go to bed with him?"

"Oh, Charles, my love, if I was only fifty years younger. I can hardly get it up for Bessie anymore, and I'm certainly not going to waste any effort on you."

"You don't know what you're missing," Charles said, wiggling his eyebrows.

Leonetta came by and handed the checks to each of them. "You know, you are a bunch of bad-ass old boys."

"Hey, I got the wrong check," said Bill.

"They should have the same totals. We all had the mix and match Grand Slams for $6.50."

"Hey fellows, don't forget to show your AARP cards. We all get a discount."

A long line formed at the cash register as everyone fumbled for money and their senior cards.

"Is anyone here named Ernest Stubbs?" came from an all-business-looking professional woman at the door.

"Hey, Ernie, there is a dame here after your body," Dick said as Ernie sauntered out of the restroom, smiling.

"I'm here, who's asking?"

"Are you Ernest Stubbs?"

"Yes, why?"

"Do you mind if we have a short conversation?"

"No, but if you're selling anything, I'm not buying."

"Not to worry, we don't plan on fleecing you. I'm Agent Tom Prentice," said the man standing next to the woman. "This is Senior Agent Sally Adams. We're from the FBI. Would you mind coming with us?"

Chapter 17
Extra, Extra, Read All About it

That night on the internet, the Old Men's Cooking Club Gazette was abuzz as the boys typed furiously on their computers.

"Ernie are you all right?" wrote Dick.

"I hope you're not in trouble," Art typed next.

"What gives with the FBI, Ernie?" Bill asked, seriously concerned.

"What's going on with Ernie?" Abe sent an email to Charles.

"I don't know. I shot him an e-mail and didn't get a response."

"I'm pretty worried," Dick wrote back into the mix. "Ernie, where the hell are you? I've been worried about you all day. Please answer."

"It's Joe here, Ernie. If you're in trouble, we want to help."

"You have us all pretty concerned, Ernie. We hope that you are okay," Steve added.

Several worrisome hours passed with no response. A barrage of panic instant messages went back and forth between the concerned friends.

Steve: "I hope they didn't arrest him."

Bill: "Maybe they took him to prison."

Fred: "He won't do well in prison."

Abe: "Ernie won't hold up under waterboarding."

Charles: "Could he be involved in some international terrorist plot?"

Dick: "Who, Ernie? No way!"

Joe: "He can't find his plastic leg by himself in the morning, let alone be involved in some conspiracy."

Art: "What will we do without him?"

Fred: "I don't know how I would get by without his chronic complaining."

Bill: "Or without his crazy political opinions."

Charles: "Or his nonsensical mutterings."

Steve: "Or his inactivity in the kitchen."

Dick: "Or his prejudiced mumblings."

Abe: "His absence would leave a black hole!"

Joe: "Yeah, who is going to keep the pot stirred?"

Even Franz had been pulled into the commotion by Art. As time passed, more and more e-mails flew back and forth.

11:00 p.m.
FROM: Ernie
TO: Fred, Steve, Bill, Charles, Dick, Joe, Ed, Abe, Art (please tell Franz).
SUBJECT: Hi Guys.

"Sorry that I didn't respond sooner. Bessie and I went out for dinner. Dick gave us this buy one, get one free coupon for Smokey Bones. I had the ribs with a baked potato and lots of sour cream; she had the pulled pork with mashed potatoes. The pork was a little tough and stringy. The ribs were much better, tender and juicy. They also serve a good salad at Bones with some secret ingredient dressing. We were too stuffed for dessert although the strawberry cheesecake looked delicious. Next time Bessie said she will order the ribs, but only if we get another buy one, get one free coupon. Otherwise we can't afford these prices. Have you guys seen the prices of dinners at restaurants these days? Eating out costs as much as buying a car: well, almost, anyway.

Oh, by the way, about the FBI agents who came by Denny's this morning. They just wanted to set up an appointment to chat with me about an old acquaintance who's involved in a case that they're working on. Gonna meet with them next Monday.

See you on Thursday.
Chao, Ernie."

"You God-damned bastard" was heard in unison across the skies of Orlando.
Joe: "That SOB had us worried for nothing."
Abe: "Maybe we shouldn't worry about him again?"
Steve: "I thought maybe they confiscated his leg."
Bill: "He has some hell of a nerve."
Charles: "Well, maybe we worry too much. After all he went out to dinner. He doesn't just sit around watching his computer like us losers. He was having fun while we gnashed our teeth and wore out our fingers."
Art: "But he made so light of the FBI?"
Joe: "Who could the old acquaintance be?"
Abe: "Ernie doesn't have any other friends."
Charles: "You think he may be hiding something?"

Steve: "Naw, he's too dumb to keep a secret."
Dick: "What are we going to do with our Ernie?"

Chapter 18
The Spy Who Came in From The Heat

Franz had such a splendid time with Art and the men of the cooking group at Denny's on Thursday that he found he was bored at his son's home. He was relieved Ernie was not in trouble, because he enjoyed him despite his puerile behavior. Now he was stuck at Harry's home in the middle of what seemed like nowhere with too many rooms to rattle around in.

Anneliese, Ingrid and the grandchildren had gone shopping, and Harry was downtown to complete some work. He puttered around with nothing to do. Franz located the morning newspaper and settled into a reclining chair in his son's bookshelf-lined den to catch up on the news. Although he felt some awkwardness when speaking English, his reading ability was good. Scanning the print and bypassing most of the articles, he came to a gut-wrenching headline:

POLICE INVESTIGATION OF DESECRATED SYNAGOGUE CONTINUES.

"The police diligently tried to find clues about the painting of swastikas on the Orlando synagogue several weeks ago. Thus far there are no leads or suspects …" The article named a few secret organizations in the area including the Ku Klux Klan and a branch of the neo-Nazi party, but none had claimed responsibility. "… law enforcement is stumped. They were ready to write off the incident as a school-age delinquent prank." His heart was beginning to ache and his hands shake as he read this disturbing news.

Feeling hungry, he wandered into the ultra-modern kitchen, and found a piece of chicken and some homemade potato salad Ingrid left for his lunch in the refrigerator. Sitting at the kitchen table to eat, he heard the phone rang. Franz didn't know where the extensions were but had seen one in the den. He hobbled there quickly, just in time to answer.

"Hallo."

"Hi, is Harry home?"

"No, he's at work. Who is this, please?"

"You must be his father. We met at Publix the other day. I'm his friend, Pete."

"Ah, yes, yes." Franz remembered he didn't like the combination of Pete and his son.

"Please tell him I called. I couldn't reach him on his cell. Tell him I will see him tomorrow at the meeting."

"Ya." Franz had not realized that Harry would not be with them again this Sunday. Harry had never mentioned anything about a meeting. No sooner had he devoured the first piece of chicken than the phone rang again. Again, he repeated his trot across the house, feeling like a runner in the 1936 Berlin Olympics.

"Hallo" came his breathless answer.

"Hello, Is Harry Smith home?"

"No, he is out at the moment."

"I tried him on his cell phone, but it was turned off."

"This is his father. Can I give him a message?"

"Tell him Henry Johnson called and the device in the plan from Otto is very effective."

"Ya."

"Did you get that, sir?"

"Ya, ya, the device from Otto is gut," Franz frantically wrote down the message.

"Very good, I'll get back to him."

"Okay. Bye."

I also know an Otto, Franz wondered. He decided to stay in the den and continue his career for the day as Harry's secretary. The chicken was not very good anyway. Franz rummaged around and decided to see if he could get the computer working. He wasn't very good at technology, but he read the news and played solitaire on his computer in Regensburg. Perhaps he could log onto the Bavarian news site. At least it would be in German.

Since it was a PC, he had no difficulty turning it on. Suddenly a video showed two men embracing and doing unspeakable things to each other. Franz watched in disbelief. Even God himself would be embarrassed by this display of sexuality, he thought. Never having seen anything quite like it, he wondered what Harry was doing on this site. He pressed a few buttons and an additional website popped up: THE AMERICAN NAZI CONSORTIUM PARTY. Franz looked through the website in disbelief. At the end of the most demented letter by the group leader was a tab to download Adolph Hitler's, Mein Kampf. Franz was distraught with old stirrings of guilt. His eyes filled with tears of sadness and regret as he sat reading the book. Still hunched over the poisonous rhetoric of the heinous dictator, he fell asleep.

Several hours later, he heard, "Franz, Franz, where are you? We're home."

Startled awake by Anneliese, he opened his eyes staring at a portrait of Adolph Hitler on the screen. Quickly he pushed several buttons to close this site before his wife came in. Franz was baffled and didn't know how to understand what he had found on his son's computer. Both websites were forms of demented perversion.

Anneliese, Ingrid, the children and the nanny carrying the baby came into the den.

"Grandpa, Grandpa," yelled 9-year-old blond-haired, blue-eyed Anna, as she ran to hug him.

"How is my favorite American granddaughter?"

"Don't be silly, Grandpa, I'm your only American granddaughter," Anna laughed.

"How is your day going, Papa?" Ingrid asked.

"Very interesting," he said half-joking.

"What did you do while we were out?"

"I worked as Harry's secretary and spent some time on the computer."

"Sounds exciting,"

"You can't imagine."

"What did you buy, Anneliese, and how much did it cost me?"

"Everything was on sale, Franz. Ingrid helped me get some wonderful bargains on clothing. I bought some sweaters for our cold winters, several pairs of shoes and a beautiful leather handbag that was 75% off."

"You are my ticket to the poorhouse, my dear." Franz was secretly pleased his wife was enjoying herself with Ingrid and the children.

"But it was such a bargain."

"What a bargain."

"Mom, Mom, what are you making for dinner?" interrupted 11-year-old Thomas.

"A reservation," Ingrid laughed at the family joke.

"That's a good idea! Let's all go out for dinner," said Anna.

"Yes, Mommy. Let's go to The Golden Corral."

"Well, I don't know, Tommy."

"Why can't we. We love it there," Tommy whined.

"I don't know if Mama and Papa would like it?"

"They'll like it, I know."

"Grandma, they have this big chocolate fountain that you dip strawberries and marshmallows in. It's so neat."

At that moment Harry came in. Franz stared up at him with steely eyes.

"Daddy, we all want to go to The Golden Corral."

"Sure, why not," Harry said. "You'll like it, Mom, Pop. It's a big buffet, lots of food."

"I would like to ask Art, my friend from the men's cooking group, to join us. He has invited me for so many meals. I would like to do something in return."

"I don't see why not," said Harry. "As long as he can meet us there in an hour, it will be fine."

On their way out, Franz handed Harry the two phone messages. Watching carefully, he checked his son's reaction. Not in the least phased by the content, he nodded thanks, shoving them in his pocket.

Since it was dinner time on Saturday night, the buffet line was out the door. Arranging a table for nine seemed to take forever and they were all starving by the time they got to the buffet. The restaurant was packed, noisy and filled with screaming children. It wasn't Ingrid's idea of dining out, and Franz and Anneliese played along, being good sports. Tommy and Anna charged over to the dessert station first. Harry had to run after them and steer them to the real food.

Art and Franz sat at one end of the table with Harry at the other end.

"I haven't been to one of these places in years," Art commented. "My eyes always are much bigger than my stomach at these all-you-can-eat buffets, but it can't compare to the food we cook on Thursdays at the club."

The buffet completely overwhelmed Franz. He was a good eater, but this was obscene. He too would have liked to rush over to the desserts but knew Harry would object as he had with the children. He grabbed a plate and perused the 50 plus item salad bar. He piled lettuce and accompaniments as high as the German alps, adding ranch dressing like snow at its peaks. Balanced in his other hand, he had an overfilled plate of steak, roast chicken, baked potato, green beans, and broccoli.

"You sure that's enough?" Anneliese asked.

"Ya, I can go back for more if I am still hungry."

Art indulged wholeheartedly too. The children quickly ate their macaroni and cheese and chicken tenders, eager to get to the sweets.

Franz was attacking a chicken leg when he looked up and saw a large man standing next to Harry. He had a long snow-white beard that was caught on his belt buckle, arms decorated with tattoos from top to bottom, and wore tight leather pants and a biker's vest.

Harry introduced everyone to this mountain man, Floyd. Art whispered to Franz that this stranger looked like one of the Oak Ridge Boys.

"Who?"

"Never mind."

"Hi ya, folks. It's a pleasure to meet you. Don't let me interrupt. Enjoy your supper. I'll see you at the meeting tomorrow, Harry."

"What meeting tomorrow?" Ingrid asked Harry.

"I'll tell you about it later, dear."

While everyone gulped down the soft vanilla ice cream, Harry brought Ralph over to introduce him to Art and Franz. Ralph was thin as a rail, wearing tattered jeans with an uneven white beard and unkempt hair. He had his fair share of tattoos as well.

"Good to meet you, Mr. and Mrs. Schmidt. Harry has told me so much about you. You folks are here from Germany?"

"Ya," said Anneliese.

"The missus and I love Germany; we were there last summer. We saved up for years to do the big trip. It was a thrill to see all the places where the Third Reich took place. We especially loved the beer hall in Munich. They must've had some raucous parties there.

Franz raised a suspicious eyebrow but said nothing. Anneliese was gracious as always.

"Sorry, but I can't be at the group tomorrow, Harry. I'll miss you guys. Happy shooting."

Franz was faced with many pieces to a puzzle his mind could not assimilate. He thought about the homosexual videos, the neo-Nazi propaganda website, the bizarre phone calls from Pete, his shady friend, and the other about the device and the plan. What device, what plan? Franz wondered. And what about these two unsavory characters, especially the one who treasured the Third Reich landmarks as the highlight of his German tour? Then there was Harry's announcement of another meeting for tomorrow. Something smelled bad to Franz. Something was terribly wrong.

"I'm glad you could join us for dinner tonight, Art. I hope you enjoyed it?" Franz said, patting his friend's shoulder as they walked out to their cars.

"Thank you, it was a pleasure to be with you and your family. It's so nice to be included. Oh boy, I'm so full I think I'm going to need a wheelbarrow to get me home."

"Art, do you think you could meet me for coffee at Starbucks Monday morning? I'm afraid we need to talk," Franz insisted. "It's very important! Something is brewing."

Chapter 19
Diamonds Are a Briber's Best Friend

Ingrid finally retired to the enormous gold-colored master suite after putting her children to bed. Harry made the rounds of the house, turning off lights, securing the doors and windows and setting the alarm.

"You're a son of a bitch," she screamed as Harry entered their bedroom.

"Stop yelling. You'll wake everyone up."

She picked up her shoe and pitched it at him. Harry ducked, and it narrowly missed him.

"When were you going to tell me: after the meeting? You were just going to disappear tomorrow?"

"It slipped my mind."

In her rant Ingrid said, "Oh come now, nothing slips your evil mind! Why on a Sunday? It's our family day, especially with your parents here."

"They love you 'libeling.' They would rather be with you than with me," Harry said.

"They've come to visit their son and as of now they are not getting their money's worth."

"I think they're getting more than that with you and the kids."

"Your kids aren't getting their fair share of the bargain either with you such an absentee father," Ingrid was seething.

"I am a good father."

"Yeah, when you remember to give them some of your precious time. You're always so busy, either at a meeting, locked away in the den on the computer, or running around with those deadbeats you hang out with. When do you spend time with the children?"

"That's not true. I have to work for a living to keep you in the lifestyle that you demand."

"Oh, so now blame me. Why can't you beg off the meeting tomorrow like that strange creature, Ralph, we met at dinner tonight? You know the one who loves the Munich beer halls and the Third Reich tourist attractions."

"I must go to the meeting. It's important."

"This is not working. You are distant, secretive, always running off to one of your hobbies. What happened to the warm, caring soul that seduced me to leave from Bavaria and come to America? I'm stuck here in the middle of the jungle with three kids to take care of. I'm a vassal; a slave," Ingrid slid into her nightgown and turned away from him. Harry undressed and eased over to her side.

"Come, come my love, it's not so bad. 'Ich Liebe Dich.'"

"You don't love me. You love the fact that I am your indebted attendant."

"Ach, Ingrid. 'Kus Mich'."

"Kiss you now? Are you out of your fucking mind?"

Harry put on his best act and went in for the full seduction.

"Oh, my love, you know how I feel about you," he tried to be delicate and passionate.

No answer. He attempted to hug her, but she quickly pushed him away. His hand slipped under the bed cover and his long fingers reached into her nightgown for her breast. With great tenderness, he caressed her nipple which always kindled a flame. Tonight, there was no response. He felt further down her body, slowly messaging her erogenous zones but tonight 'Checkpoint Charlie' was in the way and the gate was down. She was not aroused but he could remedy that if he proceeded further.

He pursued, but she was stone cold.

"I have a surprise for you, my love."

"I'm not interested."

"It's very special."

"Keep it."

"I can't tell you what it is, but I want you to go to Miami this week and buy an expensive designer gown."

"What are you talking about?"

"Just as I said," in a seductive tone, "while you are there, stop into Harry Winston. There is a little something waiting for you."

Ingrid had started to soften and slowly turned towards Harry.

"Why, Harry? What's going on?"

"In time, my darling," as he touched her lips and began to kiss his way down her body.

Slowly the gate of the taboo zone lifted, and he passed through into the heavily guarded territory.

Of course, he knew that would happen. Diamonds are a girl's best friend.

Chapter 20
The Shooting Brunch

"I am just a lonesome cowboy, and I'm traveling all alone," Ernie, wearing jeans and a checkered shirt, sang in a deep voice, trying to imitate his idol, Elvis Presley.

"Ernie, I am so worried about you," Bessie said in a panic, trying to interrupt him.

"It's a piece of cake."

"It's dangerous. Watch out."

Ernie, trying to act like the Lone Ranger, pointed one of his unloaded guns at her.

"You don't even know what to do with that!"

"They are going to teach me at the meeting. It should be fun."

"I'm a 'rootin tootin' cowboy," Ernie continued singing, making up lyrics while trying to twirl the two weapons.

"Are you out of your mind?"

"Listen, you convinced me that I should play along."

"But that doesn't mean shooting anyone."

"Don't worry, my love. I'm not going to shoot anyone."

"There are degrees of playing along. Are you sure you know what you're doing?" She was clearly distressed.

"Only a fool is absolutely positive about anything – and of that I'm sure," Ernie boasted.

Bessie looked him straight in the eye, while Ernie packed his pistols in a Publix supermarket bag. "Listen, 'pardner,' make sure that you don't mention the FBI. Promise me that you will be very careful, and please watch your mouth. It's your biggest liability."

"Yes, yes," Ernie said, shoeing away the badgering.

"What are you bringing for the potluck?"

"Applesauce."

"Applesauce? Why on earth would anyone bring applesauce to a potluck supper?"

"It's an American dish and I got five jars of Motts for the price of two."

Ernie pecked his love on the cheek, grabbed the jars of mushed apples, picked up his Publix bag and moseyed out of the condo singing "I'm a rhinestone cowboy."

Still in a jovial mood, Ernie drove the thirty miles to Christmas. Most of the gang had arrived already. The wives were invited today and were busy laying out the food. Ernie didn't know he could have brought Bessie. She would have been a comfort to him. Ernie handed over his gastronomic contribution to one of the women and joined the boys, who all clustered around him in a big circle. Once again, he became the life of the party.

"What did the sign on the door of the whorehouse say?" He asked.

"Why don't you tell us, Ernie?" Floyd said.

"Beat it, we're closed."

There were groans all around.

"Hey Ernie, you a liberal?" Floyd asked.

"A liberal, my ass," he was almost offended.

"What is a liberal?" Jim asked.

"A liberal is like a conservative who hasn't been mugged yet."

"You're always joking around, Ernie. Do you have a serious side?"

"I never take life seriously because you're never going to get out of it alive."

The conversation finally shifted from Ernie to talk about motor bikes.

Pete and Harry were enjoying a beer under a large elm tree.

"We need to be extremely cautious now," Pete said.

"We'll divide the boys up into three groups for specific tasks. It's crucial that each group is unaware of what the other groups are doing. There will be no reporting of their tasks at the meetings. We will use just one secure telephone line: no e-mails or texts. Everything must be communicated verbally. Pete, you and I will coordinate all the activities and convey the assignments to each guy individually."

"What about Ernie? I'm still a little leery of him."

"We'll place him in the tactics group and keep close tabs on him. We must teach him how to shoot. Tom will start working on that herculean task today."

"Hopefully Ernie will shoot the President and no one else."

Harry escorted Ernie to a shed behind the cabin to find the right ammunition for his obsolete weapons. He introduced him to Tom and wished them luck. Not envying Tom's job, he wanted to get out of there as quickly as possible. Ernie was very willing but seemingly oblivious to everything happening around him. The men were shooting at bottles propped on tree stumps. Ernie picked up one of his cocked, loaded weapon and pointed it directly at Tom's head.

"Whoa there, buddy. You're not Billy the Kid. Put the gun down; we need to take this slowly."

Tom patiently tried to instruct him on the operation and safety features of the weapon, but Ernie wasn't being fully attentive. He was anxious to start shooting. For the next hour, Ernie missed every target, some of the bullets barely missing his newfound friends.

"How did I do?"

"You need lots more practice," Tom said, totally exasperated.

Ernie was still raring to shoot more rounds, but Harry stopped him as he called everyone to eat. They moved to the picnic area, grabbed beers and lined up for food. The table was filled with homemade goodies from baked ham, fried chicken, meatloaf, baked beans, corn on the cob, salads, rolls and applesauce. Everyone ate heartily. After the big feed, Harry called the men together for the meeting. The women cleaned up and then settled in a group nearby.

"My good friends, it's great to see all of you here today. It's really inspiring when we come together for the greater good. Onward and upward. Onward and upward," he chanted excitedly, and they all cheered with him.

"A big thanks to the ladies for the wonderful spread," Harry said and waved to the group of loyal wives. "One thing we always do is eat well. But now we need to accelerate our work to achieve our mission. We cannot let all these liberal Jews take over the country and allow homosexuals to marry legally. I am pleased to report that our plan is fully in place. Everyone sitting together here today will have a chance to participate in a historic scheme to turn this country around. We'll be working in teams. I am going to make the assignments for each group today. Our tasks will begin immediately. Sooner than later we will succeed. Fellows, raise your beers to the common cause, onward and upward."

"Here, here."

"Here, here."

"Onward and upward," they cheered loudly.

Jim, Floyd, and Tom were assigned to The Commander Unit; Derek, Al, and David to work on The Biblical Affairs Squad, and Ralph, Lloyd and Ernie on The Tactical Division. Each posse went into a separate area to talk. Harry and Pete met with each group to start the plot rolling. Once again, they warned each member emphatically about secrecy and discretion. Everyone was now wholeheartedly enmeshed in the mission and would be prosecuted vigorously if discovered or caught.

After spending more disastrous time in the shooting area, Ernie left the function completely bewildered. He had been told that he was selected for the great honor of being the one who would assassinate the president, but he couldn't shoot the commander in chief. He couldn't shoot a duck crossing the road slowly, let alone the most important person in the world. He was totally confused, and didn't understand, but was too scared to ask for clarification. His mood turned somber and he began having a nagging ache in his stomach. He wondered if he should tell all of this to the FBI Monday? Harry warned him that he could be seriously implicated and go to jail for life if he told anyone. What a dilemma. He felt sick on the drive home, and then suddenly a bolt of lightning hit him.

""They all ate the applesauce."

Chapter 21
Venti Puzzle

At 10:00 a.m. Monday morning Ingrid dropped Franz off at Starbucks in Orlando. He looked around the crowded coffee emporium for the most secluded table. There were only a few empty ones and they would need to talk discreetly about this sensitive matter. Ordering a regular coffee with milk and sugar, he sat and waited for his buddy Art.

Art bounded in, his white mane looked unusually disheveled. Wearing creased shorts and tee shirt, he ordered a double venti latte with whipped cream and chocolate sprinkles, grumbling that "the drink cost as much as a lunch." Looking around he saw Franz and waved.

Art needs a wife, Franz thought, seeing his rumpled friend. He, of course, was impeccably dressed as usual.

"How's my good buddy today?" Art said, licking the whipped cream from the rim of his cup.

"Gut, but very puzzled. Thank you for coming, Art. I need to talk to someone."

"Happy to come. What's up?"

Franz started whispering, "I have always had suspicions about my son, Heinrich, and now I am more disturbed than ever. There is something happening, and I can't figure it out."

Art listened as he explained all the strange telephone calls and secretive Sunday meetings. He mentioned his concerns about his son's shady comrade, Pete, whom they had met at Publix and who called on Saturday. Pete had mentioned an Otto in Germany, and Franz also had a friend Otto there. Could it possibly be the same one? And the message stating, "the device from Otto is good." "What device? It's all very confusing. I also overheard a big quarrel that Harry had with Ingrid Saturday night about his constant meetings and secrecy."

"Franz, you may be overreacting."

"Why would I find homosexual pictures on his computer?" Franz asked.

"Maybe your grandson was using the computer."

"Thomas is 11 years old. He's too immature. What about the two odd ducks we met at the restaurant? The one who took his wife to see the

Munich beer halls and the places where the Third Reich ruled? Those were hardly tourist attractions."

"Yes, I must confess that was a bit bizarre."

"The worst part was the American Aryan website that popped up on his computer. It was filled with hateful messages and the most demented Nazi propaganda. Why would that be on Heinrich's computer? I don't understand why that man at the restaurant would say 'Happy Shooting'? Why would my Harry be involved in something like this, Art? I'm very worried. I tell you something is very wrong, and I do not know what to do. Please help me figure it out." Franz had said all of this without taking a breath.

"It doesn't sound good, Franz. I think you should keep a close eye on him, and I'll help you from there. But be very cautious and discrete. If there is something misguided here, I don't want you to get into trouble, my friend. We must also try to protect Harry as much as possible. We can always speak confidentially with Dick. He's a retired CIA person. Perhaps he can help us unravel the puzzle."

Franz was frantic, "This sounds like a really nasty business, Art. I am just beside myself."

"We'll work it out together. Don't make yourself sick over this. You have caring friends here, Franz. All the boys in the club really like you and I'm sure would be willing to help."

"Ya, thank God for caring friends."

Chapter 22
Will the Real Elliot Ness Please Stand Up?

Ernie was chomping at the bit and wide awake 5:00 a.m. Monday morning. He was dressed in polyester slacks, a golf shirt and a panama hat.

"Bessie, why aren't you here?" he barked into the phone.

"My God, it's the middle of the night" she said, sounding very sleepy. "The meeting isn't until 11:00 a.m."

"I want to get there early so we can get a parking space. It gets pretty congested downtown."

"But we don't need six hours. It's a ten-minute drive in traffic. Go back to sleep and I'll see you later."

Ernie was terribly restless. On the one hand he was nervous about confessing his transgressions. On the other he was excited about dealing with real FBI agents. One of his idols was Elliot Ness, a notorious FBI agent. He still hadn't made up his mind how much information he would divulge. His life could be in danger if he told too much which he had been warned repeatedly about. After all, he wasn't completely sure why they wanted to talk to him. Did they know that he was involved with the subversive group? "Big Brother had been watching them," he surmised.

He couldn't contain himself. As the time passed ever-so-slowly, his hands began to shake, and he hoped a drink of milk might help calm him. He took out the milk with an assortment of cold cuts and accoutrements to make a sandwich. Blindly he slapped salami, Swiss cheese, bologna, roast beef, lettuce, tomato, pickles, olives, relish, mayonnaise, mustard and ketchup between two slices of stale white bread. As he took the first bite of his Dagwood concoction, the phone rang.

Who's calling at 8:00 a.m.? he thought, as he grabbed the phone and heard a very pleasant female recording reminding him that he had a meeting at FBI headquarters at 11:00.

Later, as they approached the building, they looked like a reincarnation of Bonnie and Clyde. Ernie's good leg wobbled terribly as they walked along the steamy pavement with poor old Bessie trying to keep up. Ernie was furious at the pick-up truck parked in his handicapped space with no sticker. He wanted to call the police, "To give the bum a ticket" or better yet sit in his car, "blocking the bastard in." Bessie brought him back to earth, reminding him he had more important things to worry about. The office was located on the 20th floor and even though Ernie had an aversion to heights and a fear of elevators, he bucked up and paraded into the cage that would take them there.

"Ernie, promise me that you will tell them the whole story and be completely truthful," Bessie pleaded as the elevator climbed toward their destination.

"But they will kill me. I'll be dead meat."

"Trust me, you will be even deader if you don't tell them."

Ernie's excitement slowly began to fade, "Going in for my leg amputation surgery was less scary than this."

"You'll do fine. You'll do fine." She said but was feeling less and less sure.

The glass door had bold black lettering: Federal Bureau of Investigation. Ernie and his love proceeded cautiously to the front desk.

"May I help you?" Asked the attractive young greeter.

"I'm here to confess."

"I beg your pardon?" She looked at these two elderly, mismatched individuals and just stared.

"Ernie, stop that right now!"

"Better to get it over with," he said, throwing his hands up.

"Save your confession." And to the receptionist, Bessie said, "We have an appointment with Sally Adams and Tom Prentice."

"Please take a seat and I'll get them for you. Can I get you something to drink: water or coffee?"

"How about a nice large glass of arsenic with soda?"

"Ernie! No, thank you, dear." Bessie poked him. He was so nervous that he couldn't stop saying whatever came into his head.

Bessie and Ernie huddled together on the couch. The walls were gray and dominated by a huge portrait of Frederick R. Jackson, the new black director of the agency.

"If we had a white president, we wouldn't be faced with a black director. The coloreds are into everything in this administration," Ernie rambled on. Bessie, recognizing his acute nervousness, let him babble on.

"I wonder why they don't have a portrait of J. Edgar Hoover?" Ernie said.

"J. Edgar Hoover has been dead for years," Bessie replied.

"But he owned the place, and there should be a picture of Elliot Ness too."

"Hoover was just a long-time director."

"He was a fairy, you know," Ernie said, smirking.

On that note, Tom Prentice dressed in a dark suit and a striped tie, entered the lobby, welcomed them, and escorted the couple to a conference room. Agent Sally Adams in a grey suit with silver blouse, was already waiting there. They exchanged pleasantries and shook hands.

Before anyone could say anything, Ernie's mouth was off and running, "I'm a big fan of the FBI. Elliot Ness was my favorite hero. They don't make television programs like 'The Untouchables' anymore."

"Mr. Stubbs," Sally said, trying to get down to business.

"Please call us Ernie and Bessie, you know like Bonnie and Clyde."

"Okay, Ernie, but Eliot Ness was never an FBI agent. He worked for J. Edgar Hoover for just a couple of weeks," Agent Prentice explained.

"Go on," Ernie said, totally fascinated.

"He was a Treasury agent involved primarily in Prohibition work. As a matter of fact. he tried to become an FBI agent, but we wouldn't accept him. Ness wanted too much money for his work and the director thought that his connections to the press were too strong."

"Well, hot diggity, I didn't know that. So, you guys are real G-men and G-ladies?"

"I hate to burst your bubble but there was no such thing as G-men. That's another misconception. They say that Machine Gun Kelly yelled 'Gee men, I am coming out,' when he was surrounded, but he never did. The press took poetic license and made the term famous."

"I'll be damned. Wow, this is so exciting, Bessie."

The social patter time had dragged on too long and Sally Adams cut right to the chase.

"Ernie, what were you doing at the Aryan Connection meeting in Christmas two weeks ago Sunday?"

"Having pork roast, pork and beans, chicken legs, corn, watermelon, alligator tail, which was a little tough, apple pie a la mode, and applesauce."

"This is not a joke, Mr. Stubbs. We have a potential problem here and you're involved," Sally came on strong and stared right into Ernie's face.

"Ernie, please tell them," Bessie begged.

"How do you know I was there?" Ernie asked.

"We have pictures of you at the function."

Ernie panicked and began wailing, "I didn't do anything. Arrest me now. I'm guilty of being there," Ernie was on the verge of crying.

"Calm down, sir. No one is arresting you, but please tell us the whole story," Tom Prentice was much gentler than Sally Adams in trying to deal with Ernie.

Ernie confessed to everything: the barbecue, the shooting brunch, Harry Smith and the group of men. He told the agents that the organization was planning some very serious action, but he didn't know exactly what. He told them they kept emphasizing that it was "to save America."

"We were divided into three groups for different parts of the plan," he said, and explained the categories. "But they didn't give us any of the details. The only part I know is that I was being given the great honor of shooting the president. Although they said I wasn't really going to shoot him. I didn't understand that part. I was scared stiff and when I tried to ask questions, they said that I would find out soon enough. I'm so confused."

Bessie held onto Ernie's hand, patting it lovingly.

"You're doing great. Let me talk with Sally outside for a minute, and we will get back to you," Tom said. "Sure, I can't get you something to drink?"

"No, thank you," said Bessie.

"I'm going to die young, Bess."

"You are 86 years old and you are not going to die young. You did the correct thing."

"Are you sure? I'm so frightened. I need a corned beef sandwich with sauerkraut, cheese, pickles, lettuce, tomatoes, and mayo on rye right now."

After what felt like an eternity, both agents returned looking rather serious.

Sally Adams didn't beat around the bush, "Ernie, we believe that you are an innocent bystander and we want you to help your country. We need you to go undercover for us,and continue to be part of the group."

"But it's dangerous," Ernie said, whimpering. "If they find out, they'll kill me."

"Not if you follow our instructions and do what we tell you. We will protect you as long as you help us."

"I don't know. Thank you for the offer, but I'm too old and scared for this spy stuff."

"But you have a great opportunity to save the country. Wouldn't you like that on your tombstone? 'Ernest Stubbs, American Hero'?" Tom asked.

"What do you think, Bessie?"

"I think for your safety; you should do exactly what they want."

"An American Hero?" Ernie turned to Tom. "Well if you put it that way … I guess if you guys promise to protect me … I'll do it," Ernie said, starting to feel better.

"We are going to deputize you as an FBI agent. Tom, swear him in."

Tom looked at Sally as if she were crazy but followed her directions with a mock ceremony.

"Ernest Stubbs, raise your right hand." Ernie followed the directions as Tom made up some gibberish.

"I now pronounce you a volunteer deputy FBI agent."

"Oh boy, Bessie. Wait till I tell my Thursday morning cooking mates. Do I get a badge, Agent Sally?"

"Ernie, this is a secret operation. You can't carry any FBI identification. No one must know or even suspect anything about your affiliation with the bureau, or it will kill the entire plan, and probably you too," Sally lectured him. He had now been threatened by both the Aryan Connection and the FBI. How comforting, he thought. They continued talking for another hour and gave Ernie all his instructions.

He was to become an active member of the Aryan Connection and infiltrate the group. They told him how to keep in touch with the FBI who would be available day or night.

"Can you imagine me, dear, a deputy just like Barney Fife."

Sally looked him straight in the eye and said, "And Deputy Stubbs, whatever you do, PLEASE don't shoot the president."

Chapter 23
Gay Puree

First there was a cautionary tickle and then a blusterous explosion. Again, a long tickle followed by piercing propulsion of air. Dick Reynolds couldn't stop sneezing as he crossed the threshold of the Senior Center on Thursday. Immediately, he knew that Charles was cooking today.

As he passed the computer room, sure enough he was right. Charles had decorated the room with red-checkered tablecloths and in the center of each one was vases of roses from his garden. Dick, horribly allergic to roses, couldn't seem to control these blasts from his nose.

Robert had brewed the coffee. He joined the group whenever his partner Charles was cooking. Each entered in their own style: Abe bounded, Art sauntered, Bill trotted, Steve waddled, Franz marched, Ed toddled, Joe meandered, Fred moved slowly but surely, and Dick sneezed. They had a full house this morning. Ernie strutted in, as proud as a peacock. He was now surreptitiously important.

"Oh, the pansy is cooking today," Ernie blurted out nonchalantly.

"Ernie, come here," Dick beckoned, and they moved away from the group.

"You got to lighten up, especially about Charles. You know he is gay. He has been for all the years you've known him, but you never stop ridiculing him. Please Ernie, give him a break. Do it for me."

"You know I love him, Dick, not in that way, of course, I wouldn't dream of hurting him."

"But you are, Ernie. Please."

"Sometimes I just can't help it. It just comes out," Ernie was emotional. "I'll try my best; I'll even offer to help today."

"Atta boy, Ernie," Dick was skeptical, but a bit relieved.

Charles Hamilton was hardly a pansy; no one would dare accuse him of being a timid Caspar Milquetoast. Last year Charles was arrested at the age of 79. He had stood up to a biker who was verbally assaulting Robert. After looking him in the eye, he karate-chopped the macho man into a quivering pulp. The judge secretly applauded him, issuing a verbal spanking, fining him a whopping $25 and told him to be a good boy.

Charles had a difficult early life but managed through it all. He was neither fearful nor a wimp. He grew up an only child with a single mother and no male influence, believing that his homosexuality was inherited from someone in the family. Nevertheless, he preferred boys to girls from pre-puberty and displayed strong feminine gestures.

Discrimination plagued him for his entire life, but he made peace early on and accepted his sexual persuasion. Serving Uncle Sam was his biggest challenge. Not shirking his responsibility, he fought in World War ll. Keeping his feelings closeted was difficult and painful, but he was not a quitter or a deserter. He was political, church-going and had a wide circle of friends. People really adored Charles, especially the boys in the Old Men's Cooking Club.

Ernie returned to the center of the kitchen and charged over to Charles to help.

"What can I do?"

Charles stared at him suspiciously.

"No, really, I feel good today and want to help."

"Okay Ernie, you can prick the eggplant for the baba ganoush."

"I didn't know that eggplants had pricks?"

"Ernie!" Dick tossed him an icy stare.

"Pricking means punching holes in it with a fork," Charles instructed.

"I can do that. I'm going to prick away!" It was a harmless comment but coming from Ernie, it didn't seem right.

Baba ganouj with olives and lightly toasted pita bread was the snack replacing the tired weekly French bread. Charles and Ernie worked as a team. They heated the erotically stabbed eggplant in the oven, then after chopping it, mixed it with tahini, a sesame paste, olive oil, garlic, salt, parsley, and lemon juice to make the appetizing hors d'oeuvre.

The menus the boys concocted were as diverse as their personalities. Robert distributed a menu card to each.

MENU

BABA GANOUJ WITH OLIVES AND PITA
ARUGULA SALAD WITH TOMATOES AND FETA CHEESE
GUAVA-STUFFED CHICKEN WITH CARAMELIZED
MANGOES
ASPARAGUS TAGLIATELLE
SOUR CREAM CHEESECAKE

The group drooled over the selections about to be created in their humble culinary salon.

"Hey, I can't eat asparagus. It makes my pee smell bad," Ernie explained. Dick gave him another frosty look.

Ernie defended, "What? That's a scientific comment."

"Me too. Makes my pee smell bad," Abe added.

"Me three, four and five," chimed in the other members. Even Dick agreed and started to laugh.

"Well then, try eating organic asparagus. They leave your bathroom smelling springtime fresh," Charles said.

Today Charles, Robert, and Ernie did the lion's share of the cooking. The boys sat back watching Ernie in disbelief. Steve snapped pictures on his phone of Ernie at the stove boiling tagliatelles, click; at the cutting board chopping tomatoes, click; at the counter peeling mangoes, click; at the oven putting in the chicken, click; and at the microwave warming the pita. The most damaging shot of Ernie was at the sink washing dishes. They wanted to use the photos as leverage to get him more productive on a regular basis.

Art went over to the counter to pour some coffee and offered Franz a cup.

"Would you like your coffee black?"

"What other color choices do I have?" Frantz, who had gotten very comfortable with the group, was starting to let his hair down a bit.

The cooking took longer than usual, and the group mopped up the baba ganouj with pita as they sat discussing politics, sex, their cars, and medical issues while the three chefs cooked. The tables in the computer room were set with real silverware today. Charles would not allow anyone to enjoy his gastronomical gems with the usual plastic forks and knives. The good china – the plastic dishes – was also brought out. This was not to be a paper plate banquet. Real paper napkins were purchased in lieu of paper towels usually extracted from the dispenser in the men's room, and glasses substituted for paper cups. It was a classy affair.

"Fellows, fellows," called Charles as he tapped a spoon against a glass to grab everyone's attention. A wooden spoon hitting against a pot was the usual call to chow.

"I have an announcement to make: on Saturday Robert and I will be celebrating our 50 years together and as a gift to each other, we are going to New York City to get married!"

"Congratulations" resounded from every corner of the room. Ernie made no comment and was not enthusiastic. He didn't quite understand the entire concept of homosexuality, but same-sex marriage was way out of bounds.

"I didn't think that they had fags 50 years ago," Ernie commented, ignorantly.

"Homosexuality can be traced back to biblical times, Ernie. In ancient Greece they used the practice as a means of population control. All the Roman emperors, except Claudius, took male lovers."

"I didn't know that, are you kidding?"

Charles continued, "The term homosexual was established in the 1800's to describe both sexual and emotional interests in one's own sex."

"They say that most individuals have some sexual interests in both sexes," Steve blurted out. For the first time in the seven-year history of the club, the men were totally quiet.

"Not me," bellowed Ernie." I know what hole to put my pecker in."

"Sodomy, labeled as lewd and unnatural, was a capital offense in much of Europe until the 1850's, and they executed many poor souls," Charles continued.

"Ya, the Third Reich treated homosexuals the same way they treated the Jews," Franz said now more able to speak about the war. "The Nazis believed that male homosexuals were weak and too effeminate to effectively fight for the German nation. They also could not procreate purebred German children. Most of the country's gay, men were interned in the camps and huge numbers were killed."

"I heard that despite this official hatred by the government, there were many homosexuals in the highest ranks of the German government," Art added.

"Yes, there were many. Heinrich Himmler was the most fanatic homophobic member of the Nazi leadership and he worked prodigiously to rid the government of them," Franz continued.

"I read somewhere that Hitler was a closet gay and he flaunted that sexuality in his early days in Vienna," Fred said.

"That's what some say," Franz answered. "I had a close school friend in Germany, Walter Reicher, who had male sexual leanings. A lovely lad, our friendship was strong but not physical. In later years, he was made to wear a pink triangle in the street and then was arrested by the SS. I had heard that he was interned also. I searched extensively after the war, but never could find him." A tear rolled down Franz's cheek.

"I still can't fathom two guys doing those things to each other." Ernie was again entering dangerous territory, but Dick was keeping a close eye on him.

"It's not only about sex, Ernie. It can be highly emotional. It also has to do with love: two people being in love and expressing themselves physically. Robert and I have been in love for 50 years," Charles said.

"I guess that could be true." Ernie was beginning to soften.

Robert, having left the room during the discussion, returned with an ice cooler.

"In honor of our milestone anniversary, we are going to have wine with lunch, a Pinot Gris goes beautifully with this chicken," Charles proclaimed, kissing his fingers and dramatically holding them in the air.

Robert opened the cooler and produced three bottles of Canada Dry Ginger Ale filled with the fruity spirits. Everyone cheered.

"It feels like Prohibition around here," Ernie said." I hope we don't get raided by Elliot Ness."

The men filled their glasses with the non-allowed hooch.

"Which one of you is the bride?"

"Ernie," Dick started to protest.

"What! I just want to know who to make the bridal shower for."

Savoring the delectable salad mixed with arugula, sweet grape tomatoes, olive oil, and flaky feta cheese, Art suddenly remembered the homosexual comment Franz had made about his son, Harry. Franz, tasting the mouthwatering chicken breasts stuffed with cream cheese and topped with the mango slices, also thought about Harry's use of the gay website, and the scary political leanings he found on his son's computer. Ernie was still focusing on the mechanics of two men having sex as he feasted on a slice of the sinfully rich sour cream cheesecake.

"Hey guys, I have to admit something," Ernie said.

"You are gay, Ernie," Steve picked up right away.

"No such luck. I'm a 'humor sexual.'"

"Enlighten us, Ernie, what's a 'humor sexual'?" Dick asked.

"One who likes dirty jokes."

There were groans all around.

"Guys, guys, can I have your attention. We want to wish Charles and Robert our best good wishes on their coming nuptials," Abe toasted.

"Here, here," they chimed as they raised their clandestine ginger ale glasses.

"We also have something else to celebrate. After seven years, Chef Ernest Stubbs made his debut as a worker in our kitchen today. Three cheers, boys."

"Hip, hip hooray," yelled the ensemble boisterously enough to be heard throughout the area. The ginger ale substitute had had its effect.

Ernie had had a good week. First, he was deputized by the FBI, and today he was initiated as a sous chef in the kitchen. Isn't life wonderful? he thought. Dick took the first step and hugged Charles and Robert. The rest of the boys followed suit. Ernie hesitated but said, "What the hell," and participated in the male-bonding ceremony.

"What the heck is the world coming to," Ernie muttered to himself. "I wouldn't be surprised if the next president of the United States is a queer.

Part Two
"SOUPS ON"

Chapter 24
The Belle Pepper of the Ball

Ingrid was the belle of the ball. She dazzled the crowd in her poppy-red Caroline Herrera strapless gown, Jimmy Choo suede sandals bejeweled with the finest Austrian crystals, and a Judith Lieber evening purse. Glittering diamond earrings from Harry Winston dangled from her ears. Harry lamented that his subversive activities were costing a small fortune; this bribe alone amounted to more than $15,000.

The lavish dinner party was held at Number One Observatory Circle awash with lights and colors. Thousands of tiny lights illuminated the trees lining the driveway of the vice president's mansion in Washington. Enormous vehicles queued for blocks, waiting to discharge their illustrious passengers onto the red carpet.

Ingrid and Harry Smith were personal guests of the vice president and his wife. On that star-filled night, more than 500 guests enjoyed drinks and hors d'oeuvres inside the executive home, then dined and danced in a majestically lit tent on the back lawn. Ingrid in her gown and Harry sporting an expensive Adolpho dinner suit were the talk of the party. The stunning couple promenaded through the public rooms that featured masterpieces of impressionist art. Harry hoped for an opportunity to spend some time with Vice President Sid Townsend. They had become acquaintances at a political rally and truly hit it off. Of similar age, ambition, and ruthless to a point, they shared charisma and warmth. The vice president was the jewel in the crown on the winning ticket for the reelection of Herman Sharif. He swung both ways on the political scale. Publicly, he was an independent with conservative inclinations; privately, he was an ultra-rightwing affiliate with strong racist leanings. It was amazing that his true feelings about issues could be so well hidden. He had a brilliant political mind, was profoundly handsome and, at 42, was one of the youngest politicians to potentially be in line for the presidency. His wife, Ellen, also in a designer outfit, was a former Ford model. She had strawberry blond hair, was strikingly beautiful, tall and affable. They were an elegant couple that made a superb professional team.

Harry and Ingrid sipped champagne, savored caviar-filled new potatoes and were ogling at a Monet painting when Sid and his wife joined them in the living room. They chatted about the party and their families but skirted politics. Ellen took Ingrid and began to introduce her around, the two fashion queens disappearing into the crowd. The vice-president and Harry finally had a few minutes alone.

"How are things, Harry?"

"Moving along splendidly, Thanks for asking."

"Great! After dinner, while people are dancing, I'll come by your table, and we'll go upstairs to the private quarters for a chat. Enjoy yourself and see you later, buddy."

"Hello, Pete," Harry whispered into his cell phone from an alcove. "All is well. I'm meeting Sid for a few minutes later."

"That's great. I called all the men in the tactics group and we're meeting on Thursday night. I made sure that Ernie was coming as well."

"Excellent. I will be there. Is Ralph ready to proceed on Tuesday?"

"All systems are go," certified Pete. "How are the broads there?"

"Like scrumptious ripe beef tomatoes."

"Happy eating."

"Thank you, I'll report to you tomorrow. Ciao."

***

A modern-day footman circulated through the mansion, inviting the guests to adjourn outside to the marquee for dinner. The Society Orchestra played sprightly dance music as Marines in bright blue dress uniforms and white gloves escorted guests to their tables. Harry and Ingrid were matched with four other couples from the world of politics.

Pheasant en croutte, a rich paté in a pastry crust decorated with fresh herbs, adorned each place setting. A sparkling white wine complemented the appetizer.

***

As the guests wined and dined on nectar and ambrosia, telephones fifteen hundred miles away in Florida jangled. Steve, the would-be artist, sat in his studio sporting a large erection. He had his sketchpad out and, with his charcoal, copied the intimate details of a naked woman with legs spread apart on his computer screen. This was his convoluted concept of a nude live model.

"Hello."

114

"Steve, Fred here. What's up?"

"Something big," he grinned to himself at his private joke.

"I just wanted to remind you that you're cooking this Thursday."

"I'll be there with bell peppers on," he laughed.

"What are you making?"

"Something colorful. See you there."

***

Franz and Anneliese were babysitting for the grandchildren while Harry and Ingrid were at the party in Washington. They were snuggling together in the den and watching an old Cary Grant movie on the Movie Classics channel. While Anneliese got up to get a snack from the kitchen, Franz dialed his phone.

"Art, this is Franz. How are you?"

"Good for a very old man."

"I just wanted to let you know that Harry and Ingrid went to a party at the vice president's home in Washington, but before they left, they insisted that we continue our stay here. We don't have much to do back home, and a neighbor can water my precious garden, so we said fine."

"That's terrific news, Franz. Perhaps you'll be able to cook again for the group. That would be wonderful. Why don't we cook together again?" Art proposed.

"I'd love that. Art, I continue to be worried. Would you consider calling Dick to talk with him confidentially about Harry?"

"Yes, I'll do that. See you on Thursday, buddy. Bye, Bye."

***

Under the glowing tent, some of the guests danced as the white-gloved waiters cleared the first course. The couples returned to find plates filled with juicy rack of lamb, croquette potatoes, and Belgian endive a la meuniere, paired with a dry red wine. The table companions became chatty and animated as the wine flowed.

***

As the politicos partied in the nation's capital, it was a clear, moonlit sweltering night in Florida. Dick sat on his dock trying to do some night fishing. With a rod in one hand, a beer in the other and his legs dangling off the lawn chair, the retired master spy was in heaven. Then his cell phone rang.

"Hello."

"Dick? What are you up to?"

"Hi, Art, just sitting here on the banks of my lake listening to the crickets chirping, the bullfrogs ribbiting, trying to catch tomorrow night's dinner."

"Any luck?"

"Not a bite. The fish must be on vacation."

"If I knew that you were there, I wouldn't bite either."

"Watch it or I'll catch some really big bullfrogs and cooked them for lunch when it's my turn to be chef."

"I couldn't vouch for Ernie, but I like frog legs," Art conceded. "Listen, Dick you're one of the good old boys from the CIA, aren't you?"

"Yep, I put in my time, a regular James Bond."

"James Bond was M16."

"M16 or CIA, it's the same sordid baloney."

"Franz is worried about his son. He suspects that Harry is involved in some shady stuff that might have national security implications."

"It sounds serious. Well, we CIA boys took care of the international stuff, but I certainly can listen and see if I can help."

"Would you meet Franz and me for breakfast at Starbucks to talk about it?"

"Sure thing, I'll be happy to help. Pick a date and time. The wife loves having me out of the house Thursday mornings for cooking club so she will be thrilled to get more time off. Let's set it up."

"Thanks, Dick, we love you."

***

The vice president gave the signal and lights in the tent dimmed as the band boomed an old-fashioned drum-roll. A parade of servers filed in carrying flaming baked Alaska's garnished with American flags. Everyone applauded and enjoyed the sweet baked ice cream dessert.

***

Ernie was sitting on his condo balcony staring at the stars. Taking out his cell phone, he dialed a number.

116

"Hello, chief, this is deputy Barney Fife calling."

"What's doing, Ernie?"

"Oh damn! You guessed it was me?"

"It was a tough assumption," Sally Adams smirked. "Why do I have the pleasure of your call during my dinner hour on my only night off?"

"I wanted to let you know that the Tactics Committee is meeting Thursday night and I'm going."

"Be very careful. Try to remember exactly what they discuss and what we talked about."

"Do you want me to wear a wire like they do on 'Law and Order'?"

"It's too early for a wire, Ernie. Just go to the meeting and fit in like one of the boys."

"Okee dokee, boss."

"Can you meet us at 10:00 a.m. on Friday at Denny's?" Sally asked.

"You betcha, I'll be there."

"Good, Ernie. Just remember keep quiet and cool."

"Quiet and cool Ernie, that's me."

***

Back in Washington as the music picked up for dancing, the host and his wife waltzed over to Harry's table and he got up to give Ellen his seat and followed the vice president back to the main house where they went to the second floor and Sid's sitting room. The vice president locked the door.

"We don't have much time, Harry. How are the plans coming?"

"Everything is in place. We're starting operations on all our schemes. All the tasks are planned, and Henry Johnson is working on the devices."

"What about Otto and the boys in Munich?"

"They have been working with us. Otto is due here to handle the financial side of the operations."

"Excellent. What is the money situation?"

"A substantial amount has already been wired to the Caymans and we only need to request more if we need it."

They discussed more details.

"If all goes according to plan, in a few months you will be the President of the United States."

"A scary thought," Sid pondered, "I wish we had more time to talk alone."

"Can we find a private spot and get together while I'm in D.C. during the next few days?" Harry begged.

"I'll see what I can arrange. It's going to be tough with so much going on. I miss you terribly, Harry. I need you."

Both ruggedly handsome men felt stirrings, moved closer and kissed passionately.

Chapter 25
Defacing the Mind

Rabbi Joel Tannenbaum bolted into the conference room on the second floor of the Orlando Police Department's central station. A group of local authorities were already at the table; Mayor David Han, City Manager Ed Davis; Betsy Clark, the Chief of Police; Stuart Fish, the County Sheriff; and Tom Prentice and Sally Adams from the FBI. Rabbi Seymour Auerbach attended too. Tannenbaum was the head of the Jewish community in the area and one of the few clergymen who had the political clout to summon these professionals together.

He unfolded the newspaper, throwing it down on the table. The headline screamed:

SECOND JEWISH SYNAGOGUE BRANDED WITH NAZI SWASTIKAS

"What are we doing about this, ladies and gentlemen?" He was seething.

"First of all, this is a misdemeanor episode. We are doing our best," said Orlando's fiery black police chief.

"What do you mean your best? You dismissed the last defacing incident as a malicious prank by a lone individual and closed the case. But this is obviously not an isolated incident. It seems to be a well-planned attack."

"We have no clues," the sheriff intervened. "Whoever committed these heinous acts of aggression left no traces."

"What about the Aryan Connection group that operates near Christmas?" Rabbi Auerbach asked.

"We've been keeping an eye on them but have seen no unusual activity," reported FBI Agent Adams.

"Unless we catch them red-handed, or they leave a clue, we have no grounds to interfere with them," Tom Prentice added.

"Listen, rabbis, we are as concerned about this as you are. We are posting round-the-clock surveillance at your synagogues," Chief Clark explained.

"So, they will hit the temple in Maitland or Apopka next. You folks have to do more, or we will take matters into our own hands," the rabbi said loudly.

"Whoa there, rabbi. We don't want a bunch of vigilantes. All we need is unarmed, untrained congregants traipsing through the woods looking for Nazis. That's not going to sit well with anyone and it's not going to accomplish anything," said David Han, Orlando's Asian mayor.

"We are not going to stand for this kind of branding, I warn you. If we don't attack physically, we will bring you all down politically," Rabbi Tannenbaum pointed a finger at the group. "We will be reckoned with."

"Calm down, rabbi. There is a plan in motion to infiltrate the hate group. Give us some time," Tom Prentice explained.

"Should we wait for the next branding, and then act? There are some holocaust survivors who live in Orlando. We will not let them, or any of our population, become victims to vicious attacks of terror once again. Not today, and not in Orlando!"

"You will wait patiently while we all do our jobs," said Sally Adams, forcefully.

"Joel, we need to listen," Rabbi Auerbach whispered to him.

Rabbi Tannenbaum stood and looked everyone directly in the eye. His anger made him ask sarcastically, "You have another problem, ladies and gentlemen. President Sharif is scheduled to make an appearance at the World Jewish Convocation here in Orlando. How are you going to provide the security and protection for the president if you can't prevent two small synagogues from these savage attacks?"

Chapter 26
Who Ate the Flowers?

Self–proclaimed artist Steve Quentin looked ridiculous cooking in his red beret, but if show-off Abe could wear his ostentatious chef's hat, he could wear his artist's chapeau. Steve was 76 and the largest member of the group. His great passion for food had stuck to his posterior. For someone weighing more than 350 pounds, he was active and light on his feet. He was very pleased today; lunch would be a plethora of colors and tastes. Steve was strongly pro-conservatism in his political opinions and felt equally as strongly against exercising. The boys, looking out for his health, were clearly troubled by his vast size. But he explained to them, "I am in shape. Round is a shape."

Dick entered the kitchen and began to help Steve unpack the luncheon vittles.

"How's your weight loss coming, Steve?" He asked out of concern.

"Very slowly. The older I get, the tougher it is to lose weight because your body and your fat have become really good friends," Steve explained.

The boys entered the kitchen one by one, heading to the cupboard to pick up their designated mugs and then to the Mr. Coffee machine. Fred, the 75-year-old group leader, meandered in somewhat disheveled.

"I just came from the gym, had a good workout, and feel great," he reported, slightly out of breath.

"You look like you've been through the mill," Joe chided.

"I've been on it."

"You need to take it slow, Fred. You're no spring chicken," Ed said.

"Whenever I feel like exercise, I lie down till the feeling passes," the lethargic Steve boasted.

"The Japanese say that Americans are lazy. Ha. At least we cook our fish," commented Abe.

Fred explained, "W.C Fields had a great line, 'The laziest man I ever met put popcorn in his pancakes, so they would turn over by themselves.'"

Steve presented an array of fruit as the pre-meal snack, including slices of orange, green and red melons, purple and green grapes, pineapple chunks and bright strawberries, all arranged like a still-life painting.

Ernie felt cheated, "That's all healthy stuff."

"The only trouble with buying healthy food is that the prices make you sick."

"Here, here!"

"Yeah, the only food that doesn't go up in price is food for thought," Dick commented philosophically.

"Hey Ed, you're a retired chemist, right?"

"Yup."

"So, what is healthier, butter or margarine?"

"I trust cows over scientists any day," Ed laughed.

"I need help with the salad, boys," Steve said.

Abe cut up the red, yellow, orange and green peppers. Joe diced the vine tomatoes. Ed washed the several tones of green lettuce and ripping them gently, and put them into the bowl. Art peeled and sliced the carrots. Teary-eyed Charles worked on the green and white scallions. Franz thinly sliced the rose-red radishes and Bill peeled and quartered the seedless cucumbers. Steve worked on the salad dressing, a dark balsamic vinegar concoction. He also sprinkled a few edible flowers on top. The salad looked like the brightest impressionist painting.

"Ernie, how come you don't cook?" Abe said.

"If you waste time cooking, you'll miss your next meal."

"How was your week? "Art asked Abe.

"Well I got over 'hump day!'"

"You mean you have a special day to screw" was the expected response from Ernie.

"It has nothing to do with sex, Ernie. It means climbing a proverbial hill to get through a tough week."

"Don't talk dirty to me."

"It means getting through the middle of the week," Dick added impatiently.

"Hey Ern, remember to take your Viagra fast or you'll get a stiff neck," biker Joe joked.

"I don't have that problem, fellows."

"Why, are you a super stud, Ernie?"

"No, that department has shut down for the duration."

Steve recruited volunteers to help with the side dishes.

"I am going to prepare ratatouille," Steve explained.

"I thought that was a rat?" Ernie seemed confused.

"It is in the movie, but this an eggplant dish."

Joe and Bill stood at the counter to help Steve.

The dish, filled with onions, eggplant, green and yellow zucchini, red and orange peppers, and tomatoes, was set on the stove to cook for 45 minutes.

"What is the most dangerous food you can put in your stomach?" Ernie asked the group.

"Ask what's his name on Bizarre Foods," Charles said.

From Dick, "Tell us, Ernie."

"Wedding cake."

"You should know."

Art asked Dick to come have a chat for a moment.

"Can Franz and I meet you for breakfast tomorrow morning, say 10:00 a.m.?"

"Would be glad to meet with you guys but tomorrow I'm going deep-sea fishing. How about Saturday? Do you think there's a real problem?"

"It's a long, complicated story, but there are definitely reasons to be concerned about Harry."

"Isn't he the one who is investing our money?"

"Yes."

"We better get back to the cooking, but day after tomorrow will be good," Dick concluded.

When they returned, everyone was savoring the fruit and Steve was painting the herbal green chimichurri marinade over the London broil. He settled the dressed meat in the oven and announced that they would be eating in 15 minutes.

"Fellows, did you see the picture in the newspaper of Franz's son Harry and his wife at the vice-president's place?" Art asked.

"He really travels in some very fancy circles, Franz," Steve piped in.

"You must be very proud of him," Dick added.

"I think I am, but sometimes I am not so sure."

The boys stood in clusters having the usual chats when an inordinately loud cell phone went off. Each checked his pocket to see if it was his. Harry had given Franz a phone so they could keep in touch when he was out. He was totally oblivious that it was his phone that had startled everyone.

"Someone, please help me, I don't know how to use this thing," Franz said, fumbling with the phone. His hand started to shake in a nervous panic. Dick came to the rescue.

"Hallo."

"Hi, Pop."

"Oh, Harry, what's the matter? Is everything all right?"

"Fine, fine, don't worry, Pop. I forgot that tonight is Ingrid's bowling night with the girls and I have to go to an important meeting. I didn't know if you and Mom were going to be home."

"Where are we going to go at night in your secluded forest?"

"Can you and Mom watch the kids?"

"Of course. That's no problem."

"Thanks so much, Pop. I'll see you when I get home later. I love you."

Franz hung up, slumped down in his chair and his mood settled into a gloom. Another suspicious meeting, he thought. He simply didn't know what was going on with that boy. Dick and Art, sensing something was wrong, came over.

"Are you all right, Franz?" Dick asked.

"I'm really worried."

"Is it about Harry?" Art whispered.

"Ya."

"We'll talk at breakfast Saturday. We'll work it out, Franz. Fret not, old man," Dick reassured him quietly.

"Ya, ya."

"Soups on," bellowed Steve. The boys quickly lined up around the stove and Steve plated his gourmet masterpiece. The food formed a work of art with its profusion of color. A pastel bouquet of salad topped with edible flowers, a main course featuring a perfectly pink London broil, well-roasted purple potatoes and a mixed bag of reds, yellows and greens in the ratatouille. The dessert presented a bright strawberry atop a creamy shortcake. A fine impressionistic meal was presented to the fray. The food was so flavorful and aromatic that the men lined up for seconds.

"Gentlemen, did you see the paper this morning? Another Orlando synagogue was defaced with swastikas," Abe reported, shaking his head in disgust. "It's got to be something going down. One incident is a fluke, but two different hits in such a short period of time? That's a calculated operation."

"It must be that neo-Nazi, what is it called, the Aryan Connection group? It's festering somewhere in the county," said the spy master.

"They have to be involved," Art added.

Franz suddenly put two and two together and yelled, "Oh my God," and fainted!

Chapter 27
The Secrets Unravel

"I'm fine, I'm fine," protested Franz as Art and Dick, each holding an arm, walked him into Harry's house.

"Oh my God, what happened?" screamed Anneliese, trailing after them. "Bring him into the den onto the couch," she instructed. "Ingrid, Ingrid, please come quickly."

"He passed out at lunch. We wanted to call 911, but he was adamant against it. He just wanted to come home," Art explained.

"Franz, are you, all right? I must summon a doctor, or we should take him to the hospital." She spun round and round nervously.

"Please, Mama, I'm good. I feel fine," he said as they placed him on the settee.

"What's all the commotion" Ingrid cried running into the room.

"Franz collapsed at the men's club."

"Are you okay, Pop?"

"Ya, Ya, it was just an unusual occurrence."

"Why don't you rest here for the afternoon?" Ingrid said, trying to make him comfortable.

"Good idea," Anneliese agreed.

"We don't have to meet on Saturday morning. We can get together when you feel better, Franz," Art said.

"No, I insist we get together. I'll be perfectly fine."

"Okay, we'll meet as planned."

"Get some rest, Franz. I'm really worried about you," Dick said, heading out of the room.

"Take good care," Art called as he followed Dick.

Franz slept most of the afternoon. He joined the family for dinner, but then went back to the den to rest afterwards. It didn't take him long to fall asleep again.

Suddenly a rumble of noise in the hall jolted Franz out of his deep sleep. He heard Harry and another man talking. The door was open and when he looked at his watch, he saw it was 11:00 p.m. Franz slid down on the couch so he wouldn't be seen.

"Come on in, Pete. Everyone's asleep," Harry said.

"That was a great meeting. We're underway. Ernie might work out after all. He was really serious-minded tonight and listened attentively," Pete said. "Let's check some information on the computer."

"Ralph did a great job at the second synagogue Tuesday. His work is flawless. They will never find a clue or trace it to us."

"That's excellent for us. All our efforts should be so perfect."

"I'm glad we got those Jew bastards," Pete was livid.

"That goes for me too," Harry added.

Franz listened and then poked his head up from the couch. "Harry, I didn't hear you in here. I was asleep."

"Hi, Papa," Harry said slightly embarrassed as he sat next to Pete at the computer. "What are you doing in here?"

"I wasn't feeling well today, and everyone wanted me to rest in here. I just woke up."

"Are you okay?" Harry seemed a bit concerned but more important whether he had heard them talking.

"Ya, I'm fine now. It was just a little spell."

Pete said, "I'd better be going." He wished Franz well, and left.

"So, how was your meeting, Harry?" Franz asked.

"Oh, the usual stuff. Can I help you to bed, Papa?"

"That would be good, son. Thank you."

Franz tossed and turned all night. Anneliese slept peacefully miles away in the huge bed. He generally liked to snuggle next to her, but not on this monstrous bed. He thought about how much he loved her. How could our son be involved in such terrible things? We tried to be such loving parents, he thought. His suspicions about Harry had become more real, but who was this Ernie? What did he have to do with it? Suddenly he wondered, could it be our Ernie?

Chapter 28
A Fishy Tale

Ingrid protested against him going to the meeting but finally gave in and dropped Franz off Saturday morning at the usual Starbucks., Indulging in bagels with mountains of cream cheese, sipping cappuccinos Art and Franz were already there, when Dick ambled in, lugging a shopping bag.

"Hi, guys. Sorry I am late. Hope you weren't waiting too long."

"No, Art and I have been enjoying the appetizing sights, both the refreshments and the frothy frauleins that keep passing the table," Franz said.

"What's in the bag?" Art asked.

"I brought you each a present." Dick lifted out two large packages wrapped in newspaper and handed them to his friends.

"Fish. I took a charter fishing boat in the Gulf yesterday and caught these."

"That's great," said Art. "There is nothing like fried fish filets smothered in Panko breadcrumbs."

Heads began to turn as the coffee aroma began competing with the odious day-old fish.

"What do I do with it?" Franz looked at the package skeptically.

"Eat it."

Dick opened one of the packages, laid the smelly fish on the table and demonstrated how to clean and bone it with a Starbucks knife and fork. Suddenly blood and guts spilled everywhere!

"Hey, put that stinking fish away, old man. What do you think this is 'Catfish Row?'" a bilious voice came from an older man at an adjoining table.

"Excuse me?" said Dick.

"I said, 'Get rid of the fucking fish. It doesn't belong on a table in Starbucks."

Dick straightened up, even more erect than ever, barreled over to his neighbor and rapidly flashed his badge of authority: his Medicare identification card.

"Listen, old man, I am Dick Reynolds from the CIA and you are interrupting an important international covert investigation. What is your name?"

"That's okay, buddy, I didn't mean anything by it," suddenly the man shrunk down in his seat.

"Now, sit there and be quiet." And so Dick returned to Art and Franz. Both could hardly stop from laughing.

"How do you feel? You look terrible, Franz," Dick said, showing genuine concern.

"I'm very upset, but okay."

Then Franz began to tell the story about his suspicions about Harry, including the swastikas on the synagogues and the possibility of Ernie's involvement.

"Wow!" Dick exclaimed.

"I told you it might be serious," Art said.

"I don't know what to do. Should we go to the police or the FBI?" Franz asked. "How can I turn him in? He's my son."

"Let's not jump to conclusions. Take this one step at a time," Dick said. "First of all, this is all circumstantial. We don't have a shred of evidence of a plot, and we could look like fools going to the authorities. Secondly, we want to protect Harry, if possible. If he strayed, perhaps we can help him before he gets into serious trouble," Dick answered, shifting from his fishing hat to that of the spymaster.

"I totally agree," Art said.

"Where did I fail?" Franz was crestfallen, tears rolling down his cheeks. "We were such loving parents and went out of our way to teach our children about tolerance of all races and religions. We wanted them to be above that awful mindset of the war that had swept me away."

"It's not your fault, Franz. You were a good parent," Art said, trying console his weeping buddy.

Franz continued, "Harry was a difficult child and hard to reach but we gave him all our love. Was I so blind that I didn't see any of this coming? It didn't just happen overnight. Who could have been poisoning his mind? Why would he turn out like this? It's all our fault." Franz sank low in his seat, sobbing with tears moistening his bagel.

"Franz stop tormenting yourself. We really don't know what's going on. We need to be patient and find out more," Art leaned over and put his arm around Franz.

"We need to find proof that something is happening. Franz, you must be extremely vigilant around the house and try to pick up as much information as you can. See if you can get back into the computer and recheck that Aryan Connection website. Then try to get into his email to see if he had any suspicious conversations, or whether he frequents any other websites. When we get something solid, we can plan our next step. Be careful: you must not let Harry suspect anything," Dick continued. "See when the next meeting is scheduled. Maybe we can do some spy work."

"What about Ernie? Do you think that's our Ernie?" Franz asked.

From Art, "It certainly could be."

"Well, I don't suspect there are too many racist old men named Ernie in Orlando."

Chapter 29
Beating the Eggs

"Oh Lordy, Lordy, the Men's Cooking Club was already in here this month. I thought we got rid of them. What's he doing here?" Leonetta Moore was commiserating with herself as she saw Ernie enter Denny's.

"Hi, Mr. Ernie, maybe you're a little forgetful but you're in the wrong place. Shouldn't you be in the Senior Center kitchen today?" Leonetta asked, trying to escort Ernie towards the door.

"I'm here for a meeting, Lee, on official government business."

"Yeah, honey, what you got to do with the government besides Social Security and Medicare?"

"It's a big secret."

"Ooooh, we are very important now, are we?"

"As a matter of fact, I am."

Leonetta walked off shaking her head.

Ernie saw Agents Sally Adams and Tom Prentice sitting in a back booth. He glanced around and then headed towards his rendezvous.

"Good morning, Ernie," Sally greeted him.

"Hi, chief and chiefette."

The nosey waitress, seeing the trio, came right over.

"Welcome to Denny's, and what can I get for you?"

"Who's paying?" Ernie asked.

"I'll pay," Tom responded.

"In that case, I'll have a Grand Slam with grits on the side and coffee," Ernie said, licking his chops.

"I see you're not hungry. What you want in your Slam."

"Scrambled eggs well done, sausage links, red potatoes and pancakes." She wrote furiously thinking, Not again.

"I'll just have coffee," Sally said.

"For me as well."

"So, Ernie, how was the meeting last night?" Sally said quietly, getting right down to business.

"Great, great, great, Sally," he shouted.

"Ernie, please keep your voice down. Remember we need to be

discreet."

"Yeah sure, sorry."

"What do you have to report to us?" Tom was anxious.

"There's something going down. Even though this was a sub-committee meeting, they were very vague about what they are planning. It's a big operation. I'm not sure, but it could involve President Sharif," Ernie rattled off.

"Did they use any operative words like kill, attack, and bomb or assassinate?" Sally asked.

"Not exactly, although one member of the group did make a comment that Sharif, the Jew lover, was going to get his due. At our next meeting we're supposed to devise the final plan," Ernie continued. "They did talk about the president's upcoming trip to Orlando."

Leonetta was back with the food, taking her time around the table, trying to pick up any gossip.

Ernie dove into his mountainous breakfast and continued, "I think they plan to kill the president."

"Why, are you sure?" Sally asked at the edge of her seat, listening attentively,

"No one said anything specific, but there were lots of innuendos all evening."

From Tom, "Last time you mentioned that they divided the group into three sub-committees. Do you have any idea what the others are planning?"

"Not a clue. I believe they want to keep our plans separate and secretive. We cannot talk about any of the work with each other, especially what other sub-committees are doing," Ernie continued.

Leonetta was at the next table taking an order, trying to listen to the good stuff that was going down at Ernie's table.

"Here's our plan of action: Keep going to the meetings. Get as deeply involved in the activities as you can. Participate as much as possible in creating the plan," Sally instructed.

"You mean that you want me to plan how to kill the president?" Ernie asked, somewhat rattled.

"If that's what it takes to get involved. Show a lot of enthusiasm. Make them feel that you are trustworthy. Try to get Harry Smith to let you participate in the other planning as well," Tom instructed.

"Sort of like a trusty assistant?"

"Correct, Ernie."

"I think I can do that." Ernie was excited to be part of the operation, but then his hand began to shake.

Leonetta, who was biding her time in the area, asked if they wanted anything else.

"No, thank you. Just the check, please. When is the next meeting?" Sally asked.

"Next Thursday night."

"Good. We will meet back here Friday at the same time," Tom said. "If anything happens sooner, call one of us. Night or day."

Nosey Leonetta brought over the check which Tom grabbed.

"Remember, Ernie, discretion. You are doing great," Sally said, giving him a warm smile of approval.

Ernie felt proud to be serving his country once again. After they left, Ernie sat at the table sipping his coffee but now both his hands and legs were trembling out of control.

The two law enforcement officers headed towards their car.

"We need to keep an eye on him. I'm not sure that he will hold up under all this pressure. This is serious stuff. We don't want it to go too far. If we keep it contained, we will be able to foil the operation." Before they got into their government Ford, Sally added, "We have our work cut out for us."

Ernie now was a total bundle of nerves and felt more confused than ever. They had asked him to plan the assassination of the president of the United States in order to save the country. This was huge. He prayed that he wouldn't screw it up. Finishing his coffee, he barely could stand, his whole body was quavering as he wobbled to the door. Leonetta caught up to him and walked alongside of him and said, "I wasn't listening or anything but, honey, you are up to your ears in some bad ass shit."

Chapter 30
Evil Waters

Otto Schafer and Siegfried Schloss perspired profusely as they luxuriated in the hot thermal waters at a historic resort and spa in Baden-Baden, Germany. Originally a social center for the European nobility, this picturesque city was nestled between vineyards, forests and the plains of the Rhine Valley.

They were booked there for a week to conduct secret business and take the cure. Otto, 84, was hoping to treat his persistent respiratory problems which could have been better served by a weight loss program. Siegfried, 93, while appearing calm, was afflicted with a serious nervous disorder. Collectively they were a walking disaster but the comforting baths, soothing massages, gourmet food and especially the constant spirits were the prescription to be a cure all.

"I was here for the music festival in 1937. Bela Bartok was supposed to be here for the premiere of his masterpiece, Music for Strings, Percussion and Celesta, but cancelled at the last moment," Siegfried recalled. "I was 19 and had just been conscripted into the Reich service. It was quite a time."

"Ya, I served near here for a short time too" Otto confided. "I was a young assistant on the staff of Albert Haim."

"Albert Haim. Didn't they call him the doctor of death?"

"I believe so. I remember that term. He was quite notorious."

"I never met the man."

"They said he performed horrific experiments on patients. I never saw that. I believe it was all a lie. He did scientific studies to advance the cause of the Reich," Otto said.

"Didn't he die recently?"

"Ya, about 10 years ago in Cairo. He was 92, had been on the run for many years, and was the most wanted man on our list of fugitives."

"So, tell me what he was like?"

"He was a decent man who put the country's priorities first."

A blond fraulein came into the steamy room to get them, "Time to come out of the bath and dress for lunch. Don't forget tomorrow you are both scheduled for soap and brush massages."

"Are you the masseuse, beautiful lady?" Otto could only hope.

"No such luck, gentlemen."

"She can massage my muscles with soap and water anytime," the nonagenarian said, laughing.

The two naked old men resembling wrinkled prunes climbed out of their tubs, creating a wave of water and put on cashmere robes.

"What are we drinking today in preparation for lunch, Otto?"

"You know what they say, 'An aperitif stimulates the appetite.' At my age I need a lot of aperitifs," Siegfried said.

"My appetite is always stimulated, but the aperitif just confirms that."

They ambled to the changing rooms, slowly showering and dressing for their formal lunch. Requiring total privacy for their discussion, a secluded dining salon had been reserved. The intimate room had a large picture window with a lovely view overlooking the hotel's lavish gardens and hills.

"Bring me up to date, Otto," Siegfried asked, as he slurped potato soup brimming with vegetables and bacon. He dipped rye bread in to savor each drop.

"The Florida plan is underway."

"How do you know?"

"I've been communicating with Heinrich Smith in Orlando"

"I assume that your conversations are totally in the special code developed here."

"Yes, of course. Secrecy is our top priority."

"Zayer Gut."

"The mission has been divided up, and there are three teams each operating independently. The first is working on the actual logistics for the assassination. The second is scheming the simultaneous bombing of the two synagogues. The temples are across town in different directions from the convention center where the president is scheduled to speak. The decoy explosions will take place about an hour before the president goes to the podium," Otto explained. He had to stop their discussion as a waiter wheeled in a cart with their main course. The platter was overflowing with veal rouladen, rolled beef stuffed with bacon rashers. The server dished it out, filled the wine glasses with Spatburgunder, a light red fruit-flavored wine made from the best grape in the Baden region, and left. Otto tucked his napkin under his triple chin, tasted the morsels and continued to explain the plans.

"The third team is assigned to concoct a diversionary scheme that will mock the assassination and will be leaked to the FBI before the incident."

"How will they access the convention center?"

"Heinrich Smith is working with the vice president on that part of the mission," Otto continued.

"He will also have access to the exact schedule for the president's appearance."

"What about the explosions?"

"They will be two strong suitcase-type bombs that will arrive at each synagogue embedded in the earth of a tree to be planted by a landscaping crew outside the buildings."

"Who is building the bombs?" Siegfried asked.

"A professional in Daytona Beach who owns a nursery and gardening center as a front. He is using the information on the thumb drive we shipped to Florida," Otto told his partner.

"Does he foresee any problems with the devices?"

"It's a highly technical build but he feels it is achievable. Heinrich is meeting with him this week."

"What about the finances?"

"We have already wired $500,000 to the Caymans, $250,000 this past week. They said it would cost about double that. I am leaving next week for Orlando and will be responsible for the disbursement of the funds," Otto said.

"Are you sure you're up to it, Otto? It sounds like a very stressful endeavor?"

"I will throw away my cane and dance around the room to see my life's dreams fulfilled."

"Otto, just think in a matter of several months there will be a new American president who is on the same page as we are. When we return the rightful government to Germany, our biggest ally will be totally inculcated with our fundamentals. We will leave our legacy," Siegfried pontificated.

The plates were cleared, coffee and a fruited linzer torte was served with whipped cream. The wine glasses were now filled with Riesling.

"Sounds like a very complex plan," Siegfried remarked.

"They have been working on it for a very long time and seem to have every angle covered," Otto tried to reassure him.

"I will get the information from the others in our group here in Germany. We must remember that this is very top secret," Siegfried warned needlessly.

"Now we drink and get drunk in celebration," Otto said, raising his glass. The two men were still laughing and celebrating at the table two hours later, now with schnapps.

"To the Fourth Reich."

"To the Fourth Reich."

The men had advised the serving staff not to disturb them. Later, hearing total silence in the room, a hostess opened the door to the den of iniquity and found the two gentlemen leaning over the table, fast asleep and snoring.

Chapter 31
Medicare, Motorcycles and Marinades

Torrential rain had pounded Orlando all night. By the time the cooking men assembled in the morning, the rain had slowed to a drizzle. This weather brought the men aches and pain. Abe limped in carrying groceries for the lunch. His arthritis was getting the best of him today.

"What are you doing with those today? It's not your turn to cook," Fred asked.

"Ed's a bit incapacitated, so I offered to cover for him."

Ed walked in, gingerly cradling his arm in a sling.

"What's the matter, Ed? Are you okay?" Fred asked.

"I have tennis elbow and it hurts like hell! My doctor says that I need arthroscopic surgery."

"Buddy, aren't you a little too old for tennis?"

"Not table tennis."

"Looks like you're having some difficulty with your arthritis today, Abe?" Ed noticed.

"Ed, arthritis is the cruelest disease known to mankind.'

"Can't be worse than cancer?"

"Much worse, makes every single one of your joints stiff except the right one."

"I hear you," Ed commiserated.

"Make way! Make way," yelled Steve, as he barreled into the kitchen breathlessly. "I got to get to the crapper fast. It's my damn stomach again."

Dick entered the kitchen sporting a cane. "My hip is over the moon today."

"Why don't you have it replaced? It's a pretty common procedure," Ed said.

"Cause my Medicare doesn't cover all the costs."

"I know. Even with the high supplement I pay to subsidize my plan, I still have to put out plenty of cash to get almost anything done," Frugal Bill interrupted.

"Yeah, the only thing that is covered 100% is embalming," Abe said.

The high humidity affected Ernie as he hobbled in like Walter Brennan on "The Real McCoy's." "Damn fake leg is not fitting well today. It always swells up when it rains."

Steve returned to the kitchen, "Oh boy, that was a close one."

"What does your doctor say about your stomach problems?" Fred asked.

"My gastroenterologist has a gut feeling it's colitis," Steve said disappointed no one got the joke

"Are you going to be able to eat today, Steve?" Abe asked.

"Damn straight! One thing has nothing to do with the other."

"I'll buy that," Ernie chimed in.

Dick began a chorus of booming sneezes.

"Charles's not cooking today. There are no flowers on the tables, so why are you exploding so violently, Dick?" Fred asked.

"Cause the fucking pollen flies all over the place in the wind and rain and I can't hide from it. Ha choo!"

Bill is nauseous. "I'll be fine. It's just one of the side effects of my new cancer medication they just started."

"What are the other effects?" Ernie asked, quite concerned.

"Bankruptcy" came the reply from their wealthiest and stingiest member.

Art and Franz arrived together. Today their afflictions were mental; both were seriously worried over the dramatic revelations about Franz's son. Abe did a head count. Charles was away on his honeymoon with Robert in Barbados.

"I can just see those two boys lounging under a tropical palm tree and being fanned by a naked pool boy," Ernie said.

"Joe's not here. I hope he isn't ill today?" Dick wondered.

"If he is, he should be here like the rest of us. This is a regular walking infirmary," Steve said.

"Let's face it, boys, we're just a bunch of ailing old farts," Abe piped in, "but fuck that, let's get cooking."

They decided to ignore their ailments and moved to the kitchen. Abe was top chef today, and donned his white chef's hat, unpacked the goodies, and got down to serious business. Dick called Art and Franz into the computer room for a short conference.

"We're going to follow Harry to the meeting tonight. Franz, we'll pick you up at 6:30. We'll hide down the road and follow him," Dick instructed.

"Do we need to wear anything special?" Franz asked.

"A trench coat, fedora and a spy glass are the uniform of choice," Art mused.

"We don't need a trench coat and that other stuff. Just wear something comfortable. Preferably not your suit and tie, Franz."

"Did you have any problems with an alibi for getting out of the house, Franz?" Art asked.

"I told everyone I was going bowling. They laughed. It turns out that Ingrid bowls once a week, so she asked me what alley we were going to. I was at a loss, so I told her that I didn't know. I had never been bowling. So, you guys, better explain the game to me in the car."

"That will be the easy part tonight."

"I'm nervous, guys," Franz said, clearly worried. "Those Nazis can be very dangerous. What happens if they have guns?"

"We are not going to get into a shooting match. We are just doing surveillance, Franz."

"Don't worry. We'll take care of each other," Art assured him.

"Boy, this is going to be fun," Dick added.

"Maybe for you, but I never did spy work before."

Abe came into the computer room and broke up the group. "Okay, fellows, I need some help in the kitchen."

"What's for lunch today, Abe?" Steve asked.

"A Chinese-style lunch," Abe told his second and third sous chefs.

"I like Chinks," Ernie stated. "But it's been a while since I had roasted cat!"

"ERNIE!"

"The first course is the egg drop soup. We pour in freshly made chicken soup from my Bubba Esther's secret recipe, add sesame oil, salt and pepper, and very slowly beat in the eggs in a steady stream."

"That's easy enough," Bill asserted, following Abe's directions.

"Speaking of a stream, I have to go play 'hide and pee,'" Ernie announced.

As the boys fussed, Fred moseyed over to Steve, "You were involved in the theatre, weren't you?"

"Yeah, a little bit. I mostly painted scenery for some amateur theater companies," he admitted.

"All the same, what I want to know is did Romeo and Juliet have carnal knowledge?"

"In the Orlando Company, they did."

"Next, we'll prepare the Chinese pork tenderloin. The meat has been marinating for a day," Abe announced.

"What's in the marinade?" Fred asked

"All kinds of great stuff: hoisin sauce, soy sauce, fresh honey, rice vinegar, sesame oil, sesame seeds, garlic and sweet and sour sauce. Now we put it in the oven for 45 minutes."

"How do you know when it's ready?" Ed asked.

"When it reaches 160 degrees," Abe explained.

"Well, how the hell do you take the temperature of a pork tenderloin?" Ernie asked playfully.

"We let you hold the roast and then stick the thermometer up your ass," Abe responded rapidly.

Suddenly there was a loud vroom, vroom of an engine that literally shook the building.

"What the fuck was that?" Steve asked.

"Hey, guys, come outside and take a look at this," Fred beckoned excitedly.

Joseph Jones, wearing a red bandana, black leather pants and vest with his beer belly sticking out of a black Harley-Davidson tee shirt, was sitting in front of the senior center on a spanking new red Harley-Davidson trike. Everyone abandoned poor Abe to his sautéed bok choy to run outside.

"Wow, where the hell did you pick that thing up?" Dick asked.

"I just bought it. It's a new Tri-Glide Ultra Classic, the utmost bad ass touring bike," Joe boasted to the group. "It's the ultimate sex machine."

"Joe, get a grip, you're over 75. I don't know how you even get your leg over the seat, let alone connect yourself with sex and that?" Fred asked.

"It's got everything: air-cooled and a twin cam 103 engine, a stereo and even a DVD player," Joe boasted.

"How do you even hear the music with all that noise?"

"I use headphones, stupid."

"Fellows, it even has heated handlebars." Joe bragged, pointing to the gleaming hand controls.

"That's really essential in Florida." Dick said, a bit sarcastic, "especially in the summer."

"I think it's wussy," chided Ernie.

"You call me a wuss, Ernie?" Joe started getting off his seat and beginning to feel a little hot under the collar.

"No, no Joe, I just didn't think that bikers would accept that as the real McCoy," Ernie answered sheepishly.

"It keeps me on a bike at my age, Ern, and we bikers have a saying that three wheels are better than four."

"What that set you back, Joe?" Frugal Bill asked.

"$45,000," Joe said.

"That thing cost as much as my condo," Ernie was flabbergasted.

"This one was made for me. People are like motorcycles; each is customized a bit differently, and there was a six month wait for this baby."

"Wow!" Bill said.

"What's the difference between a Harley-Davidson and a vacuum cleaner?" Joe asked.

"Tell me," Ed volleyed back.

"The location of the dirt bag."

Ernie walked over to the wheels to get a closer look.

"Wanna take a ride on my bitch seat, sweetie?" Joe said kidding, fluttering his eyes at his homophobic friend.

"No, thanks, I can think of better ways to vibrate my testicles."

Abe yelled out the door to get everyone back to earth. "Food's ready, fellas. Come and get it."

The boys paraded back into the kitchen and lined up while the chef du jour ladled out the delicate egg drop soup. He then piled plates high with Asian-style roast pork over fried rice with baby bok choy. The group sat in clusters and soon their discussion returned to their four favorite topics: aches, pains, sex, and politics.

"Hey, Ernie, what's difference between a hematologist and urologist?"

"I don't know, and I go to both. Tell me."

"A hematologist pricks your finger."

"My last hospital bill was outrageous. Can you imagine, they charged Medicare $200 for an aspirin," Bill complained.

"Yeah, they now divided hospital bills into parts and labor," Ed added.

"What is the difference between an HMO and terrorists?" Steve asked.

The boys were in rare form today.

"I give up," Art said.

"You can bargain with a terrorist," Steve said and laughed at his own bad joke.

"Getting anything through congress is impossible. That institution is totally useless," Fred interjected to the boys at his table. "The aging process could be slowed down if it had to work its way through congress."

"I believe that politicians and diapers have one thing in common," Abe announced. "They should be changed regularly for the same reason." Everyone laughed.

"Ernie, are you still taking those tranquilizers?" Dick asked.

"I stopped taking those pills a long time ago when I was starting to be nice to people."

The rustling of wrappers could be heard crumbling after Abe handed out the fortune cookies.

"Hey, I got a good one, 'Your love life will reach a new plateau.' Maybe this knows something I don't. My Bella said to me recently, 'Let's go upstairs and make love.'

'Pick one,' I said, 'I can't do both,'" Ed admitted.

"Mine is interesting," Steve piped in. "'You will come into great wealth in later life.' I'm 76. I passed later life already."

"'Money talks,'" Art read his slip, "But all my money says is 'Goodbye.'"

"I got the best one, boys," Joe said. "'You will eat Chinese food soon.'"

Lunch was over, so the boys folded the chairs and helped with the washing up. This was a particularly lively session for the Old Men's Cooking Club. Despite the aches and pains, everyone was in particularly good form.

"Hey, Ernie, want to join my poker game tonight?" Steve asked.

"Thanks for inviting me, but I have to go to an important meeting this evening."

"What kind of meeting?"

"It's top secret," Ernie said, hesitating to go any further.

"Fellows, I think Ernie is a spy." Steve was being playful.

Dick listened very carefully.

"See you next week, guys." Ernie got up from his perch where he had watched the cleaning up and strutted from the kitchen as proud as a peacock.

"Hey, Joe, lots of good luck with the new trike," Franz said.

"Thanks, pal."

"Be very careful, buddy," Abe showed his genuine concern.

Art, Dick and Franz met behind a bush near the exit to reconfirm plans for that night.

"You better take a nap this afternoon, Franz; it's going to be a long night," Dick suggested.

"Good idea."

The three self-deputized spy masters sauntered out to the parking lot, arm in arm.

"We do have a good time Thursday morning," Art said, feeling rejuvenated.

"Seven days without laughter makes one weak," laughed Franz.

"If we can laugh, we know we're really alive." Dick said, as he got into his car.

142

Chapter 32
Old Voyeurs Never Die

The rain threatened once again. Aside from the sky lighting up with distant electrical fireworks, it was an inordinately dark and dreary night. Franz hardly ate a bite at dinner. He was apprehensive about what was to follow.

"You're all dressed to go out. Where are you going, Pop?" Harry asked.

"Bowling."

"With Art and Dick?"

"Ya."

"Have a great time but be careful."

"You know me, I'm going to stand around and watch mostly. Excuse me, I have to go now." Franz got up from the table and put on his least formal sports jacket and Mickey Mouse hat from Disney World that he had borrowed from his grandson. "Bye, bye, everyone."

The two co-conspirators were waiting halfway down the street in Dick's 1957 two-tone black and white Edsel Villager station wagon. The rain had started again, and the exceedingly noisy windshield wipers swished back and forth as Franz slumped in the backseat.

"What is this old car?" Franz asked.

"I've had this baby for 50 years. It was the worst piece of crap that Ford ever produced, but I love it," Dick said.

"What is it called?" Franz asked, amused.

"An Edsel. You know what it stands for? Everyday Something Else Leaks. When it was created, it was promoted to be the life-changing great car, but it sucked in the end. What do you drive, Franz?"

"An Opel Insignia, and it's certainly not as ostentatious as this thing."

"How come I have never seen this car at the men's group on Thursday?" Art asked.

"I don't take it out much, and the boys would laugh me out of the group if I drove up in this. But we'll see who has the last laugh. This four-wheel antique turkey is valued at more than $25,000."

"This is hardly a car for clandestine operations. It sticks out like a sore thumb," Art said.

"On the contrary, Art, who would ever think that we are on official business with this thing?"

The boys sat quietly waiting and watched attentively. The wipers were in perfect rhythm with Franz's rapidly beating heart. A few minutes later Harry's black Mercedes pulled out of the driveway and drove past the three. Dick trailed him, but not too closely. He had enough issues with his sight, and the constant movement of the wipers was not helping. The Edsel huffed and, puffed, moving slowly. They almost lost Harry several times on the highway. After twenty-five minutes, Harry pulled off the interstate onto a country road which led to a crowded housing subdivision sporting boats, cars and garbage on many of the lawns. "A lawn service couldn't make a buck here," Dick mused.

At the entrance, a lit sign announced they were in the Xanadu Forest Community. A warning sign noted that this subdivision was on the edge of a forest preserve, and all owners and visitors were warned about the possibility of forest fires. A welcoming thought.

They followed Harry around several bends to a cul-de-sac. There were five cars already parked in front of the house and two on the lawn including a white boxy Scion. Art thought he recognized that car with its blue and white handicap sticker. Harry pulled into the driveway of the ramshackle Florida dwelling and entered. Dick drove around the block and parked out of sight. The three spies stepped into the mud, hitched up their pants and were ready for their surveillance. They tiptoed through the grass of a neighbor's home and startled a monstrous dog that began barking in a nearby yard. Art tried to pacify the gigantic mutt, but he just yelped louder. They walked gingerly through the wet grass onto the property to survey the house. The rain waited to fall until they were there. Then it began pouring.

The front rooms were lit up. Peering through the living room window, they could see seven men seated around a table in the dining room. Since the windows had shear curtains, Dick, Art and Franz could see in. It was like a silent movie: they couldn't hear the voices, but they watched the movement. Harry Smith stood at the head, pointing to an easel with sheets that looked both detailed and complex. Hanging on the wall was a large photograph of the historic beer hall in Munich. Suddenly Harry raised his right arm straight in front to eye level with his hand parallel to his arm, and all the men followed suit.

"My God, that's the Nazi salute," Franz gasped. "I'm feeling queasy. I think I have to go to the bathroom."

"Try to stay calm, Franz," Art whispered.

"Art don't fart out here. You know what they say, 'Only you can prevent forest fires'," Dick said, trying to add some levity to the situation.

By now sheets of rain were falling and the three were totally soaked.

Art, looking around the room, motioned to his pals.

"Guys, do you see who I see? Look in the corner."

Swaying back and forth in an old-fashioned rocking chair was their Thursday morning cooking partner, Ernie Stubbs.

"What the fuck is he doing here?" Art whispered.

"I knew that car looked familiar," Franz said quietly.

"Why am I not surprised?" Dick concluded. He anticipated seeing Ernie here but hadn't told his co-amateur sleuths. Now he knew that his buddy was up "shit's creek." He had to act quickly and bring Ernie's involvement to an end before he was handed his head.

The discussions seemed very animated, and at times heated, as Harry flipped through the chart. Ernie seemed to be participating in the discussions. Ralph, the host, to whom Franz and Art were introduced at the Golden Corral Restaurant, filled the table with beer and ham and cheese sandwiches. The three musketeers had seen enough. They sloshed back to their comedy of errors car. Shivering from the dampness, they sat silently for a few moments.

"I am thoroughly soaked and absolutely beside myself," Franz finally cried out.

"This is definitely a meeting of a neo-Nazi group, and Harry seems to be the leader," Dick confirmed.

"But what is Ernie doing there?" Franz wondered, puzzled.

"Well, we know he is very prejudiced, but I thought he was just a harmless bag of wind. I guess I was fooled," Art said, shaking his head.

"Okay guys, we can sit here commiserating all night, but I think we have our first break in the case."

"What are we going to do?"

"We are going to follow Ernie home, confront him and get to the bottom of this," Dick said.

"God only knows what they are planning at that meeting," Art worried.

"Oh, when Anneleise finds out, she'll have a heart attack." Franz was once again desperate. "God, what did we do to deserve this?"

"Franz, I know this is difficult, but you must be strong. We need to figure everything out and see what we can do to fix things."

They sat in the car drying off for an hour until the guests began leaving. Ralph wished each one well with a bear hug. Harry and Ernie left together and seemed to be talking, but Dick couldn't make it out. Harry left first while Ernie took his time getting into his car and heading home. The Edsel didn't have to pick up much speed since Ernie never drove over 40 miles per hour.

It took about 45 minutes to reach Ernie's condominium. He parked his car and Dick pulled in right behind him. Then the three caballeros jumped out and followed him to the door. It was 10:00 p.m. and the rain had finally stopped.

"Hey, you," Dick, pointing a flashlight in Ernie's face, called out as he stood in a shadow so Ernie could not see him! Franz and Art crouched behind Dick.

"Who's there?" He tensed up, looking around.

"Stick em up!" Dick thought he would add a bit more tension to the already frightened curmudgeon.

"Take my money, but spare my life, I've got a couple of dollars that you can have," he begged. "You can have my fake leg and sell it. Medicare paid $25,000 for it."

"Ernie, it's me Dick, from the cooking group, and Art and Franz are here too."

"What are you doing here in the middle of the night? You nearly scared the bejesus out of me. I am old; I can't take too much scaring."

"If I'd been where you've just been tonight, I'd be scared out of my fucking mind," Art said.

"We know where you went," Dick said, continuing to point the light in Ernie's eyes.

"We were there. We saw you, Ernie."

"It was nothing, guys, just a bunch of men getting together to celebrate a birthday, we played some games and had refreshments." Ernie started to shake.

"What did you play?" Art asked.

"Party games, you know, like pin the toupee on the old guy, doc doc goose, kick the bucket and spin the bottle of Viagra."

"Ernie, cut the crap. We know what's going on," Dick spit. "We need to talk."

"Okay, we can get together tomorrow and go over everything."

"No, Ernie, NOW. Where can we go to talk?"

"There's an all-night Burger King down the road. Let me go in and pee, and I'll meet you there in ten minutes."

"Don't disappoint us, Ernie. We know where you live," Dick said, pointing a finger at his frightened buddy.

"I'll be there."

The three watched a very distressed old man hobble into his apartment.

146

A few minutes later, Art, Franz and Dick were tucked in a back booth at the happy king's palace with coffee all around. Ernie limped in, looking haggard.

"Are you hungry, Ernie?"

"Not really, but are you buying?"

"I'll buy." Art said.

"Okay then, I'll have a triple whopper with cheese, pickles, onions, lettuce, tomatoes, mayo, a small fries and a coke."

"How can you eat all that, Ernie?" Art asked as he wrote down the order.

"It's healthy, plenty of vegetables and good protein."

"It must have a million calories."

"Only 1750."

Art returned to the table with an armload of food for Ernie and ice cream all around for them.

"Ernie, what are you doing involved with that neo-Nazi group? I know that you have some prejudices, we all do, but carrying them that far is over the top."

"It's just a bunch of American boys who meet every week like the Old Men's Cooking Club to shoot the breeze."

"Or to shoot someone," Art whispered.

"Who do you think you are talking to, Ernie? I worked for the CIA for forty years, I'm not some babe in the woods," Dick was getting really upset.

"Come on, Ernie, tell us everything," Art prodded.

"How did you get involved with this group?" Franz asked impatiently.

"I can't. I'm going to get killed."

"I'm going to kill you right now with this fork if you don't spill the beans. So, either way you are dead. If you want to live a bit longer, you better start talking," Dick said, raising the plastic fork over Ernie's head.

"Harry Smith invited me to a meeting, and the boys accepted me right away," Ernie said sheepishly.

"Oh shit," Franz moaned.

Ernie felt tormented. He desperately needed to relieve himself of everything he knew to get this terrible weight off his chest. He was in too far over his head, so what did it matter. Maybe his cooking buddies could help him. So he told them all about the group, the meetings, and the plot. He told them everything except his involvement with the FBI. He wanted to buy time until he spoke to Sally Adams. The boys were horrified.

"Why don't you go to the police or the FBI?" Art asked.

"I am so scared, fellas. They threatened my life. I don't know which way to turn."

"Did they talk about a man named Otto?" Franz asked.

"Otto is Harry's uncle in Germany. He is scheduled to come to town next week."

"I knew it," Franz was aghast.

Ernie was beside himself, squirming, with tears rolling down his cheeks.

"Listen, Ernie, this has got to be so difficult for you. We are here to help," Dick said, and put his arm around his sobbing buddy.

"But you have to hang strong. We must put a stop to all this. Do you think you can continue going to the meetings and playing along? You have us. Together we will figure out what to do, old friend," Dick tried to sound soothing.

"I think I can do that. I may have my quirks and mouth off a lot about hating this and hating that, but I don't really mean to hurt anyone. The boys in that group like me and accept me," Ernie bellowed, wiping his tears.

"We do too, Ernie. We really care about you. You have true friends in the cooking group. The neo-Nazis are just using you. This is some serious business."

"Ernie, please go home. Try to get some rest. I'll call you tomorrow to check on you," Dick said soothingly.

"Is Bessie in town? Can you spend the day with her tomorrow?" Art asked.

"Yes. I feel a little bit better now that I have talked to you guys. Maybe I'll order a triple whopper to go."

The three were quiet on the drive back to Harry's. The only noise was the laboring Edsel chugging along.

"It's late and we are all tired. Let's get together tomorrow to figure out a solution. We're no good to anyone right now."

It was two a.m., but the house was ablaze with lights when Franz tiptoed in looking like a washed-out dishrag.

"Are you all right? Where have you been?" Ingrid said in a panic. Anneliese ran over to hug him.

"I was out with the boys." Franz could barely speak.

"The bowling alley closed two hours ago. I wanted to call Art and Dick but didn't know their names or numbers. I was ready to call the police. Harry drove around the neighborhood for an hour to try to find you."

"I'm really sorry. We went to a bar after bowling," he lied.

"You're no spring chicken, Franz. You have to take care of yourself."

"I promise I will," he kissed her.

A distressed old man walked to the bedroom holding hands with his beloved bride of so many years.

Chapter 33
A Heap of Ice Cream And Trouble

It was 2:00 a.m., and Ernie was slouched over in a booth at Denny's working on his Triple Whopper, fries and soda he'd brought from Burger King. He had gone directly here for the morning meeting place after Franz, Dick and Art left him. Feeling too upset to go home, he decided to wait the seven hours for the meeting with Sally Adams and Tom Prentice at the eatery. He felt so old, so drained, with pangs of depression setting in. The entire situation had gotten completely out of hand. His mind raced a hundred miles an hour. I am involved with a vicious group of neo-Nazis. They plan to kill the president of the United States, and I'm the designated assassin, but I'm not going to really shoot the commander in chief. My buddies from the men's cooking group are now involved and Harry Smith, the leader of the subversive group, is my buddy and Franz's son. Not to mention that Harry's uncle, and Franz's best friend, Otto, a Nazi activator in Germany, is involved in the plot and is coming to the States this week! This was all too much for him. The more he thought, the more he ate to try to blot out the horrors of his situation.

At 6:00 a.m. Leonetta Moore arrived for her morning shift and found Ernie fast asleep in the back booth, an empty Burger King bag in front of him.

"Mr. Ernie, Mr. Ernie, are you, all right?" she poked him on the shoulder.

Startled, he woke up, "Oh, hi Lee, I guess I must have dozed off."

"You look terrible. I'll bet you're up to your ears in that bad business I overheard you discussing with those people last week."

"Don't ask, Lee. I'm in a boatload of trouble," Ernie confided.

"What can I get you to make you feel better, Mr. Ernie?"

"How about a four-scoop vanilla ice cream sundae with chocolate syrup and nuts and don't forget the cherry."

"If that will cure your blues, coming right up."

"I don't think anything will cure those," and he promptly dozed off again.

Sally Adams arrived first, and gently tried to remove Ernie's face from the bowl of melted ice cream. His stark creamy vanilla mug made him look like Emmett Kelly, the sad clown. Sally wiped the ice cream from his face, but Ernie seemed devoid of life. When Tom Prentice joined them, they both tried to revive him.

"Maybe we should get an EMT?" Tom wondered.

"He's coming around. Give him a few minutes. He'll be okay."

"That boy don't look so good," Leonetta gave them an icy stare and added, "Honey, I don't know what you're selling my buddy Ernie, but it's sure making him sick. You should be ashamed of yourselves. I have a good mind to throw you both out of here and call the police. You are harassing Ernie."

"Calm down, dear. This is clearly not your business," Sally shot back.

"It is my business when a friend of mine is being persecuted," she turned in a huff and walked away.

Ernie could hardly speak as he described the confrontation with his three cooking buddies the previous night.

"Ernie, you're doing great. Don't worry, we're going to foil the whole plot and get all the perpetrators. We've been waiting a long time to shut down this neo-Nazi ring and you are not only going to be a hero for saving the president of the United States but also for helping us eradicate a vicious hate movement in the country," said Sally whose words uplifted Ernie.

"Just hang in there a little longer, partner," Tom Prentice said, patting him on the shoulder.

"What about Franz, Art and Dick? They have partially figured out what is going on," Ernie agonized.

"Keep them involved. Call them to a secret meeting and tell them that you are working for the FBI. Ask them to join in and help. Since I know that Dick Reynolds is former CIA, I am sure he will want to be involved," Sally figured. "There will be plenty of work for a whole bunch of guys to throw a monkey wrench into this barbarous plan."

"Make sure they are sworn to secrecy. Why don't you deputize them, Ernie?" Tom suggested.

Sally gave Tom another one of her looks but shrugged and said, "What the hell."

"Oh wow, I've got assistants!" Ernie perked up. "I'll do it. I'm beginning to feel good again."

"That's the old spirit, Ernie."

"Hey Leonetta." Ernie yelled across the restaurant.

The very concerned server came running over.

"What is it? Are you okay, my baby?"

"I want to order scrambled eggs well done, an English muffin with jam, new potatoes, pancakes with a scoop of vanilla ice cream and a side of oatmeal with brown sugar and raisins, coffee, cream, and sugar. Do you folks want anything?"

"Who's paying? Tom laughed.

"You are."

"No, thanks."

Leonetta scribbled down the order and headed to the kitchen, mumbling. "I don't know what kind of bullshit or drugs they are feeding him, but that old fart has just been risen from the dead."

Chapter 34
Behind The Sordid Bride's Veil

A half-naked pool boy swayed back and forth over the honeymoon couple fanning them with a gigantic banana leaf. Charles and Robert, distracted by this gyrating bronze statue, totally missed the breathtaking view from the cliff of their resort on the lovely island of Barbados. With piña coladas in hand, they were lounging on the private terrace of their one-bedroom villa.

"Oh, to be young again," Charles bemoaned, staring at the tanned abs of the beautiful youthful stud.

"But it's so wonderful that after 50 years, we are finally married. Charles. That certainly is reason for a huge celebration."

"Why don't we have one?"

"But we're already married."

"There is no reason that we can't have a reception for all our friends."

"That's true."

"I know of a wedding planner who works with gay couples who marry in other states and come to Orlando to have their party. I'll send her an e-mail and we'll set up an appointment," Robert said excitedly.

"Oh Robert, I love you so much," Charles declared as the warm sea breeze swirled around their heads, and their bodies were caressed by the tropical sun.

"Ernie, this is absolutely crazy... Have you lost your mind?" Dick complained. "I know you said that it was essential to meet in a conspicuous place, but this is ridiculous."

Franz, Art, Dick and Ernie, all wearing ill-fitting vintage bathing suits were sitting in gigantic black inner tubes floating on a lagoon at the Wild Surf Water Park. Dozens of annoying children were tubing around them, racing each other and splashing wildly.

"You can't be too careful these days," Ernie said.

"It would have been a lot safer at Starbucks."

Art splashed Ernie.

"Easy, Art, I can't swim," Ernie protested.

"So, what the hell are we doing here?" Dick asked.

"Yeah, what was so important that you had to drag us all the way out here and put us in harm's way in the middle of this dangerous ocean?" Art laughed.

"Okay, fellows, here's the scoop. But you got to keep this completely under your hats."

"I'm not wearing a hat, Ernie," laughed Art.

"You know what I mean. Listen, I'm working undercover with the FBI. They made me an honorary deputy," he boasted proudly. "We are going to foil the vicious plan that the neo-Nazi group is planning. I'm helping with that operation. I couldn't tell you everything until I cleared it with my chief."

"What are you doing exactly?" Dick asked.

"I've become a member of the neo-Nazi group and am gathering information about their plans for the FBI."

"That sounds mighty dangerous, Ernie. Are you sure you're up to it?" Art wondered.

"The two FBI agents are monitoring me very closely. They have assured me full protection if I do what they say," Ernie was feeling less sure of himself.

"That sounds like bribery to me, Ernie,"

"It's not, Dick. I have no choice. I want to help them. They said I would be an American hero." Ernie felt a little better. "And they asked me to enlist your help."

Dick, Art and Franz looked at each other skeptically.

"We really want to help, Ernie, but this is a very delicate situation," Franz said.

"We know that Franz's son is up to his eyeballs in this mess. We've been tracking him for a while. He unfortunately is the leader of the group," Dick said. "We need to come up with our own plan to try to rescue Harry before he gets into real serious trouble."

"Unfortunately, guys, he's already in a pickle of trouble," Ernie stated. "I don't know if he can be saved."

Franz groaned.

"I think that we are all in with you, Ernie, as long as we can be as sensitive to Harry's situation as possible." Dick tried to broker a deal.

"I'll ask Sally Adams, my FBI Agent, about that," Ernie said.

"Good."

Dick playfully gave Ernie's tube a push and sent him twirling down the rapids. Laughing, the boys followed and caught up at the bottom.

"Hey, fellows, that wasn't fair, but it was a lot of fun," Ernie cheered.

The four men started splashing each other to the delight of the children.

"So, what's the next step, Ernie?" Art asked.

"We wait for further instructions from the FBI…"

That afternoon, Harry entered the lobby of a skyscraper in Orlando and rode the elevator to the second floor. The lettering on the door read "Smithfield and Weston Wedding and Event Planners." The office was decorated poshly with life-size photographs of swanky party scenes. Harry took a seat. Across from him sat an older male couple holding hands and talking quietly.

"Good afternoon," Harry said.

"Hello."

"Are you here to plan a retirement party, perhaps?"

"Our wedding reception," boasted Robert.

"Yes, we were just married in New York City after living together for 50 years and want to throw a big bash for our family and friends," Charles continued "What about you?"

"I am here to start working on my daughter's wedding," Harry lied convincingly.

"Well, you have come to the right place; my sources tell me that this is the best party-planning service in the country."

"My name is Robert, and this is Charles."

"Harry."

"What do you do, Harry?"

"I am an investment broker." Harry got up and handed Robert a card.

"We could use a good broker. Our limited investments are scattered all over the place." Charles said.

"I'd be pleased to talk with you. Perhaps I can take you to lunch?"

"That might be nice."

"Give me a call when you're ready."

At that moment the major-domo himself, Emil Weston, strolled into the reception area and invited Harry to his office.

"Good luck, fellows, I hope that you have another 50 years of happiness."

"Thank you, Harry."

"Best wishes on your daughter's wedding," Robert said, waving.

Another voice in the room said, "Charles and Robert?"

"Yes."

"I'm Hope Smithfield, Emil's partner. It's so nice to meet both of you. Please come with me and we can chat."

Harry entered Emil's lovely office. Dark wood covered the walls with the leather upholstered furniture. The walls sported large photographs of

Emil Weston with dignitaries and celebrities from all over the world. There was even a coveted picture of this master planner shaking hands with Herman Sharif, President of the United States.

Emil Weston lived a binate life. By day, he was one of the most sought-after social event planners in the nation. His commissions took him all over the world. After work, he was a notorious covert marksman and assassin. His fees were staggering, and he accepted assignments prudently. Having no scruples or loyalties, big money talked. His covert occupation had yielded huge success in obliterating a variety of client targets including terrorists for the CIA, unfaithful husbands or wives, and mafia intruders. He was recommended to Harry by Sid Townsend, his furtive lover, and vice president of the United States.

The two men talked for an hour as Harry explained the plan including their alternative scheme to throw everyone off. Emil would receive top dollar for this most dangerous assignment. Harry assured his marksman that the financial matters would be taken care of shortly since their money man was arriving that afternoon from Germany. Although Harry would have talked more, he noticed he was late to pick up "Uncle" Otto at the airport. Harry stood and handed Emil the $100,000 down payment.

Taking the money, he warned, "Go. Harry, but make sure that he has the rest of the money with him…"

A rotund man stood at the Lufthansa luggage carousel at the Orlando International Airport. Harry hadn't seen his uncle for many years and almost didn't recognize him. Now elderly, Otto Shafer, his large beer belly protruding, stood waiting, surrounded by six matching suitcases. There was nothing small scale about this German national socialist. Harry ran and embraced his adopted mentor.

"It's so good to see you and have you here, Uncle. Are you well?

"A bit too heavy, but I am well and able."

"That's terrific."

"People say that I have a beer gut. It's not true. I have a protective covering over my rock-hard abdominals." They both laughed.

"How is your father doing?" Otto asked. "Whatever we do, we mustn't let him know I'm here," Otto cautioned Harry. "And what about your mother?"

"She is thrilled to be here with the grandchildren," Harry explained.

"And tell me about your lovely Ingrid," Otto asked, remembering how he had brought this couple together.

"Ingrid is fine. She is busy with the kids and household."

"Does she have any suspicions about your activities?" Otto asked.

156

"I don't think so, Uncle. Although I seem to be in the doghouse a lot because I have so many meetings. But I truly believe that she doesn't have a clue."

Harry put the luggage on a cart and the two men walked arm and arm to the garage.

"What's new with Hilda, Uncle?" Harry asked.

"Besides the usual aches and pains of being an old woman, she is holding her own. Her goal in life is to torment me about losing weight. She is relentless," Otto said.

"It's for your own good."

"I am 85. My own good is to let me eat and enjoy myself," Otto chuckled.

"You haven't changed a bit in all these years. Still as stubborn as a mule and cantankerous as ever."

Otto brought Harry up to date on the activities of the senior council in Germany and the financial situation of their mission. "We have been working on this plan for a long time, Heinrich. Is everything still going smoothly?"

"So far, so good, Uncle, but the next month will be telling."

"Do your members have their assignments?"

"Yes, everyone is preparing."

"What about the bomb maker in Daytona. Is he done?"

"Yesterday he confirmed that the devices were ready to go."

"And Weston?"

"I just came from a meeting with him and we discussed the actual attempt. He is raring to go. All he needs now is money, lots of it," Harry explained.

"Revolution is expensive. That's why I am here, my boy. Did you give him the small incentive?"

"Yes."

"He will receive an additional $150,000 the week before the operation with the balance deposited in a Swiss bank account after he accomplishes the goal."

"Sounds like a plan. Now that you are here, all will work and we will make history." They drove the rest of the way to the hotel in silence.

Harry checked Otto into his suite. "Get some rest, Uncle. The fun begins tomorrow."

"I may try to find some fun tonight. Perhaps in the form of a blond fraulien," Otto said coyly.

"What are you talking about, Uncle, a young blond at your age?" Harry asked and laughed.

"What's wrong with my age? You aren't the only one with a dick that works."

"What would Hilda say if she knew about your philandering?"

"She would say it was fine," Otto boasted.

"I don't believe that for one minute, Uncle."

"She would be happy that it would prevent me from eating!"

Euphoric, Robert and Charles drove home from the party designer's office. Plans had begun for the most opulent party to commemorate their celebration.

"This is going to be so much fun, Robert, my love," Charles said with one hand on the steering wheel, the other squeezing his partner's hand.

"Do you have the business card from that nice young broker? We may have to sell some stock to pay for this extravaganza."

"I was hoping we wouldn't have to sell anything but, what the hell, you only get married once," he said, handing the card to Charles.

"'Harry Smith,' that name looks familiar. As a matter of fact, he looks familiar too. Now I remember. I think it's the financial broker Bill brought to our cooking group. You know, for that investment we made. I believe Harry Smith is Franz's father. Franz's granddaughter is getting married. What do you know? It is such a small world… Hmm… but I thought Franz said he had very young grandchildren."

Chapter 35
Fish Are Jumping

Biker Joe was cooking today and it would definitely be a Southern meal. The fragrant aroma of buttermilk biscuits baking permeated the kitchen as the boys sauntered in for today's gastronomic session. Joseph Jones was a good-old country boy from Arkansas. He was one of the few members in the group whose head bore a full crop of white hair with a ponytail dangling like an appendage. His cheeks were rosy red, and he sported a distinguished beer belly. On his arms were a collision of Navy tattoos and many old age, red blood spots. A biker through and through, he had owned motorcycles for most of his life. After 40 years of marriage, and a prolific family producer of seven children, he became a widower. It didn't take him long to hook up with a new lady. His biker babe bride, Pat, was 15 years younger, at all of 60 years old. The two of them loved to ride off into the sunset on his new Harley-Davidson trike. Joe's motto was, "A good rider, has good balance, judgment and good timing … so does a good lover."

A staunch right-wing conservative, his president-bashing had the fierceness of the potatoes he worked over on his cooking days. Joe was not as vociferous as Ernie but boasted religiously that some of his "best friends" were blacks and Jews. He kept the boys aroused with his daily erotic emails on the Old Men's Cooking Club Gazette.

Joe's downfall was he constantly thought of himself as an expert and declared his strong opinions before thinking through an issue. He had a good heart and despite being an all-around smart ass, everyone enjoyed his company.

"I got fresh catfish today, boys."

"I don't like catfish," Ernie proclaimed.

"Just be a good boy and eat it, Ernie. It will grow hair on your chest," Art said.

"I haven't had hair on my chest in 60 years."

"Catfish is supposed to be healthy," Fred quipped.

"Never mind healthy, I need all the preservatives I can get," Ernie said.

Bill asked, "You know what they say the difference between a catfish and a lawyer?"

"Tell us, Bill."

"One is a bottom-dwelling, scum-sucking forager and the other is a fish."

"That was pretty bad."

"Boy, that really changed my mind about eating those scavengers," Ernie confirmed. "I used to eat a lot of natural food until I learned that most people died of natural causes."

"Coffee and biscuits are ready. Come and get it, gang," Joe boomed.

Brimming with butter, the biscuits were passed around the room.

Dick pulled Ernie into the hallway, "Any word from the FBI?"

"Heard from Sally last night. They want to meet us tomorrow morning at 9:00 a.m. at IHOP. Can you make it?"

"Why IHop? What happened to Denny's?"

"Sally doesn't like that annoying waitress, Leonetta, but I think she is a harmless old soul."

"I'll be there, and I'll tell Franz and Art." They went back into the kitchen to re-bond with the boys.

"Hey, Charles, welcome back. How was the honeymoon?" asked Steve.

"Our 50 years together have been a honeymoon. This was just an overseas extension," Charles replied, all choked up.

"That's wonderful," Dick said.

"By the way, Robert and I are planning a fun-filled wedding reception and, of course, all of you and your wives will be our guests."

"That's terrific," cooking-leader Fred said.

Charles walked over to Franz. "By the way, congratulations, Franz, I understand that your granddaughter is getting married," putting his hand out to shake.

Franz was totally puzzled. Anna was only nine years old and he didn't know of any pending nuptials.

"Thank you, Charles. How did you know?" Franz went along.

"Robert and I met your son, Harry, at a wedding planner this week. He talked about the upcoming wedding. Your son seems like a lovely boy.. He offered to take us to lunch to talk about investments."

"Yes, thank you. He is a lovely boy," he half-heartedly responded.

"I need a bunch of help today, guys. We are doing a lot of cooking," Joe announced.

"What are you serving with the catfish?" Know-it-all Abe got into the action.

"Homemade coleslaw, bacon-scallion hush puppies, and okra with stewed tomatoes; then pecan pie for dessert."

"Okra, yuk," laughed Steve. "My mother taught me how to become an adult: 'If you don't eat your vegetables, you'll never grow up.'"

Abe and Ed cozied up to the counter to start shredding the cabbage for the slaw. Steve, Bill, Fred and Joe gathered near the stove. The range-top was crowded like rush hour on the interstate. Aromatic bacon was frying, catfish sizzled loudly, and okra was boiling. The combination of smells from the gastronomic highway was dizzying.

"Hey, fellows, I saved a heap of money this week on food using coupons," Joe boasted as he sprinkled breadcrumbs on the fish.

"I always use coupons. With buy one, get one free store, and manufacturer's coupons, my wife and I save a bundle each week," frugal Bill added.

"Sometimes my wife gets really carried away," lamented Abe. "Paula gets so excited about saving money, we have stockpiles of stuff. In fact, I have enough toilet paper for two years."

"Yeah, Robert and I do too. I have 25 toothbrushes, which may be good, but I don't have any teeth. I take them out at night and put them in a jar with cleaner," Charles explained.

"My wife got so excited one week she came home with 20 pounds of cat litter that she'd only paid 89 cents for. That was a great bargain, but we don't own a cat," Dick chuckled.

"The food looks luscious Joe," Steve said, eager to begin.

"Any luck with your diet, Steve?"

"Now that food has replaced my sex life, I can't even get into my pants." They all chuckled.

"Last week I took a coupon into the drugstore for my Medicare discount on a glucose diabetes meter. The young punk snot-nose clerk at the cash register said to me, 'Are you sure that you have diabetes? I can't sell it to you if you don't have diabetes.' I offered to open my fly and give him a urine sample. It's amazing how fast he rang it up with the coupon." Ernie recounted the sordid tale.

"Good boy, Ernie," Art said.

"Can you imagine Ernie whipping out his schlong in the middle of Walgreens and peeing on the floor," Abe said.

"Nobody would see very much," Joe fired back in his usual perverted manner.

"Hey, wudda you mean. They don't call me 'Ernesto the bull' for nothing," Ernie protested loudly.

"But they don't call you Ernesto the bull with nothing, Ernie!" Steve chimed in.

"Last week was my 86th birthday and there was good news and bad news," Art said, having become much more outgoing since his friendship with Franz. "The bad news is that no one in my family sent me a birthday card."

"Oh, that's a damned shame, Art. Well, we all love you anyway," Charles said.

"Where was your family? What's the good news?" Fred asked.

"You know what they say: out of sight, out of mind. They forgot. The good news is that I got birthday greetings from Denny's, Del Taco, Fridays, Maggiano's, Moe's Southwest Grill, Friendly's, Ruby Tuesdays, Red Lobster, Quiznos, Texas De Brazil, Arby's, IHOP, McDonald's, Firehouse Subs, Backyard Grill, Perkins, Zaxby's, Houlihan's and Chili's. Gee, I didn't get one from the Olive Garden. I guess I'll have to take them off my Christmas list. Each one invited me for a free meal, providing that I spent the equal amount on a companion meal."

"Wow, how do you handle that?" Boring scientist Ed said, trying to figure it out.

"If I accepted all those birthday invitations, I would gain 200 pounds and it would cost me over $500 for free meals," Art laughed.

"Hey, Art," Dick whispered into his ear. "We're meeting tomorrow with handlers at 9:00 a.m., at IHOP. Remind, Franz."

"The food is ready. Come and get it," Joe summoned the boys by banging on a pot with a wooden spoon. He dished out some appetizing Southern comfort food, loading the plates with mayonnaise-dripping coleslaw, crispy catfish filets, hush puppies with the scent of bacon and onions, and a saucy vegetable concoction of green okra and vine-ripe tomatoes.

The cooks then filed into the computer room to eat. The room had five tables in a row. They usually sat at the first three tables, but today there was a group at the first two and at the far end of the room, Franz, Dick, Art and Ernie huddled whispering.

"The plot thickens, friends. Charles just told me that he met Harry at a wedding planner. He was there to plan his daughter's wedding, but my granddaughter is only 9 years old. There's more fishy business going on there than on this plate," Franz said.

"Put that on the agenda for tomorrow's meeting," Ernie suggested. "Will you have any trouble getting out of the house, Franz?" Dick asked.

"No, Ingrid is so happy for me to have activities, she will drive me anywhere. Otherwise, I would sit around all day and mope."

The boy's lined up for the pecan pie topped with vanilla ice cream.

Corpulent Steve helped himself to a double portion.

"If you eat all that you're never going to lose any weight, Steve," Abe said.

"I can't lose the weight anyway. I don't have to bother eating the chocolate cake. I just have to apply it directly to my hips."

"Hey fellas, lunch cost only $2.50 each today. With the coupons and discounts, I saved $25.00 on the food," Joe boasted proudly.

The Old Men's Cooking Club Chorus sang out gleefully.

"That's terrific."

"Here, here!"

"A great meal for so little."

"What a saving."

Ernie moaned under his breath, "He saved on the fish, and I'm busy trying to save the country from a big bad kettle of fish,"

Chapter 36
Planning the Pot Roast

Otto Shafer looked out of place standing below the portrait of the Munich Beer Hall in Ralph's crowded dining room. He was wearing a starched white dress shirt with gold cufflinks, a maroon ascot and dark baggy dungarees. Although he was trying to be accepted as one of the men, his outlandish clothes hampered this. Harry greeted his mentor with a bear hug and then opened the weekly Aryan Connection meeting.

"Fellas, please welcome Otto Shafer from Regensburg, Germany. He is our patron saint."

Otto walked around the table shaking hands and then they stood in unison and stretched out their arms in the nationalistic salute.

"My friends, it's a pleasure to be here," he said. "On behalf of the Fourth Reich, the future of Germany and the world, I applaud you. Your work here is monumental. It parallels the achievements that we are so busy with in the Fatherland. We are continuing the crucial work of the Third Reich. We don't have time or need for Jews, blacks, homosexuals or other non-white races. We must work as allies for the common cause."

"Haroo, Haroo," roared the gathering, banging on the table.

"We believe that there is one man who can lead your nation and is closely aligned with our ideologies and that is Sid Townsend, the vice president of the United States. That is why we maneuvered so hard to get him on the ticket with Herman Sharif. We have vast financial resources and thriving industry behind us. You are involved in a historic period. You men are the heroes who will help bring all our dreams and convictions to fruition. For that I salute you and I'm here to help." There were nods and applause all around. Ernie sat in his rocking chair feverishly trying to capture every word.

"In five weeks, we put the plan into action," Harry reiterated. "Ernie has been assigned the task of the assassination, although we need to take him back out to the shooting gallery to better prepare him. At 86, with his difficulty walking, he will be the least suspicious one and be able to pull this off with ease."

Ernie bolted upright in his chair.

"Is Ernie up to speed?" Ralph asked.

"He will be by the time we are ready to roll," Harry replied.

"How are we going to get him close to Sharif?" Lloyd asked.

"Sid Townsend is providing us access to the venue where the president is speaking," Harry told them, and then continued explaining the plan. Ralph brought a plateful of the usual ham and cheese sandwiches. They were devouring the pork with great voracity and swigging beer while Ernie sat there, a bundle of nerves. With a sandwich in each hand in a near panic, he wondered to himself. What's going on? They told me I wasn't going to shoot the president. I'm not supposed to shoot anybody.

"Hey Ernie, why are you sweating, and your hands shaking?" Floyd asked, as pieces of ham and cheese dripped from his sandwich.

Afraid to say anything, "Oh it's my old age, fellows. Don't pay it any mind. I am as steady as a rock," and he laughed, trying to slough it off.

"That's good, partner. We need to take care of you and make sure that you're okay," Pete said.

"Mr. Otto, you are from Regensburg, Germany?"

"Ya"

"Did you know that Harry's father, Franz, is also from Regensburg and he is here on vacation?" Ernie asked.

"Ah yes, I know him casually from around town, but not very well."

"I guess it's a small world, Mr. Otto."

"Ya, I guess so."

The men ate, drank, and continued to strategize. Otto discussed the funds that were being funneled in from Germany. At 10:00 p.m. Harry ended the meeting and one by one each wished Otto well and left.

Ernie, now in a complete panic, waited until everyone had left and went over to Harry who was still talking to Otto.

"Excuse me, Harry, but I thought you said that my shooting the president was going to be just a decoy. Why am I going back to the shooting range?" Ernie asked, hardly able to get his words out.

"That's right, Ernie, don't worry. You are just as a decoy. We want to make sure your part in the operation appears realistic."

"I am no good with a gun, Harry. Do you know that the last time I was at the range, I nearly killed the entire group?"

"Relax, Ernie. Trust us. It must look real, that's all. Go home and get some rest. How about meeting Tom and me at the rifle range over the weekend?"

"Okay, Harry, Okay."

***

Rabbi Joel Tannenbaum completed his prayers and removed his tefillin, a small set of black leather boxes placed on the head and arm containing scrolls with verses from the Torah worn at weekday morning services. He walked out of Beth Hamidrash, the mini auxiliary synagogue. In his office with its wall-to-wall bookcases, his colleague and dear friend, Rabbi Seymour Auerbach, was waiting.

"What are you doing here so early, Seymour? It's barely 8:00 a.m. Is everything all right?"

"Yes, yes, Joel. I just wanted to go over the plans for President Sharif's visit."

"We have been over the details many times, my friend."

"Forgive me for being a pest, but I have a disquieting feeling about the whole affair."

"Between the Secret Service and the local authorities, the security will be at its highest level. The city seems to be doing something right for a change."

"Thanks to you, Joel, because you stood up to the city fathers about the swastikas that defaced our synagogues."

"Someone had to. The president will land at the airport and then take his motorcade to the Convention Center. He plans to meet for an hour with Jewish leaders at a reception, and then mount the podium to address the World Jewish Convocation assemblage. He will speak for 45 minutes about our Jewish concerns, the rise of anti-Semitism in America, the State of Israel and the Palestinian situation. They said that he will share some information about the defacing of our temples. After the speech, he will have lunch at the center with specially invited Jewish leaders. You should have received an invitation."

"I did and also got a call from the Secret Service about their needing a background check for me."

"After the luncheon he'll head directly to Air Force One and fly out. It should be fine. I believe that everyone is on top of things, Seymour. What about we go over to IHOP and get a cup of coffee?"

"I'm sure it will be fine, Joel. I just have this gnawing feeling in my gut."

The pancake house was hopping. The two clergymen sat in a booth. Looking around, Rabbi Auerbach spotted FBI Agents Sally Adams and Tom Prentice, who were sitting with four elderly gentlemen across the restaurant. He recognized them from the meeting after the swastika incident.

Ernie ordered the largest breakfast on the menu. His nerves had gotten the better of him and he was in one of his serious eating moods. Dick, Franz, Art, Sally and Tom just ordered pancakes and eggs.

"Sally, I'm scared shitless," Ernie whispered, getting right to the point and relayed the details of the previous night's meeting with the group and Otto Schafer. Franz cringed every time Otto's name was mentioned. They all tried to console Ernie, who by now was slurring his words and trembling uncontrollably.

"You've got to get me out of this," Ernie begged, pouring eight packets of sugar into his coffee.

"Listen, Ernie, we are not going to let you shoot the president or get wounded yourself. You just have to play along," Tom Prentice said, trying to sound reassuring.

"Why don't you just move in and close down the operation?" Art asked.

"The director wants to let it play out in order to eradicate the entire operation from its roots once and for all. We can arrest one or two people now, but that would only be putting a bandage on the problem. We need to get everyone involved with the plot and need to trace it to all its sources. Who is behind it? Who is funding it? Is it just a local, national or international conspiracy? We need to do our homework," Sally explained.

"We also don't know who the actual would-be assassin is," Tom added.

"If Ernie is truly a decoy, then there is someone out there getting ready to pull the trigger."

"Are you going to pay the hospital bills from my nervous breakdown, because I don't think that Medicare covers that?" Ernie asked.

"No one is going to have a nervous breakdown, Ernie. You are going to be fine," Sally said, coming on strong.

The food arrived, and Ernie's order monopolized the entire table. He poured the coffee cream on the pancakes, the blueberry syrup on the scrambled eggs, scooped several teaspoons of oatmeal into his coffee and dropped pieces of bacon on the floor. His cooking partners had never seen him so agitated and became very concerned about his state of mind.

Franz relayed the story about Harry and the wedding planner, possibly shedding a new light on the plot.

"Dick, you're former CIA. What's your take on the situation?" Tom asked, inviting him to participate.

"Well, I agree that Ernie is being set up as a decoy to take the attention away from the actual assassin. Ernie mentioned that there are two other parts to the plan, but no one seems to know what they are. I suggest that we try to find out what else they are up to."

167

"I tried to get Harry to include me in the other parts, like you asked, but so far he has not said a word; and I don't want to be too pushy," Ernie added.

"I think it's time to use a wiretap. Ernie. How many times have you been married to Bessie and are you married, or divorced, now?" Tom asked.

"I've been married twice, and we are divorced now but the best of friends."

"I think it's time for you to get married again, Ernie, old boy," Tom said.

"What does my fucking marriage have anything to do with the price of cheese?"

"Dick, how would you like to be the best man at Ernie's next wedding?"

Dick started to laugh," It will be a pleasure to stand up for Ernie."

"Will someone please tell me what's going on?"

Chapter 37
Deceptive Wedding Bells

The mismatched elderly threesome, Ernie, Bessie, and Dick entered the opulent offices of "Smithfield and Weston Wedding and Events Planners."

"I'm Ernest Stubbs. We have an appointment with Mr. Weston," he told the receptionist. She did a double take and laughed silently, thinking the moon must be in a special orbit with all these old geezers suddenly getting married; probably a change in the Social Security laws.

"They are getting married and I'm the best man," Dick bragged enthusiastically.

"How nice, please have a seat. Mr. Weston is on the phone but will be with you shortly."

"Thank you," frail Bessie said.

"Pretty ritzy place," Ernie remarked, looking around at the enormous photographs of extravagant parties. "We can't afford this."

"Be quiet," Bessie nudged him and whispered, "We are not really getting married. Just play along."

"Are you going to wear a white dress, Bess?"

"Ernie, please behave yourself."

"I'm just trying to have a legitimate wedding conversation."

The receptionist invited the trio to follow her to Mr. Weston's office. Ernie's eyes brightened as he watched her shapely behind wiggle its way down the corridor. Emil Weston was a short, charismatic man with a poorly fitting toupee and an overly dark mustache. He wore a pink dress shirt with a Polo by Ralph Lauren monogram, gray slacks and black-tasseled loafers without socks. His smile was condescending, and there was an iciness in his eyes. He reminded Ernie of a crooked, used-car salesman.

Despite his farcical and effeminate demeanor, Emil's credentials as an event planner were unsurpassed. He organized the most exclusive parties and receptions around town. The photos in the lobby authenticated his accomplishments.

"How do you do, Mr. Stubbs," Emil said, putting out his hand.

"Just call me Ernie. This is my fiancée, Bessie Hudson, and best man Dick Reynolds."

"Okay, Ernie. It's a pleasure to meet you all."

"We want to get married," Ernie boasted nervously.

"Well, you have come to the right place. When are you planning the lovely nuptials?"

"Well at 86, I can't wait too long."

"In the spring," Bessie interrupted and gave Ernie a stare.

"How many guests are you thinking of inviting?"

"At least 200," Ernie threw out any number.

"Ernie, dear, that may be a bit too many." Bessie looked at him as if he were mad. He had two friends, a couple of kids with children, no siblings, the men in the cooking group and some questionable ones in the neo-Nazi group. Where in God's name did, he come up with that number? she wondered.

Dick surveyed the ostentatious office and walked over to examine the autographed pictures on Weston's walls.

"Oh, this photo of you and Tiger Woods looks great, but it's a little crooked." He straightened it out while attaching the most sophisticated listening device to its back. He moved further down.

"Wowee, look at this one with Mr. Weston and the president, Ernie. I'm so impressed," attaching a device to that one as well.

"I have worked with my share of distinguished people," Emil bragged proudly.

They began to discuss the details of the impending event. Ernie and Bessie argued over the choice of reception hall, invitations, food and beverages, and the choice of marriage service. Then there was more quibbling over the photographer, music, flowers and limousines. Emil Weston should have been given the Nobel Peace Prize for his diplomacy, negotiating skills, and patience in dealing with this bickering couple. Ernie and Bessie were at their theatrical best and having a hell of a ball in the process. Dick winked at Ernie.

"Emil, there are pictures in the reception area that show some really nice decorations," Ernie said.

"Let's go and have a look."

He and Bessie followed Emil out. Dick went into action, planting several more bugs including one in the telephone. Dick noticed Emil's cellphone and placed a minute device there quickly. He completed his task just as the threesome returned.

"I know we have to be more specific, and money is no object, but what ballpark per head are we looking at?" Ernie tried to sound cool and casual.

"Well, without all the details and, please don't hold me to it, I would say

I could bring it in for about $200-250 per person."

"No problem," Ernie gulped internally. That's $40,000; more than the cost of my condo, he thought. "Well, this has been great. I can't begin to tell you how helpful you have been, Emil. Looks like, with your help, we are going to have the best wedding in town."

"We aim to please."

"I have to take my little pumpkin home and go over all these notes. We have so much to discuss. Are you ready, dear?"

"Yes, love," Bess said, putting it on thick.

"So nice to meet you, Emil. I can't get over the number of celebrities you have on your walls. I'm very impressed," Dick said, acting impressed.

Emil escorted them out and watched the threesome toddle out of the office.

"That was a lively discussion, sir," the receptionist said. "I heard it all the way out here."

"I'm willing to bet that they won't survive the wedding planning process."

Tom Prentice was around the corner waiting to pick up the subversive trio. They headed to meet Sally Adams at Denny's where waitress Leonetta Moore practically barred them from the door.

"You not hurting my buddy Ernie, are you? Cause if you are, I am not letting you into the restaurant."

"No, Leonetta, we are up to only good stuff. Trust me, really good stuff," Ernie tried to pacify his food-serving protector.

"Well, praise the Lord. Go have a seat and I'll be right over to take your orders."

They ordered pie, ice cream and coffee all around. Ernie had a strange bacon-filled chocolate sundae with whipped cream topping, bacon shavings and a maraschino cherry at the summit, but at least it wasn't the kitchen sink.

By now the event planner surveillance bugs had been activated and the monitoring was turned over to a technical squad.

"Those devices may lead us to some clues about the actual assassination plot," Sally said.

"We had Emil Weston checked out and he looks pretty clean, with some mighty impressive credentials. He has a wide range of community and political connections, and is pretty philanthropic," Tom reported.

"Yeah, he gives away some of the money that he bilks from his wedding clients. I can't believe how much that man charges."

"We may be on a wild goose chase here," Sally said, "but we'll keep an eye on him."

"I looked into his eyes," Bess commented for the first time, "And there was something draconian about his stare."

"We need to try to find some indication of a Jewish connection," citing the swastika incidents, Sally said, mystified and trying to put a difficult piece of the puzzle in place. "Dick, please ask Franz and Art to keep as close an eye on Harry as they can. Monitor him to see where he leads us next."

"Harry Smith here," he answered his cellphone while trying to keep track of the numbers on the stock market tickers that were flashing by.

"Please hold on for the vice president, Mr. Smith."

Pause.

"Harry, how the hell are you?"

"Excellent, Sid, everything is copacetic. All systems are on target."

"Great, listen, Harry, I'm going to be in Orlando next Monday. I'm staying at the Bohemian Grand, speaking at the regional Orange County Chamber of Commerce dinner. Why don't you get a room at the hotel? I'll work it out to get away after dinner."

"Will do."

"See you soon."

"Operator, that's Monchengladbach, Germany, near Dusseldorf. I want to connect to Siegfried Scholes. No, not duffel bag, Dusseldorf. I can't hear you, operator," Otto Schaffer shouted into the phone.

After a long pause:

"Hallo."

"Siegfried? Otto here."

"Hallo, Otto, how are things?"

"EXCELLENT, THE PLANS FOR THIS TRIP ARE WONDERFUL"

"WHEN IS YOUR TRIP HOME, OTTO'?"

"FIVE WEEKS FROM TODAY, Siggy."

"IS THE WEATHER GOING TO COOPERATE?"

"THE SKIES OVERHEAD WILL BE CLEAR AND SUNNY," Otto assured. "I NEED A PAYMENT MADE TO MY LANDSCAPING COMPANY AT HOME WHILE I'M AWAY. WILL YOU PLEASE TAKE CARE OF IT?"

"Very good. ARE YOU PLANNING FOR A FEW DAYS REST IN THE CAYMAN ISLANDS ON THE WAY HOME?" Siegfried asked.

"YES."

"DON'T FORGET TO GIVE THE HOTEL YOUR CREDIT CARD NUMBER. How are the 'frauleins' in Orlando?" asked the 93-year-old lecherous Nazi.

"Hot, like the weather," replied the 85-year-old compatriot.

"You be careful, Otto."

"What harm can I do?"

"Don't ask."

"Please keep me posted."

"Auf wiedersehen, Siegfried."

***

Ernie grabbed a box of Twinkies from his kitchen cabinet, found his I-pad on the living room couch and collapsed onto his worn rocking chair on his screened porch. Past the point of exhaustion, he unfastened his prosthetic leg and shifted to find a comfortable position. He thought he might be ill, because he wasn't hungry or even motivated to dig into his favorite sweet for a change. There was so much going on; his head was spinning.

He was feeling slightly more secure with the outcome of this plan and beginning to trust Sally and Tom. It comforted him to have Dick, Art and Franz as co-conspirators. Ernie was proud of his involvement, yet he still felt miserable.

The next month was going to be most titillating. He prayed he would have the energy and the state of mind to see the project through. Ernie had always envisioned himself bent over and drooling in a wheelchair in the hall of some rancid nursing home at this age and never dreamed that he could be a deputy FBI agent about to foil a major anti-American plot. Although he wasn't thrilled about going to the shooting range on Saturday, it was critical for him to play along. He would do everything in his power not to shoot any of the group.

Breathing the fresh night air, Ernie got a strong whiff of meat cooking from a neighbor's barbecue. The scent reminded him it would be his turn to cook for the men in three weeks. He always took them out to Denny's for food, however feeling a brief adrenalin rush, he promised himself that for the first time in seven years, he would cook breakfast for the boys. Life was getting interesting, and the pot is beginning to boil very quickly, he thought as he plugged in his earphones and nodded off to sleep.

Chapter 38
The Yeast Is Rising

Exhausted and forlorn, Dick entered his home and hugged Ruth. Looking pale from her cancer treatment, she rose above her problems and concentrated on her tired war torn-looking husband. Feeling clammy and unsettled from his trip to see Emil Watson and the meeting with his pseudo FBI colleagues, Dick headed to the shower, but the water wasn't enough to have a relaxing effect on the former spook. He was tense and dreadfully worried about Ernie. There were too many variables floating around with nothing concrete happening. He didn't know if Ernie would survive this and while he understood how critically important the mission was, he was angry that Ernie had to go through the experience at his age and in poor health. Ernie certainly is a trouper, Dick thought, but was fearful that his resilience would not last.

He let the water shower down his frail body while trying to put some of pieces together. If his buddy wasn't going to assassinate the president, who was? If Ernie was being used as a decoy, what would they do with him after the mission was accomplished? Would they kill him? How were the desecrations of the synagogues related to the grand plan? He needed to check out the synagogue angle, thinking it might be a prime key to the puzzle.

Dick dressed in his tattered Bermuda shorts and tee shirt and joined Ruth for dinner. Both of them looked worn and bedraggled and barely able to eat the pot roast that Ruth had been cooking all day. Dick's mind was miles away and Ruth repressed her discomfort so as not to worry her mate.

"What's going on, Dick? You hardly touched your food."

"I'm very worried about Ernie. I think that he's up to his ears in a shitload of trouble and I don't see a way out."

"Please tell me what's going on. I can't stand seeing you like this."

Dick had never discussed CIA business with Ruth and had never brought his work-related tension home. He might have been the victim of a failed assassination attempt but would come home in a cheerful mood and say that everything was fine. She was used to this. So, the fact that he was so bothered made her realize it must be really serious. She took two cups of coffee and guided Dick to their living room sofa. Calmly, she talked with him and, finally, with tears streaming down his cheeks, he confided the entire mess to her. Ruth was a tough bird, but she too was moved to near tears by the seriousness and scope of the situation.

The ringing of the phone startled them. Bessie, in a state of near panic, was on the line. She couldn't find Ernie. He didn't answer his phone which was never the case at this time of night. She admitted her great fear about her best friend's predicament. Dick tried to soothe her and hung up with a promise to make sure that Ernie was safe. Ruth was sitting on the edge of the couch, listening to every word.

"You have to go and find him, Dick."

"I know. I'm on my way," he said, although he could barely get up, and headed for the door.

"Be careful."

"I will."

Dick got into his Edsel. He could have taken the SUV, but he wanted to be with his old friend for comfort tonight. He piloted the tank-like vehicle and headed the three miles to Ernie's condo. Dick was really worried when he noticed Ernie's car missing. Even though the lights were off in Ernie's condo, he cautiously rang the bell, but there was no answer. Ringing several more times, he began pounding on the door. Nothing. Getting a flashlight and his baseball bat, Dick walked around the building and counted the number of screened-in porches to find Ernie's apartment. The porch was dark too. The moon provided just enough light for him to see his buddy fast asleep in the rocking chair. A box of Twinkies sat unopened on a small table and two small speakers filled his ears.

"Ernie," Dick called. "Wake up, buddy."

"What, where…"

"Ernie, it's Dick. You need to wake up."

"What are you doing here in the middle of the night?"

"We were all really worried about you. Bessie called me in a panic when she couldn't get you on the phone."

"I must have fallen asleep with my favorite Roy Orbison tape playing and didn't hear the phone."

Ernie refastened his leg and Dick sat next to him in a beach chair.

"Have a Twinkie?"

"No, thanks. Listen, pal. I am downright worried about you. We are all concerned for your health and well-being. I'm afraid this may prove too much for you. I think it's time for you to get out while you can."

"But I can't, Dick. The FBI won't be able to prevent the attack without me."

"They'll manage, Ernie. But we won't be happy after you have a stroke, nervous breakdown or get killed."

"I need to see it through. I am a trusted undercover deputy FBI agent on a critical mission."

"Ernie, this isn't some fantasy television show. This is a very dangerous mission, and you are right smack in the middle of it. Let me call Sally Adams and tell her that you have to pull out."

"Then Sharif will get murdered."

"That doesn't sound right coming from you."

"I hate the man and would like to see him out of the presidency but not to go as far as killing him."

"Well, these so-called neo-Nazi friends of yours aren't kidding; they are planning to kill him."

"That's why I have to stay involved in order to stop it. I am committed."

"You should be committed, Ernie. You have acted heroically. You have alerted the powers that be that there is an attack brewing. Let the professionals handle it and bow out gracefully. You will still be a major hero."

"What will Sally say?"

"Thank you."

"What will I tell Harry and the boys?"

"That you are ill and have to end your involvement."

"What if they decide to kill me because I know too much?"

"We will all make sure that you are protected."

"You mean they will put me in the Witness Protection Program, change my identity, make me grow a beard and move me to the middle of the rattlesnake-filled Arizona desert all by myself without Bessie, never to be heard from again?"

"Ernie, come back down to reality; you are not going into witness protection. Come on, Ernie. Let's call Sally right now."

"She doesn't like to be disturbed at night while she is drinking."

"Ernie!"

"I don't know, Dick. I'll have to think about it."

"Think fast, my friend. In the meanwhile, you better give Bessie a ring and tell her you're okay. Tell her that you will giving all this up and prevent another heart attack."

Ernie scratched his bald head, closed his eyes and sat still. The only sound was a loon singing near the lake. Dick sat patiently to give him the space he needed.

"I've made up my mind," Ernie said forcefully. "I can't give up now. I need to do the American thing."

"Ernie."

"Are you sure that you don't want a Twinkie, Dick."

Chapter 39
Dueling Eggplants

The eleven would-be cooks were standing around the kitchen waiting for their weekly KP assignments. Ed Fisher, the persnickety retired scientist, was chef du jour. Everyone enjoyed him but weren't thrilled when he cooked. The food was always tasty, but that wasn't the issue. He was so finicky about his scientific ingredient measurements; it made all his kitchen assistants crazy. Edward fit into the younger curve of the group: he was in his early seventies. He was short, somewhat dumpy with thick spectacles, and was borderline careless with his appearance, always looked slightly rumpled.

From Long Island, he grew up a self- proclaimed "original nerd," a term he boasted was "originated by Dr. Seuss, as an individual who passionately pursued intellectual activities." Although a good soul and smart as a whip, he was incredibly mundane. Ed brought a whole new intellectual dimension to group.

"Cigars for everyone," beamed great-grandpa Abe, as he handed out the chocolate-wrapped smokes. "My granddaughter just gave birth to a baby girl."

"Congratulations, Abe, way to go. How is she?" Dick asked.

"Okay, it was a little rough; they had to do a cesarean section."

"I thought a cesarean section was a neighborhood in Rome," Ernie belted out from his Thursday morning perch.

"I'll make the coffee," Steve said, grabbing the coffee pot.

"Remember just put exactly 2 1/4 scoops of coffee in the filter," Ed instructed.

Science class was officially in session.

"I'm up to preparing the snack. English muffins today?" Wannabe-artist Steve asked.

"Make sure that you use only 12 muffins, wrap up the rest and ziplock them, a level teaspoon of butter on each, and cook them in the oven for no more than 3.5 minutes," Ed ordered.

"Yes, boss."

"Hey Ed, for Christ's sake, for once stop being such a prissy scientist and let loose," know-it-all Abe said.

From across the room came, "Did you know that Ed was a Scatologist?" Everyone turned and glared at Ernie.

"Pray tell us, Ernie, what is a Scatologist?" Club-leader Fred asked.

"Ed's specialty was the scientific study of excrement." At that point Joe started chasing Ernie around the kitchen to the cheers of the group.

"What's on the menu today, Doc?" Bill asked, as the boys finally settled down.

"We are starting with Waldorf salad which originated in 1893 at the famed Waldorf-Astoria Hotel in New York City. The salad was so popular that composer Cole Porter used the salad in one of his songs: 'You're the top, you're a Waldorf salad.' Then we move on to beef stroganoff, a Russo-Franco dish that came to us in the early 19th century and received its name from a Russian Imperial family. It will be served over noodles with roasted eggplant. For dessert we have a cherry tart, this cookie-like confection is offered up on a feast day that commemorates the birth of the Virgin Mary in Malta," Ed rattled off without taking a breath in his monotone voice.

Ernie dozed off on his chair during Ed's soporific presentation.

"Ernie has no sitzfleish," kidded German Franz.

"Speak English, Franz," good old Southern boy Art said.

"Oh, sitzfleish, he doesn't have any patience to sit and listen."

"Yup, that about sums it up," Charlie added.

"I need help with the salad, fellas."

With the fear of having to count cucumber seeds, suddenly everyone in the kitchen became busy with other things.

"I'm the dice and chop, man," Abe said.

"I'll help too," Fred acquiesced. They meticulously started cutting apples and julienning the celery. The salad was to be mixed with walnuts, mayonnaise and draped over a leaf of lettuce.

"Steve, would you please boil some water for the noodles?"

"Sure thing."

"We want a rolling boil," Ed elucidated.

"It will be rolling like 'Old Man River.'"

"How do you get holy water?" Ernie, now wide awake and raring to go, asked anyone who would listen.

"You boil the hell out of it," came Jewish partner Abe.

At that moment the director of the senior center walked in and asked for everyone's attention.

"Gentlemen, gentlemen"

Everyone began talking at once.

Dick put two fingers in his mouth and whistled loudly.

"What's up?" Fred asked.

The director began, "Have I got a deal for you: there's a Senior Cooking Recipe Contest taking place next month with the best recipe will be receiving a $500 prize. Why don't you select one of the dishes you've concocted, and I'll submit it? We can take a group picture to send with it. If you win, you would have a generous kitty for the group. I think that would be great."

The Old Men's Cooking Club Chorus sang out.

"What a neat idea."

"I think it's pretty terrific."

"We would be famous."

"We have seven years' worth of food dishes."

"Which will we choose?"

Now the pandemonium began.

Dick: "Fred makes a mean breast of chicken with spaghetti."

Steve: "It isn't fancy enough for a contest."

Fred: "Art's venison stew was a one-of-a-kind creation."

Abe: "Too rustic and the animal rights people would give us hell for cooking Bambi."

Joe: "How about the money-laundering chicken that Bill made. It was really tasty. What do you call it again ponzi chicken?"

Bill: "Ponzu chicken."

Ed: "Nah, the name is too controversial."

Art: "Franz's sauerbraten was mouth-watering."

Ernie: "Much too German."

The suggestions and rejections flew around the room a mile a minute. Each suggestion was louder and more passionate. The boys were having in a real pissing contest.

Steve: "What about the luscious guava-stuffed chicken with mango topping Charlie prepared? It was colorful and tasty."

Fred: "That's a possibility, but don't you think it's too froufrou for a bunch of macho men like us?"

Charles: "There's always the London broil Steve cooked. The meat was pink, beautiful and soft, like butter."

Ed: "Too ordinary. We need something unique."

Art: "Abe's Chinese pork tenderloin was pretty juicy and extremely flavorful."

Dick: "I guess Joe's catfish fillets wouldn't go over well."

Abe: "A bit too scary a dish."

Art: "Since when is catfish scary?"

Abe: "Cause to Northerners that is one strange-looking fish with those ugly whiskers."

The Director threw up her hands and marched out.

Joe: "What about Ed's beef stroganoff that we're cooking today?"

Ernie: "We haven't tasted it yet. We don't know if it's good."

"Ernie, that wasn't nice," three of them said in unison.

"Hey, fellows, we'll be here all day if we keep this up. Lunch is behind schedule. We have to get cooking, chop, chop," Ed broke in.

"Hey Ed, you're a pretty smart guy, so tell me why men get their best ideas in bed?" Ernie asked with his impish grin.

"I don't have a clue, Ernie."

"Cause they're plugged into a genius."

"Oh, Ernie, I think you're ready for the old age home," Ed said as he un-wrapped the beef tenderloin roast that he had pre-chunked at home. "Ernie, I have one for you. Sex is like math. You add the bed, subtract the clothes, divide the legs and pray they don't multiply," Ed rattled off with a straight face. If Ernie had recited this ditty, there would have been groans all around but since this was Ed's premiere joke of the day, the gang laughed enthusiastically out of respect.

Under Ed's scrutiny they measured the vegetable oil meticulously, patted out the butter precisely, chopped the scallions fastidiously, sliced the mushrooms vigilantly, and poured in the beef broth carefully. Because the recipe called for cognac, Ed pulled out a large silver flask from a shopping bag and carefully poured out five tablespoons.

"Look what Ed has, fellows. How about a swig?" former bartender and biker Joe said. The flask of contraband spirits was passed around and it loosened everyone up. All the precisely measured ingredients were added with loving and painful care to the saucepan. Steve whipped the heavy cream and blended it in.

Happy as a lark with his culinary masterpiece, Ed said, "I practice safe eating, I always use condiments," as he sprinkled in generous pinches of salt, pepper and dollops of Dijon mustard.

The creamy preparation was sautéed and then allowed to simmer. Art helped, basting the eggplant with olive oil and spices in a roasting pan and placed in the oven to brown.

Forty-five minutes later, Ed doled out precise lunch portions. The boys ate more quietly than usual. Even Ernie was reflective.

Art ate mechanically without tasting a bite. He was trying to put two and two together to understand all these covert activities. It was taxing his mind and body. Just a few days ago he was a mellow retiree who thought that his vegetable garden was exciting and going out for Carvel ice cream was a special treat. He felt so sorry for Franz and vowed to plough ahead and do anything he could to help his buddy.

Ernie, deeply troubled, shoveled his food into his mouth even faster than usual. The creamy sauce created rivers down his shirt. He shook his head over the dismal experience the shooting range had been the previous weekend. First, he thought, How on Earth would anyone believe that I had the capability of shooting a gun, let alone shooting the president? Then he thought about Bessie, she is such a docile soul, a wise old bird. Ever since last week she has been constant worrying about the event planner Emil Weston. "He had death in his eyes," she kept predicting. Ernie wondered what this celebration impresario could possibility have to do with the shooting of the president. Perhaps he is the shooter? He worried.

Dick was totally preoccupied too, just eating tiny morsels. He was trying to fit the pieces together about the Jewish community connection to the presidential plot and thought, was this going to be another decoy like with the assassination itself? But how was it going to work? He would have to do some spy work himself and he needed to involve Abe, the Jewish member in the men's cooking group.

Franz wasn't hungry either. His plate sat untouched and his stomach was in turmoil. He worried, what's going to happen to Harry? Everyone is pointing fingers at his involvement, but no one discussed what the outcome would be for him. Could he be killed? Would he go to prison for life? What about Ingrid, the children, and Anneliese? Harry seems involved in some heinous activities, but he is my son. Do I help him, support him, try to stop him, reason with him or betray him for the good of this country? All these thoughts depressed and confused the old man. He made it to the restroom just in time.

Gloom was rampant today and no one bothered to put the lights on in the computer dining room. The other boys sat around the tables in near darkness bemoaning the bottoming out of the stock market, the three wars that the country was involved in, funded by raiding their social security and Medicare accounts, and the overall grim political aura of the country. Unfortunately, no one really tasted Ed's delicious beef stroganoff.

"The sweet bing cherry tart dessert is served," bellowed Ed, turning on the light and trying to revive the group.

"I love cherry tart," Abe said, beginning to perk up.

"Me too," Steve said with a bit more enthusiasm.

Ed passed pieces of the colorful confection.

"This dessert brings back some very sexy memories for me," Ernie boasted. "Sixty-five years ago, I lost my cherry to a tart in Germany." That finally lit up the room.

During the clean-up Dick called Abe over to a corner of the kitchen. "Are you busy after lunch today? Could you meet me at Einstein's for a cup of coffee? There's something important that I would like your opinion on."

"Sure, Dick, I'd be happy to meet you there," he said." You know me, any chance for a bagel with a shmear of cream cheese and an opportunity to give my opinion."

As the men did every week, they gathered around Fred, the leader, before heading home. "Who is cooking next week?" asked Steve.

"We have a treat once again. Franz is the chef with Art, as his lovely assistant." Art assumed a silly grin.

"That's great," Joe said.

Ernie was still quiet, but then out of the clear blue sky, yelled, "I got it! I've got the winning recipe for the Seniors Cooking Recipe Contest. Ernest Stubbs' famous pork and beans!"

Chapter 40
Forbidden Fruits

Dick and Abe scurried around the bagel spot in search of a table among the bustling post-lunch crowd. Finally, they perched in a secluded corner booth that insured some privacy and sipped fruit iced teas. Abe munched on a bagel with a shmear of cream cheese.

"Abe, what I am about to tell you is strictly confidential."

"That's not a problem." Abe was genuinely intrigued as to why this retired CIA spook wanted his council.

Dick peered around the room, moved closer and whispered, "There is a plot to assassinate the President of the United States."

Shocked, Abe said, "What, you've got to be kidding. What's the scoop?"

"When he speaks at the Jewish Convocation here in Orlando in a couple of weeks. Franz, Art, Ernie and I are working with the FBI to try to foil it."

"You're shitting me?"

"I wouldn't kid you about something like that."

Dick went through the entire story: How Ernie had become embroiled with the neo-Nazis, all about Franz's son, Harry, their investment broker, and his involvement in the sordid business as well as the draconian plan itself. He reported the supremacists were preparing Ernie to be a decoy to take the spotlight off the actual assassination attempt. It was all very complicated, but Dick explained it in black and white. He also discussed his own suspicions that there may be another camouflaged, interwoven plan involving the local Jewish community to further throw off the actual deed.

"Unbelievable." Abe's face turned bright red. He was flabbergasted and replied. "What can I do to help?"

"Aren't you involved in the synagogue that had those swastikas?"

"Yes, I'm a member."

"Do you know the rabbi?"

"I do. Joel Tannenbaum, a real regular guy."

"Good, I want you to set up an appointment for the three of us to meet with him as soon as possible. We need to feel him out to see if there is anything suspicious. It could lead to some clues. I don't want to alarm him unduly. Let's just see if there's any indication that something may be awry."

"I'll call him today."

"Good. Remember we must keep this very quiet. I am not even telling the FBI folks about this synagogue visit."

"God help us all" was all Abe could say.

The following Monday, Harry and Otto enjoyed lunch in the opulent dining room of the grand old Orlando hotel.

Otto, on a quasi-holiday, temporarily liberated from Hilda's constant badgering about his food and health, was indulging in gastronomic suicide. His plate swelled with a mountain of greasy French fries and a juicy blood-rare, fatty hamburger sweating with mayonnaise, lettuce, tomatoes and pickles on a roll. His sweet soft drink put the finishing touches to the death-defying meal. Harry, while his food lacked the abundant caloric content, was indulging in the most extravagant item on the menu; a nine-ounce filet mignon accompanied by a double stuffed potato and roasted asparagus. In addition, he sipped an expensive red wine.

"Otto, you have to watch what you eat. That's much too rich for you."

"I greatly appreciate your concern but you're beginning to sound like Hilda," he said as he poured a heap of salt onto the burger.

"It's for your own good, Uncle."

"My own good is devouring this lovely burger with fries."

"I guess there is no warning you."

"You can tell me anything you want, just not what to eat," he chuckled.

"I spoke with Henry Thompson in Daytona today and the devices are just about ready. They are being imbedded in the soil of two large transplanting trees, one for each synagogue. They have to settle in the earth for a week before they are transported," Harry said. "We have to make payment to the nursery."

"I will make arrangements," Otto noted. "I understand that Sid Townsend will be in town tonight staying at this hotel. Will you get to see him?"

"Yes, he is delivering a dinner speech and we will meet here after."

"Excellent."

"There is no need for me to see him on this trip, Harry," Otto said.

"I agree."

"What about Weston?"

"Emil is ready to go. We have to pay him too."

"Will do. Waiter," Otto called. A tuxedo-clad server appeared. "Could I please have a triple scoop of vanilla fudge ice cream with chocolate syrup, whipped cream, and don't forget the cherry. As a matter of fact, make it two. Anything for you, Heinrich?"

"No, thank you, Uncle. I must get back to do some real work. If you need me, I'll be here this evening in Room 832."

Harry left Otto to enjoy his frozen orgy of sweet delights.

At 8:00 p.m., the hotel lobby was bustling with post-dinner activity and crawling with Secret Service. A large group of well-wishers gathered to shake the vice president's hand as he exited the Grand Ballroom. Townsend was the ultimate politician, a consummate glad hander, whose charismatic charm generated enthusiastic well-wishers wherever he went. The vice president's security surrounded him as they proceeded to the elevators. When they reached the eighth floor, Townsend asked his handlers to remain by the elevator to allow him some privacy with a major donor. He walked down the corridor alone and knocked on the hotel room door.

"Come in," Harry beckoned.

"Harry, it's lovely to be with you."

Harry had Chivas Regal, the vice president's spirit of choice, waiting. They sat in the parlor of the two-room suite, making small talk. There he brought Sid up to date on the operational plans. Sid praised Harry for his commitment and promised a White House appointment as soon as he assumed the presidency. Harry was elated. All this work will finally pay off, he thought. His major goal now was to make sure that the transition of power happened smoothly. Slowly the men moved closer and then embraced passionately. Sid rose from the sofa, pulling Harry up by the hand, and pointed towards the bedroom, "Let's consummate your new appointment, Harry."

Otto leaned against the oak-paneled hotel bar downing one drink after another, lapsing into a state of inebriation.

"You're cute, Grandpa."

"Danke," he replied, trying to focus his eyes on the striking brunette on the stool next to him.

"Where are you from, Papa?"

"Germany."

"A tourist?"

"Half business, half pleasure," his words slurred.

"What a coincidence, I'm in the business of pleasure," she took a napkin and patted his sweating brow. They talked, laughed, drank some more, and Otto brokered a staggering deal for her time. He could hardly stand but was helped by his professional companion. He reached into his pocket but could not find his room key.

"I need to stop by the front desk for my key."

Together, they sauntered to the reception desk. Otto was beaming to have a strikingly beautiful appendage that promoted cleavage on both ends. What would Harry think of him now if he saw what he had procured for the evening? He thinks there is no life left in this old battle axe, he thought. She had to physically hold him up at the reception desk as he hardly was able to enunciate his words.

"Room key, please?" His mind was a jumble. In a daze he told the clerk the room number that came to mind. Handing him a duplicate key, the very odd couple made their way to the elevators. As they exited on the eighth floor, he saluted the secret service men waving his room key as a pass before staggering down the corridor. Otto fumbled with the keypad and, with assistance, opened the door. The two of them headed straight to the bedroom. Otto almost fell but managed to open the door and to his horror saw Harry Smith in bed with Vice President Sid Townsend.

"HARRY?"

"OTTO?"

Chapter 41
Salt Peter and The Gates Of Heaven

On Tuesday morning Franz sat waiting at Starbucks for Art, Dick, and Ernie before they did the men's club shopping. He found a round table in the corner, ordered a light iced coffee, and nabbed a newspaper. Skimming the dreary world news, he read the latest daily dip in the popularity polls of the president and surveyed the ominous economic news. He chuckled at the comics and enjoyed a restaurant review of a new German Hofbräuhaus in Orlando.

Turning the page his eyes spotted a headline in the local news section:

"German Business Leader Found Dead In Downtown Hotel"

He read on in horror: 'Otto Shafer, a respected German financial mogul, was found dead late last night in his room at the Bohemian Grand Hotel. Initially the death was ruled a heart attack, but the medical examiner has some question and has not ruled out a suspicious cause. Mr. Shafer was in Orlando on business for Germany's Deutschebank and was last seen with an unidentified woman in the lobby of the hotel. He was 85 years old."

Franz was stunned, and tears began falling. Oh my God, Otto. I didn't even know that he was in town, he thought to himself. Otto was a longtime friend and former army buddy. His heart suddenly bled for Hilda being so far away, and he wondered about the mysterious women. Hilda would know that from the press accounts. He thought about his daughter-in-law, Ingrid, Harry's wife, who was like a daughter to Otto. I wonder where Harry fits in this picture, a grimmer thought. Poor Anneliesse, he grieved. She was unaware Otto was in Orlando either. Things are getting so complicated.

Art bounced into the café in a jovial mood, "Top of the morning to you, Mr. Franz."

"Oh."

"Franz, what's the matter? You look like you've seen the ghost of your mother."

Franz handed him the paper. "Take a look. That's my old buddy, Otto. It was him who was involved in this dreadful mess."

"Jesus H. Christ," bemoaned Art, skimming the article, his color changing from bright pink to dark red. He remembered Otto from his Army days as a guard and just recently had suspected that his former German prisoner was up to his eyeballs in this sordid affair. He felt genuinely unhappy for his best new buddy, Franz.

***

At the very moment Harry was in a panic, pacing in front of the windows of his penthouse office. There was no way he could eat his bagel that sat on his desk. His mind was racing, a jambalaya of emotions. Last night had been such a mishmash, ending in utter disaster. It began with his excitement at the possible appointment as a senior advisor in the White House. It was followed by a very gratifying carnal experience with Sid, which deteriorated rapidly with Otto's appearance. Now he envisioned his life and career in total ruins. Harry had believed that Otto wouldn't betray him and Sid, but there was too much at stake. Otto's discretion would cost Harry and Sid dearly. To make matters worse, Harry had more than 50 messages on his desk from clients who were panic-stricken about their portfolios in the terrible economy. "When it rains, it pours," Harry moaned.

He pushed away the untouched food, grabbed his remote-control and flipped on the local news. He was stunned to see a photograph of his dear friend, mentor, and partner, Otto Shafer. He fumbled and turned up the volume.

".... Orlando police said that it was too early to determine the cause of the German financier's death, but that they were not ruling it out that it might be suspicious."

He couldn't believe it and fell backwards into his chair, staring blankly into space. After a few moments, the initial shock began to wear off and he was plagued by a sudden wave of melancholy, relief and enormous guilt. Pulling himself out of his funk, he fought to strategize a plan. He had to call Siegfried Schloss in Germany. Franz, Anniliese and Ingrid did not even know that Otto had been in town and he would have to invent some story about that. Things were indeed very delicate. He dialed overseas.

"Ya."

"Siegfried, It's Harry here in Florida," he said sadly.

"Well, Heinrich, good to hear from you, my boy. How are things?"

"We have trouble, Siegfried. Otto died last night."

"Ach du lieber, how did it happen?"

"The press is saying it was possibly a heart attack, but they are not ruling out homicide."

"So how do we proceed from here?"

"There are no changes to be made. The finances are under control, and our plans will move forward as scheduled. I have an appointment today with our engineer. I don't want to call the police for information.

"Zayer gut. Does Hilda know?"

"I don't know. I found out through the news. I will have to call her."

"I am so, so sorry. Please keep me posted. Let me know if there is anything I can do," his voice trailed off weakly.

Suddenly, Harry had a paralyzing headache.

"Harry Smith," he said quietly into his phone.

"Hi, Harry. It's Sid," came the voice from the vice president's plane.

"Did you hear?" Harry asked.

"Yes. It's for the best."

***

Two miles down the road, Dick and Abe were in the study of Rabbi Joel Tannenbaum of Temple Tikvah, or Temple of Hope.

"Shalom, Abe, it's good to see you. How's Paula?" the rabbi said, offering drinks.

"She's fine, rabbi. Busy with her mahjong set. Meet my friend, Dick Reynolds."

"It's nice to meet you, Mr. Reynolds, welcome."

"Rabbi, thank you for taking the time to meet with us. I am just an old fool with nothing to do since I retired from the CIA. So, please just consider me a busybody, but like so many people, I have been intrigued and bothered by the swastikas on the synagogues."

"Naturally we are extremely concerned and very puzzled by these episodes," the rabbi replied.

"Do you suspect there might be something else in the works? Anything out of the ordinary you've heard lately which makes you think this is not over, or is perhaps related to something else?"

"No, nothing. We have had our ear to the ground in the community and everything comes up negative. The FBI tells us that a neo-Nazi group in the outskirts of the city is currently dormant, and not a cause for alarm."

Suddenly there is a loud knock on the door.

"Come in," the rabbi said. An assistant brought in a letter marked personal. He excused himself while he opened it and found a note from an anonymous synagogue member who was contributing a dozen trees to be planted in two weeks at front of the temple. The note said, "To enhance the beautiful landscaping for our house of worship."

The rabbi shared the note with them but couldn't imagine this would be a problem. He even speculated who had made the gift.

"It has to be Jack Cohen. He does things like that: anonymous gifts. He wants to do good deeds but doesn't want every other charity in town on his doorstep. I can't blame him."

"Is there anything else you can tell us, rabbi?"

"Dick, may I call you Dick?"

"Of course, rabbi."

"What do you suspect, Dick? You must have an idea you're not telling me."

"There is speculation that another attack is on the horizon. So, please be very vigilant, rabbi. I don't know anything else concrete right now, but I assure you that I will share any information as soon as I have it."

"I feel very nervous from this conversation, Dick. I feel that the world out there knows something I don't."

"Just be observant, rabbi. We'll figure this out. Again, please forgive this old man for butting in."

"Thank you, Dick."

"Here is my cell number. Please call me or Abe at any hour if you hear about anything suspicious. Thank you, rabbi."

"Shalom."

As the two left, the rabbi's phone rang.

"Hello, Joel."

"Hi, Seymour."

"Guess what, Joel? I received a hand-delivered letter from an anonymous congregant informing me that he was donating a dozen trees to be planted on our temple's lawn. It said, 'To enhance the beautiful landscaping for our house of worship'."

"I got the same letter, Seymour. Something is very wrong."

"What do you think?"

"I'm not sure. I'll get back to you. Hold on tight." He quickly hung up and called Dick.

Dick was late. He huffed into Starbucks apologizing for his lateness. Franz, Art and Ernie were already sitting with cool drinks looking like zombies.

"What gives, boys?" Dick asked.

"Otto Shafer is dead. I believe he was Harry's German contact for business here in Orlando," Franz said.

"How did it happen?"

"They don't know. It could be a heart attack or foul play."

"Will it spoil their operation?"

"Who knows?"

"He was my old friend and army buddy," lamented Franz. "We served as prisoners of war in the States, but he never gave up his Nazi leanings. Even today he still believed that the Third Reich would be rejuvenated and save the world." Franz became teary-eyed.

"Well, fellas, we have work to do, places to go, food to shop for. Let's pick ourselves up and get a move on," Dick said, trying to revive the disheartened troops when his phone rang. He answered, listening patiently and said "Yes, rabbi, something is really rotten in Orlando."

Chapter 42
Aisles of Adventure

Three tired old men wearing baggy Bermuda shorts and tee shirts and the fourth in suit pants and a dress shirt formed a train in their electric handicap shopping carts that rolled them up and down the Publix supermarket. It resembled a geriatric version of the Disney World Monorail. Produce Land was the first stop in their grocery adventure park. Ernie trying to add levity to their dour situation by grabbing a heavy Crenshaw melon and tossing it to Dick, almost hitting him in the head.

"That was close, Ernie," as he barely caught the pass.

"Act your age, Ernie," Art laughed, a bit revived.

"At my advanced stage, I am acting my age."

Dick put down the melon and started juggling four vine ripe tomatoes priced at $4.00 a pound. "Hey Art, catch." He tossed a tomato to his buddy. Art caught it, getting off his buggy and hobbling around the counter to tag him out.

Meanwhile, "This hothouse cucumber looks like a large dick," Ernie playfully massaged the fourteen-inch pole.

"How would you know what a large penis looks like, Ernie?" Dick asked.

"I got my share of footage. It doesn't extend like it used to, but plenty of meat is still there."

Franz was on the verge of being shocked, but after hanging out with these boys, especially Ernie, he laughed and took it all in.

Rolling further down the vegetable aisle, Franz became wildly excited to see that they had bunches of white asparagus.

"I can make 'Spargal,' white asparagus with melted butter. Wunderbar," Franz said as he fondled the bunch of the thick vegetables. He hesitated and then added, "It looks like a bunch of 'mannliches geshlechtsorgans."

"What's that?" Dick asked.

"How do you say it in English, penises?"

"We finally did it, fellows. We corrupted Franz. Shouldn't we be ashamed of ourselves?" Art cackled.

"Nah," came Dick.

"I haven't groped melons like these in 60 years," Ernie said feeling up two cantaloups.

They filled their carts with parsley, onions, leeks, carrots, celery, garlic, fresh rosemary, thyme and bay leaves.

"I need marjoram," Franz searched the shelf for a bunch of the green aromatic herb of the mint family.

"That sounds like marijuana to me," Ernie smirked.

"Why don't you try smoking it, Ernie?"

"What are you cooking anyway, Franz?" Ernie asked.

"A special dish just for you, Ernie; simmered pickled pig's knuckles." Franz tried to keep a straight face.

"I guess I won't be at the cooking group this week."

"Just joking, Ernie, I'm just joking. I'm making a special dish 'Beschwipster Huhn,'"

"What the fuck is that?"

"Drunken chicken in red wine sauce."

"Is the chicken drunk before they kill it? They don't allow drunks at the senior center, you know."

"I am also serving German potato salad, the white asparagus, dumplings, Bavarian bread, and Black Forest cake for dessert."

"Potatoes," Franz said, reaching for a five-pound bag of red potatoes.

They rode in tandem to Bakery Land.

"I need day-old bread," Franz asked the baker.

"We only carry fresh bread, sir."

"But my recipe calls for day-old bread."

Dick used some of his CIA logic with Franz. "If you buy it today and use it tomorrow, it will be day-old bread, Franz."

"Very true, I never thought of that. You're so smart, Dick."

They grabbed several packages of corn muffins as bait to keep the group satisfied while the cooking took place. Franz, an unusually honest man, decided to cheat. Guiltily, he selected a sweet aromatic, hot-out-of-the-oven Black Forest cake and added it to the cart.

The next stop was Meat Land. Franz selected bacon for the chicken dish and wavered over several different varieties of chicken thighs.

"I like my dark meat plump and juicy," Ernie explained to the group, who by now ignored the remark.

They traveled up and down the aisles. Franz was the lead engineer in this electric wagon train and Ernie's served as the caboose.

"Stop here. I need kosher salt," Franz said.

"I didn't think a former Nazi would use kosher salt," Ernie said, laughing at his own joke.

"This former Nazi does." Franz said loudly, and several nearby shoppers turned around with shocked expressions and walked away.

They tooted over to Dairy Land to get milk, eggs and butter, then passed the starches and stocked up on brown rice flour. Nutmeg, chicken broth and pepper rounded out the list.

"On to Happy Land," yelled Ernie, as they entered the home stretch to Wine Kingdom.

"We need a red cooking wine." Franz said, looking at the shelves.

"I found one. Here's a cooking wine," Art said, holding up a bottle of red wine.

"Never use wine that specifies it is for cooking," Dick said.

"I didn't know that."

"If you wouldn't drink it, you shouldn't cook with it."

"You learn something new every day," Franz said.

"Hey, guys, I found the perfect wine and it's cheap too," Ernie said as he rolled over to them, brandishing a large box of red wine.

"Ernie, there is no way that we are going to use a box wine for my cooking."

"I was just trying to be economical. After all we are not drinking it in a glass. "You're just going to splash it into the stew. Who's is going to know the difference?"

"I will."

They selected a Little Roo Cabernet Sauvignon that was promoted on the buy-one, get-one-free table and propelled their carts to the checkout. The boys then ditched their disability vehicles Ernie pulled out a wad of crumbled food coupons.

"Are any of these good?" he asked the cashier.

"They are all good, sir, but you have to buy the products for each."

The checkout line stretched up the aisle as the sweating cashier looked through the 50 or so coupons, trying to match products. He finally gave up and included most of the discounts. Ernie was pleased with his accomplishment.

As Franz and Dick left the store, Frank noticed Harry and Pete talking to a strange-looking short man standing by a green Ford pick-up truck. Harry handed an envelope to him and continued chatting.

"Doesn't he ever work?" Wondered Franz.

"This looks suspicious." Dick scrutinized the scene. "Listen, Franz, you and the boys go to your cars and stay out of sight. I'm going to meander over and see if I can hear anything." He crouched down and slipped into a lane near the truck.

The short farmer explained about the delivery and clarified the tree-planting process. The men shook hands, and the gardener headed off. Dick scrambled back to the group.

"I couldn't hear everything, but it was something about a tree delivery and installation," Dick said and then remembered the rabbi's anonymous letter to the temple and the call from the other rabbi. These were significant clues, he deduced. He didn't have all the details of the plot, but he did write down the name and address of the culprit from his truck:

Hidden Garden Nursery and Landscaping Corporation, Daytona, Florida

Henry Thompson, proprietor

Dick quickly dialed his cell.

"Can we get them by tomorrow morning? We need four of them. Wonderful, you're a love. I owe you one.

Chapter 43
High, Low, High, Low, It's Off to Cook We Go

"It's a beautiful day in the neighborhood. A beautiful day for a neighbor. Would you be mine? Could you be mine? Please won't you be my neighbor?" Fred Davis, not Fred Rogers, sang loudly as he strolled towards the weekly cooking extravaganza. It was a magnificent day: the lemon-yellow sun was shining high, the cerulean sky was clear, and the usual virulent humidity was hardly hanging in the air. The aches and pain meter would be registering in the lower range of the medical Richter scale. The boys almost bounced into the kitchen in relatively jovial moods. Fred happily began filling the weathered coffee pot. "Is there life before coffee?" he sang out.

"Don't make it too weak," Steve asked.

"Don't criticize the coffee, Steve You may be old and weak someday."

"We are old and weak," Charles added.

"How do you know that man, not woman, made the coffee in biblical times?" macho biker Joe asked.

"I didn't know that you were a religious man, Joe?" Abe said.

"I'm not, just answer the fucking question."

"Okay, we give up" came a chorus of anticipated groaners.

"He-brew."

Franz stood at the counter, unpacking the groceries for his feast. Aside from his traditional uniform, a starched white shirt and brown striped tie, he wore Ingrid's red polka dotted apron. The merry old cookers took every opportunity to make cracks about his culinary garb. Everyone thought Franz looked good in red. The boys became suspicious when Art waltzed into the kitchen wearing a blue dress shirt with silver cufflinks, a grey striped tie and slacks followed by Ernie who practically gave away the mission, wearing a red and white dotted bowtie on a freshly pressed white shirt, dress pants and his Sunday best red suspenders. No one had ever witnessed these guys in anything but ragged shorts and faded tee shirts. Speculation about this fashion parade were rampant.

"Okay, what gives, fellas? This isn't Halloween," Joe pitched the first low blow.

"Are you guys going to church after lunch today?" Bill asked.

"Dressed like that they should be asking for forgiveness," came wise-cracking Abe.

"We are going on a mission," Ernie bellowed. Art gave him a sharp look to be quiet.

"Sounds suspicious. Anything you care to enlighten your best cooking buddies about?" Charles asked.

"Let's just say it's a pastoral pilgrimage and leave it at that," Art said.

"My God, they are turning religious," Jewish Abe said, making the sign of the cross on his chest.

Joe threw in a zinger, "Maybe Ernie is converting to Judaism?"

"Not in this lifetime," Ernie rapidly returned the volley, continuing "Hey Franz, what do they call their pastors in Germany?"

"I don't have a clue."

"German Shepherds."

It was going to be one of those mornings.

"Stop fooling around, friends. We have a lot of work to do to get lunch on the table," Franz said, finally taking command.

At that moment, Dick came running in like a house on fire. He was also dressed semi- professionally in a white shirt and red tie. "Sorry I'm late, fellows, I had to make a stop. How are we doing with lunch?"

"There is way too much intrigue around here today. I'm exhausted from all this," Charles piped up.

Boring scientist Ed plated the corn muffins in precise straight rows on a platter and set them by the coffee pot. Each member owned private equity in the kitchen: an individually labeled coffee mug.

"First, we'll create the 'semmelknoedel,'" Franz told the group.

"Don't talk dirty to me, Franz," Ernie said.

"Sorry, Ernie. It's Bavarian bread dumplings."

"Ed, would you please rip the bread into small pieces."

"Sure thing, chef."

"You're using moldy, stale bread," Ernie said.

"It's day-old bread, not stale bread, Ernie; I just don't want it to be too soft."

"Abe, how about sautéing the onions, parsley, marjoram in butter for me?"

"Next, we'll stir in eggs, onions and nutmeg with the breadcrumbs and let it set. For the potato salad, we cook the potatoes in their skins for 20 minutes," Franz filled a pot with water, dumped in the potatoes and placed them to the stove. "Preparations for the Drunken Chicken in Red Wine

Sauce commence now. We start by frying some bacon that we will also use for the potato salad." The boys were standing around very engrossed. This was turning out to be an intriguing cooking class.

The potato salad was assembled, and the chicken was inebriated with wine before being laid to rest in the oven.

"I love cooking with wine," Franz beamed cheerfully.

"Sometimes you even put it in the food," Steve laughed.

"That joke is as old as you are, Steve," Abe said.

"You're not old. Ernie is old."

"Thanks a lot, fellows."

"Ernie is so old that when he goes into a restaurant and orders a three-minute egg, they ask for money up front," Joe added.

"Very funny. Just hilarious," Ernie said caught slightly off guard and taking some of his own medicine.

"You know there's an old saying, 'what wine will not cure, there is no cure for,'" Charles said, burying the empty bottle in the bottom of the trash can.

"Frank Sinatra said, 'I feel sorry for people who don't drink. They wake up in the morning and that's the best they are going to feel all day,'" Abe said.

"I don't drink much. What about you guys?" Fred asked.

"Robert and I drink wine every night," Charles said.

"Red wine is good for your heart" came Ed the scientist.

"Why don't Jews drink?" Spewed another Ernie special.

"This better be good," Abe said with a skeptical look.

"Because it interferes with their suffering."

"Ernie, you are incorrigible."

"I drink only beer and have an authentic belly to prove it," Joe bragged, jiggling his bulging stomach.

"I feel euphoric when I drink," Steve said.

"Speaking of euphoria, I won a free eight-day Caribbean cruise for Bella and me," Ed reported gleefully. "I never won anything before in my life."

"So, what was the catch?" Charles asked.

"They told me we just had to go to a presentation, with no obligation to buy."

"That sounds like the old timeshare scam," Abe shared.

"No, this was for a travel club. So last Sunday we went to a hotel near Disney World to collect our prize."

"I went to one of those," Abe quipped. "It was a brutal experience."

"This three-hundred-pound gorilla badgered us for three hours. He

199

reminded me of a carnival barker: loud, brash, oleaginous with a patter faster than a speeding bullet."

"What the hell is OLOGINOUS?" Ernie asked.

"Oleaginous means slimy."

"Oh, like most attorneys."

"Anyway, during the long travel club presentation, I learned everything about his personal life and hardly anything about travel. They wouldn't reveal the membership price."

"They are supposed to do that to make you feel comfortable," Abe spouted again.

"Well, let me tell you, it was starting to make me feel very uncomfortable. So, I called out, 'what does the program cost?' He went on to explain about all the wonderful travel bargains that would be ours. He then told us that renewing each year would only cost about $200 or $150 if you let them take it out of your bank account automatically."

"I wouldn't let anyone near my bank account," Ernie said.

"I thought you kept all your money hidden in your spare plastic leg, Ernie," came Joe.

"So, Bella and I looked at each other," Ed continued. We couldn't afford much, but certainly a couple of hundred dollars a year for all these travel bargains sounded good. 'What's the membership fee?' I called out again. He gave me an icy stare. He was going to tell me when he was good and ready."

"Yeah, they hold you captive and play by their time rules," Bill agreed.

"He went on about himself and I was getting impatient listening to him pontificate about his sex life. Then he gets to the bottom line and tells us that this is a reduced membership fee for ten years of service and it is only good today, tomorrow it doubles, of course. He proclaimed it to be the bargain of a lifetime at only $8900 payable in cash, check or credit card."

"Wow, that's highway robbery," from frugal Bill.

"Well, Bella and I are out of our chairs faster than his verbal projectiles but are barred at the door by this snot-nosed kid salesman who has us sit with him for a talk in the lounge."

"That's where they try to get you," Abe said.

"Yeah, they put on all the heat."

"'Did you ever see a better deal?' the sales punk said, so excited for me," Ed continued. "We listened politely and then I told him that I needed to think it over and wouldn't be able to decide today. 'Why not?' he pushed repeatedly. 'Cause I won't,' I kept saying, but he wouldn't listen and keeps hammering, pushing and prodding at me. My blood pressure is stirring like lava in a mountain and Bella is looking at me, waiting for the volcano to explode. He was relentless. Finally, I yell out so everyone in the room can hear, 'What don't you understand about I have to think it over?'"

"I would have punched him," Ernie said, up in arms.

"I had the same exact experience," Abe said, reliving a painful memory.

"'I want to go home' I finally said. 'Well I'm just trying to do my job,' he pushed. 'You are doing your job, but I have had enough of you doing your job.'"

"You must have been exhausted," Steve said.

"Drained would be more like it. Anyway, he disappeared and returned with this big burly man who was introduced as the manager. 'How was our presentation?' he asked. 'Much too pushy and upsetting,' I respond. 'I am so sorry.' He is trying to be humble. 'I don't train my boys to push over the line.'" He then went on to push harder and continued by telling us that he could arrange financing today and even let me pay half today and half in six months.

Franz had left the stove to came over to the boys standing around Ed. Suddenly the smoke alarm went off with a piercing siren. The boys rushed over.

"I guess the chicken is ready," said Ernie.

"Is anything burnt?" Joe asked.

"Everything is fine," Franz assured them, pushing the smoke from his face. "Lunch will be ready very soon."

"So, what happened with the free cruise?" Steve asked.

"Well, now the manager is relentless and goes on and on. I finally say, 'Give me my fucking cruise so I can get out of here.'

"I never heard Ed say fuck before, fellas. He must have been seriously pissed," Abe said.

"Yeah" came Charles.

"Did you get the trip?" Ernie was curious.

"Yep, and we only have to pay $350 per person for taxes and port fees if we want the eight-day cruise."

"That must have been a grueling experience," Bill said.

"It was horrendous."

"So, where are you going on your vacation?" Abe asked.

"Who can afford the $700," Ed said, and they all laughed.

Lunch was dished out. Franz filled each plate with the bread dumplings, laid out the intoxicated chicken, rich potato salad, and white asparagus, as Franz put it, that looked like penises.

It was such a beautiful day that Franz, Art, Ernie, Dick, and Abe took their plates outside to the picnic table. This assured an idyllic lunch and some privacy from the rest of the boys. Considering the stress, they were experiencing, their moods seemed stable, for the moment.

"Abe, you are one of us now, and we can't emphasize discretion enough," Dick said.

"I am totally with you guys."

"Well, after lunch, the four of us are off to Daytona on a very delicate mission," Dick continued and explained that he suspected explosive devices might be attached to trees that were being anonymously donated to the two synagogues. It was their mission to gather some evidence and turn it over to the FBI.

"Dick, that's a brilliant assumption about the landscaping explosives," Art exclaimed. "You must have been a cracker jack CIA operative."

"Aw shucks thanks, Art, it was nothing. To tell you the truth, I read the premise in one of bestselling author David Baldacci's espionage thrillers."

The well-fed picnickers hobbled back into the kitchen to join the group patter.

"Hey, where were you guys?" Steve asked.

"You boys have a secret or something?" Joe questioned.

"Can't a person get some fresh air on a beautiful day in Florida," Ernie asked.

"Ernie, you are so full of hot air that no amount of fresh air could possibly help you," said Joe.

Slices of the store-bought chocolate Black Forest cake with a crown of whipped cream were passed around to all.

"That was a great meal, Franz. I ate much too much and am starting to get some heartburn." Joe was uncomfortable.

"I have some Tums," Charles said, searching his pocket.

"Thanks, but no thanks. I'm all excited. I finally found a dish that gives me heartburn directly after I eat it instead of at three in the morning."

"Speaking of heartburn, I have chronic indigestion from following the stock market," Fred said.

"Yeah, my acid reflux dances up and down as fast the stocks in my portfolio," Bill admitted.

"Who's got a portfolio these days?" Steve asked. "I have a brown envelope full of worthless stock certificates."

"I got plenty of nothin' and nothin's plenty for me," Abe started singing and everyone laughed.

"Hey Bill, how is our group investment doing?" Ed asked.

"I don't know. To tell you the truth I haven't been able to reach our broker, Harry Smith, in a week. The economy is so volatile that he must be jammed up."

"At least someone is making money. Brokers do well in the best and worst of times," Steve said.

"Bill, you're the money man. What's the latest dope on Wall Street?" Fred asked.

"My son," replied Bill.

"Congress is all fucked up too. Looks like we are going to have a civil war on the floor of the House of Representatives," Joe piped in.

"I call it the House of Reprehensibles," Ernie added.

"That was a delicious lunch," Charles said to Franz. "You need to move here permanently, so you can cook for us all the time."

"You truly flatter me, boys. I am deeply touched." A tear of emotion started trickling down the German's face.

"Who's cooking next week?" Bill asked.

"Ernie," Fred announced.

"I guess it's Denny's again," someone piped up, joking.

"No, fellows, I am cooking," Ernie boasted proudly.

"What?" from Abe.

"I think I'm going to faint from shock." Steve said theatrically.

There was dead silence in the room. This was a historic moment for the Old Men's Cooking Club.

"Someone snap a picture of this Kodak moment," Dick said.

"I didn't know you could cook, Ernie," Charles ventured.

"I can't. Let me tell you about my cooking. When I go into the kitchen, the onions cry." They all laughed. "But you guys have been so good to me, and put up with so much, I am going to take the plunge and cook lunch."

They all lifted their plastic water cups in unisson and said. "Here's to the stomach pump."

Dick rounded up his three partners in crime suggesting they all leave together. Franz dished out the leftovers for the boys to take for their wives to sample. The other guys finished the washing up, put the folding chairs back, and started heading for their cars.

"Sorry that you had such a bad experience with those travel shysters," Abe said to Ed as they left the Center.

"Thanks, Abe. Let me tell you something, my colonoscopy was more fun."

Chapter 44
The Great Tree Imposters

The four imposters headed to Daytona. Ernie persuaded Dick to use his black SUV for this mission. "It looks like the vehicles used by the agents on 'CSI – Crime Scene Investigation.'"

"Hey Dick, where's the Edsel?" Franz asked.

"It's in the quiet comfort of its home, my garage. That's where I should be right now."

As they breezed along at 70 miles per hour, Dick handed out the fake identification cards his friend had produced overnight.

"Hey, look at this; 'Ernest S. Stubbs, Senior Inspector, Department of Agriculture, State of Florida.' What do you know? First, I am a Deputy FBI agent, and now an official Senior Inspector for the government. Well, they got the senior part correct, but I don't have a clue about vegetation. I even make Bessie do my produce shopping."

"That title will look good on your resume, Ernie," Art said with a straight face.

"Resume, shmesume. What do I need a resume for? I haven't worked in 25 years."

"You never know, Ernie, things could get bad, and you might have to go back to work."

"Who in their right mind would hire a one-legged, eighty-six-year-old, the cream of the crop of the American workforce?"

"No one, that's for sure," Art said.

"Things are bad, fellows. The government is all fucked up and congressmen are only out for their own political gain. My taxes are going up, my benefits are going down. They are diddling around with my Social Security and Medicare programs. It's so depressing. All this intriguing spy work has given me a new lease on life. But to tell you the truth, a couple of months ago I was so depressed that I didn't rule out putting an end to things."

"Ernie, that doesn't sound like you," Dick said.

"Things looked mighty bleak. So, one night I even called one of those suicide hotlines. The first thing I had to press was one for English. Then I got connected to a call center in Pakistan. I told them I was suicidal. The counselor got all excited and asked me if I could drive a truck."

"Ernie, I don't believe that one iota."

"I was just putting you on, guys. I'm here for the duration."

"Okay, fellows, you need to focus here. You are all senior inspectors from the State Department of Agriculture," Dick instructed.

"How do I speak intelligently about trees and greens? I have the opposite of a green thumb. I don't keep plants in my house. Bessie has the green plants. They just don't live for me. Some of them don't even wait to die; they see me coming and commit suicide."

"I have a little garden at home in Regensburg. We have all kinds of vegetables and flowers." Franz began longing for his safe home surroundings and idyllic garden back in Germany. "But gardening requires lots of water. Most of it comes from the sweat pouring down my forehead."

"Knowledge is knowing that a tomato is a fruit; wisdom is not to put it into a fruit salad," Art laughed. The four elderly cooks were having fun.

"All right, fellows, let's get down to serious business," Dick said trying to refocus them.

"What's our mission?" Art asked.

"As you know, I suspect they're developing major explosive devices somewhere on the grounds of the landscaping business. I believe that several bombs are being built to attach to trees which will be planted on the grounds of two synagogues in Orlando. Putting two and two together, I believe that these explosions will be used as a tactic to divert attention from the real plot to assassinate the President when he speaks at the Jewish Convocation in a few weeks. Now, all of this is a hunch but there are a number of clues that point in that direction."

"So, what are we inspecting for?" Franz asked.

"Undercover, we are looking for any possible indication that a laboratory or workshop exists there to build the bombs. We need to comb the entire property and note anything that will lend credibility to my theory."

"But we need to have a cover to make the inspection legitimate," Art said.

"The 'Halyomorpha Halys,' gentlemen."

"The what?" Came Ernie.

"The brown marmorated stink bug. We are investigating the infestation of this vegetation-eating pest that is killing trees and plants up and down the East Coast and has just spread into Florida. While the bug mostly attacks fruit trees and berry plants, and is not harmful to people, it is such a new specimen in the state that I'm sure our landscaping folks won't have heard about it. Therefore, we will tell them that it is dangerous to humans and gets into homes causing all kinds of damage, giving us an excuse to inspect inside their buildings as well."

"Why do they call it a stink bug?" Ernie piped up.

"Because it stinks."

"I'm nervous, Dick, we don't know enough about this 'Halle Berry Bug' to appear to be experts," Ernie said, showing his seriousness.

"Just look around and act very suspicious of everything, I'll do most of the talking."

When they approached their destination, Dick told them more about the wildlife and the property they were to inspect. He had Googled the site plan and had a good lay of the land. They drove into the parking lot of Hidden Garden Nursery and Landscaping Corporation, got out and formed a posse that looked highly professional and mighty intimidating. The four phony inspectors moseyed side by side down the main drag of the dirt parking lot, looking like a scene out of "The Gunfight at the O.K. Corral."

"Henry Thompson, please," Dick inquired very professionally.

"Who's asking?" an unfriendly young farmer-type asked.

"Inspectors from the State of Florida Department of Agriculture."

"He's busy."

"Well, tell him to become un-busy," Dick bullied.

"I can't do that."

"Don't beat around the bush with us, son. Tell him that he can come out and meet with us now or meet with us in the state capital after we padlock the center and confiscate all the plants and trees. Does that make it clear? Men get ready to close the place down," Dick was growling like a tiger and shot the impertinent young clerk an icy stare. Ernie, who had never seen Dick so enraged, was shivering in his boots and almost peed in his pants. Franz and Art looked at each other earnestly, trying hard not to laugh.

"Boy, that guy is as welcoming as a skunk at a lawn party," Ernie managed to whisper under his breath.

The officials were escorted into the office and asked to wait. Twenty minutes later the cranky proprietor, Henry Thompson, charged in and faced the government representatives. Dick was furious about the wait. He and the boys showed their ID's. He explained about the infestation of the pest that could be very harmful to his business and customers, then took a very aggressive tact keeping the landscaping guru on the defensive. Dick demanded a comprehensive tour of the property. Mr. Thompson got a golf cart for them to inspect the grounds. They traveled through hundreds of acres of plants, trees and flowers. The boys played their roles cleverly, searching for the smelly critter that probably wasn't there.

Dick insisted on inspecting the interior of the buildings. The arduous, time-consuming tour and pseudo inspection was taxing, but the inspectors were troopers and plowed on. To break up the monotony, and add to the drama, Ernie, cool as a cucumber, picked a leaf from a tree, tasted it, and spit out the bitter-tasting poisonous membrane. They traipsed through the endless acreage.

"I hope there aren't any snakes here," Ernie whispered to Art." I'm terrified of those slimy creatures."

"There are no snakes here," Art said.

"You got to look out for Burmese pythons. Some of them can grow to 26 feet," Ernie continued his discourse on reptiles.

"Ernie, they are in the Everglades three hundred miles away. We are in Daytona Beach."

"Well, you never know."

"How would they even get here?" Franz asked.

"Well, they got to the Everglades from Burma, didn't they?"

"Ernie, just behave a little longer, you're doing fine," Dick said, trying to get Ernie and Art to refocus on the mission.

Henry Thompson was painstakingly making life difficult for the four officious officials. They had spoiled his work for the day, and he was doing his best to do the same for them. He was suspicious of the group but complied since they could disrupt his business.

At the far end of the fields they saw a large barn.

"What's in there?" Art asked.

"Just storage," the pugnacious farmer responded.

"We need to inspect."

"You're not going to find anything that grows in that building."

"Open it up."

"Suit yourself." He walked over and dialed the entry combination.

"Why do you keep it locked?" Franz asked, acting very professional.

"'Cause I keep expensive equipment in there."

When the team entered, they did indeed find costly farm and landscaping equipment. They searched every inch, looking for a door or anything that might give them a clue. On one wall Dick found a keypad.

"What's this?"

"It opens the front door. I keep it locked at all times, even when I am in here," Thompson rallied, thinking quickly.

Dick was suspicious but moved on. They spent another 30 minutes checking out the property but didn't find any indications of wrongdoing.

Thompson drove them back to their car and the boys were totally exhausted after the long, hot experience. Dick reported that the property appeared to be clear of the nasty critters, thanked the proprietor, and handed him his card with instructions to call if he noticed any pests. The four drove off into the sunset. Thompson was dubious about the entire escapade. These old fools didn't quite match the profile of state agricultural inspectors. So, he sat at his computer and typed in: Brown Mamorated Stink Bug. Indeed, there was an insect of that variety. It was invading the Eastern corridor, but it hadn't hit Florida yet.

They were aching, overheated, exhausted, and dying of thirst. In addition, Ernie had to pee. Dick pulled the spy mobile into a McDonald's.

"I'm not too hungry. Just order me a double quarter pounder with cheese, fries, and a coke. Oh, and add a dollar vanilla ice cream cone," Ernie listed as he headed off to the men's room.

"I guess he really isn't hungry," Art laughed, and the other boys ordered snacks. They had spent three hours casing the grounds and hadn't found any concrete evidence. There didn't seem to be any unattended shacks, hidden doors into the ground or anything to indicate that a workshop was in operation. However, the chief spook's Professional antenna was still sending him signals.

"I have some concerns about that large barn. Why did it have a combination lock both inside and out? Also, did you fellows notice that the area on the inside of the barn was about a quarter of the size of the total physical structure?"

Chapter 45
No Reservations

The following morning, Denny's was jam-packed with breakfast customers when Ernie dragged himself in. He hadn't slept much and was exhausted from their grueling Department of Agriculture escapade. As always, his gal, Leonetta came waltzing over.

"Hi, hon, you here to make a reservation for your cooking group. It's about that time of the month."

"Not this month, Lee. I'm cooking for the boys this week," Ernie said with a big smile.

"Did I hear you correctly? YOU are cooking?"

"What's wrong with that?"

"I didn't know you could cook."

"I can't, but I'm going to anyway."

"Lordy, would I like to be a fly on the wall in that kitchen."

Ernie was joined by Dick, Franz, Art, and FBI Agents Sally and Tom. Boring scientist Ed came in, looked around and saw his cooking mates. He was about to be initiated into the scheme of things. They sat at a circular booth in a back corner which gave them some privacy to discuss the sensitive matters.

Meager breakfasts were ordered with Ernie taking the prize for volume as usual. Last night, after he returned from Daytona, Dick took matters further into his hands by calling Ed and bringing him into the fold. Ed had vast experience as a chemist working with explosives and Dick felt he would be a great adviser. Although Dick wouldn't tell him everything on the phone, Ed was shocked at what he heard and agreed to meet the boys at Denny's.

The usual pleasantries were taken care of, and the group got right down to brass tacks. Sally was not pleased when Ed appeared. She felt things were getting out of hand, and that a dangerous precedent was being set by expanding the secret group. Dick convinced the FBI agents that they were necessary resources to stop the dangerous plot. He filled them in on the visit to the rabbi and the anonymous donation of the trees for the two synagogues. He described the meeting between Harry and Henry

Thompson, the landscaping boss, where they exchanged what appeared to be money, and their inspection adventure to Daytona.

Sally had mixed reaction. On one hand she was livid that the boys had taken so much initative but was secretly grateful for the work and information. She agreed that they were such a conspicuous-looking group of old men that no one would suspect they were involved in the scheme. From the information they presented, the agents agreed that explosions were probably planned for the synagogues to coincide with the president's visit.

They talked with Ed about the various types of bombs that could be manufactured, attached to trees, and detonated remotely. They questioned whether the bombs could be installed on site without danger of exploding by a hidden remote. They discussed strategies to thwart the plan. There was no concrete proof, only supposition. They might assign 24-hour surveillance for the synagogues and nab the culprits in the act. Another option would be to raid the manufacturing operation in Daytona. They were cautious since foiling the plan too early could affect the rest of the plot. Dick's experience suggested they catch the planter red-handed. They would be caught off guard and not be in position to detonate. They assumed that Henry Thompson would be supervising the planting, and, with his capture, they could eliminate the bomb-making operation. Sally and Tom listened carefully and promised to take all their information under consideration.

Breakfast was served, and the group dined on Denny's delectable morning offerings. Ernie's order took up a sizable portion of the table. Everyone watched in awe as the old man devoured so much food. Afterwards, they shook hands, vowing to keep in touch. The countdown had begun with a little less than two weeks till D Day.

Ernie and Dick followed the FBI agents to their car.

"What's happening with Emil Weston?" Dick asked.

"Not much. I'm afraid. There's been nothing out of the ordinary from the wiretaps. Even his cell phone conversations seem to be clean," Sally reported.

"I'm still very suspicious."

"We are keeping a close watch on the situation. Ernie, continue doing what you are doing and keep us up-to-date."

"I keep going to these hate-filled meetings where they talk about the plan, but they never give any details."

"They are doing that on purpose, Ernie," Tom explained.

"Keep playing along. The agency is completing the strategy of how they will handle the actual day that the president is in town. Remember the goal is to capture everyone involved. Be patient, Ernie. You're doing a terrific job.

210

Thank you," Sally sounded almost human for a change.

***

"Harry,"
"Hi Pete,"
"The deed is done."
"How?"
"A very anonymous tip."
"Great. We're really cooking with fire."

***

The Men's Cooking Group Internet Express was blazing. Each man sat at his computer typing furiously sending copies to everyone.

Fred typed with one finger: "Remember cooking group on Thursday this week, fellas."

Dick, shaking his head: "Is Ernie really cooking or was that a bad dream that I had?"

Fred: "Believe it or not, Ernie is the Chef-of-The Week and he is cooking."

Dick laughed: "I'll believe it when I taste it."

Joe stroking his handlebar mustache: "Ernie can't cook. He doesn't even butter his own bread. He considers that cooking."

Bill, the frugal one: "Maybe we better eat before we come?"

Art jumped in: "That'll cost you double, Bill."

Abe, laughing to himself: "Here's to the stomach pump."

Joe; "If he doesn't poison us first."

From tedious Ed: "Remember, arsenic is only edible once."

"Hey, fellas, give me a break. Can't a guy even offer to cook a good meal these days?" Ernie shot back with rapid speed.

Joe: "Good and meal are not synonymous with you, Ernie."

Ernie, typing feverishly: "That was way below the belt, fellas. You guys remind me of my earlier days when I was young and stupid."

Dick: "No comment."

Charles, nosy as ever: "So, Ernie, what are you making?"

Ernie: "It's a big surprise."

Bill: "More mystery meats?"

Abe: "Steve, you finally are going to lose some weight. Ernie is cooking

211

raw pork and rancid tuna."

Ernie: "The last time I cooked, hardly anyone got sick."

Fred, smirking: "Well, I am glad that Ernie's cooking. If it's not take-out from Denny's."

"Fellas, if you don't like my cooking, lower your standards," Ernie zinged back on the keyboard.

Dick: "Hey, guys, ease up on Ernie. You're not helping matters. Remember complaints to the cook can be hazardous to our health."

.   Dick laughed, turned off his computer and headed towards the bedroom. The boys had their fun at Ernie's expense. It was the comic relief, he thought, before the beginning of the final and most dramatic act.

Chapter 46
Action, Camera: Breakfast

Bessie helped Ernie carry the groceries down the corridor into the Senior Center kitchen, and then she went down the hall to the Line Dancing Class. After raiding the Yoga room, and pilfering a tall bar stool, Ernie unpacked the bags, spreading the ingredients out neatly, perched himself atop the high seat, and waited for his guinea pigs to wander in. Ernie was making breakfast; it was the rational thing to do. The other boys created large feasts that were difficult to digest at 10:30 a.m.

Who can eat meatloaf, liver and onions or spaghetti bolognese first thing in the morning? Why didn't anyone else think of cooking breakfast before? Ernie wondered to himself.

The boys were in a rapturous but cautious mood today about the phantom meal. Ernie was glad their feelings and humor about his cooking had been aired in advance on the internet.

Desperately wanting to please his peers, and hoping to provide a tasteful and memorable meal, he prayed that things would be peaceful. He was in a constant nervous state these days. With the assassination plot fast approaching, and his so-called involvement, he was a mess. Ernie now trusted Sally and Tom, and Bess was truly his life-saving support. He also felt good about his close relationship with his cooking buddies, especially Dick, Art and Franz.

He had never really experienced dear, good friends before, and at 86, he was developing relationships that felt both foreign and exciting to him. Despite all the kidding and kibitzing, he believed the boys really liked him. This was crucial for Ernie since he was feeling so conflicted, both in turmoil and at peace deep down.

Art wandered in first and Ernie asked him to wipe down the counters where the food would be prepared.

Abe rolled in next and danced over to the counter to peruse the food selection. "It looks like makings for breakfast. Great, Ernie, old boy, I love breakfast. How can I help?"

Like a movie director with a beret and a megaphone, Ernie began to direct his gastronomical epic: action, camera, breakfast.

"You can do the oatmeal, Abe."

"Right on, Ernie." Abe grabbed a large pot, filled it with water, mixed in the oats and set it on the stove to boil.

Steve arrived next, "Wow, breakfast, my favorite meal. What can I do?"

"Percolate the coffee, Steve," the director ordered.

Ed sauntered in, praised the breakfast menu, and was directed to lay out the boy's private equity holdings: the coffee cups.

Art was directed to fry the bacon. He pulled out a frying pan from the cupboard and got to work. The aromas of sizzling bacon gave everyone a high. Charles, also pleased about the breakfast menu, sliced the English muffins, dowsed them with butter and garlic and sequestered them into the oven.

Bill and Fred were delegated to create the egg concoction. They diced the ham, cubed the cheese, cracked more than two dozen eggs, added a splash of milk, stirred the mixture, and poured it gently into a large skillet.

Franz was relegated to cook the patty sausages and Joe was commissioned to make the cheese grits. Eggs and cheddar cheese were combined in the pan and the whole mixture was placed in a casserole to bake in the oven.

"Joe, don't forget to sprinkle butter over the top," bellowed Ernie from atop his perch.

"Right on, chief."

"Dick, would you please set out the plates, forks and napkins," Ernie thinking that Dick could not mess up this job.

"Consider it done, Ern."

The boys started chanting an off-key chorus of "Whistle while you work." It was pure and simple teamwork. There was none of the usual banter and barbs under Ernie's watchful eye, just the creation of a sumptuous breakfast.

Abe ladled out the first course, pouring milk and sprinkling raisins and brown sugar atop the oatmeal. The boys sat around slurping up the sweet porridge.

"We grew up very poor," Ernie told the assembled diners. "But we always had three meals a day; oatmeal, miss a meal and no meal."

"Hey, Fred," Abe chastised, "You spoiled my entire evening last night."

"What did I do? I was in home in bed with my wife."

"You sent me that e-mail with the 75 clips from the golden age of television."

Fred chuckled.

"I watched that blasted thing for three hours."

"I watched that recently too. It is great," Steve agreed.

"Those were the days," Charles waxed nostalgia.

"Do you guys remember 'The Ed Sullivan Show'?"

"Are you kidding?" Abe jumped up. "Religion in my house wasn't going to temple on Saturday mornings but prostrating in front of our television every Sunday night at 8:00 for 23 years. Do I remember 'The Ed Sullivan Show'!"

"I loved when Elvis Presley was on," biker Joe reminisced.

At that point Steve took center kitchen and gyrated his hips while mimicking, "You ain't nothin' but a hound dog."

"Well, that was a sight for sore eyes," Charles joked. "I mean, it makes my eyes hurt to see that from you, Steve."

"I liked it when Elvis Pretzel sang 'Heartburn Hotel,'" Dick said.

"You know what killed Elvis?" Ernie asked

"We give up."

"Butter."

"The Beatles were my favorite," Fred continued.

"They were such a nice, clean-cut group of kids when we first saw them on TV," Art remembered.

"So, what happened?" Bill asked.

"They became a bunch of potheads," Ernie beamed from his director's chair.

"I got a good one. What would it take to reunite the Beatles?" Ed asked.

"Enlighten us, Ed," from Abe.

"Two bullets."

"Red Buttons was my favorite comedian on the show," Charles said.

"That is certainly a name from the past," Fred agreed.

"His best line was, 'Never raise your hand to your kids, it leaves your groin unprotected."

"My wife used to swoon every time she heard Eddie Fisher singing 'Oh My Papa'," Abe said.

"Elizabeth Taylor used to swoon as well," came the slightly perverted Joe.

Suddenly out of nowhere, Abe sang out, "How much is that doggie in the window?"

"Arf, arf," came the chorus from Art, Dick and Fred, meshing their heads together.

"The one with the waggly Tail."

"How much is that doggie in the window?"

"Arf, arf,"

"I do hope that doggie's for sale," all the boys joined in and ended up laughing.

"Patti Page," Art said. "I loved her. Those were the days when people could sing."

"I like Lady Gaga," Ernie boomed.

"Are you crazy? She's a walking carnival, Ernie."

"Did you know that Lady Gaga took her name from a burlesque queen from the 1920s?" Know-it-all Abe informed the group.

"I didn't know that," Ernie said.

Ernie continued to hold court from his director's chair while Joe plated the main course. The plate was a visual delight: an egg, ham and cheese creation, crispy bacon, juicy sausage, mouthwatering grits and English muffins with butter and jam. The boys were in hog heaven. For a brief few moments between the nostalgia discussion and Ernie's perfect breakfast, they all forgot the problems of the day.

"Ed Sullivan wouldn't last an hour on television today. He was homely, couldn't get his words out straight and had no personality. Can you imagine him hosting 'American Idol'?" Abe said.

"I liked the Grateful Dead," Ernie spoke out.

"The Grateful Dead never appeared on 'The Ed Sullivan Show'," came Mr. Knowledge.

"Oh, you're right, that was the Dr. Kevorkian Show."

"ERNIE."

"Sometimes I think that Ernie is a few peas short of the casserole," Ed said.

From Joe, "Just sometimes?"

"I think the greatest moment on the 'Sullivan Show' was Irving Berlin singing 'God Bless America'." Charles raised his coffee cup in salute and the boys followed suit and sang a chorus of the American hymn together.

All agreed it was the best Old Men's Cooking Club session of the year. The meal was perfect, and the fellows entertained themselves grandly. Some of them even felt guilty about giving Ernie such a hard time about his cooking. They patted each other on the back and continued reminiscing as they washed up. Ernie remained on his perch yelling orders and doing nothing.

Suddenly, the director of the center walked in with two gentlemen in suits.

"Ernest Stubbs?" came a deep, menacing voice.

"Yes, Stubbs is my name, but I'm not to blame," Ernie joked as he climbed down.

216

"Would you please put your hands behind your back. You are under arrest for the attempted murder of the president of the United States."

"Huh?"

The officers cuffed Ernie and Mirandized him. His face turned a deathly shade of white and had a sheepish expression. The boys all stood paralyzed with their mouths open as the accused presidential assassin was led out of the center.

"Help me, fellows," he yelled, "I'm too old to be raped."

Chapter 47
Stubbs Busters

Stunned, Fred, Dick, Steve, Joe, Ed, Abe, Charles and Franz sat glued to the television in the lounge of the center watching the midday news. They were all in a state of shock.

BULLETIN BULLETIN BULLETIN BULLITEN

"This late-breaking story news. Eighty-six-year-old Orlando resident Ernest Stubbs was arrested today accused of creating a possible plot to kill President Herman Sharif. Police said the plan involved assassinating the president during his visit to Orlando when he speaks at the Convocation of Jewish Leaders in a few weeks. Stubbs, a local resident for more than 40 years, is a vocal advocate for change in government. He confessed to police he was the sole culprit in this plot and that no one else was involved. Stubbs was held without bail.

Law enforcement officers have recommended he be given a psychiatric evaluation to determine if dementia played a role in his planning or if Stubbs is part of a larger plot. More news about this developing story as it unfolds."

"Did anyone know about this?" Fred asked.

"I had some inkling," Dick said, trying to avoid giving more away. "But nothing specific."

Fred said, "Ernie's all mouth. I can't believe that he could be involved in such a sinister plot."

The opinions were flying around.

Bill looking totally puzzled: "He wouldn't step on an ant."

Art continued playing along: "What was he going to do kill Sharif with, his plastic leg?"

Charles, the food maven, added: "Today's meal was so good. And it was his first time up at bat."

Steve was completely dumbfounded: "Unfortunately, it looks like it was his last hurrah in the kitchen."

Franz in the know: "Poor Ernie."

Fred asked: "Does he need a good lawyer?"

Dick: "Let's see what we can do."

Ed jumped in: "Someone needs to call Bessie."

"I'll do it," Dick volunteered. "We need to see him and make sure he is all right."

"Dick, with your connections, can you try to arrange something?" Fred asked.

"Federal lock up for his crime is pretty serious stuff. I'll see what I can do."

At that moment the door crashed open and in ran a breathless Leonetta Moore, their favorite waitress from Denny's. "I just heard the news. What happened to my boy, Ernie?"

"He was arrested," Dick said.

"I knew that those people he was hanging around with were up to no good and I told him so. That old geezer couldn't kill a fly. He wasn't going to shoot the President. Lordy, Lordy. He is in a load of shit."

***

"Hello." Harry said, picking up his phone.

"Pete, here."

"It worked."

"Now we can proceed with the real business at hand."

"All systems are go."

***

Dick helped Bessie up the stairs to the Seminole County Jail. He had pulled strings to have a private visit with Ernie. The entourage sat around a table in the lime green, cinder block room under glaring fluorescent bulbs. Having aged dramatically in the last few days, Bessie was noticeably shaken. She knew that Ernie was involved, but no one expected this glitch in the plans. A metal door opened and Ernie, in an orange jumpsuit, was escorted in by two officers, both laughing at some remark he had made.

"Hi, everyone," Ernie said, almost jubilantly.

"Oh, Ernie, I have been so worried about you." Bessie ran over, bursting into tears, hugging and kissing him.

"Please step back, you can't touch him, ma'am," an officer interceded and eased them apart.

"I'm fine, Bessie, really. It's good to see you, Dick. How do I look in orange?"

"What's going on, Ernie?" Dick asked.

"They caught me," with that Ernie gave Dick an animated wink indicating that he couldn't talk but all was well. "The police arrested me, but the FBI is coming in later today to interrogate me."

"How are they treating you?" Dick asked.

"Are you cool enough? Is the bed comfortable for your bad back? What about your medications? Are you eating?" Bessie couldn't stop.

"I'm okay, Mama. They aren't treating me too badly. As a matter of fact, the inmates are all looking up to me as if I was an idol. They said, that anyone my age who has the balls to shoot the president is all right with them. My block mates all lined up to shake my hand. They treat me like a king, and this 300-pound gorilla has even offered me free protection. Life is sweet in jail. How is Ruth doing, Dick? Did she get her medication approved by Medicare yet?"

"Not yet, Ernie. It's a real cliffhanger."

"Send her my love. If you need money, Bessie knows how to access my dough."

"Thank you, Ernie, but right now we are terribly concerned about you."

They talked for half an hour, and Bessie, still very emotional, clung to Ernie's every word, not wanting to leave.

"Is there anything we can do for you?" Dick asked.

"Yeah, tell Fred that there will be one less for lunch next Thursday."

Email
TO: Fred, Bill, Abe, Joe, Steve, Ed, Art, Charles and Franz
FROM: Dick
SUBJECT: Ernie

We saw Ernie this afternoon. He seems to be doing well. He was waiting to talk to the FBI, expecting some interesting developments. Keep tuned to your emails for updates.

220

Ernie was marched back to the meeting room a second time later that day. Sally Adams and Tom Prentice stood as he entered.

"So, you caught me," Ernie boasted gleefully.

"We didn't get you, Ernie. There was a leak to the police that you were involved in a plot," Sally said.

"What happens next?"

"The tip was anonymous, but we surmise it was from the subversive group that you are working undercover with. This is what they meant by using you as a decoy. With you arrested, they assume that the plot has been discovered, and we will let our guard down, so they can continue with the real plan," Tom explained.

"In other words, they've thrown me to the wolves."

"Precisely and well calculated. The bottom line is that we still have a potential assassin on the loose," came Sally.

"What about Emil Weston, the so-called party planner?"

"The only thing that we know is that he is managing the luncheon for the Jewish leaders and the president at the Convention Center," Sally said.

"He is our number one suspect, but we need to get closer to him," Tom jumped in.

"How do I help if I'm stuck in here?"

"Be patient. We will take care of things," Tom said, trying to be reassuring.

"Since there are now six men in your cooking group who are involved, we want to recruit the rest to help us with a plan to foil the assassination," Sally explained.

"I'm sure that won't be a problem. They are a bunch of the most patriotic men in the country. Just tell me what we are supposed to do," Ernie was flattered and eager. "What's the plan?"

"You'll know soon enough. In the meanwhile, we want you to just sit tight," Sally advised.

"That's the way I have to sit here in jail."

Email
TO: Fred, Bill, Ed, Joe, Steve, Ed, Abe, Art, Charles and Franz
FROM: Dick
SUBJECT: URGENT: The Old Men's Cooking Club

Ernie needs our help. Everyone, please attend a meeting on Thursday. We will have a picnic at Alexandra Springs Picnic Area in the Ocala National

Forest at 11:00 a.m. Bring a dish to share. Be there or be square. Dick

Chapter 48
Music of The Night

Sounds of snoring were the music of the night in the dimly lit cell block corridor at the Seminole County Jail. Having a restless night, Ernie watched the big and small hands on the clock rendezvous at midnight. The novelty of his arrest was over, and the enormity of the situation was beginning to sink in. Although believing he had played an important role in potentially foiling the heinous assassination plot, he still felt like a failure because the real perpetrator was still out there and might carry out the mission. He hated President Sharif and all his liberal Democratic cronies with a deep passion. He believed the country was going to hell and back, just thinking about it made him angry.

Without thinking he had opened his big mouth once too often about his political views and now he was on a lumpy mattress in a four-by-eight cell with a stainless-steel toilet at eye level. Deep down he had no desire to see the president dead, just out of the Oval Office. He lamented that Dick, Art and Franz were now involved in this mess. Dick had his own problems with his wife's illness; poor Art had the right to enjoy his retirement puttering in his vegetable garden and no parent should endure what Franz was going through with his son up to his eyeballs in the plot. Bessie didn't deserve this mess, or him, for that matter.

Sally assured him that he was doing the right thing, and was helping enormously, but Ernie felt trapped. He needed to be out there fulfilling his role as a Deputy FBI Agent Stubbs, capturing the culprit rather than being locked away like an animal in a cage. Sally hadn't told him the plan, leaving him emotionally and physically helpless. At wit's end, Ernie began to cry.

Hearing a key in his cell door, he began to panic. "Who would be coming at this hour?" He didn't recall the jail serving midnight snacks. Is this where Bubba comes in to rape him? Perhaps he was going to be the midnight repose. There was a bigger fear: that some of Harry's neo-Nazi partners had connections in the jail and were going to kill him to get him out of the way. A chilling thought, he covered his face with the sheet and feigned sleep but could not control his shaking. Two correction officers entered and roused him, telling him to get dressed. Ernie fastened his leg and slipped into his prison jumpsuit.

"Where are you guys taking me?" he cried, hardly able to stand up.

"You are being moved. Don't ask any questions; just come with us."

Ernie did not know these guards, who were unfriendly unlike the day shift with whom he had developed a camaraderie. He thought about screaming but didn't cherish a beating and anyway, who would come to his rescue? He closed his eyes, prayed, gathered his few belongings and followed them. They marched him down several corridors and shoved him into another almost bare cinder block room, telling him to wait there and be quiet. Ernie looked; there were no windows and no way to escape. The tears running down his cheek merged with the rivers of perspiration coming from his forehead.

An eternity later, Tom Prentice opened the door.

"Thank God it's you. I thought they were taking me out to kill me."

"Ernie, don't say a word and get into these clothes and come with me." Handing him a pair of jeans and a denim shirt which he struggled into. Tom handcuffed Ernie and they left the room and met Sally Adams. The agents showed identification and signed Ernie out as a prison transfer. The steel door of confinement buzzed open and the trio walked into the warm Florida night air. They made Ernie comfortable in their government Ford and removed his cuffs, heading towards the interstate.

"What's going on? Can I talk now?" Ernie babbled.

"Sorry, Ernie, we needed to make your transfer look as realistic as possible," Sally explained, trying to soothe their flustered volunteer deputy. They told Ernie that he was being relocated to a safe house until it was time for the plan. Twenty minutes later, they pulled up in front of a ranch house by a lake.

"This place seems very familiar," Ernie said, looking around.

"Hi Ernie," Dick said, opening the front door.

"What are you doing here, Dick?"

"I live here, Ernie."

"What am I doing here?"

"You are going to stay with Dick and Ruth during the operation. But Ernie, NO ONE, but NO ONE must know you are here," Sally said with great authority. "Bessie can come to visit but that's it."

"Come on in, Ernie, and sit down. I'll make some coffee." Ruth said and led her new boarder in. They all sat around the table.

"Are you hungry, buddy?" Dick asked.

"Am I hungry?"

"I guess that was a dumb question."

"Well, I could have a little something. What you got? I had a pretty good dinner tonight; Cold meatloaf, mushed potatoes with brown gravy and lots of peas. Oh, and my favorite dessert, applesauce. Food was very salty, though."

"I'll fix you a sandwich, Ernie," Ruth said, asked around the table for other takers and headed to the kitchen.

The agents told Ernie that he was not to leave the house or talk with anyone. Bessie would bring him clothes in the morning. Sally began unveiling the plan to him.

"Ernie, this is what I want you to do.................." she explained in detail.

"You're kidding, Sally."

"Not in the least."

"There is no fucking way that I'm going to do that!"

"Ernie!" Dick jumped on him.

"It violates my constitutional rights, my freedom of religion," Ernie yelled.

"We are going to violate your freedom to breathe if you don't cooperate." Dick was being unusually hard on him, but it had to be done.

"I'll be the laughingstock of Western Pennsylvania."

"Ernie, you haven't been home to Pennsylvania in 60 years. Buck up, buddy. Get with the spirit. It's important."

Ruth brought out snacks and they completed talking about the plan. Then Sally and Tom got up to leave.

"Thanks for everything, Dick. Have a good night, Ernie," said Tom with a sympathetic nod.

"Yeah, SHALOM, Ernie," Sally said with a big grin.

"BAH HUMBUG!" Ernie growled.

Chapter 49
Teddy Boys' Picnic

Carting Art and Franz, Dick drove his Edsel station wagon up and down the few rolling hills of Florida to the secluded picnic spot. The two elderly partners-in-crime lugged an ice cooler from the trunk, and Dick followed with the hamburger meat and hot dogs for the grill. Joe exploded into the parking lot on his shiny red Harley-Davidson trike with Abe, a sight for sore eyes in his goggles, riding the bitch seat. Bill, with Ed and Steve in tow, came sputtering down the hill in one of his clunky junkyard jalopies and parked nearby. Robert drove Charles in their lovely new Lincoln.

All the culinary contributions were turned over to club leader Fred who agreed to be picnic chef and laid out a flowered plastic cover on the table. Joe brought a vat of pork and beans. Everyone wondered how he made it on the motorcycle with that mixture in his lap. Abe carried the hot dog and hamburger rolls in a knapsack. Steve provided two Dutch apple pies and an ice chest containing a gallon of ice cream. Bill tendered the creamy coleslaw. Ed dispensed a large serving platter filled with greasy fried chicken. Ruth sent corn on the cobs with Dick and Art supplied the utensils, napkins, cups and condiments. This was a royal picnic for a very regal bunch of guys.

There was a bit of nervous anticipation; no one had any real information other than to meet in this secluded spot. The members were glad to be out of the kitchen for a change but had a lot on their minds as a shroud of mystery prevailed.

"How's Ernie?" Steve asked.

"We don't know," Fred answered.

"I hope Bessie is okay," said Ed.

"She was teetering when we saw her at the jail the other day," Dick said. "This is a lot of stress for her."

"She's really a good woman, putting up with Ernie for all these years; and going twice to the altar and twice to divorce court," Fred added.

"I would hardly call her 'the gay divorcee,'" Charles piped in.

Dick and Joe lit the fire in the grill and the others spread out the food.

"I'll bet there are lots of God's creatures in these woods: snakes, bugs and alligators galore," Steve said, sounding less than thrilled.

"There's only one good place for God's creatures," Joe yelled across the picnic ground. "Right next to the mashed potatoes and gravy."

"No one brought fruit or vegetables for my diet," Steve lamented.

"Yeah, fruit and vegetables are a must on a weight-loss program: carrot cake, zucchini bread and apple turnovers," Charles laughed.

"Steve believes in a balanced diet: a drink in each hand," Abe chuckled.

"A waist is a terrible thing to mind, fellows," Steve said.

"I love nature. It's nice to take a deep breath of fresh country air," Franz said.

"Yeah, Impotence is nature's way of saying no hard feelings," Joe quipped, and everyone laughed.

"What are we doing here anyway?" Ed asked impatiently. "I could eat all this good food without ants and mosquitos in our kitchen, thank you very much."

"Our instructions are to gather, start eating and wait for further instructions," Dick told the group.

"Well, I'm getting damn thirsty: pass the beer," Joe said.

"You were supposed to bring the beer, Joe," came Fred.

"Bill said he was bringing it."

"Cheap Bill wouldn't spring for beer. You should know better than that," Abe said.

"Hey, that wasn't fair, Abe," said Bill.

"Well, it's true."

Bill didn't respond.

"Well, this is a fine howdy you do, no beer," Joe bellowed.

Suddenly, like a burst through the clouds, two late-model black Ford Crown Victoria's with tinted windows sped toward the picnic area, kicking up a mountain of dust.

"What the hell?" Abe looked puzzled.

"Looks like we're being raided by the cops," said Steve.

"I guess Ernie wanted company in jail," Joe said smirking.

"It's a set up to arrest us all," meek Art jumped in.

"Take it easy, fellows. Nothing's going to happen," Dick said.

Sally Adams and Tom Prentice got out of the first car and opened the door of the second. Out stepped their convict buddy Ernie and the love of his life Bessie, snuggling close to him.

"ERNIE," A loud cry of happiness and relief bellowed the strong male chorus.

"We're so glad to see you, buddy."

"We've missed you, sport."

"There's no one with a leg like yours to stir our stew."

"How did you get out?"

"What's going on?"

"We're very confused."

The group rushed over to the happy couple and gave them a big group hug. The two FBI agents who had brought the heroes stepped aside, enjoying the reunion.

"Three cheers for Ernie, boys," Abe yelled, and they broke into the most ragged barbershop harmony rendition of "For He's a Jolly Good Fellow."

If they had been 30 years younger, they would have picked up Ernie and Bessie, put them on their shoulders and paraded them in a triumphant march.

"Come on, guys, I'm hungry. Let's eat," Ernie said, waving his hands like a king on the throne.

Dick introduced FBI agents Sally and Tom to the rest of the Men's Cooking Club. Sally had made brownies for the feast, which for those who knew her saw as another notch toward her humanization.

"I brought something to contribute to the potluck," Ernie declared, pulling out a can from a supermarket bag and holding it up. "Spam"

"Spam? Who the hell eats Spam?" Responded the gourmet Charles.

"It's the number-one selling food in Hawaii."

"This ain't Hawaii. That's a different tropical paradise, Ernie," Art said.

"Come and get it," yelled master barbecue chef, Joe. Everyone lined up to load their plates with perfectly grilled burgers and dogs.

"Let's eat, enjoy the food and we'll talk afterwards," Dick commanded, setting the tone.

Bessie clung to Ernie as he filled a plate of goodies for her. They sat side by side, chatting and laughing with the group.

"I was watching this bizarre food show the other night. The host was somewhere in South America in a remote village and the tribe was cooking scorpion. He asked the head of the clan, 'What does it taste like?' To which he responded: 'penguin,'" Steve joked.

"Dick, where did you get that relic of an automobile?" Junk-dealer Bill said, eyeing Dick's proud possession.

"The Edsel? That's my baby."

"That's supposed to be the worst piece of automobile shit ever produced."

"Well, that so-called piece of crap is still running like new after 53 years."

228

"I like old cars: that's all I ever drive," Ed said.

"I used to hope for a BMW: now I just hope for a BM," Ernie rattled, with a straight face.

"Ernie's back to normal, fellows. Thank God," said Abe.

"Gentlemen lift up your water cups to toast our Ernie," Fred proposed. "Here, here."

They filled their bellies with hearty food. The restlessness in the air was palpable as all were truly itching to know what was going on.

"Don't forget the desserts, everyone," Steve said.

"Did you know that desserts spelled backwards, is stressed," said Fred.

Charles jumped right in, "Well, that's very appropriate to the current situation."

Finally, lunch was finished, and they were sitting around schmoozing when Dick called the formal proceedings to order.

"You all know that Ernie was arrested for what the media claimed was a plot to shoot the president. Ernie never had any intention of shooting anyone. He has been working undercover with the FBI to unveil a demonic assassination plot. There is a subversive neo-Nazi group, the Aryan Connection, operating in the woods east of Orlando that has been plotting this action for a long time. Ernie infiltrated and has been monitoring their activities. They, in turn, accepted Ernie but only to use him as a decoy to divert attention from the real plan. A scapegoat. They leaked to the police that Ernie was the sole planner and instigator of the attempt, and he was arrested. They thought that if Ernie was suffering from dementia, he would be tucked away in jail, probably be sentenced to life in an old-age home or psycho ward. In the meanwhile, they could continue their activities. They have plans to execute their mission in two weeks when the president will be in town to address the Jewish Leaders Convocation at the Convention Center. That brings you all up-to-date in a nutshell. Let me turn the meeting over to Sally Adams to explain more."

"First of all, let me say I am extremely proud of Ernie, Art, Franz, and Dick who have been helping. Normally we would go in and catch the culprit and that would be the end of it. But that wouldn't remove all the cancer. We're planning one fell swoop to put the entire organization out of business and bring all the perpetrators to justice. That's why we've asked you here today."

"We need your help, all of you." Tom continued. "First, you all must swear to total secrecy. One misspoken word and the entire operation can go down the drain. Second, no one knows that Ernie's out of jail. We are keeping him out of sight and under protection. We have a detailed plan that requires everyone's assistance. Time is of the essence, so we need to jump on this right away."

"Is it dangerous?" Charles asked cautiously.

"It could be," said Tom.

"Are we really going to save the president of the United States?" asked Abe.

"You better believe it, fellows," Sally was strong. "Who is willing to help?"

"I'm in, fellows. Who's with me?" Dick said, taking the lead.

The anti-President Sharif conservative Republican cooks all signed on without hesitation. They were raring to go.

"Why don't you swear the boys in as deputies, like you did to me?" Ernie burst forth with what seemed like a great idea.

"Yeah, Tom, why don't you swear them in?" Sally mocked Ernie.

"What? Oh shit, okay."

Tom created a mythical oath making everyone raise their right hand and swear allegiance. The boys of the Old Men's Cooking Club were now ad hoc FBI deputies. Sally again took over the meeting and went into detail about the plan. She gave an assignment to each man based on their abilities which took another hour. Then they whisked Ernie and Bessie away and the men continued talking.

"I can't believe that we're actually going to do this," Fred said to Ed.

"It's the craziest thing I ever heard of."

Chapter 50
Sacred Plans

A white van pulled up to the entrance of the office complex in Orlando. Six ultra-religious orthodox Jews (Hassidim), sporting long grey beards, dressed in full-length black coats, white tieless shirts, brown fur-trimmed wide-brimmed black hats, and payot (long side curls in front of their ears), got out and stood together in a single line. The group from left to right included:

Rabbi Yankel Schwartz: (Ernest Stubbs, anti-everything and bigoted curmudgeon).

Rabbi Mendel Goldstein: (Joseph Jones, beer-bellied redneck biker).

Rabbi Heschel Finkelstein: (Franz Schmidt, reformed former Nazi soldier).

Rabbi Avram Cohen: (Dick Reynolds, retired CIA operative).

Rabbi Hymie Stein: (Art O'Neil, just plain good-old Southern boy).

The transformation was perfect. After they stopped laughing and bellyaching with their usual comic and caustic witticisms, they had donned their authentic disguises and quickly got down to serious business. By now the FBI had significant reasons to suspect Emil Weston was the assassin. The mission was to gain as much information about him and help the bureau take him down before he had a chance to do his dirty deed. The disguises were appropriate for the Jewish Leaders Convocation.

"Listen, fellows," Sally Adams said, as the five cooking boys were dressing for their mission. "We're not making fun of the sacred religious sect but using this highly respected and devoutly religious group as a cover that would be accepted and blend in with the other attendees at the Conference where the president is scheduled to speak."

The five discombobulated-looking beadles sauntered into the event's planning office of "Smithfield and Weston" to meet with Emil Weston under the guise of planning a major event. The receptionist took a long double take. The over-dressed Hassidim were all over the reception area looking at pictures and talking a mile a minute.

"My white pantyhose is killing me in the crotch," Ernie whispered to Rabbi Dick.

"Get a grip, Ernie, tough it out."

"Who told you to wear tights?"

"I saw them get dressed in a Mel Brooks movie and they wore white tights." Rabbi Yankel (Ernie) said.

"White sox," they volleyed quietly back and forth.

"My pants are slipping down over my beer belly." Rabbi Mendel (macho man Joe) complained.

"These silly side curls are tickling my face," Rabbi Hymie (Art) joined in trying to hide his Southern drawl.

"Cut it out, guys. You're all a bunch of old wussies. This is serious business. Act your age," Rabbi Avram (retired spy Dick) chastised them quietly.

"We are," Rabbi Yankel shot back.

Emil Weston strolled out from his office and was totally taken aback by the congregational assemblage of black-clad elders. They must be dying of the heat, he thought.

"Rabbi Cohen?" he called out and there was no immediate answer. "Which one of you distinguished gentlemen is Rabbi Cohen?" he tried again. Rabbi Hymie nudged Rabbi Avram.

"I am so sorry, Mr. Weston. I'm a little hard of hearing," Dick said, recovering from the near mishap.

"Welcome. Why don't you all follow me to our conference room?"

He led the bearded gurus down the hall where they filled seats around a large table.

"What brings you distinguished gentlemen to Orlando?" the event planner asked, more than a little curious.

"We are here to attend the World Jewish Convocation."

"Ah, you are going to hear the president speak?"

"Yes," came the sacred choir.

"It's a small world. I have planned and am managing the hospitality for that entire event, including the reception and luncheon," Emil boasted.

"I told you we came to the right place," Rabbi Hymie (Art) interjected, in a sing-song manner and nodding his head up and down.

"Baruch Hashem ('blessed be our god'), very good," came a chant from the chorus of spiritualists. Abe had done a good job coaching the imposters.

Rabbi Dick (Avram) explained that their religious sect was from Brooklyn and some of their traditions.

"We are 'Hasidim,' which means loving kindness. Our mission is based on the joyful observance of God's commandments." He had done a great deal of research and was totally convincing explaining their history that

232

dated back to the 17th century. They were a bunch of "tzadikim," or righteous men. As Dick spoke, the others bobbed their heads as if praying.

"We would like to plan an affair," said Rabbi Mendel (redneck Joe).

"I'd like to plan an affair," Rabbi Yankel (Ernie) jokingly whispered to Rabbi Joe (Mendel), who kicked him under the table.

Rabbi Avram continued. "We would like to plan a three-day conference next June for our members from around the country. We expect around 1000 people and it must be 'glatt,' kosher, in other words, the food must be processed under the strictest kosher laws."

"We can do that," Emil was immediately interested due to the size of the project and began to envision large dollar signs. "Have you been to the Convention Center yet?"

"No, the Convocation starts in a few days," said Rabbi Avram.

"I believe that would be an ideal setting for your meeting. We can take care of your 'glatt' kosher needs. As a matter of fact, the luncheon with the president and the Jewish leaders will be 'glatt' kosher. Are you by any chance attending?"

"We are," answered Rabbi Avram.

"Why don't we meet at the Convention Center during the function and I can show you around."

"We don't want to put you out," said Rabbi Hymie (Art) who was fighting hard to mask his Southern drawl.

"Won't you be very busy?" Asked Rabbi Avram.

"I have an excellent staff, and by then, everything will be taken care of."

They talked further and the righteous men invented details as they talked. After asking many questions the FBI had fed them, the rabbis, very satisfied, arranged a tour of the Center, thanked their host and waddled out, continuing to talk incessantly. The final piece of the Chinese puzzle may have been placed in their devout laps.

***

While the disguised rabbis were solving one problem, FBI agents and police officers were hiding around the two central synagogues in Orlando, waiting for the explosive sapling deliveries. Rabbis Tannenbaum and Auerbach were ensconced with the law enforcement officers at their evacuated religious institutions. The bomb squads were poised several blocks away from each synagogue. Undercover patrol cars had been posted around the clock within view of the synagogues and as the landscaping trucks drove up to plant their deadly cargo, the full forces were mobilized.

As anticipated, Henry Thompson was in charge. He drove the green open bed landscaping truck with four workers. The cargo: two dozen young saplings, a dozen to be planted in a row in the front of each temple. Each tree had a sizable ball of earth. One tree for each synagogue carried an explosive device that was potent enough to destroy the entire house of worship. The plan was to set off the devices an hour before the president's speech.

The truck pulled up in the front of Rabbi Tannenbaum's synagogue and the workers began turning over the dirt, staking out the location for each tree. The pursuers surreptitiously circled the temple waiting for the signal to apprehend. The great fear was that Henry Thompson had the detonator with him, and at the first sign of impending danger, would set it off. There was some doubt about this possibility since the top brass felt that Thompson would not risk blowing himself up too. The mobile bomb squad moved closer and the moon-suited professionals were ready and out of sight. As the last shovels of dirt were unearthed, a swarm of law enforcement agents rushed in and overwhelmed Thompson and his gardeners, and the explosives remained forever undetonated. Another piece of the puzzle had fallen into place.

***

"Answer the phone. Answer the God-damned phone," Harry was pacing nervously in his office, trying to connect with Pete.

"Yes."

"Pete, they got Thompson and the bombs."

"Will he talk?"

"I don't know."

"Well, at least they don't know about our major player. He's working alone. Even our group doesn't know the plan. We're good to go."

"Yes, there is no stopping now."

***

The five fraudulent clergymen rode in the white van to Dick's house, their base of operations. They planned to disrobe and meet Sally and Tom for lunch at their old stomping grounds, Denny's. Ernie could be with them under close surveillance. Sally requested that he stay with the group for lunch. Leonetta Moore was as happy as a lark to see the group and couldn't stop fussing over her boy, Ernie.

"All this undercover spy work makes me hungry," Ernie informed the group.

"Everything makes you hungry," Dick said.

"Well, I feel like piss and vinegar since I started this operation."

This was hardly a 'glatt' kosher lunch: Rabbi Yankel (Ernie) ordered a double bacon cheeseburger.

"I'll have a ham and cheese on rye," requested Rabbi Mendel (Joe). Rabbi Heschel (Franz) ordered sausage and eggs; and Rabbi Hymie (Art) asked for a pulled pork sandwich. Rabbi Avram (Dick), the leader of the group, tried to stick as close to the dietary laws by ordering a turkey sandwich with a glass of milk.

Sally and Tom reported, "We got the synagogue bomber this morning and raided his den of operations in Daytona. He and his accomplices, his three sons, were arrested, and we padlocked the nursery. His operation was highly technical and very sophisticated. So far, he won't talk, but at least we eliminated one large part of the sordid operation."

"We're about to go in for the big kill," Ernie babbled excitedly.

"God forbid, Ernie. The object is to prevent anyone from being killed," Sally contradicted. "Are you fellows ready? You all have your instructions?"

"Ready as ever, Sally." Dick confirmed.

"Remember, no heroics. We will be right behind you," Tom reiterated.

"The Old Men's Cooking Club charges into action," bellowed Ernie rising from his chair waving his fork in the air. "It's showtime."

Chapter 51
The Pressure Cooker Boils Over

President Herman Sharif strutted down the steps of Air Force One at Orlando International airport, climbed inside his bullet-proof presidential Cadillac limousine and headed downtown towards the Convention Center. Today's speech was an important engagement for the chief executive. There was a surge of anti-Semitism in the nation. Hate groups had become more vociferous lately and had begun acting on their longtime threats. While Sharif was an avowed Christian, the rumor mill about his Muslim heritage still churned out of control, damaging his image. It didn't help that the president was passionately committed to the creation of a Palestinian State in defiance of the nation's strongest ally, Israel. The top of today's agenda was damage control with the American Jewish community. The presidential motorcade crippled traffic for miles as the commander-in-chief proceeded to his morning engagement.

Five miles away, Harry was pacing nervously in his office. It was D Day. All the hard work was resting on the outcome of today's plan. There had been some monumental bumps in the journey; the death of his Uncle Otto, a major organizer and financier of the plan and the unexpected arrest of Henry Thompson, the bomb-maker. However, Emil Weston was all set to go and, if all went according to plan, the country would have a new president this afternoon, and the Commander-in-Chief would have a new top adviser. Harry reached for his cell phone.

"Pete, Harry here. All systems are a go. I spoke with Sid, and he's ready. Hold on a moment someone's knocking on my door."

"Someone's at my door too. I'll call you back," Pete replied.

"Harry Smith?" Asked one of two FBI agents.

"Yes. You can't barge in here like this," he protested as the two dark-suited law enforcement officers charged into his inner sanctum.

"Yes, we can. You are under arrest for plotting to assassinate the President of the United States," as they grabbed Harry's arms, cuffing him from behind, and reading him his Miranda rights.

As an angry Harry Smith was marched through his office, there were looks of horror from his staff. FBI agents swarmed the area like bees and in one large sting, raided homes and offices arresting Pete, Ralph, Floyd, Al, Derek, and a slew of other members of Orlando's Aryan Connection.

The Hasidic quintet cleared security at the Convention Center without a problem. Rabbi Yankel (Ernie) relinquished his white tights for the more traditional white socks under black dress shoes. Everything was bothering Ernie. His dress shoes, which he'd only worn to funerals, were killing him. He dreamed about a triple scoop ice cream sundae with chocolate syrup, whipped cream and three large red cherries. Ex-Third Reich soldier Rabbi Franz was tottering. His age had caught up with him in all this turmoil and his mental stability was in limbo. The mission was emotionally draining by itself, but the extra pressure of his son's involvement was weighing heavily on him. He kept convincing himself he was doing the right thing, but was it right to go against his son? Rabbi Dick's juices were stirring. He was about to relive a moment from his active and dangerous days in the CIA. Rabbi Joe felt as if he was back in the streets of Arkansas, and ready to rumble as part of his old biker's gang. Passive Rabbi Art, wondering how he'd ever got involved in this mess, wished he was back in his garden tending his cucumber and tomato plants.

The disguised men meandered through the cavernous, crowded lobby mingling with religious peers, undercover FBI agents and Secret Service officers, but feeling out of place spiritually. Rabbi Dick caught sight of Sally Adams and Tom Prentice. The old boys had been warned by their handlers not to get in the way of the capture, just stick as closely to Weston as possible, letting the professionals come in for the kill. The religious garb worn by the deputized cooks would enable the agents to track the shooter's whereabouts.

Emil Weston, dressed in an expensive black suit and silk tie, greeted the religious entourage, escorting them through the lavish public rooms explaining how they would be suitable for their conference. The reception area, filled with Jewish leaders eagerly waiting in line to shake hands with the commander-in-chief, was off limits to the tour as was the enormous ballroom set up for the luncheon. The zealots had created an array of questions and Emil was animated in his answers. From Emil's total coolness, it seemed inconceivable that this professional would attempt to shoot the president in a few minutes. Rabbi Dick worried that they were on the wrong track but knew he had to stick to the plan.

The party planner shepherded his guests to the door of the auditorium where the long-awaited keynote speech was about to take place. He wished them Godspeed, arranging to meet back in his office before they left town.

More than twenty-five hundred religious leaders streamed into the assembly hall, stumbling over each other, searching for their reserved seats. The five elderly pretenders walked in the auditorium and Dick, Ernie, Joe rapidly turned around and headed towards the exit to follow Emil. They got caught up in the crowd pushing down the aisle and were fearful they might lose their culprit. Luck was on their side as they saw a waiter roll out a catering hamper and pass it to Emil at the other side of the vast hall. The three pursuers followed cautiously as he rolled the hamper down a long-deserted corridor. The Center was crawling with Secret Service officers. Emil had building clearance, and, as manager of the function, he could go anywhere.

The shooting caterer was feeling confident as his timing and moves were planned to perfection and the execution should be flawless. The hamper was light and rolled easily along the hallway towards a ramp that would take him to the second floor. As he started to travel up, he was startled by a sudden bump followed by a kerplunk, kerplunk, kerplunk sound. A piece of the plastic wheel broke loose from the hamper creating a ragged movement and a loud distracting noise. Emil surveyed the situation and rapidly tore off his necktie to wrap around the damaged wheel so it would spin. His cucumber-cool demeanor started turning red-pepper hot as sweat poured down his forehead.

The religious actors trailing the assassin ducked into an alcove in the nick of time to prevent detection. The FBI agents lost the costumed clergy and headed in a different direction following another trio of real religious zealots on a mission to find a men's room. The three cooks were now completely on their own. Emil moved the injured hamper alongside the wall and turned down another deserted hallway. The rabbis crept to the corner and peered around to see their perpetrator pushing back a floor-to-ceiling drape that hid a door. The door, which he had unlocked earlier was now locked, another glitch in the foolproof plan. Rummaging through his pocket for his Swiss Army knife, he deduced that the Secret Service had found the door open and locked it. Sweating profusely now, he tried to pick the lock and roll the injured wagon into a hidden lighting slit. The lighting catwalks above the auditorium were swarming with Feds but the small room with access to the catwalks remained empty. Emil positioned the hamper there and opened the slit two inches that accessed the catwalks and was directly above the podium. There was just enough room to aim his silencer-clad rifle.

Rabbis Ernie, Dick and Joe edged towards the door.

"Ernie, you wait here and keep an eye out for the Secret Service. Joe and I will go in," Dick instructed.

"May God be with you," Ernie babbled nervously.

Dick banged on the door. There was no answer. He knocked again.

"Who's there?" came a flustered Weston.

No answer.

Another loud bang.

Emil opened the door slowly to find Rabbi Avram and Rabbi Mendel standing there staring.

In a panic he said, "What the fuck are you doing here?"

"SO! We want to finish our tour," Rabbi Avram recovered.

"We saw you coming up this way and figured this was a part of the building that you didn't show us. We wanted to see the whole megillah," redneck-biker Joe blurted out, sounding more Southern than deep in the heart of Borough Park, Brooklyn.

"What are YOU doing here?" Rabbi Joe asked as he and Rabbi Dick pushed their way into the lighting booth area. The loud commotion of the anticipating crowd in the auditorium below could be heard through the slightly open slot. Rabbi Ernie stayed outside and listened.

"WE know your game, Weston," Dick said, staring him straight in the face.

In a rapid-fire movement, Emil slipped a large rifle with the silencer out of the banquet hamper and pointed it at the two rabbis.

"I was intent on shooting one person, but I guess it will have to be three." He motioned for them to stand against the wall, hands in the air.

"You will never get away with this, Weston."

"I should have known you were a phony bunch of religious fanatics."

"A wise bunch who was able to fool you," Rabbi Avram asserted. Their goal was to keep him talking and buy as much time as possible. The two wise old men, also sweating profusely, removed their fur-trimmed hats. When Dick made an abrupt move, Emil fired at him, hitting him in the leg, which knocked him to the floor. Joe took advantage of this split-second movement, and tackled Emil, and wrestled him to the ground, trying to wrestle the gun away. The scuffle was fierce. Emil achieved the upper hand, and cracked Joe on the head and then aimed the gun and began to pull the trigger. Suddenly out of nowhere he was hit over the head, repeatedly, from behind with a strange object. Emil, his eyes bulging, fell to the floor unconscious. Ernie, standing there in all his religious glory leaning against a lighting pole and balancing on one leg, had pummeled Emil on the head with his prosthetic leg.

Just then a religious leader welcomed President Sharif to the podium, lukewarm, skeptical applause could be heard when the door crashed open, and Sally Adams, Tom Prentice and several other Secret Service agents charged in, with guns drawn and positioned themselves to shoot. Dick was on the floor, fully conscious, but bleeding from the bullet in his leg. Joe was stirring, holding the spot on his head where he had been clobbered. Ernie was sitting on top of Emil Weston waving his fake leg around in a victory gesture.

"We just saved that Muslim bastard," shouted Ernie.

"You sure did, champ, you sure did," Sally said, as she cuffed the unconscious catering assassin's hands behind his back.

"Oh my God," Ernie yelled and fainted on top of the culprit.

Chapter 52
A Time to Stew

The Chinese take-out boxes adorned with fire-spitting dragons and featuring square silver handles were spread out on the mahogany dining room table, but the chopsticks remained fastened together. The moo shoo pork and beef chow fun sat unopened, as Franz and Art, still wearing remnants of their rabbinic white beards, sat trying to console Ingrid. The boys were on the brink of exhaustion while Ingrid was beside herself with grief. The doctor had just left and Anneliese, sedated, was in bed. Harry's mother had been shaken by the recent news of Otto Shafer's death and completely devastated when told of her son's involvement in the sinister plot to assassinate the president. Harry and his cronies were arrested earlier in the day and arraigned on federal charges.

Dick was rushed to the hospital for the bullet to be surgically removed and admitted for a few days. Joe's concussion was treated in the Emergency Room and he was released with a throbbing headache. Ernie and Bessie went home together for the first time in weeks. Art and Franz, unaware of what happened in the lighting booth, stayed for the lackluster presidential speech and attended the luncheon.

"Was Uncle Otto involved?" Asked Ingrid with tears sliding down her cheeks.

"I'm afraid so," Franz replied solemnly. "He and Harry were the masterminds of the scheme."

"Were there more people involved in Germany?"

"Unfortunately, there was a ring called the Fourth Reich that was responsible for the plan. It has been in existence since the decline of the Third Reich sixty years ago. Uncle Otto was the head of one of its branches."

"Do the authorities know?"

"They do now."

"What about all the meetings Harry went to?" Ingrid quizzed Franz.

"Harry was the leader of an American Aryan hate group that handled the work for the German organization. All the local neo-Nazis in the group were apprehended as well."

"What will happen to Harry?" Ingrid asked.

"I don't know. It's very serious. I suspect he will be tried for attempted murder and conspiracy and sentenced to a long prison term," Franz answered, careful not to mention the mandatory life sentence for a presidential assassination attempt.

"I knew that he was up to something but couldn't figure it out. Perhaps if I showed more interest, I might have been able to prevent this."

"Don't torture yourself, Ingrid, it had nothing to do with you," Franz said trying to soothe his daughter-in-law.

"I was the one who neglected Harry." Franz bemoaned. "I should have suspected that he spent too much time with Otto over the years. I knew about Otto's radical leanings, but I ignored them. He brainwashed and manipulated Harry to do this evil. It's all my fault."

"It's not your fault, Franz. It was destined to happen," Art got up from his chair and went over to put his arms around Franz.

"What am I going to do, Papa," Ingrid wept.

"Mama and I are here to help you. We talked it over and decided to move here to help take care of you and the children," Franz explained.

"That's wonderful, Franz," Art burst out. "Now you can become a permanent member of the Old Men's Cooking Club."

"The heroic Old Men's Cooking Club."

Later that night downtown, Ernie toted a bouquet of drooping yellow daffodils down a colorless hospital corridor. Bessie, his Sancho Panza, hobbled beside him.

"We're looking for Dick Reynolds," he said.

"Room 369, down the hall to the left," the nurse said, glancing at a chart and sent them in the right direction.

Dick was propped up in the hospital bed, his leg in a cast hanging from a pulley. Ruth was fussing around him when the couple came in.

"Hey Dick, how's it hanging?" Ernie boomed out enthusiastically, only to be shushed by old-school Bessie who remembered the days when no one spoke above a whisper in hospital rooms.

"What, Bess, I'm asking him about his leg. Here, I brought you dinner," Ernie said handing Dick the bunch of wilting flowers.

"Looks better than the salad they served for lunch."

Ruth took the blooms, placed them in a vase and invited Bessie to go for a cup of coffee.

"Behave, boys," Ruth said with a twinkle in her eye.

"Yeah, we'll try not to blow up the hospital," Dick fired back. "So, Ernie, have you calmed down yet?"

242

"I'm still a bundle of nerves and I damaged my best leg, beating up that son-of-a-bitch."

"It was for a good cause, Ernie."

"Yeah, I guess so," Ernie said slowly but sounding iffy.

"Why? Do you have any reservations about what we did?"

"Well, I really do dislike Sharif. It would have been a good opportunity to get him out of the White House."

"Ernie, you don't really mean that, do you?"

"I don't know," he said coyly.

"Do you dislike his politics or him because he's black."

"He's a black Muslim."

Dick didn't have the strength to correct Ernie for the thousandth time.

"I like blacks and I like Jews, as long as they don't get too close."

"Ernie, you said a number of times that you didn't believe that the Holocaust existed. You were in Europe directly after the war. You must have seen the horrific destruction and the signs of the near annihilation of the Jewish people."

Ernie was quiet for a moment then tears started flowing and he began sobbing.

"What is it, my friend?" Dick said, reaching for Ernie's hand and trying to console him.

Ernie began speaking slowly and quietly. "I was in Germany right after the war. I saw the destruction, the devastation. The camps were empty, but I saw the bodies, both dead and what remained alive, the walking dead. I walked into one of the gas chambers and saw the ovens and the mass graves."

Dick reached over and grabbed a handful of tissues for his pained friend.

"You don't have to tell me, Ernie."

"I want to. I was nineteen years old. We were excavating land for a bridge and discovered a mass grave with hundreds of decomposing bodies piled one on top of each other. I was devastated by the sight and others that I saw, and I suffered horrendous nightmares. I still can't get the smell out of my nostrils. I became immobile and was hospitalized. The doctors told me that I had had a nervous breakdown from witnessing the horrors. I spent time in an army hospital and then they shipped me home and discharged me from the service. I was given psychiatric therapy, medication and even shock treatment, but I buried the devastation deep in my mind. It was easier for it not to exist or to deny it," Ernie said, wiping the tears from his cheeks.

"Oh my God, Ernie, I had no idea."

"My family knew, but they hated the Jews and made me feel like it wasn't such a bad thing. I couldn't talk to them about it. I am still affected, Dick, I get so angry."

Dick leaned over and put his arm around Ernie who was bent over crying like a baby.

"Does Bessie know?"

"Why do you think she put up with me all this time?"

"I'm so sorry, Ernie. I saw plenty of hatred and destruction during my years at the CIA and I can fully understand how easy it is to push the evil deep within your mind. But you did an amazing, heroic deed this week. You saved your country from serious disaster. You need to look at the positive side now."

"I try, Dick, but a lot of things make me really mad and as I got older, my mouth has gotten bigger and gets the best of me sometimes."

"You'll be all right, Ernie. You have good friends and we'll all take care of you," Dick said with a smile as a nurse came to give Dick some pain medication.

"Hey, is that Viagra?" Ernie popped out. "You're not supposed to get him all revved up."

"Looks like you old boys can get pretty revved up by yourselves," she fired back.

"Why don't you give him a massage or a sponge bath," Ernie was starting to be Ernie again.   "He's in a lot of pain right in the groin joint where his leg is being lifted up."

"I could use a bit of stimulation," Dick said winking at his friend.

"Yeah, but if you give him a sponge bath, you would have to take your uniform off. No sense getting it wet."

"You are a bunch of dirty old men. Keep your Peters in your pants, boys," she said, smiled and left the room. Dick and Ernie laughed, joked more about sex or their lack of it and lots of other topics including Dick's horrendous cooking at the Old Men's Cooking Club. And so Ernie's secret went back into deep hibernation.

"Tell me, Dick. How is Ruth? Where you able to get her cancer, medication covered by Medicare?"

"It's touch and go. We're still waiting for a decision. I'm not sure what I will do if they turn her down."

"Remember, buddy, I've got some money for you. All you have to say is that they turned you down."

"Thank you, partner. I knew there was a little good hiding under that grumpy old exterior."

244

Ten minutes later when the two women returned, they found their two American heroes fast asleep.

Chapter 53
The Soufflé Rises

Euphoric pride filled the air as the standing-room only crowd in the shabby lounge at the Orlando Senior Center gathered around the giant television screen to watch the proceedings. Yammering away a mile a minute, the elderly fans abandoned mahjong, Zumba, and knitting to cheer on their boys.

"Shush everyone, it's on." All focused on the larger-than-life picture. A deep male voice announced:

"We now take you to the East Room of the White House where President Herman Sharif is about to honor eleven American heroes. These selfless and devoted patriots undertook a difficult mission, foiled an attempt on the life of the president and saved the nation from a sinister plot to interfere with our democratic way of life. Ladies and gentlemen, the President of the United States."

There stood the men from the cooking club. Everyone started talking at once.

"Look at Abe and Fred. They look so handsome all dressed up."

"Even Ernie is all spiffy in his shiny gray suit and red bowtie."

"Those are our boys," they pointed proudly to each other.

At the White House, the East Room was filled to capacity for this distinguished ceremony. Sally Adams and Tom Prentice sat gloating in the front row. Bessie was next to them, brimming with affection for her Ernie, and Robert couldn't hold back his tears of joy for Charlie and the boys. Biker-babe Pat gave thumbs up to her macho-lover Joe, and Ruth was grateful that Dick had recovered so well. The other wives filled the VIP seats, proud as peacocks. The members of the Old Men's Cooking Club stood at attention in a row on a royal-blue carpeted platform under the dazzling chandelier in front of a portrait of George Washington. Dick sat in a wheelchair next to Ernie. With their chests swelling and wide beaming faces, the boys were on their best behavior.

President Sharif went over to each of the heroes, shook their hands and then proceeded to the podium.

"Today we salute a group of men who risked their lives banding together to protect and save our country from a national calamity. This is a group of dedicated individuals who bond together weekly, cook for each other, and try to settle the world's problems. These friends are strong patriots of the American way of life."

"Well, we didn't do such a good job solving the world's problems by electing this raghead," Ernie whispered to Dick.

"Be quiet, Ernie," Dick smiled at the camera.

The Commander-In-Chief went on, "Each member of this group comes to us from a diverse background, has disparate political affiliations and religious persuasions. Yet here is a group of men who set aside their differences and formed a unit to work together selflessly in the service for their nation. I understand that they throw together a mean meatloaf as well."

Fred felt a hint of heartburn with memories of the disastrous food fight witnessed by the vice president; Dick rolled his eyes while Ernie held his head down in shame.

"It is my distinct honor to present each one of them with a Special Presidential Medal."

The president approached each and placed a red, white and blue ribbon with the silver presidential medal around their necks and shook their hands again. There was Fred, the leader, with red cheeks beaming like Santa Claus, Ed, the scientist who saluted the chief, Bill the frugal finance guru wondering about the value of the medal on the silver market, Abe the self-proclaimed know-it-all who was temporarily speechless, Art the good-old-boy gardener, trying to act cool as a cucumber, Steve, the artist, dazzled by the ornate surroundings of the mansion, Joe, the biker, previously decorated with a mountainous bump on his head, who couldn't wait to share his medal with his babe, Charles, Robert's husband, who was proud of Sharif's stance on gay rights, Franz the former Third Reich soldier, who couldn't believe where he was and Dick, the government liaison, sitting in a wheelchair, taking it all in stride. Then came Ernie, an anti-everything curmudgeon who was daydreaming about the lunch that they were about to be served.

"Look at our Ernie; he's wiggling his red bowtie," said a retiree jumping up and down on her perch in the Orlando lounge.

"Why is he wearing white socks with his suit?"

"That's because he's Ernie."

The president stopped at Ernie, singling him out. "A special kudo goes to Ernest Stubbs. He infiltrated the adversarial group from the start of the operation, working tirelessly under difficult conditions to lead the group and save the day."

"Three cheers for Ernie" came the Florida seniors.

"Hip hip hooray, hip hip hooray, hip hip hooray," they chanted, bursting with pride and dancing around the room.

"I'd like to say something." Ernie stepped forward. All eyes froze on him in horror. This was not in the pre-planned script; the boys were instructed to restrict their comments to "Thank you" during the ceremony.

"Oh, oh! What is he up to?" Fred whispered to Dick.

"Mr. President, on behalf of my buddies of the Old Men's Cooking Club, I would like to thank you for honoring us. We are very proud to be Americans and were fortunate to have had this opportunity to serve you and our country."

"So far so good," Charles said quietly to Abe with a sigh of relief.

"We would also like you to invite you to become an honorary member of the Old Men's Cooking Club of the Orlando Senior Center. You can come and cook for us anytime."

"Thank you, I am flattered. What would you like me to cook for the group?" the President chuckled.

"Moroccan couscous."

Chapter 54
Salvaging A Broken Egg

Harry was incarcerated in isolation at the Seminole County Jail. Allowed only one hour a day out of his cell, the rest of the time he was left to stew in his own juices. The prison guard escorted him to the visitor's room. He was a high-security detainee and Dick had arranged this visit through Sally Adams. Franz had to endure meeting with his son through a glass partition. Feeling old and beaten up, Franz leaned against the partition, awaiting their confrontation.

When Harry was brought into the room, he could not look his father in the eye. Franz noted that his son had aged in the short time since his arrest. He appeared gaunt and exhausted; his once-blond hair had sprouted gray with an uncut lawn of stubble covering his face.

"Heinrich, are you, all right?"

"Not really."

"Are you being treated well?"

"As well as can be expected."

"Your mother and I are sick with worry about you."

"How can you be worried about me, Papa, when you were actively involved in my downfall?"

"I did the right thing, Harry."

"By plotting against me?"

"By stopping you from committing a senseless murder and putting a halt to the vile practices that have consumed you."

"I was protecting the American Dream."

"The American Dream is not only for the white majority. It is for everyone. That's what makes this country so special. You were taken in as a guest here and allowed to assimilate, to take advantage of the democratic way of life. Yet you chose to change the rules and introduce the evil practices of your past to your new surroundings."

"I wanted to ensure supremacy to our way of life."

"You wanted to enhance the dreams of a group of evil men who were living in the past where they had thrived on power, destruction and greed."

"You were part of that group, Papa."

"I was fooled years ago like everyone. Then I had no choice and suffered through the horrors as I waited for the devastation to end."

"What about Uncle Otto? He believed the work of the Third Reich was worthy and needed to be preserved and continued."

"Uncle Otto was a fool and a narrow-minded bigot."

"But he was your best friend."

"Yes, my great mistake was accepting him and blocking out the bad and accepting the good of all people. Sometimes even the smartest people are duped."

"What about your Old Men's Cooking Club? Are they all good people?"

"I don't agree with all their affiliations or political persuasions, but at least they are open and honest and put aside differences to form a bonded group. I would trust my life with every one of those boys." Franz wanted desperately to end the political squabbling. "This is altogether my fault. I should have been more observant of the time you spent with Otto. I knew his leanings but I completely ignored them. I wasn't open enough with you, didn't support you enough, Harry. I should have seen the handwriting on the wall."

"Papa don't beat yourself up. I'm a big boy, totally responsible for my actions, and will have to pay for my deeds."

"We are both going to pay, Heinrich, for the rest of our lives."

"How's Mama?"

"A wreck."

"And Ingrid?"

"A trooper but starting to crumble."

"And the children?"

"They're feeling their share of the pressure as well."

"It's such a fucking mess. How will they survive?"

"Your mother and I have decided to move here to help take care of the family."

"You don't have to do that, Papa."

"Yes, we do, Harry. I can start a vegetable garden here as well. I have good friends now, like Art and the boys in the cooking group, and will be able to make a life here. Your mother will have the grandchildren to dote over. We will miss our other children, but they all have the means to visit us here."

"I don't know what to say."

"Is anything new with your case?"

"The lawyers predict a long, hard struggle. The outcome is not promising."

250

"Harry, I abhor what we did. No one deserves this, but always remember one thing: you will always be my son and I will always love you," he concluded, with tears in his eyes, Franz grabbed the glass wall in an attempt to hug his son.

Harry was dozing in his cell when a corrections officer came to get him for the second time that day.

"Harry Smith, you have another visitor."

"For the life of me, I can't imagine who that might be," he said as they headed back to the visitation area. A distinguished-looking gentleman in a blue suit and striped tie sat on the visitor's side.

"Harry? I'm Paul Stanfield. I'm an attorney from Washington, D.C. I am joining your defense team."

"I don't understand. I don't have the means to engage you as well."

"I am here at the request of Sid. I am meeting with your team tomorrow. He sends you a message."

"Yes?" Harry asked eagerly.

"Sid says he'll take care of things."

Chapter 55
Cherries Jubilee

Fragrant aromas of garlic and onions wafted from the kitchen as Dick, sporting a cane topped with an alligator handle, limped into the Senior Center for the weekly Old Men's Cooking Club. The computer room was decorated for celebration with red, white, and blue balloons, and streamers hanging from the ceiling. The tables had been arranged into one that would accommodate the sixteen guests. Elegant white tablecloths and vases with fresh flowers direct from Charles' garden adorned the feasting table. The kitchen was like an apiary of activity which added electricity in the air.

The leader Fred was tinkering with the worn-out coffeemaker; Abe was dicing beefy tomatoes and chopping sweet Vidalia onions for the salad. Steve was plating fruit arranged in a bouquet of colors.

Modeling his hero's medal, Ernie asked "Who's cooking today?" as he strolled in with Bessie on his arm.

"Charles and Robert," answered Ed.

"Oh good. It's 'La Di Da' food." Ernie was being atrocious as usual.

One by one the boys filed in, each wearing their silver medal.

"I'll make the garlic bread," Bill volunteered.

"Sorry, Bill, No garlic bread today. We're having canapés to start the festivities," Robert divulged.

"My word, fancy shmancy," Ernie interjected.

Joe, who was growing a beard, dressed in a black-and-orange Harley-Davidson shirt with a red bandana on his head, was filling pitchers with iced tea.

"Hey Joe, you shouldn't be growing that fuzz on your chin," Dick primed Joe's ego.

"Why the hell not?"

"Cause President Sharif is going impose a tax on beards."

"I wouldn't be surprised, but where did you get that cock and bull story anyway?"

"It was in this morning's paper."

"About Sharif?"

"No about Peter the Great who imposed the beard law in Russia on this day in 1698."

Dick became occupied peeling the large white spuds for the potato pancakes. "This reminds me of my army days, boys." Peels were flying all over the kitchen and onto the floor.

"Hey Dick, I guess you were a bad boy a lot in the service," Fred kidded.

Charles, mallet in hand, was pounding the chicken breasts for the chicken cordon bleu.

"Easy, Charlie, you're supposed to caress breasts, not beat them to death," Joe chided.

At that moment, two of the luncheon's special guests arrived: Sally Adams and Tom Prentice.

"How are my national heroes today?" Sally asked, hugging each of the boys.

"Great, Sally, we are pleased as punch that you are here today," said Art.

"How can I help?" Sally was ready to dig in.

"Let's give her potatoes to peel," Dick volunteered to give up his chore for his country.

"No KP duty for Sally. She's a guest. However, I do have a good job for her," Abe jested.

"Hors d'oeuvres are ready," Robert chimed in, passing around the silver platter. The enticing-looking canapés included salmon with asparagus, eggplant and shiitake mushrooms, crab with cumin, deviled eggs, sushi rolls, goat cheese, Spanish olives, and crème cheese. Robert really had outdone himself.

"Hey, what's that one with the little stripes?" Ernie asked.

"Rattlesnake!" and Joe laughed.

"Sprats," corrected Robert.

"Aren't that what fancy men wore on their feet in all the gangster movies? I saw George Raft wearing sprats."

"That's spats, Ernie. Sprats are in the sardine family."

"What about that little critter?" Ernie said pointing to another canapé delicacy.

"That's sushi, Ernie."

"Oh, I don't eat raw fish," Ernie shivered.

"Hey, Ern. What's the difference between eating sushi and eating pussy?" Joe was at his best being erotically playful.

"I give up, Joe. What?"

"The rice." Groans came from around the room.

Steve was frying the potato pancakes. Ed was preparing the asparagus by tossing them in olive oil, garlic and lemon juice. Abe was finishing the salad, and Robert was mixing his secret salad dressing after completing the surprise appetizer. Charles layered the gruyere cheese and ham and folded the chicken into a jelly-roll shape. Bill took the roulades and dusted them with a flour, salt, pepper, thyme, oil and a breadcrumb concoction. He passed them to Ed who dipped each piece in an egg and water wash combination. The asparagus accompanied the chicken into the oven and in 20 minutes, the feast would be ready.

Art and Franz tended to the banquet table. Everything had to be just right. Charles brought in fine cutlery, good china, and crystal glasses. Everyone fussed over Bess and Sally, since it was a rare treat to have female guests and the boys were truly enjoying the diversion.

"Lunch is served," beamed Charles and everyone headed to the quasi banquet hall.

"Cowabunga," yelled Ernie, "look at that fancy table."

"Where in heaven's name did you get that word, Ernie?" Abe asked taken aback.

"Shame on you, Abe. Don't you know your history?"

"I guess not," know-it-all Abe admitted meekly.

"That's what Chief Thunderthud used to yell when he was excited on 'The Howdy Doody Show.'"

All were positioned around the table with Ernie and Bessie at the head. The director of the center joined the group for this celebratory lunch, but there was still one empty chair. Suddenly the French doors swung open and a vision appeared. It was the theatrical floor show, Leonetta Moore, their favorite Denny's server, dressed to the nines. She was wearing dark glasses, a fire-engine red dress with a black feather boa around her neck, a wide brim hat piled high with peacock feathers and carried a black-and-white checkered sun umbrella. All she needed was a long cigarette holder.

"Am I late, boys? I wouldn't have missed this doo for the world." Everyone laughed and welcomed her with open arms.

"Look who's here. If it isn't our black Mae West," Ernie spouted off.

"Ernie," Dick exclaimed.

"Sorry."

With napkins positioned on each lap and iced tea poured, Robert entered with the mystery appetizer: Escargot, sloshing in melted butter and garlic.

"Now what are these nasty-looking things?" Ernie asked in a near panic.

"Escargot: snails, Ernie." Robert explained.

"I'm not eating any of those disgusting-looking slimy creatures."

Bessie kicked Ernie under the table.

"Come on, Ernie, they're delicious. We caught them in our garden this morning." Abe was trying to be funny.

"Yeah, Ernie, you're a man of the world now. You are old enough to try the snails."

The men's chorus sang out loud.

"Yeah, Ernie, eat the snails."

"Snails."

"Snails."

"Snails."

"Snails."

"Oh all right, but if I die…"

"Drum roll, fellows," Abe yelled, and Joe banged out a drum roll on the table.

"Tatum."

"Tatum."

"Tatum."

Everyone waited with bated breath. Like a condemned man about to take his last bite, Ernie dramatically lifted the morsel and slowly brought it to his beak. All eyes watched as he swished the slimy mollusk around in his mouth.

"Don't spit it out on the floor, whatever you do," Bessie whispered. He created one large swallow, made his famous discontented curmudgeon face, shook his head from side to side, and said: "That was really tasty. Let me have more" at which point everyone laughed and took cubes of French bread to dip into the buttery sauce.

Robert had volunteered to be assistant sous chef and waiter for the feast. The next course was the mixed green salad. He passed bowls filled with a garden of colorful vegetables sprinkled with a homemade Asian sesame dressing.

"Hey Ernie, you know that you and Bessie aren't allowed to live in sin in the State of Florida. You have to be married. It's the Florida Cohabitation Law. It's been on the books since the 1800's. You can face up to six months in jail and a $500 fine," Joe informed the happy twice-divorced couple.

"You're joking, Joe."

"No, honest injun. Go look it up."

"No need reporting it to the FBI," he said, pointing at Sally. "There's no hanky panky going on between us. At 86, sex is like shooting pool with a rope," Ernie laughed, but seemed resigned.

Bessie joined in the laughter as well.

"Speaking of sex: so I say to my wife, I don't know why you wear a bra, you don't have anything to put in it. And she says to me, you wear brief underwear, don't you," Steve quipped.

"Lord save us, Jesus," bellowed Leonetta, "and I'm wearing my Sunday church-going clothes for this."

When the salad plates were cleared, Robert brought out the main course. The plates were filled with sumptuous chicken breasts stuffed with ham and cheese, citrus-flavored asparagus, and sizzling potato pancakes right out of the skillet.

"Wow, it looks so rich. I'm never going to pass my annual blood tests tomorrow," Ed bemoaned.

"I had my tests recently and the results indicated abnormal lover functions," Abe laughed at his own joke.

"My doctor called me this morning and told me that my check came back," Art told the group.

"So, what happened?" Dick was curious.

"I told him that my arthritis came back."

"That was a horrible joke, Art," Bill said.

"It was funny when Henny Youngman told it," Art defended.

They savored the delicious chicken, asparagus, and thoroughly enjoyed the fried potato treats. They ate, bantered, and toasted each other with their iced tea glasses.

"How is Annillese, Franz?" Charles asked.

"She is not doing well, but hopefully, she will come out of it. It will take time."

"I'm so sorry."

"Hey, attention everyone. Franz and Annillese are moving here permanently," Art announced.

"That's terrific," Abe acknowledged. "It will be great to have Franz as a permanent member of the group."

Clink, clink, clink, a spoon was tapped against a crystal goblet. The director of the center stood to get everyone's attention.

"I am guilty of constantly accusing you guys of breaking the Center rules, making too much noise, getting food all over the carpets, sneaking in wine, and commandeering the computer room for your feasts. But today I am going to put my job in jeopardy and disobey the law. Robert, are you ready, please."

On that note, Robert, tangoed in from the kitchen carrying two bottles of French champagne and began pouring.

"Let me propose a toast: To the best, baddest, bunch of bodacious buddies in the entire United States. We are all so proud of you. L'Chiam."

"I would like to say a few words," Sally said, on her feet in a flash, and raising her glass of bubbly. "You are a most remarkable group of men and Tom and I are so proud to have the opportunity to work so closely with you. Remember, we made you deputies. We want you to keep those ranks and hopefully you will be able to work alongside us together again soon. We love you, boys." No-nonsense Federal agent Sally, totally out of character, was choked up. There was applause all around.

"Folks, I have something to say."

"Speech, speech."

"Keep it clean, Joe."

"That would be a novelty," Ernie said.

"On behalf of the boys in the Old Men's Cooking Club, we want to thank you, Sally and Tom, for your trust and good guidance. We never could have accomplished these goals without your constant nurturing and leadership. We, too, loved working with you." Joe was refreshingly serious and sentimental for a change. "We would like to make both of you honorary members of the Old Men's Cooking Club."

"Here, here."

"Make them take an oath," Ernie yelled out.

"We don't have one," Fred countered.

"Well, make one up. They invented a doozy when they deputized us," Ernie joked.

"One moment, folks, we just have one more item to attend to. Since the group is exclusively a men's organization, we're making a major exception by taking you in, Sally. We have a little gift for you and ask you to wear it whenever you attend our group." Joe handed Sally a rectangular box wrapped in gold paper with a red ribbon. All the boys looked at each other in total confusion. No one had a clue. Sally shook the box and listened for a bomb.

"Force of habit," she said, then tore open the box, looked in and started to laugh hysterically. In front of the eager audience, she lifted out a full length, strikingly real-looking, naturally colored hand-painted (with all details including pubic hair) penis necktie.

At that moment the lights in the computer room dimmed.

"What's going on," yelled Abe.

"It isn't even raining outside," Art confirmed. They sat in the dark looking around when Robert burst in carrying a flame lit cherries jubilee. There was more cheering, whooping and hollering.

"As I said before, a waist is a terrible thing to mind," the ever-dieting Steve said to Dick as he dug into the sinfully rich dessert.

Suddenly a cell phone rang as the feasting party was enjoying the luscious dessert. Everyone reached into their pockets simultaneously, but Dick hit the jackpot. He answered and listened carefully, nodding at the message. There was a deadly silence as everyone focused on their unshakable buddy as his eyes swelled with tears and his body sank down into his chair. One could have cut the tension in the air with a knife.

"What's the matter, Dick?" Ernie ventured "You look like you've seen a ghost."

"I'm all right, Ernie."

"Is something wrong. Did something happen to Ruth. Talk to me, buddy?"

Crying like a baby, Dick uttered, "Something is very right, my friend. Medicare is going to pay for Ruth's cancer treatments."

There was a collective sigh of relief and a whooping around the table for Medicare.

Ernie hugged Dick, "I'm so happy for you, buddy. Ya didn't want my money, huh? It was too tainted for you."

"Ernie, you are too tainted for me," and he laughed.

"Hold it a moment, everyone, I said that I had a special job for Sally and Tom," Abe said reaching into a shopping bag and pulling out two frilly-laced green aprons. "These are for you to do the dishes." The stack of dishes from this meal was enormous and the two FBI agents bellyached but dug into the suds and did their duty.

"This is criminal for us to do dishes," Sally complained.

"Yeah, our job description forbids us to do windows as well," Tom jested as he sloshed dirty plates through the murky water.

"Look, guys we CIA boys always said the FBI was washed up," Dick said as he cheered on the two law-enforcement officers.

The group members hugged each other and began to leave. Dick and Ernie walked to the parking lot together. Bessie and Leonetta followed.

"Did you hear that President Sharif wants to cut our Social Security?" Ernie complained to Dick.

"He wouldn't dare," Dick was belligerent.

"Yup, give to the rich and cut from the poor. He means it. Can you believe it? That Muslim bastard gave me a medal." Ernie shook his head from side to side. The two partners in crime put their arms around each other and walked toward their cars. Bessie looked at Dick and Ernie and said to Leonetta, beaming with pride, "The boys are back in town. Business as usual for the Old Men's Cooking Club."

"Yes siree, bob," Leonetta sighed and laughed.

258

Ernie stopped at his white Scion and faced Dick.

Dick opened his arms and hugged his buddy, whispering in his ear, "You know, Ernie, I think this is the beginning of a beautiful friendship."

Ernie, totally out of character relaxed, accepted the hug graciously and said, "Didn't Humphrey Bogart say that sometime during the war in India?"

"It was in 'Casablanca' Ernie."

"Africa, India. What's the difference? Those folks all look alike!"

"OH ERNIE!"

SECRET RECIPES FROM THE OLD MEN'S COOKING CLUB COLLECTION*

*The author of this book is not responsible for these recipes, because he doesn't have any clue where the cooking boys got them from!

Chapter 1: FROM FRED'S MENU

BROWNIES

YIELDS
15 small squares

INGREDIENTS
2 sticks plus 2 tablespoons unsalted butter, plus lots more for the pan
12 ounces bittersweet chocolate, coarsely chopped
½ cup all-purpose flour
1 teaspoon baking powder
3 large eggs
1 1/4 cups packed light-brown sugar
1 cup macadamia nuts, coarsely chopped

DIRECTIONS
1. Preheat oven to 325 degrees. Butter a 7-x-11 ½ inch x 2 inch baking pan. Line it with parchment paper and put it aside.
2. Put butter and chocolate in a microwavable bowl and cover. Microwave for 30 seconds at a time till it melts. Let it cool. Whisk flour and baking powder together in a bowl and set it aside.
3. With a hand mixer, beat the eggs until they are thick and creamy, about 5 minutes. Gradually beat in the sugar. Continue beating until the mixture is thick and pudding-like, about 3 minutes more. Gradually fold in the chocolate mixture alternating with the dry ingredients. Fold in the nuts.
4. Pour batter into the prepared pan. And bake it until the top is firm to the touch, about 45 minutes. Remove from the oven and let the pan cool.
5. Cut into squares in the pan.

RECIPE NOTES:
According to Ernie, if you added a bit of marijuana, they would be qualified to be called Alice B. Toklas Brownies.

Chapter 3: FROM ART'S MENU

VENISON STEW WITH RED CURRENT JELLY AND BACON

<u>**YIELDS**</u>
8 servings

<u>**INGREDIENTS**</u>
A three-pound venison (deer) roast cut into 1 ½ inch cubes
Salt and pepper
3tablespoons olive oil
1 large Vidalia onion diced
8 oz. piece of streaky fatty bacon, diced
2 stalks celery, sliced
6 cloves garlic diced
3 tablespoons of all-purpose flour
2 tablespoon tomato paste
2 cups dry red wine
3 cups chicken broth
2 sprigs fresh thyme
2 bay leaves
1 ½ pounds of new potatoes quartered
4 carrots slice
4 tablespoons red currant jelly
One cup frozen peas

<u>**DIRECTIONS**</u>
1. Put venison in a zip lock bag with one cup red wine, thyme, salt, pepper, 2 cloves of garlic diced.
2. Seal and marinate for four hours.
3. In a large Dutch oven, heat the oil and add the onions, smoked bacon, a sprig of thyme, carrots, celery. Season with salt and pepper. Cook until the onions are soft and light brown.
4. Put the venison in with the liquid.
5. Add garlic, tomato paste, bay leaves and cook for 3 minutes. Mix flour in and thoroughly cook for another four minutes.
6. Add the chicken broth, one cup red wine, the new potatoes and the red currant jelly

7. Cover and cook on medium for 45-75 minutes until the meat falls apart easily.
8. Let it rest a few minutes before serving add frozen peas.

RECIPE NOTES
Art advises that the deer be totally dead before cooking.

APPLE STRUDEL

YIELDS
One loaf

INGREDIENTS
1 Granny Smith apple, peeled, cored and coarsely shredded.
3 Granny Smith apples, peeled, cored and sliced.
1 cup brown sugar
1 cup golden raisins
1 sheet frozen puff pastry
1 egg
¼ cup milk

DIRECTIONS
1. Preheat the oven to 400 degrees.
2. Line a baking sheet with parchment paper.
3. Place the apples in a large bowl. Stir in brown sugar and golden raisins, set aside.
4. Place puff pastry on a baking sheet.
5. Roll lightly with a rolling pin.
6. Arrange the apple filling down the middle of the pastry lengthwise.
7. Fold the pastry lengthwise around the mixture.
8. Seal the edges of the pastry by using a bit of water and rubbing the edges together.
9. Whisk the egg and milk together, and brush onto top of pastry.
10. Bake in preheated oven for 35 to 40 minutes, or until golden brown.

RECIPE NOTES
Art wants to remind you that June 17th is National Apple Strudel Day. Get your ingredients early so you have plenty of time to celebrate! He also

recommends staying clear of holocaust discussions before serving!

CHAPTER 5: FROM BILL'S MENU

PONZU CHICKEN

YIELDS
Serves 6

INGREDIENTS
3 chicken breasts (split in halves)
2/3 cup Ponzu Mixture: juice from 3 limes and 3 lemons
2/3 cup soy sauce
1 tablespoon brown sugar
¾ cup water
lots of fresh garlic
salt: generous coating
toasted sesame oil

DIRECTIONS
1. Brush the Ponzu mixture on the chicken breasts and salt it heavily and marinate for about 30-60 minutes.
2. Set your oven to 425 degrees.
3. Put your chicken breasts in a small cast-iron skillet or similar pan. Add the crushed garlic to the pan.
4. Roast for about 30 minutes until nicely browned.
5. Take the breasts out of the oven, transfer to a cutting board and let rest for a few minutes.
6. Put skillet with the drippings on the stove over medium heat.
7. To the skillet, add the water, the soy sauce, brown sugar, and a splash of the Ponzu mixture. Boil and stir until the sugar is dissolved.
8. Add sesame oil.
9. Slice the chicken breasts into half-inch slices and arrange in serving dish. Pour sauce around the breasts.

RECIPE NOTES
Bill wants to make it perfectly clear that this delicious dish has nothing to do with the financial scam Bernard Madoff pulled off.

SPOTTED DICK*
Note: This English Nursery Pudding Recipe Is Rated "G" For All Ages

YIELDS
Serves 6

INGREDIENTS
10 ounces flour
2 teaspoons baking powder
5 ounces shredded suet
3 ounces sugar
4 ounces currants
1 lemon (use zest only)
7 ounces milk
7 ounces whipping cream
6 egg yolks
3 ounces sugar

DIRECTIONS
1. Place the flour, baking powder, shredded suet, sugar, currants, and lemon zest into a bowl and mix to combine.
2. Add the milk to make a soft dough.
3. Grease pudding mold with butter and spoon the mixture into the mold.
4. Cover it with a piece of parchment paper.
5. Tie a string around the edge to secure the paper and cover it with a damp dish towel.
6. Place the mold into a large covered saucepan and fill the pan up two-thirds with water.
7. Cover the lid and bring it to a boil and then simmer for one hour.
The Custard
1. Place milk and cream in a saucepan and bring to a simmer.
2. Place the egg yolks and sugar in a bowl and whisk together until light and frothy.
3. Pour the hot milk into the eggs, a little at a time, and stir well.
4. Pour the mixture back into the pan and cook over low heat, stirring with a wooden spatula until it thickens.
5. Pour the custard onto the spotted dick when you are ready to serve the dish.

RECIPE NOTES

Ernie says that he would handle a Spotted Dick dessert differently by going to the grocery store and buying a can of Heinz Spotted Dick!

CHAPTER 7: FROM ABE'S MENU

GRANDMA BETTY'S BORSCHT

YIELDS
6 Servings

INGREDIENTS
2 cups chopped fresh beets
2 cups chopped carrots
2 cups chopped onion
4 cups beef or vegetable broth
1 can (16 ounces) diced tomatoes, undrained
2 cups chopped cabbage
½ teaspoon salt
½ teaspoon dill weed
¼ teaspoon pepper
Sour cream, optional

DIRECTIONS
1. In a large saucepan, combine the beets, carrots, onion and broth; bring to a boil. Reduce heat; cover and simmer for 30 minutes.
2. Add tomatoes and cabbage; cover and simmer for 30 minutes or until cabbage is tender. Stir in salt, dill and pepper. Top each serving with sour cream, if desired.

RECIPE NOTES
Abe wants you to know that this is a non-sectarian soup. In other words, you don't have to be Jewish to enjoy it. Grandma Betty said, "This soup cured all ills better than chicken soup."

STUFFED CABBAGE

YIELDS
8 Servings

INGREDIENTS
The Stuffing
1 large head cabbage, frozen
2 pounds ground beef
1 teaspoon salt
1/2 teaspoon pepper
2 large eggs
1/3 cup ketchup
½ cup uncooked rice
1 finely chopped small onion

The Sauce
35-ounce can chopped tomatoes
2 tablespoons tomato paste
2 tablespoons sliced onions
½ cup ketchup
2 lemons
1/3 cup brown sugar
1/3 cup raisins
1 tablespoon oil
salt and pepper

DIRECTIONS
1. Defrost cabbage the night before. Separate the cabbage leaves.
2. For the stuffing: Mix the ground beef, salt, pepper, eggs, rice, ketchup and chopped onion in a large bowl.
3. Set one large tablespoon of the stuffing on each cabbage leaf.
4. Fold the ends in and roll them up like a big cigar.
5. Set them, open side down, in a 6-quart casserole dish.
6. For the sauce: Cook the onions with oil in a saucepan for a few minutes.
7. Add tomatoes, tomato paste, salt, pepper, onions, ketchup, the juice of one lemon, brown sugar, and raisins.
8. Bring the mixture to a boil, cover it and let it simmer for about 15 minutes.

9. Pour the sauce over the cabbage.

10. Cover the dish with foil and bake at 350 degrees for one and a half hours.

11. Then uncover and continue to cook for an additional half hour.

12. You may add water if it seems too dry.

13. Squeeze the remaining lemon juice over the dish if you feel if it's not sweet and sour enough.

RECIPE NOTES

Abe wants you to know that it tastes even better leftover the next day, so make lots of extra.

MACAROON COOKIES

YIELDS

Servings 12

INGREDIENTS

8-ounce tube of almond paste

1 cup sugar

3 large white eggs

¼ teaspoon vanilla extract

½ teaspoon almond extract

3 tablespoons flour

½ cup of confectioners' sugar

A pinch of salt

DIRECTIONS

1. Break up the almond paste into a mixing bowl.

2. Mix the almond paste, sugar, egg whites, 2 extracts in a food processor for about one minute.

3. Add the remaining ingredients and process the mixture for another minute.

4. Cover several baking pans with parchment paper.

5. Take a tablespoon and drop almond mixture onto pan.

6. Use a dampened finger and flatten the dough.

7. Let the pans stand uncovered for an hour.

8. Pre-heat oven to 300 degrees.

9. Put pans in oven and bake for about 15-20 minutes or until cookies are

golden.

RECIPE NOTES
Abe says you can't just eat just one of these morsels. You're going to gobble them up before you put them out for your company, so make plenty.

CHAPTER 11 FROM DICK'S MENU

DICK'S IMPOSSIBLE-TO-RUIN MEATLOAF

YIELDS
6 servings

INGREDIENTS
1 1/2 pounds ground beef
1 egg
1 onion, chopped
1 cup milk
1 cup bread crumbs
salt and pepper
2 tablespoons brown sugar
2 tablespoons mustard
1/3 cup ketchup

DIRECTIONS
1. Preheat oven to 350 degrees.
2. In a large mixing bowl, combine the beef, egg, onion, milk and breadcrumbs.
3. Season with salt and pepper.
4. Place mixture in a lightly greased 5 x 9-inch loaf pan.
5. In a small bowl, combine the brown sugar with the mustard and ketchup.
6, Mix well and pour over the meatloaf.
7. Bake at 350 degrees for 1 hour.

RECIPE NOTES
Charles wants you to know that anyone can make this recipe, even our veteran retired CIA spook Dick without burning down the kitchen, at least once.

274

CHAPTER 13 FROM FRANZ'S MENU

SAUERBRATEN

YIELDS
14 Servings

INGREDIENTS
2 teaspoons salt
1 teaspoon ground ginger
4 pounds beef stew meat
1/2 cups water
2 cups apple cider vinegar
1/3 cup sugar
2 onions, sliced
2 tablespoons mixed pickling spices
1 teaspoon whole peppercorns
8 whole cloves
2 bay leaves
2 tablespoons vegetable oil
15 gingersnaps, crushed

DIRECTIONS
1. In a small bowl, combine salt and ginger; rub over roast. Place in a deep glass bowl.
2. In a large bowl, combine the water, vinegar and sugar.
3. Pour half of marinade into a large saucepan; add half of the onions, pickling spices, peppercorns, cloves and bay leaves.
4. Bring to a boil. Pour over roast; turn it to marinate.
5. Cover and refrigerate for two days, turning twice a day.
6. To the remaining marinade, add the rest of the onions, pickling spices, peppercorns, cloves
and bay leaves. Cover and refrigerate.
7. Drain and discard marinade from roast.
8. Pat roast dry. In a Dutch oven over medium-high heat, brown roast in oil on all sides. Pour 1 cup of reserved marinade with all the onions and seasonings over roast. Bring to a boil. Reduce heat; cover and simmer for 3 hours or until meat is tender. (Cover and refrigerate remaining marinade.)
9. Add enough reserved marinade to the cooking juices to make 3 cups. Pour into a large saucepan. Bring to a boil. Add crushed gingersnaps

10. Reduce heat and simmer until gravy is thickened.
11. Slice roast and serve with gravy.

RECIPE NOTES
Franz says he realizes there are many steps, but it's worth the work for this heavenly treat!

CHAPTER 23 FROM CHARLIE'S MENU

BABA GHANOUJ

YIELDS
10 Servings

INGREDIENTS
1-pound eggplants, halved lengthwise
1/4 cup olive oil
1/4 cup tahini
3 tablespoons fresh lemon juice
1 garlic clove, chopped
Sprinkle of smoked paprika (optional)
Pita bread

DIRECTIONS
1. Preheat oven to 375°F.
2. Generously oil baking sheet. Place eggplant halves cut side down on sheet. Roast until
eggplant is very soft, about 45 minutes. Cool slightly.
3. Using spoon, scoop out pulp from eggplant.
4. Place eggplant pulp in food processor. Add 1 tablespoon olive oil (more if necessary), tahini,
lemon juice, and garlic. Process until smooth.
5. Season to taste with salt and pepper.
6. Transfer to small bowl. Cover and chill
7. Can be made one day ahead.
8. Bring to room temperature before serving. Sprinkle with smoked paprika.
9. Serve with pita bread.

RECIPE NOTES
Ernie advises not to forget to ganouj the baba.

GUAVA-STUFFED CHICKEN WITH CARAMELIZED MANGOES

YIELDS
6 Servings

INGREDIENTS
¾ cup olive oil
1/4 cup fresh lemon juice
6 garlic cloves, chopped
3 tablespoons fresh parsley, chopped
2 tablespoons fresh thyme leaves
6 large skinless boneless chicken breast halves
3 ounces cream cheese, at room temperature
2 tablespoons guava paste (about 1 1/2 ounces)
2 ½ ounces fresh spinach leaves chopped (2 cups loosely packed)
2 tablespoons canola oil
½ cup dry white wine
½ cup chicken broth
4 tablespoons butter
1 large mango, halved, pitted, peeled, cut into 1/2-inch-thick slices

DIRECTIONS
1. Whisk first 5 ingredients in large bowl, add chicken breasts. Turn to coat.
2. Cover chicken breasts and marinate 4 hours, turning 2 or 3 times.
3. Mix cream cheese and guava paste well. Stir in spinach. Cover and chill for 2 hours.
4. With a sharp knife make a pocket in the chicken breast and fill with cream cheese mixture.
Close with toothpicks Can be made 4 hours ahead. Cover and chill for ½ hour.
5. Bake in 350-degree oven for 20 minutes till internal temperature reaches 165 degrees.
6. Transfer to cutting board. Let chicken rest for 10 minutes
7. In a skillet, add juices from the roasting pan, wine, broth and boil until it is reduced to about ¾
cup.
8. Meanwhile, melt butter in another skillet over medium-high heat. Add mango slices and sauté
until brown, about 2 minutes per side.

9. Slice chicken diagonally into 1/2-inch-thick slices. Arrange chicken on a platter.
10. Drizzle sauce over chicken and surround with mangoes.

RECIPE NOTES
Ernie's guide to taking the temperature of a chicken. You shove the thermometer up its.........!

SOUR CREAM CHEESE CAKE

YIELDS
12 Servings

INGREDIENTS
1 ½ cups graham cracker crumbs
¼ pound butter, melted
1 cup sugar
2 eggs, beaten
16 ounces cream cheese, softened
dash of salt
1½ tsp vanilla
1 cup sour cream

DIRECTIONS
Crust
1. Stir together graham cracker crumbs, melted butter and ¼ cup sugar in a medium bowl.
2. Press into the bottom of a 9-inch spring-form pan. Refrigerate while making filling.
Filling
1. Combine cream cheese, 2/3 cup of sugar, salt, eggs and ½ teaspoon vanilla in medium bowl. Beat at medium speed with a hand mixer for 5 minutes. Pour the filling into the prepared pan.
2. Bake at 350 degrees for 25 minutes. Cool 30 minutes before adding the sour cream topping.
Topping
1. Mix sour cream, 3 tablespoons sugar and 1 teaspoon vanilla in a small bowl.
2. Pour and spread on top of the slightly cooled cheesecake.

3. Bake for 5-10 minutes at 350 degrees.
4. Cool to room temperature and then place in refrigerator to chill before serving.

RECIPE NOTES

Charles suggests that this should be topped by a fresh fruit.

CHAPTER 26 FROM STEVE'S MENU

CHIMICHURRI LONDON BROIL

YIELDS
Serves: 4-6 servings

INGREDIENTS
1 cup packed fresh parsley leaves
3 garlic cloves
1 shallot, peeled
½-1 jalapeno, depending on how hot you like it, seeds removed
½ cup red wine vinegar
¾ cup olive oil
1 teaspoon kosher salt
½ teaspoon black pepper
1 (approximately 2 lb.) London broil

DIRECTIONS
1. Combine all ingredients except the meat in the bowl of a food processor. Pulse until there are no more large chunks of garlic or shallot.
2. Place meat in a ziplock bag and pour about ¾ of the sauce in. Place in the fridge to marinate for at least 4 hours, or overnight. Reserve the remaining sauce.
3. Once meat has marinated, place it, with about ½ of the marinade, in a 9 x13 pan. Broil on high for about 5-7 minutes per side (for medium-rare), depending on the size of the meat and your preferred doneness.
4. Let the meat rest for about 7-10 minutes before slicing.
5. Drizzle reserved marinade over steak before serving

RECIPE NOTES
Steve warns this may be too hot for your palate.

RATATOUILLE

YIELDS
4 Servings

INGREDIENTS
1 onion, thinly sliced
2 garlic cloves, minced
5 tablespoons olive oil
¾-pound eggplant, cut into ½-inch pieces
1 small zucchini, scrubbed, quartered lengthwise, and cut into thin slices
1 red bell pepper, chopped
¾-pound small ripe tomatoes, chopped coarsely (about 1 ¼ cups)
¼ teaspoon dried oregano, crumbled
¼ teaspoon dried thyme, crumbled
1/8 teaspoon ground coriander
¼ teaspoon fennel seeds
¾ teaspoon salt
½ cup fresh basil leaves, shredded

DIRECTIONS
1. In a large skillet, cook the onion and the garlic in 2 tablespoons of the oil over moderately low heat, stirring occasionally, until the onion is softened. Add the remaining 3 tablespoons oil and adjust heat to moderately high until it is hot, but not smoking.
2. Add the eggplant and cook the mixture, stirring occasionally, for 8 minutes, or until the eggplant is softened.
3. Stir in the zucchini and the bell pepper and cook the mixture over moderate heat, stirring occasionally, for 12 minutes. Stir in the tomatoes and cook the mixture, stirring occasionally, for 5 to 7 minutes, or until the vegetables are tender.
4. Stir in the oregano, thyme, coriander, fennel seeds, salt and pepper to taste and cook the mixture, stirring, for 1 minute.
5. Stir in the basil and combine the mixture well.
6. The ratatouille may be made one day in advance, kept covered and chilled, and reheated before serving.

RECIPE NOTES
Ernie suggests not using live rats for this concoction.

282

STRAWBERRY SHORTCAKE

YIELDS
6 Servings

INGREDIENTS
1 ½ pounds strawberries, stemmed and quartered
5 tablespoons sugar
2 cups all-purpose flour
2 teaspoons baking powder
¼ teaspoon baking soda
2 tablespoons sugar
¾ teaspoon salt
1 ½ cups heavy cream

Whipped Cream:
1 ½ cups heavy cream, chilled
3 tablespoons sugar
1 ½ teaspoons vanilla extract
1 teaspoon freshly grated lemon zest

DIRECTIONS
1. Preheat the oven to 400 degrees.
2. Mix strawberries with 3 tablespoons sugar and refrigerate at least 30 minutes, so juices develop.
3. Sift together the flour, baking powder, baking soda, remaining 2 tablespoons sugar, and salt in a medium bowl. Add heavy cream and mix until just combined.
4. Place mixture in an ungreased 8-inch square pan and bake until golden, 18 to 20 minutes.
5. Remove shortcake from pan and place on a rack to cool slightly.
6. Cut into 6 pieces and split each piece in half horizontally.
7. Spoon some of the strawberries with their juice onto each shortcake bottom. Top with a generous dollop of whipped cream and then the put-on shortcake top. Spoon more strawberries over the top and serve.

Whipped Cream:
Using a mixer, beat the heavy cream, sugar, vanilla, and lemon zest until soft peaks form, about 1½ to 2 minutes.

RECIPE NOTES

Steve advises not to cut things short.

CHAPTER 31 FROM ABE'S MENU

CHINESE PORK TENDERLOIN

YIELDS
4 Servings

INGREDIENTS
1 (2 lb.) whole pork tenderloin, well-trimmed
½ cup water or chicken stock
¼ cup light brown sugar, packed
2 teaspoons kosher salt
½ teaspoon Chinese five spice powder
2 tablespoons soy sauce
1 tablespoon dry sherry
1 tablespoon yellow miso
2 teaspoons fresh garlic, crushed
¼ teaspoon red food coloring
Sesame seeds
Mustard for dipping

DIRECTIONS
1.Place the pork in a large ziptop bag.
2. In a small bowl, stir together the rest of the ingredients until the sugar has dissolved.
3. Pour into the ziptop bag; remove as much air as possible and seal shut.
4. Refrigerate for 6 to 36 hours
5. Preheat oven to 375 degrees.
6. Remove pork from the marinade (discard remaining marinade); place on wire rack in a shallow baking pan. Insert meat thermometer.
7. Roast about 30-40 minutes or until the internal meat temperature reaches 165 degrees.
8. Remove from oven and allow to rest on wire rack for 15 minutes before removing thermometer and slicing.
Enjoy it by first dipping a slice into the mustard, then into the sesame seeds.

RECIPE NOTES
Abe cautions not to cut the mustard.

CHAPTER 35 FROM JOE'S MENU

HUSH PUPPIES

YIELDS
8-10 Servings

INGREDIENTS
vegetable oil
1 ½ cups white corn meal
¾ cup self-rising flour
¾ cup sweet onion (about ½ medium onion), diced
1½ tablespoons sugar
1 large egg, lightly beaten
1 ¼ cups buttermilk

DIRECTIONS
1. Pour oil to depth of 3 inches into a Dutch oven; heat to 375°.
2. Combine cornmeal and next three ingredients. Add egg and buttermilk; stir until just moistened. Let stand 10 minutes.
3. Drop batter by rounded tablespoonfuls into hot oil, and fry 2 to 3 minutes on each side or until golden.
4. Keep warm in a 200° oven until ready to serve.

RECIPE NOTES
Joe recommends this dish as a perfect side with roadkill.

CRISPY FRIED CATFISH

YIELDS
4 Servings

INGREDIENTS
vegetable oil, for frying
2 cups buttermilk
3 tablespoons hot sauce
8 boneless catfish fillets
3 cups all-purpose flour

2 cups yellow corn meal
2 tablespoons Old Bay Seasoning
Kosher salt

DIRECTIONS

1. In a large Dutch oven, or heavy-bottomed pot, heat 2 inches of oil to 350 degrees over medium-high heat.
2. While the oil is heating, whisk together the buttermilk and hot sauce in a large bowl.
Add the catfish and let soak for 15 minutes.
3. Meanwhile, combine the flour, corn meal, Old Bay and 2 tablespoons salt in a large bowl.
4. Remove the catfish from the buttermilk, drain off any excess liquid and transfer to the flour mixture. Thoroughly coat the catfish on all sides, tap off the excess flour and transfer to a plate.
5. Fry the catfish, 2 to 3 fillets at a time, in the hot oil until the fish is cooked through and the breading is crisp, 7 to 8 minutes.
6. Transfer to a paper towel-lined plate, season with salt and repeat with the remaining catfish.
7. Serve hot.

RECIPE NOTES
Bottom feeders are best.

PECAN PIE

YIELDS
1 nine-inch pie

INGREDIENTS
1 (15-ounce) package refrigerated pie crusts
4 large eggs
¾ cup sugar
1 cup light corn syrup
½ cup butter or margarine, melted
¼ cup firmly packed light brown sugar
1 teaspoon vanilla extract
¼ teaspoon salt
1 cup pecans, coarsely chopped

DIRECTIONS

1. Preheat oven to 350 degrees.
2. Unfold 1 piecrust and roll to press out fold lines. Fit into a 9-inch pie plate according to package directions; fold edges under, and crimp.
3. Whisk together eggs and next 6 ingredients in a saucepan over low heat until well blended.
4. Pour into pie crust; sprinkle with pecans.
5. Bake on lower rack for 30 minutes or until pie is set.

RECIPE NOTES

The Gospel according to Joe it's pronounced pee-can not pecan.

CHAPTER 39 FROM ED'S MENU

WALDORF SALAD

YIELDS
4 Servings

INGREDIENTS
6 tablespoons mayonnaise
1 tablespoon lemon juice
½ teaspoon salt
Pinch of freshly ground black pepper
2 sweet apples, cored and chopped
1 cup red seedless grapes, sliced in half
1 cup celery, thinly sliced
1 cup slightly toasted walnuts, chopped
Lettuce

DIRECTIONS
1. In a medium bowl, whisk together the mayonnaise, lemon juice, salt and pepper.
2. Stir in the apple, celery, grapes, and walnuts.
3. Serve on a bed of fresh lettuce.

RECIPE NOTES
This recipe only works if you measure carefully.

BEEF STROGANOFF

YIELDS
4 Servings

INGREDIENTS
5 tablespoons butter
1-pound
top sirloin or tenderloin, cut thin into 1-inch wide by 2 ½-inch long strips
1/3 cup chopped shallots
½-pound cremini mushrooms, sliced

salt to taste
pepper to taste
1/8 teaspoon nutmeg
½ teaspoon dry tarragon, or 2 teaspoons of fresh tarragon, chopped
1 cup of sour cream at room temperature
16 oz egg noodles

DIRECTIONS

1. Melt 3 tablespoons of butter in a large skillet. Increase the heat to medium-high and add the strips of beef and cook quickly, browning on each side. You may need to cook it in batches. While cooking the beef, season it generously with salt and pepper. When both sides are browned, remove it to a bowl and set aside.
2. In the same pan, reduce the heat to medium and add the shallots. Cook for a minute or two, allowing them to soak up meat drippings. Remove to the same bowl and set aside.
3. In the same pan, melt another 2 tablespoons of butter. Increase heat to medium high and add the mushrooms. Cook, stirring occasionally, for about 4 minutes. Season with nutmeg and tarragon.
4. Reduce the heat to low and add the sour cream to the mushrooms. You may need to add a tablespoon or two of water, or stock, to thin the sauce if it seems too thick. Mix in the sour cream thoroughly. Do not let it come to a simmer or boil since the sour cream can curdle.
5. Stir in the beef and shallots. Add salt and pepper to taste.
6. Serve immediately over cooked egg noodles.

RECIPE NOTES

Ernie says forget the stroganoff, where's the beef?

SWEET BING CHERRY TART

YIELDS

8 Servings

INGREDIENTS

9 graham crackers
¼ cup sugar plus 2 tablespoons
6 tablespoons unsalted butter, melted
6 ounces cream cheese, at room temperature

½ teaspoon pure vanilla extract
¾ cup heavy cream
1-pound fresh sweet cherries, pitted and halved
1 tablespoon seedless raspberry jam

DIRECTIONS
1. Preheat oven to 350 degrees.
2. In a food processor, pulse graham crackers and 2 tablespoons sugar until finely ground. Add butter, and process until combined.
3. Transfer mixture to a 9-inch tart pan with a removable bottom. Using the bottom of a dry measuring cup, firmly press mixture onto bottom and up the sides of pan. Bake until browned, 10 to 12 minutes. Let cool completely on a wire rack.
4. Meanwhile, in a large bowl, using an electric mixer at medium speed, beat cream cheese, vanilla, and remaining ¼ cup sugar until light and fluffy.
5. Gradually add cream and beat until soft peaks form. Spread mixture onto cooled crust. Scatter cherries on top.
6. In a small saucepan, combine jam and 1 teaspoon water. Heat over low until liquefied, about 2 minutes. Using a pastry brush, dab cherries with glaze.
7. Refrigerate tart for at least 30 minutes or covered to up to 1 day.

RECIPE NOTES
This one brings back fond memories for Ernie.

CHAPTER 39

ERNEST STUBBS'S FAMOUS PORK AND BEANS

YIELDS
4 Servings

INGREDIENTS
1 can pork and beans

DIRECTIONS
1. Open can and pour into pot.
2. Heat until hot!

RECIPE NOTES
Fart alert.

CHAPTER 43 FROM FRANZ'S MENU

BAVARIAN DUMPLINGS (SEMMELKNUDEL)

YIELDS
14 dumplings

INGREDIENTS
5 Kaiser rolls (about 1 lb.), thinly sliced
3 tablespoons olive oil
1 small yellow onion, minced
2 cups milk
¼ cup parsley, minced, plus more for garnish
¼ cup flour
½ teaspoon freshly grated nutmeg
3 eggs, lightly beaten
kosher salt and freshly ground black pepper, to taste
Hot pork gravy from braised pork recipe for serving

DIRECTIONS
1. Preheat oven to 325°.
2. Spread sliced rolls onto 2 baking sheets and bake until slightly dry, about 12 minutes; transfer to a large bowl, and set aside.
3. Heat oil in a 4-quart saucepan over medium-high heat. Add onion and cook, stirring occasionally until golden brown, about 10 minutes; transfer to the bowl with the bread, and set aside.
4. Add milk to the saucepan; bring to a boil over high heat and pour over bread. Add parsley, flour, nutmeg, and eggs; season with salt and pepper, and using your hands, mix until evenly combined.
5. Bring an 8-quart saucepan of salted water to a boil over high heat. Moisten hands with cold water, and form bread mixture into 2" balls (about 4 oz. each); set aside.
6. Working in batches, add balls to boiling water, and cook until firm, about 15 minutes.
7. Using a slotted spoon, drain briefly on paper towels, and transfer to a serving platter; sprinkle with parsley, and serve in bowls surrounded by gravy.

RECIPE NOTES
For dumplings of all ages

DRUNKEN CHICKEN AND MUSHROOMS

YIELDS
4 Servings

INGREDIENTS
1 ½ pounds boneless, skinless chicken breasts, cut crosswise into 1-inch-thick pieces
kosher salt
Freshly ground black pepper
1 tablespoon all-purpose flour
2 tablespoons olive oil
1 ½ pounds cremini mushrooms, sliced 1/4 inch thick
1 medium shallot, minced
1 cup low-sodium chicken broth
1 cup dry white wine
2 tablespoons fresh tarragon leaves, coarsely chopped, divided in half
Juice of 1 small lemon

DIRECTIONS
1. Season the chicken on both sides with salt and pepper. Place in a shallow dish or bowl, sprinkle with the flour, and toss lightly to coat.
2. Heat the oil in a large frying pan over medium-high heat until simmering. Add the chicken and sauté until browned but not completely cooked through, about 4 minutes. Transfer the chicken to a plate.
3. Reduce the heat to medium, add the mushrooms and shallot to the pan, season with salt and pepper, and sauté until browned and tender, about 5 minutes.
4. Add the broth, wine, and 1 tablespoon of the tarragon. Simmer until reduced by half, about 8 minutes.
5. Return the chicken and any accumulated juices to the pan. Continue to simmer until the chicken is cooked through and the liquid thickens into a sauce, 8 to 10 minutes.
6. Taste and season with salt and pepper, as needed. Sprinkle with remaining tablespoon of tarragon and lemon juice.
7. Serve over cooked pasta, rice, couscous, creamy polenta, or on its own in shallow bowls to hold the sauce.

RECIPE NOTES
Make sure the chicken is sufficiently inebriated before serving.

CHAPTER 55 THE FINAL BANQUET

ESCARGOT

YIELDS
4 Servings

INGREDIENTS
1 cup (2 sticks) European-style butter, room temperature
1 tablespoon dry white wine
1½ teaspoons kosher salt
½ teaspoon freshly ground black pepper
Pinch of ground nutmeg
12 garlic cloves, very finely chopped
1 large shallot, finely chopped
¾ cup parsley, finely chopped
24 large empty escargots shells
24 extra-large canned escargots, preferably from Burgundy

DIRECTIONS
1. Preheat oven to 450°.
2. Using an electric mixer on medium, beat butter in a medium bowl until smooth. With motor off, add wine, salt, pepper, and nutmeg, then beat on medium until incorporated.
3. Reduce speed to low and add garlic, shallot, and parsley; mix just until combined.
4. Transfer butter to a disposable pastry bag or a resealable plastic bag and snip off end (or 1 corner if using plastic bag).
5. Place shells in a single layer in a shallow 2-quart baking dish and pipe about 2 tsp. garlic-parsley butter into each. Tuck a snail inside each shell, then pipe in more garlic-parsley butter to fill shell and mound over top. Bake until snails are sizzling and garlic in butter no longer tastes raw, 10–15 minutes.

RECIPE NOTES
Recommended highly by Ernie

CHICKEN CORDON BLEU

YIELDS
4 Servings

INGREDIENTS
4 chicken breasts, skinless and boneless
4 thin slices prosciutto di Parma
½-pound gruyere, grated
¼ cup all-purpose flour
kosher salt and freshly ground black pepper
1 cup panko breadcrumbs
4 sprigs fresh thyme, leaves only
1 clove garlic, peeled and finely minced
2 tablespoons unsalted butter, melted
2 eggs
extra-virgin olive oil

DIRECTIONS
1. Preheat oven to 350 degrees.
2. Lay the chicken breast between 2 pieces of plastic wrap. Using the flat side of a meat mallet, gently pound the chicken to 1/4-inch thickness. Remove the top sheet of plastic and lay 2 slices of prosciutto neatly over the top to cover the breast and sprinkle a quarter of the cheese over the prosciutto. Tuck in the sides of the breast and roll up tight like a jelly roll inside the plastic wrap. Squeeze the log gently to seal and twist both ends tight to form a nice log. Repeat with remaining chicken.
3. Season flour with salt and pepper.
4. Mix the breadcrumbs with thyme, garlic and salt, pepper, and melted butter. The butter will help brown the crust.
5. Beat the eggs and season with salt and pepper.
6.. Remove the plastic wrap from the chicken. Lightly dust the chicken with flour, then dip in the egg mixture and gently coat in the breadcrumbs.
7. Coat a baking pan with olive oil and carefully transfer the roulades onto it.
8. Bake for 20 to 25 minutes until browned and cooked through. Let rest before serving.

CHERRIES JUBILEE

YIELDS:
4 servings

INGREDIENTS
1-pint vanilla ice cream
1-pound fresh, ripe sweet cherries, such as Bing
½ cup sugar
1 lemon
1/3 cup golden rum

DIRECTIONS
1. Evenly scoop the ice cream into 4 dishes or decorative glasses and put in the freezer until ready to serve (this can be done up to 4 hours ahead).
2. Wash and pit the cherries. Put the cherries and sugar in a large skillet. Peel 2 strips of zest from the lemon in wide strips with a peeler and add to the cherries. Squeeze the juice of half the lemon over the top. Stir to combine evenly. Cover and cook the cherries over medium-low heat until the sugar dissolves, about 4 minutes. Uncover and cook over medium-high until cherries get juicy, about 5 minutes more.
3. To flambé the rum: If cooking over a gas flame, pull the pan off the heat and add the rum. Ignite the alcohol with a long match, or one held with tongs. Swirl the pan slightly until the flames subside, about 30 seconds. (3A). If cooking over an electric stove, put the rum in a small saucepan. Warm it over medium-low heat and carefully light it with a long match, or one held with tongs. Pour the lit rum over the cherries, and swirl the pan lightly until the flames subside, about 30 seconds.
4. Ladle the cherries and their juices over prepared ice cream. Serve immediately.

RECIPE NOTES
Keep a fire extinguisher nearby.

About the Author

 Arnold Breman is a retired Impresario, author and speaker. During his long career he served as Executive Director and Artistic Director of four major Performing Arts Centers including: The Raymond F. Kravis Center for the Performing Arts in West Palm Beach, Florida, Ruth Eckerd Hall in Clearwater, Florida, The Clemens Center in Elmira, New York and the Klitgord Center Auditorium in New York City. He also was the Executive Director of the Joffrey Ballet Company. From 1999 -2009 he served as a professor of Arts Administration at Columbia College in Chicago, Illinois.

He worked with and presented more than 2,000 artists and attractions including some of the biggest names in the entertainment business including: Ella Fitzgerald, Duke Ellington, Liza Minnelli, Cary Grant, Lucille Ball, Benny Goodman, Beverly Sills, Itzhak Perlman, Isaac Stern and Sammy Davis Jr. to name a few. He currently lectures to audiences about his journey into the backstage world of the performing arts.

His first two books **LAUGHTER IN THE WINGS** and **MORE LAUGHTER IN THE WINGS** feature more than 100 humorous stories of what took place backstage to get the curtain up for some of the most famous performers of the 20th century.

For more information visit: www.arnoldnbreman.com

THE FUN CONTINUES
COMING ATTRACTIONS

THE OLD MEN'S COOKING CLUB SERIES

Book Two **APPLE PIE IN THE SKY** – (spring 2020)
The lay old chefs become involved in a terrorist plot to blow up the largest passenger plane in the world with two of their members aboard

Book Three **THE ART OF THE TART** (Fall 2020)
Stolen Impressionist Art Masterpieces and the illegal trafficking of women keep the old chefs busy in this one

Book Four **THE OFFAL TRUTH** (Spring 2021)
Murder and the sale of body parts embroil the old chefs in this comic caper

Made in the USA
Columbia, SC
16 September 2019